THE KEY OF THE CHEST

for Peter and Ena

Neil Miller Gunn (1891–1973) was born in Dunbeath, Caithness, one of the nine children of 'bookish' Isabella Miller, ambitious for her sons, and James Gunn, a fishing skipper of local renown. At thirteen, Neil was sent away to live with a married sister in Galloway. At fifteen, he went to London as a boy clerk in the Civil Service. In 1911, he began 26 years as an excise officer, many of them at whisky distilleries in the Highlands and Islands. When the Great War broke out, two of his brothers were killed and one died later of war-related injuries. Gunn was particularly close to his brother John, who was badly gassed, and in later years John's war experiences were incorporated into *Highland River*. In 1921, Gunn married Jessie Frew. Tragically, their only child was still-born.

Gunn's duties in Inverness (1923–1937) left ample time for writing and for activity as a leader in Scottish Nationalist politics. The first of his 21 novels, *The Grey Coast*, appeared in 1926. The fourth, *Morning Tide* (1930), was a Book Society choice in 1931. In 1937, the acclaim won by his seventh, the prize-winning *Highland River*, encouraged him to resign his excise post and write full-time.

Notable among his other novels are *The Green Isle of the Great Deep* (1944), *The Well at the World's End* (1951), *Bloodhunt* (1952), and four epic recreations of Highland history, with *Sun Circle* (1933) for ancient times, *Butcher's Broom* (1934) for the Clearances, the hugely successful *The Silver Darlings* (1941), and from modern times *The Drinking Well* (1946). Gunn also published short stories, essays and plays. His last book, *The Atom of Delight* (1956), is an autobiography which reflects his lifelong and Zen-like fascination with the elusive spirit of life, wisdom, and delight.

Gunn's wife died in 1963, and he lived alone in the Black Isle until his death in January, 1973. Since then, his standing as one of Scotland's great novelists has grown even more firmly established, and the Neil Gunn International Fellowship was founded in his honour.

Neil M. Gunn

THE KEY
OF THE CHEST

*

Introduced by J.B. Pick

CANONGATE
CLASSICS
84

First published in 1945 by Faber and Faber Ltd.
This edition first published as a Canongate Classic
in 1998 by Canongate Books Ltd, 14 High Street,
Edinburgh EH1 1TE. Introduction © Introduction
copyright © J.B. Pick 1998

The publishers gratefully acknowledge general
subsidy from the Scottish Arts Council towards
the Canongate Classics series and a specific grant
towards the publication of this volume.

Set in 10 point Plantin by Hewer Text Composition Services, Edinburgh. Printed and bound
by Caledonian Book Manufacturing, Bishop-
briggs, Glasgow.

British Library Cataloguing-in-Publication Data
A catalogue record for this book is available
on request from the British Library.

ISBN 0 86241 770 8

Introduction

Neil Gunn was born in Caithness in 1891, son of the skipper of a fishing boat. He had worked for more than twenty-five years in the Excise service when he threw up his job to live by writing.

For too long he was short-sightedly categorised by critics as simply a regional novelist writing about the lives of crofters and fishermen, yet from the beginning each book had a theme and the themes were universal. In 1944 he published *The Green Isle of the Great Deep*, a profound fable which dealt not only with the spiritual corruption resulting from the use and abuse of power, but with the disintegrating effect of accepting the primacy of intellectual analysis over emotion. Gunn had come to see freedom as fundamental both as an individual drive for discovery and expression, and as an operative principle in society. But individuals and communities interact, and if the community is too oppressive or individual behaviour too unbridled, both suffer.

In *The Key of the Chest*, which followed immediately in 1945, he engaged with the essential nature of community, and the divisions in human society caused by damaging it. Because Gunn is a Highland writer, the community explored is a Highland one.

As so often with Gunn, the basis for the novel is a short story written long before. In this case the story is 'The Dead Seaman', published in *The Scots Magazine* during 1931, but he has used the plot for a new purpose, deepened its effect and widened its scope, just as he has used the narrative drive of the mystery story to explore the need for human beings to sustain one another.

The action of the novel is paramount, and never slackens; yet it is under scrutiny from many viewpoints. The tale

is set back in time from the date of writing. No period is
specified, but the doctor operates a somewhat primitive
motor-cycle, and there are no automobiles to be seen in the
district. The fact that characters are introduced whose
function is to comment on the action emphasises the
philosophical intention. The transitions from one view-
point to another are managed with unobtrusive elegance,
and the impression given is less one of detachment than
one of balance and control.

The situation is this: Charlie MacIan has thrown up his
course of training for the ministry because of loss of faith,
and returns home a failure. His failure is especially shame-
ful because he has been helped to university by the community, and in particular by his brother Dougald, shepherd
to the community sheep club.

When on a night of storm a ship is wrecked on the coast,
Charlie rescues a seaman, who dies. Medical examination
shows that he died from strangulation. Was his death
accidental? The seaman was clinging to a chest, but the
chest is almost empty, so why did he save it? Did it once
contain money? How is it that Dougald is suddenly able to
buy sheep of his own?

On one level the focus is on the mystery – but there are
other levels. There is the basic level of nature, with the
moods of the weather and the behaviour of birds and
animals continually observed; there is the community
regarded as an organism; there is the level of relationships
– Charlie with the minister's daughter, Flora, the relationship of the brothers with one another, and of the two
brothers with the society they have offended. There are
outsiders observing and analysing the community and its
behaviour. There is action and commentary on the action.
Finally, there is the metaphysical dimension of meaning.

At the end the doctor reflects:

And suddenly, from the excess of his baffled mood, there
flashed something like a vision, and he saw figures . . .
moving over a twilit landscape, a timeless landscape, and
they were the people of the community, and they had their
way of living, the right way and the wrong way, distilled out

of numberless ages, so that the right way and the wrong way
became native to the blood, like an instinct, an instinct
protecting the community, and this instinct, known also to
the very birds and animals that lived together, this conscience, this thing that needed no words, was – morality.

The idea of morality as a protection for a total community of men, birds and beasts is an interesting one, which
may derive from notions of co-operation within species
for survival, as developed by Kropotkin in *Mutual Aid*, a
book for which Gunn had both respect and affection.
There is always in his work the sense that the inter-
dependence of natural life has a metaphysical as well
as a physical reality.

It is said during the story, 'A living community always
meets.' This community meets in two centres: Kenneth
Grant's shop, where business is conducted, and Smeorach's house, for social gatherings. Kenneth Grant is the
organising brain of the community, the driving force
behind not only the co-operative sheep club, but most of
the progressive moves in the place.

Smeorach's is the only house where the thrawn Dougald
calls when he comes to the township. Smeorach is an elder
of the tribe. He is not authoritative, but a smoother, an
easer of social life, who has a feeling for the traditions of the
community, for courtesy and hospitality.

Several times, though, he is seen suffering from a kind of
ennui and despair which the Highland community as a
whole has endured since the Clearances, when whole areas
were cleared of people to make room for sheep.

Smeorach lifted his eyes to the blind window, and it seemed
to him that life was all shadows, and the movement of
shadows, and blindness, and had no meaning, and when
you hearkened for its sound, it had no sound.

Throughout there is a sense of the community as an
organism with eyes – 'Eyes, many eyes, looking round
corners'. Someone is watching when the outsider, Michael
Sandeman, takes his prying photographs of birds and

people. His camera is watching them, and they are watching him.

The boy Hamish is innocent of knowledge, yet he seems to be everywhere, seeing everything. He is watching when Michael goes over the cliff and it is Hamish who calls for help.

When Charlie MacIan secretly meets Flora, the doctor sees them.

When Dougald MacIan is driving home his suspect sheep, Hamish sees him.

When Dougald clashes with the minister, there are eyes everywhere.

The doctor sees Flora's final parting from her father.

Typically: 'His mother heard him coming a long way off. As indeed did the neighbours, who would be wondering what had kept the doctor all day.'

The seeing is intrusive, but it saves Michael from death on the cliff, and saves his boat from disaster when he sets out in a storm to seek Charlie and Flora.

So it breaks both ways: curious eyes are always watching, to help or to harm. Everyone knows everything – or nearly everyone, and nearly everything. What they don't know, they want to find out. Community is at once a protection and a prison.

When an event occurs, people gather naturally: 'A man here and there found he wanted an ounce of tobacco at Kenneth's and some of the women thought they might as well buy their messages early, for it was a fine morning.'

The men of the community attend the seaman's funeral:

> The mourners for this foreign seaman had the extra feeling of hospitality for the stranger to quicken their natural respect for the dead . . . As they would be done by, so would they do.

But there are those in the community who are not fully of it, set apart by their position and function: the minister, the doctor, and the policeman.

The policeman has his duties in connection with the

seaman's death, but he knows that if he is too officious he
will not be able to live easily with his neighbours. He meets
with resistance when he enquires where Dougald got the
money to buy his sheep. He is worried by the affair not only
for his own sake, but for the community's.

And there is the strange position of the minister. The
community meets in the kirk on the Sabbath, but does it
feel entirely at home there, as it does in Kenneth's shop or
in Smeorach's house?

The minister is shown at his best and his worst within a
few pages. First, he is praying with a dying woman and her
family, giving spiritual sustenance and comfort. But as he
leaves the croft he sees Dougald driving those dubious
sheep, and lo! it is the Sabbath.

> A faint darkness from a flush of blood came over the
> minister's vision. Rage at what he saw, black hatred of its
> abominable desecration, had him in an instant. That a man,
> already accursed, should so dare!

And later, in the pulpit:

> Wrath in its streams and rivulets poured into the minister
> and Mr Gwynn had the impression that he began visibly to
> swell as he took upon himself the powers of judgement and
> condemnation, under the avenging hand of God.

Gwynn is the other outside observer, a friend of Michael
Sandeman's, and a philosopher. He says of the minister in
relation to the community:

> 'He is pulling the boat widdershins . . . He is doing it
> deliberately. He is going to smash the superstition. That's
> his job. But the superstition stands for a whole way of life.
> He is therefore smashing that. And what is he offering in its
> place? Not a new way of life, here and now, in relation to sea
> and land . . . but . . . the salvation of the soul *in a future
> life* . . .'

The minister, then, is at once an anchor for the community,
and a threat to it. He should be a link between the

community and the spiritual reality of God, but his God is a judging and divisive God, so that religion, instead of uniting people in community, splits them into righteous and unrighteous, elect and damned, into theological categories not natural to the old way of life.

The minister's relationship with his own daughter is in question. He has repudiated Charlie because the young man disrupted Flora's respectable university life. But there is a strong element of the sexual in the minister's possessiveness. (The method of revealing this, oddly enough, is through a dream of the doctor's, yet the dream affects the reader as an authentic perception.)

When the minister loses his daughter, he collapses and is lost. He finds his way to Smeorach, the elder of the tribe – the old tribe, not the new, the tribe whose values were established before the coming of the God of wrath and judgement.

The doctor is the other link. In a sense he is a link with the outer world of education and science. But he is one of the community, too. He is, as a result, the book's central figure: 'The doctor was well liked and considered very able. Women talked of him confidently among themselves. For a bachelor, some of the older women thought he had a great understanding.'

But he is set apart by his position, his advisory and authoritative function – and by his relationship with the outsiders Michael Sandeman and Gwynn.

There is continual reference to the doctor's habit of distancing himself from people and events; from the Procurator Fiscal, for instance, who comes to investigate the seaman's death: '. . . though [the doctor] recognised the necessity for officials and their procedures, he usually adopted in their presence a cool and precise form of talk or answer.'

The doctor distances himself, too, from the intrusive Sandeman. When he sees Michael's photograph of the dead seaman, this is his reaction: 'Deep in him there was a movement of that sense of shock, which causes at a still deeper level, a cold stirring of the elements of hostility.'

He reacts against the sophisticated abstractions of the

philosophical Gwynn. He is always afraid of 'giving himself away', of letting Gwynn and Michael inside his mind.

Although demonstrating his own skill at rational analysis, the doctor distrusts it, reflecting at one point that it can become an effort to explain away what is important, in the interests of the mind's comfort. He senses that if analysis goes too far, separation of individual mind from community is complete, and both are in danger.

Michael Sandeman, the first of the outsiders, is accurately placed in relation to the community. He occupies the Lodge which belongs to the land-owning family, but he is not a respectable tenant – he is the black sheep, a remittance man in Highland exile.

He is something of a clan warrior without a clan. He is also a natural artist. His photographs are odd and alarming; they produce shock and surprise. His insight is real, but contains a destructive, disintegrating element.

When Michael is forced to recognise the existence of community, as the result of twice being rescued from death by the men of the district, he reacts with a kind of half-humorous generosity, giving the boy Hamish his fishing rod, but making the mistake of offering his rescuers money. Erchie, his ghillie, reports:

> 'To tell the truth, Norman, I did not know what to say, and the words came out of me without thinking, and I said you were not the kind of men to expect to be paid for saving anyone's life, not at sea.'

Michael is forced to acknowledge the existence of a code which has power for the whole social body, and he resents the fact.

Gwynn, the other outsider, has a concern and a thesis. He is looking at the community for elements of the primitive, because, he says, '. . . in that early tribal or primitive society . . . life was completely integrated'.

In the modern world:

> The spontaneous belief that gave wholeness was gone. Now if we could grow a new whole out of scientific inquiry and

material phenomena alone, then we could see our way
ahead. But apparently we can't.

Indeed we can't, and that is one of the main themes in
Gunn's writing from this time on. Gwynn refers to:

> The old primordial goodness of the human heart . . . and
> you can measure its strength by its evil opposite, its
> perversion . . . The need to feel good must in nature have
> an outlet. When it doesn't get it . . . then it bursts through,
> with mad scaldings and bloody wars.

This is an explanation for evil which would be shared by
Kropotkin, Mencius, and Chwang Tzu, but not by the
theology of original sin. You cannot convincingly advocate
freedom without a belief in 'the old primordial goodness of
the human heart'. To liberate human beings you must trust
them. Authoritarians prefer original sin.

Throughout the book the mythic is brought in to deepen
events, and as a balance to the abstractions of Mr Gwynn.
In the minister's case, Gunn writes:

> Dark and archaic words out of the mouths of prophets, with
> the power in them of the sign and the symbol. Not the
> power of daylight and order but the avenging power that
> hunts the fleeing heels of sin into death's uttermost abyss.

Dougald is said to be 'challenging the forces of the night',
and is proven to be indeed 'his brother's keeper'. Although
he resents the vain sacrifice he made to send Charlie to
Edinburgh, he will protect him not only against the community but against death itself.

Of Charlie's playing the pipes we hear that:

> When an old pipe tune was so profound in its revelation of
> human experience, of inexpressible sorrow, that its creation
> was clearly beyond human power, the folk knew that the
> masters could have got it only from some other power, and
> they talked of . . . the small wise people of the green hills.

Again and again there are characterisations which depend

upon poetic force rather than intellectual clarity: 'Death, dark and round-shouldered with hidden face'.

The total effect of the book is multi-layered, but it is an effect of unity, a unity established within the author's mind. The Highland community was failing throughout Gunn's lifetime (he died in 1973) because it had not come to terms with the economic organisation necessary to life in the twentieth century and because the psychological disruption of the Clearances had damaged the fundamental culture. But more than this, he had the sense that community was failing all over the Western world, and the strength of the State was no substitute, for community cannot be imposed from above. And community embodies values which as a species we cannot afford to lose. The comment is made about the Highland people:

> Their social pattern – getting torn. So they appear dark and gloomy, as individualists. Why? Because they are so intensely social. They prove . . . that man can fulfil himself only in social life.

But what is the meaning of social life in a dying community? The book charts how individual behaviour relates to communal values, and how the two balance. We cannot start from scratch, we must use what we have, and realise its meaning.

Charlie tells the doctor at the end: 'Even if I had children, and grandchildren, they would still be known as coming from me, and beside me always . . . would be the strangled seaman and the money.'

It is the mythic, the symbolic, which he cannot overcome. Yet whenever the intellect makes all the secrets of a community and a way of life too clear and shallow, the community dies. A community lives by myth and legend as well as by morality.

The doctor reflects that human tragedy lies 'with the inevitable, in the things that cannot be "put right"', and turns his eyes away to the wild duck arriving back to winter quarters:

Out of the bright air, first like a silent singing and then with
a whirr of wings, came the wild duck in a wide circle, heads
out-thrust on long necks, eager, out of the heart of life . . .

Their arrival breaks the doctor's despondent mood. Life
goes on, and his life must go on. But the long descriptive
passage, with its profusion of commas and clauses, seems
forced, as if the author is pressing too hard for a positive
ending.

Is it indeed a positive ending? Is it enough for the doctor
to live with his mother and tend the sick? Is the community
more likely to flourish at the end rather than the beginning
of the story? It's to the outsiders, Michael and Gwynn, that
the doctor turns for conversation, not to the people of the
community, and Michael and Gwynn are birds of passage.
What is left?

Michael at one point says that he has had 'a premonition
of wholeness'. But this personal wholeness, if ever
achieved, will be achieved elsewhere. What is 'wholeness', anyway? Gwynn never defines it. If we don't know
what it is, how can we attain it? How do we know it is worth
attaining?

I think the word 'premonition' is a good one here. The
sense of wholeness – an experience of living fully in an
accepted universe – although momentary is also timeless,
and provides a premonition of a state of being which seems
at once essential and perfectly natural. It is a matter of
experience, not of theory, and to define it is to miss it.

For a community, of course, wholeness is an accepted
way of life which provides a sense of meaning and fulfil-
ment for its members, and may begin to break up when
questioned and analysed.

Neither Gwynn nor Gunn is advocating a return to the
primitive, which would be impossible as well as undesir-
able, for the realisation of individuality has been the greatest achievement of civilisation.

The Key of the Chest is based on his knowledge of the
Highland community when Gunn was a boy, and of the
Highland community in decline, when he was writing the
book. It cannot be said to have anything as straightforward

as a message. The integration of the individual helps a community to thrive, and one function of a thriving community is to help the individual towards wholeness, towards being able to stand on his own two feet and gain an understanding of the world. But if the individual must attain personal integration and then live in such a way that community is restored, the process will be so long and difficult that before anything is achieved the community itself may be swallowed by history and lost for ever, and if community were to vanish from the world, mankind would vanish with it.

The book leaves us with a sense that the search for meaning and integration will go on because it's essential for the human psyche that it does, and that whatever happens to a particular people in a particular place, community will restore itself because the species requires it. There is room for faith as well as hope.

J.B. Pick

All day the sea had boomed in the rocks from the storm outside in the ocean. Now the cliff rumbled under his feet and the grey sky flattened still more. Thrusting his red-bearded face over his shoulder, he stared at the approaching horizon. The wind came in a wild scurry among the heather. The lean intelligent black collie with the white star on her chest kept close to heel.

When next he glanced over his shoulder, the brow of the horizon had lowered and he saw the sea's teeth whitening in the storm's mouth. This time he stopped. But his cottage was lost to sight. His features closed in a sardonic twist as he saw his brother putting more peat on the fire and taking out his chanter. No doubt he would lift the tune onto the full stand of pipes now that he was alone. He liked playing to himself!

A solitary spit of rain hit an eyeball between the narrowed lids. The track was rough but he stumbled rarely, for the moor was native to his feet as a ship's deck to a sailor's.

Another hour, and his eyes focused on Cruime. It was a village or township with a huddle of houses in the middle and others thinning out along the curve of the shore and upon the slopes behind. They were mostly straw-thatched but two or three had slate roofs and a few more the black of tarred felt. Hummocky bents overlooked the sweep of brown sand with its high-tidal marks of old dark tangle. On the near side the strand finished in the low cliff root; on the far side, amid a welter of skerries, a few massive boulders in some olden time had been levered together into a primitive but useful jetty. Nine open boats of about fifteen feet were drawn up well beyond the dark tangle. They stood in a row, supported on even keels, their sterns to the sea and their dumb bows lifting to the land. In that dream they had been for many years, though one or two of them still got a smearing of tar and even a lick of blue paint round the gunnels.

But lower down, four lay usefully on their sides. Round one of them six dark figures were grouping and heaving. The tide would be high enough to-night on top of the storm, though the stream was falling under a growing moon.

His eyes swept everywhere with little movement of the head. The more men about the boat, the less of them in the village. The smother of dusk went with him down past the near houses.

But first one little boy saw him and then another. A woman with a black shawl round her head straightened herself to look at him as he passed. He was on the hard public road and the scattered houses stood back from it, aloof under their brown curved roofs.

Two boys began whispering together as they followed at a respectful distance. Two little girls joined them, but in a moment stood by themselves, letting the boys go on. Another little boy came rushing up, then another. They began to chatter, but with repressed voices.

At last the houses gathered more confidently towards the public road, and here was the shop with the slate roof and the name KENNETH GRANT on the long green signboard. It had a large window with shelves of goods, and between the shelves one could look into the shop and see the heads and shoulders of those serving and being served.

As the man stopped on the middle of the road all the boys stopped. The dusk was thickening quickly under the approaching storm, and the man stood detached and ominous as his low-set head twisted over his shoulder and stared at the window.

A match was struck inside the shop. The clink of a lamp funnel was thinly heard. A yellowish light pervaded the shop. The man looked round and saw the boys. They stood dead still. There was no one else about and the man went into the shop.

As the bell tinkled above the door, the shopkeeper paid no attention until he had satisfied himself that the round-wicked lamp, suspended from the ceiling, was burning evenly. Then he turned, blinking a little from the strong light. When he saw his customer, he said in an expressive cheerful voice. 'Hullo, Dougald, is it yourself?' He was a well-set-up fellow in his thirties, dark and energetic, with a keenness in his features. Now he was cheerful and friendly, putting his visitor at his ease. 'And how are things out with you?'

'That same way,' answered Dougald, taking a folded sack from a poacher's pocket.

'I was east-the-country the day before yesterday,' said Kenneth, 'and there's talk of the lamb sales improving still more.'

'It was about time,' muttered Dougald.

'It was indeed,' agreed Kenneth, briskly slapping his hands as if dusting them of the paraffin smell. 'High time. That was a terrible snowstorm last spring in the high parts of the country. I met one flockmaster who lost fifteen hundred.'

'A terrible loss, that.' Dougald stood staring before him.

Kenneth glanced at him. 'It is. But we must take things as they come, and what may be one part of the country's loss may be another part's gain. Not that it would have been all gain for us had it not been for yourself.'

'Och,' mumbled Dougald, with an abrupt movement of his body.

'All the same, it was enough,' said Kenneth. 'Our ground is low-lying and the sea around helps to keep the snow away, but we had it bad enough. A few of the Committee were just saying as much no later than last night, when I was telling them the news.'

'Oh well,' said Dougald.

But Kenneth was not deterred, for he fancied that though Dougald could not readily find words, he might like all the same to get what news was going and even a word or two of genuine praise if they could be passed across naturally enough. Besides, it would all help the Sheep Club, of which Dougald was the shepherd.

Kenneth was secretary of the Club, in which all the crofters had a share. He, himself, had a large croft in addition to the shop, but keener at the moment than his personal interest in his own portion was the thought of a favourable balance sheet for the annual meeting and share-out. Years of debt had given the whole undertaking a gloomy air.

So he talked on, teased a little, too, by the enigmatic presence before him standing like a slab of red sandstone, a little above medium height, with a short neck. The reddish whiskers were bushy, at the longest no more than two to three inches, but so natural a growth on his weathered face that they might never be trimmed. His eyes, of a greenish blue, were remembered as a glisten of light between narrowed lids. He was forty-five.

A flurry of rain hit the window panes.

'You could hardly have used your weather lore to-day!'

'I knew it was coming.' Dougald looked at the laden shelves.

'Well,' said the shopkeeper, taking a pencil from his waistcoat pocket, 'we'd better get a move on. Though I'm afraid you're going to have a nasty night.'

'Four quarters of bread,' began Dougald.

Kenneth wrote down on a fold of wrapping paper each item of Dougald's order. Dougald never hesitated, not even over the final item, which was a brown earthenware teapot.

'Been breaking the crockery?' asked Kenneth as he cheerfully thumped the loaves on the counter.

'He broke the spout off it,' mumbled Dougald as he opened the sack and shoved in the bread.

Kenneth, about to say something, thought better of it. Perhaps Dougald had had a row with his brother Charlie.

After twisting the neck of the sack, Dougald deftly heaved it over his shoulder. More rain hit the window on a whine of wind.

'Here,' said Kenneth, 'I'll wrap some of the things up for you. Bread and tea—'

'It's all right,' said Dougald, making for the door.

'I'll give you another sack anyway—'

Dougald went on.

'Good night,' called Kenneth.

'Good night.'

The door rattled against the jambs, the bell tinkled.

Kenneth stood motionless looking at the closed door for a time. About to move away, he saw the pencilled order on the wrapping paper. He took the day-book from under the counter and began entering up the items.

CHAPTER TWO

Outside it was now quite dark. A gust of wind steadied Dougald and then fled past, leaving the sting of rain on his face. The children had gone from the window and there was no one about.

When he had gone up the road a little way, he paused. The moon would not rise for another hour. Time meant nothing at all, and the habit of calling at Smeorach's exerted its pull. It was the only house at which he ever did call.

He stood quite still, until his head turned and lifted slightly in the direction of his home across the moor. Whereupon he left the road and followed the short path to Smeorach's cottage. There was the groping scratch of his hand for the iron sneck, the thump of his bag against the door as he entered, and in a moment old Smeorach's voice rising high and thin in welcome:

'Is it yourself, Dougald? And what a night you have brought with you! Come away in, man, come away in. I'm glad to see you.'

The only light in the cottage came from the peat fire. It was soft and warm on the living faces until they turned from it and created their own shadows. Then the bodies stood up to make room for the stranger whom Smeorach approached in welcome, approached a few steps and then turned back, offering the best chair and talking all the time.

Smeorach was about eighty, spare and almost quite straight, for he was not very tall, with a white beard and brown living twinkling eyes. His voice was thin and high-pitched but with a clear quality in it like a bird's. Even when it went husky or ragged, this quality persisted, and no doubt accounted for his nickname, Smeorach, which meant Thrush, though it was old enough now for its origin to be forgotten. It never even occurred to children to wonder what his real name was. He lived all alone and was so full of lore and stories and brightness that men and boys of a night drifted into his house more naturally than into their own.

When Dougald had dropped the bag by his chair and sat heavily down, Smeorach, whose voice had never stopped, said he must get the lamp lit,

'Don't light the lamp for me,' said Dougald in a voice that was like a gruff order.

'Och,' said Smeorach hospitably, 'it will brighten the room a bit.'

'It's bright enough,' said Dougald.

'Very well, then,' agreed Smeorach, 'very well. Perhaps, like myself, you find the peat fire more friendly. For it's a strange thing, and indeed it's a strange thing, and I've noticed it often, that the steady light of the lamp will empty the mind and hide away from a man what he had been wanting to find. But you'll have a cup of tea, for it's a long road—'

'I had my tea before I left,' said Dougald. 'You'll put no water in the kettle for me.'

'Are you sure?'

'I am.'

'Are you quite sure now, because it will be no bother at all but only a pleasure?'

'I am. I'll be going with the moon.'

Smeorach withdrew his hand from the kettle. 'I'm thinking you'll be lucky if you find the moon this night.'

'There'll be enough,' said Dougald.

'Very well,' said Smeorach. 'And how did you leave your brother Charlie?'

'He's all right,' answered Dougald flatly.

'That's fine,' said Smeorach. 'That's good.'

As he sat down, the storm broke over the roof. There were three other men in the house and two of the boys who had followed Dougald to the shop. One of the three said, 'It's as well we got the boats up, I'm thinking.'

'It is,' agreed Murdo, a quiet man.

The storm blew two other men into the house. They came in dark and tall, shedding the storm from them.

'Phew! that's going to be a night,' said one, smiling and jovial. 'Is it yourself, Dougald?' he cried. 'By the lord, you'll catch it to-night, boy!'

Dougald did not answer.

'Eh?' continued William, making a joke of it. 'What brought you east to-night?'

'The same,' answered Smeorach, 'as would bring your-self: food.'

'There's something in that,' agreed William, aware that Dougald had not answered.

There was a shifting of bare wooden chairs and stools. The two boys were chaffed by William for keeping so far back from the fire, but they did not speak.

When they were all seated, one or two took out their pipes, and Smeorach courteously accepted a roll of black twist tobacco from which he cut a few flakes before handing it back.

They began discussing the storm. They had known all day it was 'outside' and spoke of the signs.

'It would have been pretty bad off the Point to-day?' said Murdo to Dougald.

'It was,' answered Dougald. 'It was restless yesterday.'

His tones, being almost easy, brought every eye upon him and faces lightened. He sat hunched on his chair, his eyes on the fire. The momentary silence pulled his head round and Smeorach at once started talking about the worst storm he had ever known.

They all knew the story and its dread marvels, but, as the wind howled round the house, it might have been quite new to them. Indeed the far years gave to its moving parts a dark and legendary body.

Their mood soon became fully attuned to the storm, and as the rising whine carried beyond the house, they were stirred as by the sea itself, the thresh of it on the black rocks, and the scream of the harrying spinning wind. Deeds of the past were like flotsam tossed, and the dark flotsam had faces and bodies, which fate overtook. All this had hap-pened to them or to their kindred, and pressed in upon the gable-end and the roof.

The more their spirits swung with the elements the more

they became aware of that solid hunched figure by the fire, dumb as an outcrop of rock on his own moor. In a strange almost perverse way his presence excited them, urging them to tell more tales, so that they could ignore him, forget him.

Storms and wrecks and dead bodies washed up by the ocean, lonely old women living in cottages by the tide, foreign sailors, theft, and voices in the night.

Smeorach produced the curious fantastic incident of the black man. A stormy night in the dead of winter and a voice shouting outside his father's window in a strange tongue. They were in bed, the fire smoored. He himself was only a lad of six. Then came the thundering of bare fists on the door. His father got up and cried, 'Who's there?' The wild voice outside jabbered in a way that sounded full of threats and terror. His father took the iron tongs from the fire and approached the door. 'What do you want?' he called through the door in a fighting voice. At that there was silence. He slid the bar and pulled the door open. Outside a whole moon was driving against a rushing sky and there, standing back from the door, was a big man with a face black as hell's soot. The white cloth tied about the black neck made no doubt of the blackness. No doubt in this world or any other. It staggered his father for one terrible moment, then he gripped the tongs hard and with a yell advanced. The figure let out a queer screech enough – God between us and all harm – and took to his black heels. 'For nearly a mile my father pursued him, and he was a good runner as any in the place, but he was not so good as the black fellow. And at last my father stopped, and he came home. Well do I remember that night in the kitchen. But the black man was never seen again. No one saw him. And that night, so far as we ever knew, no ship foundered.'

As Smeorach finished, Dougald gave a grunt. Smeorach swung round on him with a high sharp animosity. 'But I tell you it's the God's truth. Wasn't I there? Don't I know? Didn't I hear what I heard and see with my own eyes?'

All the others looked at Dougald with the same gleam.

Dougald's mouth opened a little, saying 'Uh?' as he glanced back at them. 'I was just thinking it's time I was going home.'

'Home!' echoed Smeorach, taken aback, for now he knew that Dougald's grunt had been no ironic comment. 'Home? On a night like this?'

'Yes, home,' said Dougald. 'It's about time.' He bent over and caught the neck of his sack.

'Home?' cried Smeorach. 'Is it leave of your senses you've taken? Do you think you'll find your track on the moor and it black as the Earl of Hell's riding boots? Eh?'

'I'll manage,' said Dougald, getting up.

'You'll find no moon this night, if that's what you're thinking of,' said William.

'I'm no woman – to need the moon,' said Dougald.

So unexpected was the stroke that even the jovial William forgot to laugh.

But Smeorach laughed. 'And if you feel tired you can sit down and put your head under the sack, for the rain will have masked the tea and melted the sugar and turned the bread to brochan. You should fare well.'

A terrific blast of wind tried to flatten the house, failed, and fled inland to the mountains carrying Smeorach's high mirth in its hound's throat.

Dougald, who had got to his feet, looked down at the brown jute sack. So accustomed were they to the sounds of the sea that they rarely consciously heard them, but now into that moment of silence came the muffled thunder of waves breaking on the strand. A swirl of rain beat on the small window like a shower of gun pellets.

Dougald turned his head slightly towards the blind wall as if better to see the night and his path. Then he looked down again at the bag.

'It would be difficult to keep it dry,' he admitted slowly. Then he sat down. 'It may take off.'

'Do you think so?' asked William, in the innocent voice of polite irony.

'It may be no more than the tail-end of the storm outside,' said Dougald.

'I have heard of the tail wagging the dog,' said William.

Faces brightened and smiled, with a quick glance at Dougald, but none laughed.

Dougald looked at him. 'I have never seen a tail wagging a dog.'

Everyone burst into laughter.

Dougald's eyes narrowed and his colour seemed to darken. But no one could say whether he was amused or angry, though they felt the presence of the state that lay between.

Murdo said calmly that possibly Dougald was right. The centre of the storm lay to the nor'-ard in his opinion and was maybe passing them by as it drove on its course.

Then they heard it coming, heard the earth being flattened. Their muscles grew taut and held on. Their faces turned to the blind window. The floor rumbled under their feet. But the house held and the pressure eased.

Murdo lifted his eyes to the window again. 'God help all those at sea this night,' he said quietly with a seaman's reverence. Then he got up.

They all got up, for byre and barn roofs might suffer and women would be anxious. Smeorach got the door open. William called the two boys by name, Hamish and Norrie, and caught a grip of them. He was passing their homes. Smeorach got the door shut and shoved home the wooden bar.

'What a night!' he said, returning to the fire which he began banking up with peat. 'It's a good thing for you, Dougald, that you're not on that moor this night.'

'It may be as well,' said Dougald.

But Smeorach did not mock him now. Nor did he ask him if he wanted a cup of tea. Water he put in the kettle, lifting it with a tin jug from a zinc bucket in the dark passage, and swung the kettle on the crook.

Smeorach did nearly all the talking, but he liked talking, and if Dougald had had easier manners, it would not have been difficult to entertain him. There was a time, indeed, when the core of the man must have gone soft and responsive; but as, suddenly realizing this, Smeorach looked at his guest, he felt that he had merely forgotten the man and been talking to himself. He grew suddenly tired, feeling his age. They sat in silence for a long time, gazing at the fire. The thunder of the sea-storm came about them and they were isolated.

As Smeorach's head drooped, the storm sounds went through it . . . flung bodies without shape or face, hunting the void of this world and the void beyond. A cry issued amid them and above the cry a gleam of two red eyes. The two red-streaming eyes shook his substance together and his head jerked up.

There was a queer smile on Dougald's face. 'I'm keeping you from your bed,' he repeated.

Smeorach stared at him. 'What's that?' he stuttered, like one lost. 'Eh? . . . Dear me, was I nearly asleep?'

'You were,' said Dougald, and a simple humour stirred on his face.

But Smeorach said, 'Is it laughing at an old man you are?'

Dougald looked at him and then settled back in his chair. 'I wasn't laughing,' he muttered. 'I don't want to keep you out of your bed.'

'Bed, is it? Well, well. You will excuse me for wandering. And it's high time indeed that we were in bed. Come, and I'll show you to the room. I'll light the lamp.'

'Not for me,' said Dougald. 'I'll just sit where I am.'

Smeorach gaped at him.

'The storm will take off,' said Dougald. 'When it does, I'll go.'

And in the end Smeorach had to accept the position and get to his bed, which was a boxed wooden structure set against the wall opposite the fire. His legs were lean and he slept in his shirt. But he had been a seaman and everything in the house was tidy and shipshape. A niece did his washing and occasionally brought him soup and meat. The two short print curtains were fresh and the pillows white. He spoke for a little while, but wearily, and soon he fell asleep.

When he awoke the storm was still raging. From the fire he knew he had been asleep less than two hours. Dougald was still sitting in his chair, but his head had fallen forward and plainly he was fast asleep. The flame had all but died from the peat, and the body was solid as a boulder in the reddish glow. Smeorach looked at it for a long time. It wakened him fully.

Then his head fell back on the pillow and he sighed, staring unseeingly at that mystery of life of which a man could make so little, however long he lived.

He awoke once or twice again, though in the following daylight hours he half-wondered if he really had awaked, so lost were the occasions in the hollow of the night.

But in the end he was startled from sleep by the sounds of that figure moving in the kitchen. Dawn was in the window and a stillness on the world.

'Is that you Dougald? . . . Are you going?' Smeorach got up on his elbow, his round eyes peering from above his whiskers in solemn wonder. 'It sounds a calm morning.'

'It's calm now,' said Dougald. He swung the sack on to his back.

'Wait, man, and I'll make you a cup of tea,' said Smeorach, and he threw the clothes back.

'No need,' said Dougald. 'I'll be going.'

'What's your hurry?'

Dougald paused by the end of the bed, but he said nothing and went on and out. They had seen the last of him now for a few weeks.

Smeorach's head fell back. There was something graceless in the man that couldn't be got over.

CHAPTER THREE

But in the forenoon, Smeorach, straightening his back from the cow's tether and slowly looking around to take the autumn sun and bright air, saw a man and a dog coming from the cliffs. 'Here,' he called to the policeman who was passing on the road, 'that's not Dougald MacIan coming there?'

The policeman turned to the moor. 'It looks like it,' he said.

'I wonder what on earth he can have forgotten that would be taking him all this way back at once?' Smeorach took a neighbourly step or two towards the policeman. Before Dougald would get home again he would have walked twenty miles in a morning, for it was six if not seven to his cottage.

They waited together in silence until Dougald came up. Smeorach was about to cry a humoured greeting when he saw Dougald's face.

'Can I have a word with you?' Dougald asked the policeman. They both walked away from Smeorach, of whom Dougald had taken no notice.

Coming to a halt at a little distance, they stood talking together so earnestly that soon all eyes within sight were secretly watching them.

Presently the policeman was seen clapping his hand to his breast pocket, but though he had on his blue trousers, he was wearing an old tweed jacket, and the notebook he had plainly reached for was not there. He took out his watch, put it back, and stood thoughtfully. Then all at once he started down the road, but stopped again, and, giving a shout to Dougald, overtook him.

They walked up the road together until their ways parted, Dougald heading back for the moor and the policeman striding on to the house with the dark blue slates and the unobtrusive notice: Police Station.

Within five minutes he was out again, properly dressed, with his wife calling to him a few final words from the door. He did not answer her, but strode steadily down the road to Kenneth Grant's shop.

Kenneth, who was serving an old woman, saw his head pass the window and heard him go into the small room that was the post office. Presently the communicating door opened and the policeman's head looked round. 'Can I see you a minute?'

Kenneth dropped his scoop in the tea-chest and went into the post office, for which he was responsible.

'I want to send a telegram,' said the policeman.

'I'll give Sarah a shout. I hope there's nothing wrong?'

'It's a dead body.'

Kenneth stared at him.

'I want the doctor first,' said the policeman.

'The doctor?' repeated Kenneth. 'He's not past yet. I've put a sign out for him – for Widow Macrae. The nurse was here a minute ago.'

'Are you sure he'll be passing? No time must be lost.'

'Certain, I should say. But you'd be as well to say a word to the nurse. It's not – anyone – we know?'

'It's a dead seaman. But I cannot say anything until I have investigated the case. I'll see the nurse and you get hold of Sarah.'

At that moment Sarah came in, a slim girl of twenty, with dark attractive eyes.

'I'll be back,' said the policeman, and out he went, striding down to the nurse's cottage, which lay some twenty yards below the road.

As crime was almost unknown in this part of the world, the whole township was soon aware of the policeman's activity. Folk did not approach him in any way, but stood back watching.

Soon he was seen setting out for the moor, and in a few minutes everyone knew he could be heading only for Dougald's cottage at Sgeir. A man here and there found he wanted an ounce of tobacco at Kenneth's, and some of the women thought they might as well buy their messages early, for it was a fine morning.

The moor was an extensive sweep of land, jutting broadly into the sea. At one time it had contained three small townships, one on the northern side, along which the policeman was now proceeding, and two on the southern. Some of the ruins of these townships could still be seen. Their inhabitants had been forcibly evicted from them over a century ago to make room for sheep. The cottage in which Dougald now lived had, in fact, been specially built for a shepherd from the Border country.

As the policeman continued on his lonely way he was very full of his 'case'. It was the first dead body he had ever had to deal with and he was anxious not to make a slip in his report or to omit from it any point of official importance. He was a tall dark man of thirty-two, broad-shouldered and fresh complexioned. 'At 10.50 a.m. on Wednesday the—' (he could not remember the day of the month with certainty, but the calendar would soon settle that) – 'I was approached by Dougald MacIan, shepherd, of Sgeir . . .' The postal address, parish, county, what he said. He took out his notebook, and put it back. There was plenty of time. No good hurrying a thing of this sort.

Though the sea sparkled under the sun it still pounded the cliffs. Obviously the wrecked vessel had come through heavy weather, perhaps been driven along with it. There might be other bodies, even survivors. It could easily be a very complicated and important case.

The policeman looked about him. Now the rocks gave on a gully with sloping braes. There were cairns of stones and raised green rectangles where the grass had grown over the foundations of some of the ancient cottages. Sheep were nibbling on the other side of the small stream, which came from a loch set in broken land in the middle of this broad promontory. There were some marshes in there, too, good wild duck and snipe country.

The policeman, however, had no thought for anything but his duty and when at last he drew near the cottage, he was feeling all keyed up and ready. Dougald appeared round the gable-end and stood against it, waiting.

The strangeness of this remote dwelling rose suddenly upon the policeman. With no woman about the place, what a queer life these two men must lead. No wonder there was talk! However, that was no business of his, so after he had greeted Dougald he asked, 'Where's your brother?'

'He's inside,' said Dougald, 'with the body.'

As they entered the living-room the policeman peered hither and thither through a yellow gloom of the dead that gripped him. The air, too, was heavily tainted. His eyes fastened on a figure that rose slowly from a chair near the fire.

'Fine day, Charlie,' said the policeman softly and solemnly.

'Fine day,' answered Charlie, and a thin smile spread over his pale face. It was a sensitive face, good looking, and the fair hair had a touch of yellow. Indeed there was something of Charlie's college days in the face even at that moment. The tall body had straightened itself from the stool with a lazy grace, and as the eyes rested on the policeman they glistened against the dim light.

After the bright freshness of the world outside, the policeman turned to the small window and found it mostly obscured by a piece of brown cloth. As he faced into the room again he discerned the hump of the body on the bed in the inner corner.

He asked Dougald to take the blind from the window, and when the light flowed in he went over and removed the white sheet from the face, putting the flat of his hand at the same moment on the forehead. The hand drew back quickly, surprised by the cold, and the policeman began to stare at the face.

It was a face with distinct cheek bones and a fair pointed beard. The bedclothes were drawn up under the chin so that the face, thus cut off, held a strangely isolated, suppressed power of personality. A slight furrowing between the eyebrows still caught the intolerance, the anger, of a final command. A small man, but a masterful spirit. Death had done no more than trap the spirit, had frozen its nobility in a darkly congested, even menacing way.

The policeman gently removed the bedclothes and

exposed the chest. The body was naked and the skin fair
except for one or two discoloured patches that clearly spoke
of the fight with the sea. As he replaced the clothes and
turned from the bed, Charlie's eyes shifted from him to the
window and stared far out to sea.

They were silent for a little and then the policeman said
that it was a sad and a tragic business, for the dead man's
darkened face so affected him that he forgot for the
moment the importance of his case.

'It must have been wild here last night,' he added,
remembering the storm.

'It was,' said Charlie.

Then the policeman stirred. 'Come,' he said, 'you'll have
to tell me how it all happened from the beginning. In that
way, we'll get it in order.'

'All right,' agreed Charlie. He found the policeman a seat
at the table near the window, pushing back some crockery
so that he would have a clear place for writing in his
notebook. He had the ready movement and ease of expression which his brother lacked.

'You can sit down,' said the policeman.

Charlie sat down, and as he went on answering the
policeman, Dougald, standing with his back to the fire,
kept staring at his face. When Dougald's eyes shifted for a
moment to the policeman there was no movement of his
head.

'Now tell me, when did you have the first intimation of
it?'

'Just on midnight,' Charlie answered. 'A little before I
saw the light I looked at my watch, wondering if Dougald
was coming home. It was then ten minutes to twelve.'

'Have you your watch on you?'

Charlie took out a silver watch, and suddenly listened to
it. 'It's still going,' he said. 'I don't remember winding it.'

'You're twelve minutes fast,' said the policeman, repla-
cing his own watch. 'Very good. Now you said you saw a
light?'

'Yes,' said Charlie, winding his watch automatically. 'I
was sitting by the fire and thought I saw a dull glare in the
window.'

The policeman looked out of the window and saw a series of low rocks beyond the Point. The sea was still breaking over them. As the blue heaved the sunlight was reflected radiantly. When the policeman had recorded how the rocks could be seen from the window, Charlie shifted his eyes from him and continued. 'I knew it was not lightning, and when I got to the window and looked out I saw it was flares from a ship caught on the outer spit.'

'What did you do then?'

'I went out. It was blowing very strong. But I managed down to the shore. I had been down in the first of the night making sure of my boat. At that time there was no sight of any vessel.'

'Now what did you observe when you went down?'

'I saw that a vessel was on the outer spit and that nothing could save her. I heard cries. They came through the noise of the storm. I felt from the high sound of them that she was going down fast.'

'Did you actually see the vessel?'

'Yes, I thought I saw her black side and a wild heave of her masts in the red flare, but that was when I was climbing down. By the time I was down, the flare was gone.'

The policeman wrote down all that Charlie said in a clear round hand. It took time and sometimes he asked Charlie to repeat his last words.

'Very good. And what happened next?'

'I could see nothing now. But I shouted at the top of my voice once or twice. I felt it might guide some of them. It was all I could do. But the noise of the sea drowned everything.'

'Was it pitch black?'

'No, not pitch. The moon was hidden but there was a sort of near greyness, though the spray was blinding. But I could see nothing, and now I could hear no voices. I was crouching under the lee of a rock. Then suddenly I heard a cry—'

'Wait a minute . . . Yes?'

'Then I thought I saw something. It was like a seal – in the swirl – but when I went nearer I saw it wasn't. It was close to me, but the swirl was treacherous. Then I thought I saw a head, and hands holding on to something. I waited my chance and went in. I got a grip. I was swept off my feet, but got bottom again. In the end I managed to drag the man ashore. But he lay unconscious. I had got a mouthful or two myself.'

'He was not dead then?'

'No.'

'How do you know?'

'I heard him in the water. If I had thought he was dead I would hardly have tried to carry him up in the dark, for it was not easy.'

'Good! That's fine,' said the policeman. 'So you carried him here and then——?'

'I stripped off his wet clothes and put him to bed to try and get him warm. The breath seemed to have gone out of him, but I felt his heart move.'

'What did you do next?'

'I warmed a blanket and wrapped it round him. I had kept the kettle near the boil for Dougald, so I tried to get hot tea between his teeth.'

'And then?'

'Then,' said Charlie, moistening his lips, 'I saw he was dead.'

The policeman wrote in his notebook with growing confidence. The climax had at last been reached and now everything was surely clear. He turned back the pages and, rereading them, nodded as each point was made. Dougald watched him. Charlie looked far through the window, like one exhausted by the long night, and now feverishly awake.

His chair scraped as the policeman squared himself once more to his notebook.

'Now tell me, what did you do next?'

Charlie's chest filled with air. 'What more could I do?'

The policeman looked up. 'You just stayed in here, because of the storm?'

'No,' answered Charlie. 'I didn't stay in. I thought there might be others of the crew. This time I took a burning peat with me from the fire. The rain soon put it out. I got down

to the shore. There was no one there. There was nothing –
except the chest, which he had been hanging on to. So I
took it back with me.'

The policeman wrote. 'So I took it back with me,' he
muttered. Then he looked up into Charlie's face almost
with surprise. 'So you have it here then?'

'Yes,' said Charlie, getting up. 'That's it.'

The policeman rose and went over to the wall by the head
of the bed. He saw a small box no more than a couple of feet
long and about a foot and a half wide and a foot deep. He
lifted it and brought it to the table. It was a smooth neat job
in cedar wood and had two small brass handles at each end
which folded down flush into the wood. The seam between
the lid and the box could hardly be seen, so perfectly did
the lid fit.

'It's locked,' said the policeman.

'I think so,' muttered Charlie.

'Didn't you try to open it?' asked the policeman.

'Can you open it?' asked Charlie, with a weary smile.

The policeman tried again, but the box appeared one
solid piece. 'No,' he said, turning it round in his hands.
Then he found a tiny opening for a thin flat key and,
scraping it with his nail, exposed a small brass lock. The
policeman scratched his cheek. 'Where's his clothes?'

'On the chair there.'

The policeman turned to the fire and started methodically going through the pockets. A cigar cutter, a piece of
white string, a foreign silver coin and a florin. No papers,
nothing else, and certainly not a key.

The policeman stood looking at this miniature seaman's
chest. It was not very heavy and might contain documents,
the ship's papers, perhaps in a foreign tongue. It would
have to be broken open – but that could wait meantime. Let
the investigation be finished first.

He returned to the table and entered in his notebook an
account of the chest, its discovery, and its voluntary
exhibition by Charlie.

'And what more did you do?'

Charlie slowly sat down. 'What more could I do – until
the daylight came?'

'I know,' said the policeman. 'I'm only asking you, just to get it all down. Did you go out when the daylight came?'

'Yes. I went down to the shore again. There's some timber. I saw some planks washing along the rocks. But I saw nothing else and there's no sign of the vessel. With the body in the house, I had to wait for Dougald. I was feeling pretty tired, too. So in the end Dougald went for you.'

Presently the policeman drew a quick line in his note-book.

'Your evidence is very good and clear. You did well. And indeed you must be feeling tired after such a night.'

'To tell the truth, I am,' said Charlie, and he stretched himself. As he yawned his jaws quivered. Then he smiled with the weary satire that suggested it was not the sort of night one would like to have often. But he appeared more cheerful as he got to his feet.

'Are you too tired to come down with me to the shore for one minute?' asked the policeman considerately.

'Not a bit,' said Charlie.

The policeman thanked him and added: 'When we come back you'll just go and take some sleep.'

Dougald led the way to the door and, as he went out, filled his chest with air. The other two followed him to the brink of the descent. At first there were clearly defined steps worn through long usage in the grassy brow, but soon one had to pick one's footing carefully in the rocky zig-zag down the irregular cliff.

At one point the policeman paused and asked, 'Did you carry him up this?'

'I did,' said Charlie.

The policeman showed his admiration of the feat.

It was a small creek, with rounded stones on its slip of beach, sheltered on the right hand by a reef of low dark rock which at ten yards dipped, to rise again, to dip and rise once more, until the outermost spit set the swell boiling. On the left the broken cliff wall fell slightly away to come again more boldly in a headland called the Point.

Charlie's open boat was drawn up and lay on her side. Lobster creels, a mast and sail, oars, were tucked away in a low opening or cave at the root of the rock which they had descended. By the cave's mouth was an old rusty winch for hauling up the boat.

'Was it here you took him in?' asked the policeman.

Charlie nodded to the spot. 'Just there.'

The policeman climbed up on the skerry and looked about him. A low black reef, with the sea sucking white from its fangs to rise again in a drowning spout. From somewhere near the Point came a regular explosive boom. The cliffs were sheer, and, beyond them, the sea again.

The policeman jumped down. 'They hadn't a chance.'

They all stood silent for a little.

Suddenly Dougald turned to his brother. 'Go away home,' he said gruffly. 'You're looking grey.'

Charlie closed his mouth firmly as if his teeth had been chattering, and the smile was only in his eyes.

'Do you that,' said the policeman warmly. 'Have a rest before the doctor comes. There will be the customary formalities. But if you answer as you answered me, there should be no difficulty for any of us.'

'All right,' said Charlie, 'if I can be of no more use to you—' He turned, sidestepping for a moment like a drunk man, and left them.

'Your brother went through a lot last night,' said the policeman, looking after him.

'He did that,' said Dougald, looking at the policeman.

CHAPTER FOUR

Two hours later, as the doctor drew near on Kenneth Grant's pony, the policeman went to meet him, leaving Dougald at the gable-end of the cottage.

The doctor dismounted and they stood talking together for a long time. When the doctor had heard the whole story, he said, 'Good, we'll have a look at him.'

The doctor was an athletic figure, thirty-seven years old, with an alert quiet face and an easy manner. 'It was a wild night last night,' he said casually, the slight Highland intonation conveying a natural friendliness.

'It was that indeed,' agreed the policeman, feeling now fully supported. The doctor was well liked and considered very able. Women talked of him confidently among themselves. For a bachelor, some of the older women thought he had a great understanding. The nurse, a hardy active brown woman of over fifty, who had had some training in midwifery, talked of him as 'very skilled'. The policeman glanced at the cool expression and saw the grey eyes taken up with the appearance of the cottage in its slight hollow, a sheltering outcrop of lichened rock beyond it.

The doctor did not appear to think Dougald's manner unusual, but there were a few seconds when his eyes rested on the weathered whiskered features.

'You can tie up the pony, Dougald,' said the policeman.

The doctor paused to clap the beast as Dougald led it towards the byre, then he opened the door, stooping a little from force of habit, and went in.

At once his attention was drawn to a body stretched out stiffly before the fire. Laying his hat automatically on the table, he went directly to the figure and stooped. The policeman, entering behind him, stood for a moment unable to speak. As the doctor's hand touched him Charlie wakened and in no time was on his feet, his teeth showing, and his disordered hair giving a strong impression of fright.

The doctor, who had stepped back, said with humoured restraint, 'I thought there was a mistake somewhere!'

There was a wildness in Charlie's confusion as he glanced away from the doctor's eyes. 'I was asleep,' he muttered.

'You'll have to go to bed properly,' said the doctor. 'You need it.'

Dougald's footsteps paused on the threshold. The doctor turned to the bed and was at once attracted by the face of the dead seaman. He studied it minutely; then he swept the bed-clothes off the body and gave it a careful examination, his back to the three men, who stood clear of the window light. When he had finished with the body, he drew the clothes over it, took a thoughtful step or two forward, then paused and said to Charlie in a normal conversational tone:

'You say the body was alive when it came ashore?'

'Yes.'

'Uhm.' The doctor withdrew his eyes for a moment, then looked at Charlie again. 'How long would it be from the time you carried him up here until he died?'

'Not very long.'

'An hour? Two hours?'

'It could hardly have been an hour,' Charlie replied after thinking for a little.

The doctor glanced at his watch. 'Say he died at one in the morning – that would be about it?'

'Yes,' said Charlie.

'Fourteen hours,' murmured the doctor, and he nodded thoughtfully.

'I understand he was alive when you brought him in here?'

'Yes.'

'How do you know that?'

'Well, I felt a movement in him.'

There was a certain easy humour in the doctor's face as he asked, 'Would you be prepared to swear to it?'

Charlie's brows gathered a trifle and he looked through the window but did not answer.

'Anyway, you're quite sure he was alive in the water?'

'Yes,' said Charlie, now with a certain reserve.

'How were you sure?'

'Because he used his voice and was kicking with his legs.'

'That's usually enough,' agreed the doctor. 'What did he say?'

'I don't know. It sounded like a foreign language. But he didn't say much.'

'He lost consciousness as you got him ashore?'

'Yes. It was not easy. There was a back eddy coming off the cliff.'

'Did it nearly get you?'

'It did.'

The doctor was silent for a moment. His voice had been dry and matter-of-fact but quite friendly.

'Then you carried him up here?'

'Yes.'

'He's over ten stone, I should say – a pretty good lift.' He looked at Charlie, not as it were to observe him but thoughtfully. 'How did you carry him?'

'On my back.'

'Where was his head?'

Charlie moved restlessly. His reserve had set a thin smile on his haggard face. 'His head? – somewhere about here,' and he raised a hand towards his right shoulder. 'I just got under him and took him on my back.'

The doctor thought for a moment. 'Fourteen or fifteen hours ago – that could be about right.' Then he added, 'Would you mind leaving us for a little? We must consider our official reports.'

The brothers withdrew and closed the door. The doctor listened carefully to their footsteps receding in the direction of the byre, then he turned to the policeman and without any emphasis said, 'It seems a clear case of strangulation.'

As the policeman's eyes opened wide, their innocent blue caught a lot of light and were suddenly in striking contrast to his black hair and full rosy face. He turned them on the doctor in silent absolute astonishment.

'Here,' said the doctor, clearing things off the table, 'give me a hand. . . . You take his legs. The light is too dim in this bed.'

The body was quite stiff and easily carried to the table. A certain dark congestion in the features was much more discernible under the clear light of the window. The doctor's attention was concentrated and objective. He might have been examining a piece of mechanism which had ceased to work, an engine that had broken down, whose parts he knew intimately and rather liked looking at and touching. 'Some bad bruises. He got nipped there, and a real good blow there. See that? . . . Now, see the bruise marks here. Across the throat and under the ears. He was gripped there. That stopped him breathing. You can see the congestion of the features as he was choked.'

'My God,' breathed the policeman, 'do you mean – he was murdered?'

The doctor smiled into the policeman's intense expression. 'I said choked, strangled – not murdered. We mustn't fly too far ahead.'

'But – you mean he was strangled by someone's hands?'

'Strangled anyway. Beyond doubt.'

The doctor's easy manner had its steadying influence. 'You can see the marks for yourself, can't you?'

The policeman began to look at them again. 'Yes. Will I put it down—'

'Don't bother meantime. Give me a hand.'

They carried the body back to the bed, where the doctor lingered a moment looking at the face. 'Quick-tempered, but able. He didn't stand fools gladly.' He drew the sheet over the face.

'This changes everything,' said the policeman. 'I'll have to get in touch with the Procurator-Fiscal at once.'

The doctor agreed. 'Is this the chest?' He lifted it on to the table and began to examine it as he had examined the body. 'It's beautifully made,' he said. Then his eyes were held. 'What's this?'

'No, no,' said the policeman. 'I did that, scratching for the lock. There wasn't a mark there.'

The doctor crouched down and got his eye on a level with the lock. Then he stood up, finished with the chest.

'That's about all we can do meantime. I want to have a glance at the shore and the place he said he carried him up.'

'What about this chest?'

'We could force it. Or do you think it would be better to wait for the Fiscal?'

'I think so,' said the policeman. 'I'll carry it home with me. I'll put word to the Fiscal at once. He could be here to-morrow.'

'That would do,' said the doctor. 'Of course – not a word to them meantime.'

'No, no,' said the policeman. 'Not to anyone.' His voice was still inclined to whisper and his breath to ball.

'By the way, show me that money?' The doctor examined the foreign coin. 'A Swedish kroner. I thought he was a Swede. Well, shall we go?' He lifted his hat and the policeman followed him.

The policeman saw Dougald's head protruding from the byre door. Dougald uttered a hoarse word and emerged, followed by Charlie. In an instant, the policeman got a completely new and unhuman view of the two brothers. Dougald looked uncouth as some primeval animal and Charlie had something peculiar in his face, the haggard nonchalant grace of one who had committed a crime. Despite his six feet of pliant, powerful body, he looked light and grey. They approached in what seemed a shambling, stumbling way.

'I just want to have a look at the shore,' called the doctor lightly. 'Then we'll be off.' And he started out, followed in single file by the others.

'You did pretty well carrying him up that,' said the doctor to Charlie, on their return to the cottage. 'And what you need now is a real good sleep.'

The policeman had hardly spoken to the brothers. 'We'll be out in the morning,' he now said. 'And that reminds me. I'll have to arrange for the burial.' He looked at Dougald. 'Have you a measuring rule?'

'You can take it,' said the doctor as he mounted the pony, 'at five feet eight. And now, if you give me hold of that box—'

'Not at all,' said the policeman, 'I can easily carry it.'

But the doctor had his way, and called over his shoulder to the brothers, 'To-morrow forenoon, then.'

The policeman walked beside the pony for about a couple of miles. They discussed what had to be done next. The seaman would, of course, have to be buried in the churchyard. The policeman would get in touch with the Sanitary Inspector, see to everything, so that all would be done, and charged for, according to law. He had never had such a case before.

'I'll look in and see the minister on my way home,' the doctor volunteered.

'That would be a great help, thank you.' The policeman was grateful. They went on in a thoughtful silence.

'Do you think you could carry this now?' asked the doctor. 'I have still one or two calls to make.'

The policeman lifted the chest off the pony, and, after a final few words about meeting at the police station in the morning, the doctor set the pony to a trot on the open moor.

CHAPTER FIVE

'I hope it's nothing serious at Sgeir, Doctor?' asked Kenneth Grant, as he took the pony's reins.

The doctor straightened himself. He was not used to riding. 'A dead seaman,' he answered. 'Apparently a ship went down last night off the Point.'

'My God!' said Kenneth. 'Any of them alive?'

'Not at Sgeir. She piled up on the spit.'

'Last night! On the outer spit!' Thought held Kenneth's breath. 'Not much hope in that case.'

'Afraid not. I must be off.'

His motor-cycle, in these early years of the century, was still new to Cruime. A high single-geared affair, it was not easy to start when the engine was cold. But presently he had made a final call and was roaring along the highway towards the next township, where he lived with his mother. A crofter took his horse and cart off the road when he heard the roar approaching. The horse danced and the crofter had difficulty in holding the beast and at the same time saluting the doctor.

About a couple of miles out of Cruime, he came on a church, with its cemetery and manse. The manse was a fairly tall building, with a plantation of old trees shutting it off from the church and cemetery. It stood at a little distance from the road.

The doctor stopped his motor-cycle on a slight declivity, so that he could waddle it off easily, and, entering at the iron side gate in the wall, went up through the trees to the manse. He hesitated before he knocked, looking in through the open door upon the small hall and the pitch-pine staircase. The house always gave him a feeling of polished bareness, as if it had never known the warmth of living which gathers odd gear and scatters it about. Clearly not so much a case of frugal living, or even of austere living, as a reflection of some uncompromising attitude of mind to necessity.

The doctor had just given the first rap with the black iron knocker – there was a brass bell-pull but he had entered a pace by this time – when two women appeared simultaneously, the daughter of the manse upon the stairs and the grey-haired old housekeeper from the kitchen.

The doctor, who appeared not to notice the housekeeper, turned with a smile to the young woman as she descended the last step and came towards him. The housekeeper slowly withdrew.

She was twenty-six years old, with dark-brown hair caught back into a knot behind her head. The simple sweep of the line of her hair was like all the lines of her body, in which there was an easy flowing movement. The clear skin of her face caught a slight flush and her blue eyes a light that glanced and shone.

The doctor held her hand firmly. It was rather a large hand.

'Is your father in?'

'Yes. He's in the study. Will you come in?'

'Well, I thought I'd come and see him – about an unfortunate business.' As he said this, he turned and hung up his hat. But he did not move on. She stood waiting, anxiety slowly draining away the warm colour.

'I have been out at Sgeir,' said the doctor. 'It was very stormy last night. You would have felt it here?'

'Yes.'

He regarded his hands, as if to make sure they were reasonably clean. Thought or feeling showed on her face so readily that she could do nothing about it.

'It was a shipwreck,' he said in his easy voice. 'None of our own people. Apparently she was a foreign boat.' He looked at her again.

'Were they saved?'

'Afraid not. There's one body. That's what I wanted to see your father about.'

She looked past him through the open door. 'That's dreadful,' she murmured.

It was this deep note in her voice that was most characteristic. Not that it was really deep so much as rounded
and warm. But he found it impossible to describe. It held
for him an extraordinary attraction, and he now knew that
he was making conversation in order to hear her speak, and
at the same time to observe the responses of her face and
even of her body. One could deliberately blow colour into
her face.

'Of course, we may yet hear something better from the
other side, around Balcreggan. The gale was blowing in
that direction, and she seems to have been carrying timber.'

'Oh, I hope so. It's terrible. Poor men!'

And for the first time the loss of living seamen touched
him imaginatively. Normally the expression 'poor men' (as
he would yet hear it so often in the district) showed a
sympathy too facile to touch him. When accompanied by a
mournful inflection, he disliked it.

He became aware that her eyes were on his face and had
caught him looking at her objectively, feature by feature. At
once he said, 'Yes it is terrible,' as if he had been regarding
her absentmindedly.

A door behind her opened.

'Ah, it's you, Doctor.' The minister came forward and
the doctor met him and shook hands.

The minister was tall and broad-shouldered, with a
tendency to an unnatural stoop from listening to the
troubles and petitions of his flock. His characteristic
welcoming smile now held and lingered like a mask. He
had a clipped moustache, bushy eyebrows, and a strong
growth of grey-dark hair.

'I hope it is nothing very serious that has brought you to
see me,' he went on. 'Though I suppose I can hardly expect
it to be anything else.'

'Well, I'm afraid—'

'Won't you just come into the study,' continued the
minister, and in no time the doctor found himself behind
the closing door. No attention had been paid to the girl,
whose footsteps he now heard ascending the stairs. Of
course, it was all perfectly natural, but he had the momentary feeling that she was hardly a schoolgirl.

'Now, you'll take this chair . . .'

When at last the minister sat down, the doctor proceeded to tell about the shipwreck at Sgeir.

'Ah, just so. Very sad. Very sad indeed. I was afraid we would have bad tidings from the sea. It was very wild about one o'clock. I heard a great crash. I went out – but it was no more than a tree blown down. Fortunately it was no more than that. Ah yes. So the body, you say, is still in the shepherd's house?'

'Yes. The policeman is making arrangements, but as he's busy at the moment I offered to let you know, seeing I was passing.'

'Quite so. Quite so. Yes. The day is getting on.' His eyes almost disappeared as the eyebrows and lids closed thoughtfully.

Feeling the minister was contemplating an immediate visit to Sgeir, the doctor at once said, 'Of course, they're not expecting you there. I merely wanted to let you know the position, so that when it came to the burial – I suppose he will be buried here – anyway, I thought I'd tell you.'

'I know they will not expect me at Sgeir,' said the minister with his smile. 'That does not mean I may not go.'

'Of course,' said the doctor formally.

'I suppose it must be many years since either of them entered at a church door, and I can hardly expect they will extend that active reverence to the dead which, as a people, we consider it our duty to do.'

The doctor remained silent – and suddenly in doubt. It was no concern of his what the minister did. That he himself did not go to church, any more than the two brothers, was an added thought in front of the minister's smooth tones. He got up. 'Well, I'll have to think of my report for the Procurator-Fiscal. So I had better be getting along.'

'The Procurator-Fiscal!' said the minister, who had also risen. He now looked directly at the doctor. 'You don't suspect . . . I hope there is nothing wrong?'

'The Procurator-Fiscal would have to come in any case, I should say. This is a complicated matter, a shipwreck. There's a box – ship's papers. The body may be the captain's. These matters will have to be looked into officially.'

'Of course – if that's all it is?'

'It's a fair amount,' said the doctor, with a small dry smile.

'Oh, yes, indeed. But when we hear of the Fiscal being called in, we in our ignorance are inclined to think that there may be some doubt as to – the cause of death itself, or shipwreck, or whatever the occasion may be. I am glad to be assured by you that there is no such suggestion of criminal taint.'

The doctor knew he hadn't directly assured him of any such thing, and as it was almost certain, whatever conclusion should be reached by the Fiscal, that some version of the actual state of affairs would circulate among the people, it might be at least unneighbourly for the doctor not to give a hint to the minister who, after all, was the other leading professional man in the district.

Yet he found himself extremely reluctant to do so, and he knew, though no expression showed on his face, that the minister was already suspicious of his hesitation.

'It's really no more than a professional matter. The cause of death – and I hope you understand that I give you this in all confidence – was not entirely due to drowning. A storm is a pretty violent affair. I am not suggesting anything of a suspicious nature. It's just simply that there is a formal method of procedure and it's not yet complete. That's all.'

'Of course. I see,' said the minister. 'And if that's all you can tell me, I quite understand. And they found, you say, the body on the shore?'

'Yes. Charlie found it and carried it up to the house. Then Dougald came along for the policeman, who, of course, informed me. We are just back from their house.'

'Thank you,' said the minister, 'for calling and letting me know. It was very good of you, and you such a busy man.'

'Not at all,' said the doctor, 'and please don't trouble coming out.'

But the minister accompanied him to the outside gate and there shook hands.

As the doctor waddled off down the decline, he kept a

grip on the exhaust lever so long that when he at last dropped it, the machine shot forward and swerved. He straightened it up, aware of his irritation.

It is almost certain, he thought, that he will go to Sgeir this very evening. He would go alone, on his round-bellied pony, and he would see to it that both Dougald and Charlie were present while he held his service for the dead. A gathering of the elect!

But not before he had first probed every detail of what had happened out of them. A sudden and extreme dismay so gripped the doctor that he actually stopped his machine. 'Damn it!' he muttered, and his skin paled. It was very unusual for him to use an oath of any kind. His grey eyes gathered a stormy look.

The one thing the doctor had not told the minister was that Charlie had said the seaman was alive when he took him out of the water. And, of course, it would be the very first thing that the minister would find out from Charlie himself!

Having found that out, the minister would at once remember what the doctor had told him about death being due not to drowning but to some other cause. What cause?

The doctor half turned his machine on the road, then stopped, astride it. He could not go back and forbid the minister to do his duty by the dead. That was quite impossible. The minister would rightly regard it as blasphemous presumption. All he could do would be to tell the minister everything and ask him not to question the brothers in any way. But would that stop him from putting his own kind of circuitous questions? Not it!

The doctor took out his silver cigarette case. His features resumed their characteristic still cast of thought, as he breathed out the tobacco smoke. Having turned the whole position over, he decided nothing could be done about it. At least he had not mentioned the word strangulation and that was a positive and favourable point.

Then the doctor remembered that the minister had trained in his early days to be a medical missionary. Many of the old and holy folk still preferred him to any doctor.

This was the real reason why his predecessor in the practice had left. In fact, his predecessor had warned him about the minister, and, being a hot-headed man, had been a trifle lurid over the ministerial 'mumbo-jumbo' not to mention love of power. Apparently there had been one or two stand-up rows.

The minister would probably have sufficient knowledge to recognize strangulation – if he was curious enough!

The doctor threw the half-smoked cigarette from him. Nothing could be done. Not a thing. For the minister would want his triumph over Charlie. And what an utterly appalling triumph it might be!

The doctor pushed his cycle to a level stretch, then, running alongside, leapt on as the engine fired, and the manse fell rapidly behind.

Had it been anybody but Charlie!

Though he had not appeared to be looking at Flora when he had first referred to an 'unfortunate business' at Sgeir, he had been completely aware of the momentary arrest-ment in the girl. He had felt a standing still, a waiting, in every cell of her body. She was too easy to read. It would have been brutal to have looked at her searchingly. So the old trouble was not all over and done with, at least not in the girl's mind!

She was naive. She was simple. That was the real fact. And a disturbing fact because the quality of her simplicity was in some absolute way feminine. He had felt it to-day, quite strongly. Not that she was 'simple' in the silly sense. The very opposite. She had manners, a native grace, a living warmth. She could become powerfully attractive to a man, decided the doctor, and his mind for a moment grew somewhat vague about that region which lay beyond intellectual assessment, because it was already suggesting that he himself had called not altogether for the pleasure of seeing the minister!

The minister, who had come out to interrupt their talk! His daughter was, of course, all he had. So they said. The poor man had had a great concern for his wife. She had hardly ever left the house. At the time of the trouble between Flora and Charlie in Edinburgh, she had gone down with a chill, caught pneumonia, and died. As simple as that. The doctor's smile caught a dry assessing quality.

He topped a slight rise and was at once aware of a horse and trap a short distance ahead. He lifted his exhaust valve and closed the throttle. But the figure in the trap was shouting and waving to him to come on. It was the young owner of Ros Lodge. The doctor, however, knowing his man, stopped dead. Michael Sandeman drove off the highway onto the road leading down to his house, whose roofs could be seen at some distance amid a plantation of pines. The horse was already restive and when at last Sandeman leapt out and got it by the head, the doctor thought: That's a bit better! Thereupon he started off, but with caution, and just before reaching the junction stopped again, but now managed to disengage the clutch and leave the engine roaring.

Michael Sandeman was twenty-seven, very dark, slim, and with that extreme force of will that knew no end to a wild fight short of defeat or conquest. But the mare was young and the fight at the road junction became such a rearing, bucking, dancing madness that the doctor, sensing the beast was about to bolt or smash everything, stopped his engine. Whereupon, still fighting, Michael yelled angrily, 'Keep the damned thing going!'

The doctor smiled. It was exhilarating to watch this man almost at any time, and the doctor liked him. Soon Michael had the trap fair and square on the side road with the mare's head just short of the highway. The beast was quivering and wild-eyed.

'Start up! Come on!'

'No fear!' called the doctor. 'You hold her there a minute.'

Presently, astride his silent machine, he let it run slowly down, then stopped three or four yards away. 'We'll let her have a smell of it,' he said.

'You and your smells!' cried Michael with a flash of his white teeth. But he was laughing now. He saw the doctor's point.

Pushing off with his feet, the doctor drew slowly nearer, talking in his easy normal voice for the beast's sake. 'She must see that it's a harmless contraption. It would not reassure her if I started roaring past like the hammers of hell. Not to mention that I should still like to live for a short while.'

'Why?' asked Michael, who, however, was also giving his attention to the mare. There was something in that wild liquid eye, in the hot lather of the curved gleaming neck and shoulders, which the doctor suddenly admired. It was certainly a natural background for Michael Sandeman, who, despite the excess of his will at such a moment, had an intuitive apprehension of the nature of wild life. So no doubt he could quarrel with it occasionally! He was now clapping the mare's neck and talking to her about the doctor and his bag of tricks in gently derisive tones.

The doctor crept nearer, until he was almost under the mare's head. She backed and quivered, but now Michael was in the mood to calm her, for he knew he had her in hand, if not beaten. Neither suggested that the engine should be started up.

All at once the doctor began to waddle off. 'Here endeth the second lesson,' he said.

'Wait!' cried Michael. He turned the trap at the junction and got the mare facing home. 'Come down to-night. I want to show you something.'

'Not to-night,' answered the doctor. 'Perhaps to-morrow.'

'Right!' He got smartly into the trap. 'Let her go!'

The doctor pushed off again, dropped the exhaust, and shot forward. Looking back over his shoulder, he beheld man, mare and trap going flat out for Ros Lodge.

The crofting district of Ardnarie now spread before him. Away on his right gleamed the sea. He had crossed the root of the bluff promontory of Ros, near the far tip of which Dougald had his cottage.

Ros Lodge had in the first place been built for the Border sheep farmer who, when the Ros had been forcibly cleared of its inhabitants, had taken it over at a rent which paid the landlord very much better than the sum of the crofting rents and was collected with less trouble and more certainty. What happened to the evicted tenants, whose forebears had been on this land longer than any story told, was not a matter of economic nor therefore of any other importance. Some of the old people along the coast had news of descendants of the evicted in places as far distant as America and New Zealand, but it was based on hearsay, and altogether that old race of the Ros had disappeared.

Just as the sheep farmers and their kin had in turn disappeared, when imported wool and mutton from the colonies made sheep rearing on the Ros uneconomic. But the landowner was again lucky, for wealthy men, who made their money in all kinds of industries from coal to table condiments, were prepared to pay handsome rents for sport. So the square sheep farmer's house grew wings and became Ros Lodge.

Nor was that the end, for in turn the Highland landlord found it necessary to sell most of his ancient estate and the Sandemans had bought the Ros outright, while continuing to hold a lease of a neighbouring deer forest. When the lease expired the Sandemans made no effort to purchase the forest.

They were losing interest in Highland sport, for fashion had its moods and changes, and were on the point of selling the Ros, prompted if indeed not stung thereto by an agitation (which gained considerable publicity through the Press) by the poor crofters of Cruime to have the Ros as a common sheep grazing, when the second son of the Sandeman house dramatically changed the parental intention.

Michael's career at Oxford was irregular enough, but thereafter his conception of how life should be lived in all its phases was so completely shocking to his parents that a crisis was reached. As a boy he had been passionately fond of hill sports, and on more than one occasion had had search parties scouring the mountains for him. His excuse had always been simple: a wounded stag or a rare bird, darkness or mist.

So at the moment of crisis, the ultimatum was made very clear. Either Michael would reform and take his appointed place in the family fortunes or he would be banished to the

Ros on the meagre but utterly rigid allowance of £2,000 a year, payable quarterly through the bank. He would understand, however, that if he elected to be banished, his debts and misalliances would alike be utterly ignored.

Michael had chosen the Ros.

So much the doctor had gathered from odd phrases let fall by Michael when recounting some amusing experience of the past. Whether that final scene had been a painful irrevocable one or whether it had been tempered by a father's secret hope that a few years' banishment beyond the civilized pale might help an irresponsible youth to find a man's feet, the doctor could not be sure. But Michael had been at Ros Lodge now over two years, and there seemed to be no early prospect of his departure. His advent pleased the crofters very well, for they got the sheep grazing at a moderate rental and Michael retained the sporting rights.

But here were the first houses of Ardnarie, Maclean's shop with its pile of wooden packing cases, old Alie with his grandchild at his heels, a long thatched croft house here, another there, a wash of gold on the corn, flowers on the potatoes, and now at last the white harled walls of the doctor's house.

His mother had heard him coming a long way off. As indeed did the neighbours, who would be wondering what had kept the doctor all day.

She was a tidy white-haired woman of seventy years, active, with colour in her cheeks.

'David, what's kept you?' she asked on a sharp note of concern.

'Oh, the usual,' he replied, with a tired smile.

'Have you had anything to eat since the morning?'

'Eat? No.'

'Oh dear me, will you never learn sense?' and she retreated hurriedly into the house.

CHAPTER SIX

With chisel and hammer, the small seaman's chest was opened the following day in the policeman's parlour. There were documents, including the ship's log, but as most of them were in Swedish their examination did not take very long. It was, however, quite clear that she was a Swedish vessel of some 800 gross tons, bound from a port in Finland to the Clyde with a cargo of wood pulp and timber. Entries in the log no doubt fully described the weather and how the vessel had fared in the storm. There seemed to be nothing of an unusual nature – and, anyhow, the documents would, of course, have to be studied in the proper quarter, as they would provide the basis for all considerations and claims, human and financial. The policeman's wife had put a fire in the parlour and now the Fiscal was carefully drying some of the documents. The doctor was examining the chest. Remarkably little sea-water had seeped through. 'A very neat job,' he murmured, fingering some fine oilskin lining. But the way the inner wood-work tightly overlapped when the box was closed, so that even the keyhole, small as it was, did not go right through, held his attention.

The policeman, who was assisting the Fiscal, glanced at the doctor, for they had already decided that the box had definitely no appearance of having been tampered with. The doctor was merely having his last look at the ruptured lock. His motor-cycle had given him an interest in mechanisms.

Presently there was the noise of Kenneth Grant's gig outside, and when the policeman had locked away the chest and its contents, they prepared to set out for Sgeir.

The Fiscal, a stout man, with a clear mind and a rather thin but precise voice, was a Bachelor of Laws with about thirty years' experience of all kinds of legal work. The policeman had already warned him that the gig would be able to proceed at only a walking pace, and that indeed often they would have to get out and walk themselves, the track was so rutted and rough.

Now as his eyes took in the tall policeman, the doctor, the man who sat respectfully with the reins in his hand, and his own weight, the Fiscal began to laugh softly, almost without sound. Without a word, they all saw the humour of the heavily laden vehicle with the single horse on the impossible road. Then they got in, and every eye within sight – and that meant most of the eyes in Cruime – watched them set off.

The easy confidence of the Fiscal, the complete absence of anything in the nature of importance or stress, greatly heartened the policeman. No further reference was made to the inquiry, but the Fiscal asked quite a lot of questions about the history of the Ros. The doctor found the journey much more agreeable than he had anticipated, for, though he recognized the necessity for officials and their procedures, he usually adopted in their presence a cool and precise form of talk or answer. Now he found himself smiling and chatting in a friendly way. The Fiscal had already thanked him for the extra trouble he was giving himself and the doctor had replied that he was really interested in the case.

The heather was in full bloom. Its purple wash lapped hillock and boulder and ran inland with the eye. So naturally pervasive was it that the policeman did not consciously observe it, but the Fiscal, in a moment of sudden realization, was silent in surprise. There was such a lot of it, and as it receded from him in slow waves, it gathered the mist and bloom of purple. The freshness that had followed the storm was still in the air, was warm under the September sun, and the fragrance of the heather was an exquisite memory of wild honey. The track dipped and here were ruins, strangely still and silent. So silent indeed lay those ravaged upturned faces that involuntarily the ear listened for their immortal speech. Here and there, amid a green fume of bracken, hung a frond yellow as a woman's hair. But much of

the bracken had been scythed and the short stalks stuck
up like thin brittle bones.

'Who cuts the bracken?' asked the Fiscal.

'Dougald MacIan,' answered the policeman. 'Whatever
else he may be, he's a good shepherd.'

The Fiscal said no more, and when the gig faced the
opposing slope they all got out and walked.

With the freshness alive on the blue sea they came at last
in sight of Dougald's cottage.

The policeman, with solemn face, introduced the Procurator-Fiscal to the two brothers, and at once in the air
was born the knowledge that here men were come together
in their several functions to decide issues of life and death.

They became separate from one another in a curious
quietude. The Fiscal looked about him and said he would
like first to see the shore. The policeman led the way,
followed by the Fiscal, Charlie, Dougald, and the doctor.
Sandy Grant (Kenneth's younger brother), who had driven
the trap, stood at the horse's head gazing at that silent
procession of men in single file until they disappeared over
the cliff-head.

On the shore, the Fiscal questioned Charlie in a direct
natural way. Charlie had shaved but his face was still rather
grey. His manner was reserved but he spoke clearly and
intelligently, for he had been a bright schoolboy before
going on to take the divinity course at Edinburgh University where he studied for over two years.

The Fiscal grew deeply interested in the terrific onset of
the recent storm, considered how the great seas smashed
upon the skerries, how an incoming current was set up that
met the face of the opposing cliff, was turned toward the
small bouldered shore, to ebb under the lee of the near
skerry – a sort of slow vast whirlpool.

Upon this heaving movement of water the seaman had
come: into it Charlie had dashed and got a grip of him, lost
his feet but held on. There was some confusion until they
fetched against the skerry. Charlie pointed to the jagged
outthrust of rock that anchored them long enough for him
to get his wind and fight his way back, taking the seaman
with him.

'You still had him by the clothes at the back of his neck?' asked the Fiscal.

'Yes,' answered Charlie.

The Fiscal looked around upon the wild scene. 'I see. Then, I suppose, you grabbed him with the other hand and hauled him up?'

'Yes.'

'Was he still holding on to the chest?'

'Yes. He was. I—'

'Yes?'

'It was a bit in the way.'

'That's how you remember it? I see. I am merely trying to get a picture of the whole thing. Did you haul him out then by the one hand or did you use your other?'

Charlie hesitated and for the first time his brows gathered. 'I just hauled him out.'

'Is it difficult for you to remember precisely?'

As Charlie remained silent, the Fiscal went on, 'You must not think we are doubting what happened. This is an official inquiry, and questions have got to be asked and answered. You understand that?'

'Yes,' answered Charlie.

'Very good,' said the Fiscal quietly. He turned and looked towards the outermost spit. 'Have you been out to see if the vessel is there?'

'No,' answered Charlie.

'I think we might pull out and have a look,' said the Fiscal.

The boat was launched and Charlie and Dougald took an oar apiece.

They found her in deep water on the southern side of the spit. From her position and a knowledge of the direction in which the gale had been blowing, it was not very difficult to see where she must first have struck. They discussed the time and the state of the tide, and then the Fiscal asked about lighthouses on the coast.

Charlie told him of the nearest lighthouse to the north by which the master of the vessel could have been guided.

'Do you think the weather was so thick that he could not have seen the lighthouse?' the Fiscal asked.

'I don't think so,' answered Charlie.

Thought gathered about the Fiscal's small eyes. It seemed to the doctor that he was on the verge of speaking but then decided to hold his tongue. A curious silence fell on the boat. The doctor regarded Charlie's face for a moment, then looked over the side with the others, and, through the clear water, saw dimly the dark hull of the vessel. A lighthouse, a light, thought the doctor, and his mind tried to rationalize a vague but ominous inrush of fantasy from forgotten tales of wrecks and wreckers. There was no tradition on this coast of vessels being lured to their doom. The notion was preposterous, absurd. For the moment, his reason balked. The Fiscal ordered the boat to be rowed back, and they went all the way to the house in silence.

When the Fiscal and the doctor had finished with the body, the doctor went to the outside door and called to the brothers. As they came up he turned to Dougald: 'Was the minister here last night?'

'He was,' said Dougald.

The doctor felt the suppressed force in the man coming at him. It was elemental, terrific. He had not spoken one word until that moment. The doctor asked Charlie to enter and followed him with a queer irrational need to smile. Everything was on that level, with the possibility of incalculable eruption. The quietness of their procedure was acquiring the automatic in a fatal way.

The Fiscal sat in the chair which the policeman had occupied on his first visit, laid some papers on the table, then turned towards Charlie, who was sitting with the light on his face.

While the Fiscal was making his cautionary remarks about the need for truth and the nature and use of evidence, the doctor, who was sitting opposite him and had the back of his head to the window, was able to watch Charlie's face.

It was an interesting face, with its fair clean skin and that elusive gleam of yellow in the hair. That the fair skin could, contrary to fair skin generally, go a trifle grey, suggested a capacity for introverted thought. At the same time there was about the face, as its native inalienable characteristic, a certain gallant careless air. The man was well made, tall, with an easy swaying movement of the body. About thirty years of age. It was not difficult to understand how attractive he could be, given the moment, with desire in himself.

Methodically the Fiscal traversed the evidence, as it had in all important detail already been given to the policeman, until the moment arrived where Charlie again asserted that the seaman was alive in the cottage.

'Are you prepared now, or in a court of law, to take your oath on it that the seaman was alive?'

'I thought he was alive.'

'Listen to me. Are you prepared to state on oath that he was alive in the water when you rescued him?'

'Yes.'

'You are absolutely certain of that?'

'Yes.'

'Are you prepared to state on oath that he was alive in this room?'

Charlie hesitated.

The doctor actually felt his own heart beat as he saw Charlie's face assume an inner dourness. He knew well the attitude of mind. He had seen it locally too often. Having said something, the man would stick to it whatever the consequences. Yet Charlie was troubled in some other subtle way that the doctor could not follow.

The Fiscal waited, his solid bulk unmoving.

'I thought he was alive,' answered Charlie at last.

'Are you prepared to swear to it?'

The Fiscal's thin voice gathered a certain body, remorseless and without any colour. The moment became still and solemn.

Charlie twisted slightly on the hard wooden chair. And then, almost as if drawn out of him against his very nature, he said, 'No.'

The Fiscal moved.

After a few more questions concerning Charlie's direct dealing with the body and the absence of any reaction to the warm blanket and the hot tea, the Fiscal asked him if he had seen or been in contact with any other living person during the night.

Charlie looked directly at him. 'No,' he answered, and seemed to wait, as if something suspicious were about to be revealed.

'I have to put to you a very direct question,' said the Fiscal solemnly. He looked at Charlie steadily. 'The medical evidence would seem to suggest that this body has been strangled.'

He paused, and the doctor, in a silence in which each breath was held, watched Charlie's face as the eyes stared. The mouth fell slightly apart and the underlying bone structure of the face was revealed. Then the eyes roved but came back to the Fiscal's face.

'Did you strangle the body of this seaman?' asked the Fiscal quietly.

The chair scraped back from the straightening of Charlie's legs as he arose. 'So that's what it's all about!' There was a bitter derision in his voice.

'Please sit down,' said the Fiscal.

But Charlie went towards the fire and turned round. His face was completely drained of blood. It was in a way as if he had not heard the question, had not yet realized its personal import. So this was what it was all about! And yet the doctor, had his life depended on it, could not have sworn that Charlie was now reacting naturally. It was extremely like the way in which a Highland temperament, such as Charlie's, would react in all the circumstances: the staring amazement, the derisive intolerance, the pallor of anger behind; but somehow the doctor was left with a feeling of uncertainty, of something concealed in Charlie's mind.

'Will you answer my question?' asked the Fiscal in his even, unavoidable voice. 'Did you strangle this seaman?'

Charlie looked at him. 'No,' he answered in a voice suddenly cool as his own.

'To your conscious knowledge you did not in any way bring about his death?'

'No.'

The Fiscal at last withdrew his eyes and wrote for a

minute or two. Then again he looked at Charlie. 'Are you still prepared to assert that you thought he was alive in the cottage?'

'I thought he was alive,' said Charlie at once.

'But you may have been mistaken?'

'I may.'

'Can you give any idea at all of how the seaman may have met such a death?'

'No.'

'Yet you were the only one in his company from the moment you found him alive until his death?'

'Yes.'

'Is it possible that you may have, all unknown to yourself – and please understand that I *mean* all unknown to yourself – that you may have brought pressure about his throat in the struggle and confusion of getting ashore?'

Charlie stood rigidly staring through the window. 'I don't know,' he said tonelessly.

'Think,' said the Fiscal. 'You are an educated man. Do you mind if we attempt a reconstruction of what happened on the shore?' He got up. 'Perhaps,' he said to the police-man, 'you wouldn't mind acting the seaman?'

For so heavy a man, the Fiscal very deftly reconstructed the scene, with the policeman on the floor gripping a stool which was just about the size of the chest. It took time, and Charlie who, in the beginning, showed reluctance, finally did as he was directed in a passive manner. But apparently he was not quite certain exactly how to grip the policeman's clothes behind the neck. One or two holds were tried. This took a little time, but the Fiscal was in no hurry and appreciated certain choking sounds which the policeman made when he himself took a grip. But Charlie refused to have any opinion about the throat strangling. Clearly his natural urge was to deny it – and at this point, again, the doctor was invaded by his tantalizing feeling of uncertainty.

In the end the Fiscal thanked him, saying he quite realized how Charlie must feel, particularly in view of his statement, which, indeed, his actions in this tragic business would seem to bear out, that what he had done, at grave risk to himself, was to attempt to save the seaman's life. At the same time, Charlie on his part would understand that the law demands certain procedures which it was his duty, as Procurator-Fiscal, to carry out.

The policeman led Charlie from the room and brought back Dougald.

Dougald came shambling to the threshold and stood, his eyes going from one to the other in quick thrusts.

'Come in,' said the Fiscal, 'and take a seat.'

By the way Dougald came forward and sat down the room might have been strange to him and none too secure. The doctor turned his eyes away and looked through the window.

'Well, Mr. MacIan, as you know I am holding an inquiry into the death of this seaman. All I want from you now is just exactly what you saw when you came back here in the morning from Cruime, what your brother told you, and any other circumstance attending the matter.' The Fiscal's voice was precise and friendly, but when it finished Dougald sat still and silent.

'Let me see,' said the Fiscal. 'You stayed the night in Cruime with – with—'

'Smeorach,' said Dougald.

'Good. Now you left there – about what time would it be?'

In this way each simple fact had to be drawn out of Dougald. Sometimes he knew the answer, sometimes he didn't. When pressed for an answer as to the hour, he told the height of the sun. The Fiscal was patient, and the picture grew.

The first complete sentence uttered by Dougald came in answer to the question why his brother Charlie had not gone for the police before Dougald appeared in the morning.

'He would not be wanting me likely to come home alone and find a dead body in the house.'

Out of his harsh voice there came an extraordinary effect of satire, but whether this satire was directed against Charlie or against the question and those present, the doctor could not determine with certainty. Probably, therefore, against both. And that was interesting in the light of rumours that had gone around about the relations between the two brothers.

Why precisely had Charlie, after smashing his career in Edinburgh and wandering heaven knew where for some years, come back to his brother in this miserable shepherd's cottage? That folk were almost afraid to ask Dougald about his brother, told its story far more radically than would any mere theory of brotherly relations. In such cases, folk awareness was extraordinarily subtle. When, by a chance politeness, Dougald was asked how Charlie was keeping, he would grunt. That Charlie helped with the sheep occasionally was known, for the communal flock was growing under the long-sighted secretaryship of Kenneth Grant. But his real job was lobster-fishing. He worked the boat alone and usually brought his lobsters to Cruime, where he kept them in two floating but submerged fish boxes until he had a sufficient number to dispatch by bus to the distant railway station.

This enigma of the brothers had naturally bred all kinds of rumours, and women, talking together, with the manse in the hinterland of their minds, would often wonder how they managed 'in the house'. And something a trifle dark and distant and even unholy came through to childish ears. 'I am Red Dougald MacIan,' a boy would declare and try to look like the Devil as a roaring lion. His companions would laugh at the boast and run on.

The doctor, quietly sitting in his chair while the Fiscal pursued his course with so simple and sure a touch, tried to read Dougald's face, to resolve the man's nature, to separate the basic primordial element from the uncouth superficialities, from the instinctive wariness, but found it very difficult. Quite impossible, in fact. There was a whole wood in one's own mind, a sheer growth of the intellectualities, that had to be cut through in order to get at that place where response would be unconditional and immediate. Like trying to sheer through Dougald's very face, with its thick growth of reddish whisker, its weathered skin and bushy eyebrows, its half-hidden eyes with the glint that glittered a moment as it was caught by the sunlight in the window.

'I see. So Charlie did not mention to you that the body was alive in the house?'

'I don't know what he did.'

'Didn't you ask him?'

'No.'

'But you said that he told you the body was alive?'

'He said something like that.'

'Did you gather that the body was alive in the house here?'

'The body was dead when I saw it. I don't know what he'd been doing.' Impatience was growing in the bushy figure.

And then the Fiscal came away with the intelligence that physical evidence suggested the seaman had been strangled.

The effect on Dougald was in its silent way very dramatic. His eyes became round and fully visible. The lips, too, became visible as they separated, creating a curious, stupid gape in the beard. The act of thought could be seen struggling to birth, wrinkling the skin around the eyes, concentrating the eyes themselves on the Fiscal's face.

The doctor had been uncertain in Charlie's case, but here clearly so consummate a piece of acting was utterly impossible.

When the Fiscal spoke again, Dougald did not answer. He was still thinking, trying to realize the news.

At last the doctor saw Dougald almost physically tuck away this startling piece of intelligence into some deep hole in his mind. Then he was ready again. The doctor was aware in himself of a slight physical sensation like a shudder.

Dougald provided nothing new. What he said in the main confirmed Charlie's account. After all, he could clearly have been only a short time in the house and equally clearly the seaman had died hours before he had appeared on the scene.

When, at the Fiscal's bidding, he got up and stumped out, the Fiscal, looking after that uncouth physical withdrawal, which momentarily gave the effect of emptying the room, laughed in his soundless way. And for one moment the doctor was aware that the withdrawal and the comment on it were of the same kind. He smiled in response, as did the policeman, but no word was spoken.

'Well,' said the Fiscal, the glimmer of humour still in his expression as he gathered his papers, 'what do you make of it all?'

'It's very complicated,' said the policeman.

'Eh, Doctor?' asked the Fiscal.

'Complicated seems to be the word,' agreed the doctor, 'short of adopting a theory.'

'Such as?'

'That he was strangled unknowingly in the water.'

'Quite so,' said the Fiscal, and the humour passed from his face. 'But immediately we assume that as a possibility, and it plainly is a definite possibility, what other kind of assumption can we set up against it? In other words, supposing we were to accuse Charlie of having strangled this man in this house, what evidence could we adduce in support of our accusation? Charlie denies it. There were no witnesses. And, as far as we can see, there is no motive. Can I make out a case that the Crown could possibly sustain, or even wish to support, in view of the simple facts of the case? For let us consider them. Assuming Charlie is the kind of man who would strangle for strangling's sake, then why go through all this labour of bringing the body up here, when he could simply have disposed of it by throwing it into the sea without anyone's being a bit the wiser? His whole story of the rescue would be utterly pointless. That kind of criminal does not keep the evidence that would incriminate himself and then inform the police. Any such line of argument, in view of Charlie's assessable character, is manifestly absurd. Assuming next that he strangled the man for some sort of gain which we cannot determine – and which we could hardly therefore put forward to proof – again, why keep the body? For if he is capable of murder, surely he is capable of slipping the dead body over a cliff? If the body were washed up thereafter even on his own little shore, nobody would think anything of it. We, in fact, expect a body or two to be washed up in various stages of decomposition. As it is, even this body has sufficient bruises upon it not to preclude entirely the possibility that it may have been choked by an unknowable agency – such as, for example, the chance crushing together of planks of timber in the wild welter of wreck and storm. Would you deny that?'

The doctor thought for a moment. 'I should say it is extremely unlikely – and besides, Charlie says the man *was* alive, and he heard him shout.'

'Take your first point: you say "extremely unlikely". Could you say "impossible"?'

'Well, no.'

'The second point: Charlie says he heard cries *before* then. Now remember he would be in a highly worked-up condition. Someone might have cried who was going down directly behind this seaman and Charlie would naturally have thought the cry came from the seaman. It was dark. Remember also the set or flow of the water. It was a back eddy from the cliff. Once a seaman had swum or struggled far enough he would hit the cliff and then be carried inshore on the back eddy. That is, if he had something to hang on to, like a chest, or could still swim strongly enough not to get drowned in the smother at the cliff-foot. Do you see the picture?'

'Yes. I admit even the possibility of deception in the matter of the cry,' replied the doctor. 'But what is not quite so clear is how a body which had been strangled would then hang on to a chest.'

'You think that would be quite impossible?' asked the Fiscal.

'Well, don't you?'

'I just don't know enough,' confessed the Fiscal. 'You're the expert there. I merely wondered if a man mightn't hang on rigidly to his precious box when life was gone, particularly if the box had got lodged across his chest in a balanced buoyant position. However, all I wanted to suggest is this: we have no certain evidence at all that the body was alive when it was drawn from the water. From that moment, no positive movement of life is alleged – except for the supposed movement of the heart in the house. That's about it, isn't it?'

'Yes.'

'Now about the movement of the heart – what's your opinion, Doctor? Do you think Charlie could have been mistaken?'

'The heart-beat must have been faint and fairly difficult to feel with an unpractised hand at that moment.'

'But a layman might *fancy* he felt it. I know I have sometimes been in doubt when feeling for my own! Now think. Psychologically, why would he fancy he felt it move, if it didn't? Remember, in the circumstances, as he gave them.'

'Presumably because he wanted it to move.'

'Precisely. It's the most revealing point in the whole story.'

'But I could imagine circumstances in which he would be so afraid that the body was *not* dead that sheer fear would make him fancy the heart moved.'

'Certainly. But that could only be if he wished the body dead for some very strong reason. In this case, because he had strangled it. But if he had strangled it, then he had a very simple way of getting rid of the body. And in any case surely then the very last thing on earth he would do would be to insist in such a dogged way that the heart did beat? For so to insist would be to incriminate himself.'

'I agree. Except for this point. Assuming he had over-looked the possibility that it could be discovered from medical examination that the body had been strangled?'

'I admit the point. It is one among any number of possible assumptions. He has some education, but one may assume any degree of ignorance here. In the end the only thing we can do against assumption is to apply common sense and probability. And here we have the simple straightforward story of one man's brave attempt at rescuing another. Take it absolutely as it stands. Take it that the seaman actually cries, and is alive and hanging on to his chest. Charlie dashes into that whirlpool. He grabs the man behind the neck. He gets swept off his feet and momentarily goes under. It's very dark. But he hangs on and with his free hand strikes out blindly. They are bashed against the skerry. He still hangs on and tries to lift the man's head out of the water. Remember, the wind is roaring, the sea smashing, the spray flying, and it's black night. Think of the inferno it was; put yourself in Charlie's position. He fights his way to shore and at last *drags* the seaman, now unconscious, after him. He is nearly unconscious himself. You saw the neckband of the seaman's shirt and that sealskin waistcoat that buttons up to the throat. Charlie had a grip of them at the back of the neck . . . It would not take us long to dress the body again. We could then see how pressure could be applied from a grip.'

The doctor, without dressing the body, quite simply tied the top button of shirt and of sealskin waistcoat round the throat and then turned the body over on its face. Each of the three men tried the grip and agreed that if Charlie had hauled the full weight of the seaman for one minute, the result could easily have been strangulation. Not to mention the final solid hauling up the beach.

The doctor was meantime examining very closely the back of the neck. He fitted the knuckles of his right hand against certain discolorations.

'Exactly,' said the Fiscal. 'Charlie's knuckles where the hand, entering between neck and clothes, then gripped the clothes. And Charlie's clothes are as salt as the seaman's. Everything fits.'

When they had got seated again, the Fiscal continued: 'So far Charlie's story could be reasonably established. But what happens next? Charlie comes fully to himself and realizes the man has passed out and may be dead. His natural instinct, if he was really anxious to save the man, would be to get him into a place of safety and warmth. The only place, of course, was his own home. And now starts that remarkable climb, in the storm and dark, up the rock face, with the dead man on his back. He comes in here. Strips the clothes off the body. Wraps a warm blanket round it. Feels for the heart, and is so anxious for the man to be alive that he imagines he feels the heart beat. So at once he brews some hot tea and tries to get the man to take it. *Now*, Doctor, there was tea in the mouth on your examination, which means, I take it, that the man was already dead when Charlie tried to force the tea into him.

Had the man been breathing, he would have choked or shown some reaction. Charlie says he didn't. But Charlie also says he felt the heart beat. Therefore, either the heart-beat was an illusion on Charlie's part, or the man died *naturally* in bed in the minutes between Charlie's having felt the heart beat and administering the tea. If you do not agree that the man died naturally in bed, then Charlie's experience of the heart-beat was an illusion. We have seen the tea stains on the bed sheet, with a clean space, corresponding to the head, between them. All clear?'

The policeman moved his whole body in a certain wonder. The doctor nodded thoughtfully.

'Next Charlie wonders what more he can do. There may still be others. He goes down to the shore again. He will naturally look into the whirlpool. He comes therefore against the chest. There is no one more to save. He brings the chest back. What more can he do? It's so wild a storm that even his brother, who is clearly pretty tough, has been prevailed on not to face the walk from Cruime. Besides, the man being dead, there is no point in Charlie's trying to reach Cruime. For all he knows, his brother may come staggering in at any moment. He waits for the dawn and then sets about searching the cliffs, like a sensible and responsible man. By that time he is so exhausted that his brother undertakes the journey. And here we are.'

There was silence for a few moments. The policeman stretched back in his chair, relieved and confident again in his own judgment now that the Fiscal had substantiated so clearly what he himself had felt to be the truth in the first instance.

'Well, Doctor?' asked the Fiscal.

'I presume you have been putting forward the case for the defence. Frankly, I cannot see anything that would stand against it.'

'And I have to look at it in that way. I am responsible to the Crown and shall, of course, report fully. But naturally the Crown hesitates to implicate any citizen unless the Crown can make out a reasonable case. In your opinion – and, I may say, in mine – the Crown cannot.' He paused and his eyes twinkled. 'Not even the Crown Agent in

Edinburgh, who might call for a Public Inquiry just for
the sake of being contrary—' His smile lit up a private joke.
Then seriously he continued: 'Actually, to take the thing to
its logical conclusion, it would hardly do to put a man on
trial whose clear and unassailable story is that, at risk of
death to himself, he strove almost superhumanly to save a
foreign seaman's life. Good men among the public would,
not unnaturally, think it monstrous.' The Fiscal turned to
the policeman. 'What do you think about it?'

'I agree with you. It would be an awful thing. It would be
enough to make decent men afraid to rescue anyone or
report a dead body or anything.'

'However,' said the Fiscal, 'that is for the Crown to
decide, in view of all the facts as we three have them
and shall report them. But it might be as well for us to
be clear in our own minds, as to what we genuinely think
about it. Supposing I were to put it to you like this, Doctor:
do you really believe, in your own mind, that Charlie saw
the flares, went down to the shore, rescued the seaman
substantially as described, brought him back here, and tried
to revive him?'

'I do.'

'Again taking all the circumstances of the case into
account, together with any private assessment you may
have made of his character and of his answers, do you
believe that he strangled the man consciously?'

The doctor sat quietly for a moment. 'No,' he answered.

'You hesitated?'

'Not really,' said the doctor. 'For what other answer
could I make, in all the circumstances? What touched my
mind was your reference to flares. And I thought again of
the lighthouses – and your sudden silence, in the boat.'

The Fiscal looked at the doctor and just stopped short of
his silent laugh. 'You noticed that? Wreckers and wrecks?
The notion that the brothers may have arranged by means
of a light to lure the ship to her doom and then to steal her
wealth?'

'Well?'

'No,' said the Fiscal. 'Too far fetched, and again no
evidence. Though there is no reason why our friend here

need not make very discreet inquiries along the coast. Assuming the man lying there was the skipper – and that can be established, so we might have a photograph of him—'

'Very good,' said the policeman, as the Fiscal paused.

'Then his anxiety,' proceeded the Fiscal, 'to save the ship's papers, and particularly the ship's log-book, becomes understandable on the assumption that the log will tell its tale of a terrific storm and engine-trouble or other disabling factor. That would not only clear the master, but be very useful to his owners when they come to deal with the insurance brokers. If the master had merely let his vessel drive on a lee shore, with lighthouses flashing about, he presumably would not be so very anxious to save his log and hardly at the risk of his own life. It is my opinion that that box was made water-tight in a disabled ship some little time before she struck.'

The doctor smiled. 'Very neat,' he murmured.

'But with the log, yet to be translated, behind the neatness,' said the Fiscal.

Presently they got up and had a quiet, careful search through the two rooms of the cottage. In the second room, which was Charlie's, the doctor came on a photograph in a tin trunk. It was a snapshot, slightly faded, of Flora, and though she seemed to stand back into student days, and though her features were anything but clearly etched, she came alive in the doctor's hand in a way that sent a soft thresh of blood to his head, as if he had stooped too quickly. Very slightly his hand shook, and for a few moments he remained in his crouching attitude, unable to move.

The search revealed nothing, and presently the Fiscal said he would like to have a few reassuring words with the two men alone; then they would get back, for he was starving.

CHAPTER SEVEN

Michael Sandeman stood in the library door. 'Thought you weren't coming!' He was wearing a dinner jacket that looked extremely black against the lively pallor of his face. As the doctor passed in, he added, 'I have a guest. Hence the correct garb, which I hope you will overlook.' Plainly Michael was subduing a condition of excitement.

The guest was standing before the fire, with a mild smile on his face, at first glance a benevolent rather small figure in the fifties. He came forward to meet the doctor.

'With gifts in his hands he came,' declared Michael, holding out a box of cigars. The room was already drenched in the rich mild aroma and the doctor took a cigar.

'You like a good one,' said Mr. Gwynn, handing the doctor a matchbox.

The doctor, who had been unaware of the way he had fingered the cigar, answered the smile with one of his own.

'I suspect,' said Michael to the doctor, 'that he has been sent here to spy on me, but you needn't pay any attention to that.'

'I have come to spy out the land,' said Mr. Gwynn, 'which is perhaps not quite the same thing.'

The man's simplest words had overtones of meaning or humour out of an easy cultured background. There was more than mere manner to it, however, for the doctor now observed an intellectual quality so native to the face that it flickered with the smile in the match flame. His hair was grey and thin on top, but apt to the face as to a priest's.

'Arrived to-night?' asked the doctor.

'Last night,' answered Mr. Gwynn, 'but enough has happened since then to make it feel much longer, very much.'

'I had him out at Sgeir,' said Michael.

Without a word, the doctor turned his look full on Michael.

'Sit down,' said Michael. 'Sit down. We've been longing for you to come.' He laughed at the doctor's expression. 'Now! Tell us all about it.' He stuck out his legs, an elbow on each arm of the chair, the cigar smouldering from his locked hands.

'About what?'

'Oh, climb off it! We were *there*. Who's been an' done it?'

The doctor blew out some smoke slowly, while his left eyelid quivered very faintly.

'The trouble with Michael has always been,' said Mr. Gwynn, 'that he has no very clear notion of what constitutes professional etiquette.'

'Oh!' Michael moved his head impatiently from side to side. 'That's Gwynn all over. Instead of being one of our most brilliant literary men, he is trying to become a philosopher. A philosopher!'

'Merely the new fashion in reaction against the 'nineties. It doesn't really mean much,' explained Mr. Gwynn.

The doctor smiled.

'The Welsh league and the Highland covenant,' cried Michael. 'But to come to the burning point – how was the seaman throttled?'

'It's a matter,' said the doctor, 'that is still *sub judice*.'

'God!' said Michael, probably at the Latin phrase.

'There's one thing,' said Mr. Gwynn, who looked as if he might now enjoy the doctor's company. 'I don't quite understand the procedure through this legal official with the magnificent title of Procurator-Fiscal.'

'It's different from your English system.'

Michael suddenly laughed. 'Please carry on. Gwynn merely has theories about his remote Welsh origin – dating all the way back to Charles the Second.'

'In the English system,' said the doctor, as if Michael hadn't spoken and with an innocuous look at Mr. Gwynn, 'you sit publicly on any dead body found lying about. In Scotland, we may refrain. We leave it to the Procurator-Fiscal, who is a servant of the Crown, to investigate all the circumstances. If the circumstances warrant a public inquiry, there is one; if not, not.'

'Very interesting,' said Mr. Gwynn. 'But do you mean that a body might be found with evidence upon it of rough usage, and yet there could be no inquest, no jury?'

'Yes.'

'I had heard of differences between the Scotch and English. Seems to be fairly radical.'

'Probably he means that the Scotch system is barbarous,' said Michael.

'I don't know that it is,' suggested the doctor. 'What you probably want to know is whether a man who was discovered in the company of an alleged throttled seaman will be taken before a jury?'

'Dropping the alleged, you've got it dead right.' Michael sat up.

'If the Procurator-Fiscal's report and the Crown's decision on it warrant such a procedure, he will. But if they don't, he won't. Inquest by a Coroner's Court is not in Scots law. There's no such thing.'

'And do you find your system – efficient?' asked Mr. Gwynn.

'Very,' replied the doctor. 'The Procurator-Fiscal is a highly trained legal man of proven repute, acting for the Crown.'

'But, good heavens,' cried Michael ironically, 'surely the principle of being brought for trial before your peers is sacrosanct to justice!'

'Oh, you get tried by your peers all right,' replied the doctor, 'if any reason is established for such a trial. But not otherwise.'

'Look here, do you mean that Charlie may not be tried at all?' demanded Michael.

'Possibly,' said the doctor somewhat vaguely.

'But—' Michael stared at him.

'I think I have got it now,' said Mr. Gwynn. 'If your Procurator-Fiscal decides there is no case against – let us call him – Charlie, there simply will be no public inquest? And that's the end of the matter?'

'That's about it,' agreed the doctor. Then he added,

'Apparently the idea is that if there is no case against a man, then the coupling of his name with a monstrous deed in any court is – unnecessary.'

Mr. Gwynn had a quiet pleasant laugh. 'The terrible logic of the Scot, that is so humane.'

'I suppose it is another way of doing the thing, but it *is* efficient,' said the doctor simply.

'Efficient! Oh God!' Michael got up. 'What did you think of his face?'

'Whose face?' asked the doctor.

'The seaman's. The dead seaman's.'

Now all along the doctor had been just a trifle uncertain of how much all this apparent badinage was meant to convey. It was their way of conversing, so he was prepared to join in and do what he could to keep the talk going. Obviously one could not go altogether by the words that were spoken. But now a definite feeling of uneasiness touched him.

'An interesting face,' he answered, looking up at Michael.

'Interesting! You positively babble information!' Michael laughed, and his teeth gave their characteristic flash. Probably their white was specially noticeable because of the very black hair, which went back from the forehead in a wave. But the whole face was now alive, full of verve, with a glitter in the dark swiftly-glancing eyes. 'Come on, and I'll show you just how interesting it is.'

The doctor automatically got up.

'It's all right,' Mr. Gwynn assured him. 'I think you will be astonished,' and he politely waved the doctor on.

The doctor had been many times in what Michael called his gallery. The house was lit by electric light, an engine, complete with accumulators, having been installed in an outhouse, whenever Michael had found this to be necessary for his photography.

In the beginning, the doctor would have been willing to lay any bet that Michael's interest in photography would evaporate fairly quickly. It just did not fit in with a character which he politely assessed as too dynamic for so static a pursuit. In this he had, so far, been completely confounded, and Michael now and then teased the doctor for having launched him on so desperate a hobby, particularly when he failed to get the precise effect he wanted. He would then storm up and down, but also swear that, by God, he would get it yet.

It was through a bird that Michael had first introduced himself. The maid returned from answering the door and said in a low voice, 'It's Mr. Sandeman from the Lodge.'

And there in the surgery he was waiting. He was extremely sorry to trouble the doctor, he said, but he felt that it was perhaps time he had introduced himself as a neighbour. When Michael was being polite, his manner could be very attractive. Indeed, behind the flash of his animation, there seemed to be a sensitive, engaging shyness. He stood there smiling, with his cap in one hand and a dead golden plover in the other.

The doctor was on the point of inviting him into the sitting-room to meet his mother and have a cup of tea when Michael, with his smile, looked at the dead bird and thus silently presented it.

The doctor turned the bird over in his hands, extending the wings and testing the articulation of the legs. 'You're wondering how it met its death?'

'I am.'

So this was why he had called. Interesting, thought the doctor, probing away. 'Nothing outwardly wrong,' he said. He smoothed the disturbed feathers; of a greyish black, spotted with bright yellow, white above the eyes, with the white running along the sides of the neck into a mottled dark and yellow; and then, right from the throat underneath, that distinguishing splash of black which could never be mistaken.

'Death by natural causes?'

'Well,' said the doctor, and he smiled.

'You don't believe there is such a thing as a natural death?'

'I suppose every death is natural to nature.'

'You know all the same what I mean?'

'Yes. Would you like me to have a look inside?'

Michael hesitated, then stood utterly still as the doctor,

with a surgical knife, cut the bird open and, isolating each organ, carefully examined it. There was no obvious evidence of disease, and the doctor was inclined to place the trouble in the crop, adding, 'Probably because I don't know much about crops, but it seems a too solid mass. It's a known trouble among hens. There's a woman here who cut open the crop of a dying hen the other week with a pair of scissors and sewed it up with a needle and thread. The hen is laying again.'

Michael looked at him for a moment and did not quite laugh.

'True,' said the doctor. 'Where did you find this bird? Seems rather an old sinewy fellow.'

'On the Ros, near Loch Geal. I knew it would be an abuse of your time to trouble you, but – I was curious. It's the first bird that ever got me into trouble. You know its note – a single rather haunting note?'

'Yes.'

'I was about fifteen, and one evening – not on the Ros but in the forest, up on the moor behind the slopes of Garuvben – I heard it. I had gone to meet some men and had just decided to turn back, for I could see no sign of them and the light was beginning to go. I thought first of all it was a peewit that couldn't finish its cry. This affected me, so I thought I'd try and get near it and see what was wrong. At first I could not spot the bird at all. The cry came from here, and then from there, but always near – and always the same plaintive, sad, yet strangely penetrating cry. Are there any legends about it?'

'None that I know.'

'Odd. I should have thought there would have been.'

'Why?'

'Anyway, it drew me on. At last, of course, I spotted it. A low short flight, and then down, not directly away. And then, though the light was really going, I spotted this black under-body, just as if someone had tarred it, and I knew, of course, that it was no peewit. What was it? The cry was so like a lost cry, as if the bird had landed on the wrong planet. The cry sometimes, too, came from the wrong place, until I realized there were two birds. It was pure luck got me back before the search party actually started.'

The doctor smiled (for Michael had spoken with an amusing animation) then turned to wash his hands. In the end, he introduced Michael to his mother, who had tea ready. She had been flattered by the young man's polite attentions and his liveliness. Then the doctor had produced a periodical in which there were some interesting studies of birds in flight.

Michael had gazed at these for a long time. 'I see now,' he said to himself. His face had that extraordinarily concentrated look which made the doctor's mother regard him once or twice out of her woman's eyes. She had almost forgotten the stories about him.

He laid the periodical aside, saying conversationally, 'The carefully painted studies – they lack movement and life.'

No more was said about birds, and presently Michael took his leave, with the polite hope that the doctor and Mrs. Stewart would call on him.

A couple of months after that, happening to meet the doctor on the road, Michael had invited him there and then to have a look at some photographs of wildlife which he had taken. He was still at the stage of sending his plates away to be developed, but clearly the three studies which he showed to the doctor had pleased him, for he had had them enlarged.

The doctor regarded the photographs critically and in silence. Technically they were no doubt averagely good, but there was also an unusual angle of vision, an effort at composition which had a slightly startling effect.

In his calm way the doctor expressed his praise. 'I think you are getting at something here.' He seemed both arrested and troubled a little.

No method of criticism could have pleased Michael better.

'You feel that?'

'I do,' said the doctor. There was something . . . and then it occurred to him. He smiled as he spoke the words. It was not really gross flattery. For why should the idea have flashed into his mind at all? 'You're hunting the cry of the golden plover,' he said, looking into Michael's eyes, with a certain detachment behind his smile. It was the detachment, the objective regard, of the medical man. Michael realized that the photographs had – as indeed they had – produced that unexpected exploring look, and was subtly flattered.

But also into the doctor's mind had come the thought that here, against all the chances, might be a source of interest for this wild spirit. It would not last, but it might see him through what might well be the most critical and decisive period in his life – the early months of his isolation.

It had seen him through much more than that, and often to the doctor's frank admiration, and even astonishment. There was one photograph of a common gull that had haunted him for quite a time before it became part of his mental life. There was nothing picturesque or 'dramatic' about the photograph. The gull was simply standing on its two legs – and a gull has a very solid stance – on the verge of a high cliff. Its head was turned a little sideways, its eye looking straight at the beholder. The doctor had tried to analyse the effect the picture produced. There were four main elements, he decided. First, the unexpected nearness of the bird. This produced the physical sensation of pause before the act – in this case, the act of flight. Second, this suggestion of arrested movement, of a spell, was also conveyed by the height of the cliff, the dizzying depth, and the presence of a current of wind against which the bird visibly leaned. Third, there was the whiteness of the plumage, an unearthly white, for ever without taint. And fourth, that round, wild, yet cold eye, to which the human eye always came back.

This analysis exercised the doctor quite a lot in the more solitary wanderings which his profession laid upon him. It gave him odd moments of insight into the value of analysis itself, but more particularly it made him aware of that border line beyond which analysis is blind, and, being blind, destructive. There was something in the picture which no analysis could touch. At this point, analysis became a dodge, an effort at explaining away the 'something', in the interest of the mind's comfort and 'normality'. He decided that this was at least what his own mind had been attempting to do. And this, again, carried him on beyond the indefinable spell or magic, which presumably must constitute the moment of arrestment in art, to those anthropological considerations with which he was much more familiar, particularly as they affected the spells and magics of what were called primitive peoples.

Thereafter he found himself looking at gulls, and Michael was paid his highest compliment when one day the doctor asked to see the photograph again. 'I had wondered,' he murmured, gazing critically at it, 'if you had actually caught some of the cold yellow in the eye.'

So that now in Ros Lodge, as he preceded Mr. Gwynn, and followed Michael, into the gallery, he was beset by a feeling of profound uneasiness, for he not only knew of Michael's capacity absolutely to ignore convention but also of his sheer drive, almost his need to capture 'the unlawful'.

However, no matter what he might think of their talk or ways of behaviour, he was not now going to permit these two men to transgress beyond the proper limit in this affair which concerned him professionally. He felt his body grow cool, his mind take on a certain protective chill.

The gallery was no more than a living-room which had had an extra long window let in on the north side. The curtains were drawn and the high-powered electric bulbs arranged. Michael had set his stage.

There was nothing theatrical in the way he snapped on the lights; but if his aim had been to surprise, to astonish, the doctor, quite clearly he succeeded.

The doctor stood very still, his face unnaturally pale in the flood of white light, a glitter in his eyes, with a slow constricting and hardening of the features visibly taking place.

The picture was disposed on a painter's easel. It seemed slightly larger than a life size of the dead seaman's face and bare shoulders. But just as, in a sense, the doctor had never seen a gull until he had first seen Michael's photographic study of one, so now it might have been that he had never really seen the dead seaman's face until this moment. It was not that the face was 'paraded'; it was simply and overpoweringly there. By some effect of the light, the brow gleamed dully as in a faint exudation of sweat or agony. The intolerance, again as if touched with agony, of the lines in which the eyebrows met, held still a native nobility. The straight nose, the cheeks, the pointed beard. And the whole was cunningly taken at an angle which told that the dead body was on its back, as it lay in death. The hair under the chin could be partly seen, as could the neck, and the light caught dull gleam-points on the bared shoulders.

The doctor could not speak. Deep in him there was a movement of that sense of shock, which causes, at a still deeper level, a cold stirring of the elements of hostility.

But Michael was now excited. For him the doctor's response had been the highest tribute, and, from watching the doctor's face, he strode forward into the full glow of the lights, at once emphasizing the black and white of his person in an extravagant way, which achieved the fantastic in a remoter movement of shadows.

Pointing to the intolerant expression of the eyebrows, he cried, 'Take that away!' (sweeping away at the same moment his own hand and its shadow) 'and see in its place the smooth brows of the man who was crucified, and you would have – the Swedish Christ!'

And to the doctor in that moment – of all hostile moments – there was no doubt about it.

The doctor did not speak until he was quite sure of his voice. Then he asked, 'How did you manage to get it?'

They were both looking at him. Mr. Gwynn said, 'He always did like his dramatic effects. You can't consort with new movements in the theatre, really new, unless you have definite notions of this kind.'

Michael seemed baffled by the doctor's cool expressionless manner. He had had the 'story' all ready of how he had managed to get the remarkable photograph, but in the enthusiasm of the moment had forgotten it, and, like an artist, did not think it of any consequence compared with the 'work' on the easel.

'Feel I have been poaching on your preserves?'

'It's not altogether a question of that,' replied the doctor, again without any expression.

'No?' probed Michael. 'What do you think of this one?'

He removed the photograph from the easel and placed another in its place. Again of the dead seaman but now more obviously in a recumbent position, for one looked along the body at the face, seeing the throat, the pointed beard, the nostril holes, the eyebrows. It was solid as a carven figure on a tomb. The doctor found his eyes fixing on the throat.

'Or this?' Whipping away the second photograph, Michael replaced it by a third – where the sensitive lens had looked down upon the extended body completely naked.

Almost it was too much even for the doctor who had dissected a few dead bodies in his time. For this exhibition had clearly nothing to do with a professional or scientific interest. It was palpably a mixture of gruesome curiosity and a reminiscence of medieval religious paintings of the Christ. There was an intimacy about it that was horrible.

The doctor knew Michael was watching him, was waiting for the behaviour by which he would give himself away. All at once he had an extreme prescience of Michael's mood, ruthlessly prepared to find its humour in the doctor's professional or provincial reaction, now that the 'work' had not received the right kind of exclusive attention.

And standing quietly between them both, but a little behind, was Mr. Gwynn, who could have eased the situation, but did not.

'You haven't missed a great deal,' said the doctor evenly.

It was a little too much for Mr. Gwynn, whose breath of appreciation could be heard softly in his nostrils.

'But what I should like to know is how you managed to get them,' the doctor added.

'You would, wouldn't you?' challenged Michael.

'I would,' said the doctor, turning his head slowly and looking at him.

'By God, you're deep!' declared Michael, his mood changing in a moment. He laughed.

'It's a professional matter,' said the doctor, his tone

hardening. 'I have my responsibility, as the medical witness. The case is still under consideration by the legal forces of the Crown – as I tried to explain to you.'

'And you think I have rushed in?'

'Well – haven't you?'

'No,' answered Michael. 'I, too, am acting for the Crown.'

The doctor's eyes half-closed, but Michael held them with a brilliant satire. He was now beginning to enjoy himself in quite another way.

Suddenly the doctor remembered the Procurator-Fiscal's words to the policeman.

'You mean – the local policeman asked you to take them?'

'Solved at last!'

'In that case,' said the doctor drily, 'you would seem to have met all possible requirements.'

Michael and Mr. Gwynn laughed outright, and the doctor knew that the hostility which he had felt, and must in some measure have shown, was recognized as a natural element of the moment even as it was being wiped out in laughter.

'You see, I told you he had kept me on the run ever since I arrived,' explained Mr. Gwynn. 'First, round to the scene of the wreck by sea, then on to – to—'

'Cruime,' said Michael, 'where we ran into the policeman. We were naturally wanting to hear all about it. After all, it's my first shipwreck on my own land. But we hardly got a word out. The policeman was gaping at me as if I had risen from the wreck. "Excuse me," he said. "Have you got your photographs?"'

They both enjoyed the memory. There had been some slight confusion until it was made clear that what the policeman had been hunting and could not find in Cruime was a man with a working camera. The policeman had known the schoolmaster possessed one, but had forgotten that he might not have plates. He was sweating with anxiety, for time, in its race against decay and the coffin, was running short 'on him'.

As Michael never went to sea without his camera, it was a

simple matter to bundle the policeman into the boat there and then.

'All out, she has over eight knots in her,' said Michael, referring to his thirty-foot launch. 'The light inside the cottage wasn't good enough, of course, but the policeman carried that stiff body in his arms as if it was his child. An earnest officer. A sound man.'

His laughter was now growing hectic. He was full of the wildest detail, observed with a precision so vivid that it gathered attributes of the mythical. The policeman's battle in bringing out the table, legs first. The stretched naked body, with its intimations of decay, under the vivid blue sky in that wild setting. The glimpse of a face. The humped back of the cottage.

'Whose face?' asked the doctor.

'Wait!' said Michael, and with swift movements had in no time set a new photograph on the easel.

It was the incredible illustration to a grotesque, uncouth folk fable. Round the corner of a wall a hairy face was peering and beyond it a lean cow was gaping with out-thrust neck. In the enlargement, the features of the human face had gathered a weird transparent vagueness, though the doctor instantly recognized Dougald.

Perhaps had he not known Dougald and been aware of the present atmosphere surrounding the cottage, the photograph might not have had the same impact upon him. Now the grotesque scene held not only the comic but also the peril that is concealed somewhere in every fable.

He was surprised to hear his own voice saying quite clearly, 'Remarkable.'

'You're wondering what that blemish is there,' said Michael, thrusting his hand and its shadow at a dark claw-like blur on the left margin. 'I did not mean it to be there, of course. It's the toes of the dead man's near foot.'

The talk went on. There was one more photograph. As Michael placed it in position, he said, 'The principal in the case.'

It was Charlie, cut off at the waist by the gunnel of his own boat. He was not looking at the camera, but towards the sea. His body was isolated in an extraordinary stillness, emphasized by the blackness of the skerry.

'They don't know I took these, of course,' remarked Michael.

'They're not to be exhibits in the case,' said the doctor, after a moment. 'They are very good.'

'Are you trying to damn them by faint praise or what?'

'I thought you'd have known by this time, Doctor,' said Mr. Gwynn, 'that the artistic temperament demands a certain kind of response.'

'On the contrary,' said the doctor, 'I do. But when it is a very artistic temperament, the response must not be too obvious. Or perhaps I'm wrong?'

'Perhaps you are,' said Mr. Gwynn, as he glanced at Michael.

Michael laughed, if a trifle erratically, and damned them both.

In this mixed, laughing mood, Michael switched off the lights and they retired to the library.

Mr. Gwynn talked of drinks. Affable and quietly courteous, suffusing an air of ease, he produced a bottle of whisky. 'I got some of this particular brand in Inverness. I was assured it was the pure dew of the heather. Are you expert in the national drink?'

'No, not exactly,' answered the doctor.

'A nice distinction.'

Michael got the glasses out.

'The truth is, I really must be going. I only looked in for a minute,' said the doctor.

'Do sit down,' pleaded Mr. Gwynn, 'and support me. After all, as you can see, I've had rather an exhausting day.' He poured a drink. 'Soda?'

'No, thanks.'

Michael handed the doctor a jug of water. 'He prefers to add the water himself.'

Mr. Gwynn watched the doctor add a very few drops of water. 'So!' he said.

When the doctor pronounced the whisky to be 'fairly good' Michael laughed.

The doctor did not mind Michael's erratic somewhat

congested mood – it could hardly be called sulky – but he did wonder for a fraction of a moment if Mr. Gwynn was subtly aware that he needed the drink, that there was in him a weakening feeling of nausea. He did not want to sit down. He wanted to go away. And, in particular, he had a distinct dread of having to continue the recent conversation, lest he fail to maintain his normal calm.

So he answered Mr. Gwynn's questions about whiskies, about the brands he thought good and not so good, until at last the liquor began to have its reassuring effect and conversation was almost lively. Then he got up.

'I suppose there's no end to your day?' said Mr. Gwynn.

'No certain end,' the doctor agreed. 'The other night I was out all night.'

'Bringing the living into the world.'

'Or showing the dead out of it?' suggested Michael.

The doctor smiled. 'Good night,' he said. 'And thanks for showing me the photographs.'

'You do think they are pretty good?' asked Michael, bringing the inner forces to a last focus.

'As photographs, they are marvellous,' said the doctor, getting into his raincoat in the hall.

From the library door, Mr. Gwynn laughed quietly. 'That's right, Doctor. Good night again.'

'Good night.'

And the doctor was out in the dark, with all that was suppressed, the images and the feelings, coming welling up in him, and the night itself reeling slightly, with dark words issuing from a struck mouth.

CHAPTER EIGHT

The joiner was an old grey man with a heavy limp. Time
had developed in him the serious thoughtful expression
that comes from looking at wood, and the grain in the
wood, before deciding whether it can fulfil his purpose. His
assistant, Jimmy, a sturdy fair lad of nineteen with a full
flushed face, was standing at the foot of the coffin. The two
fishermen, being tall straight men, could see the features of
the dead seaman from where they stood by the fire. The
entrance passage was darkened by the waiting figures of
Dougald and Charlie.

The joiner cast his eyes round the interior margins of the
coffin. Satisfied, he stooped for the lid and Jimmy at once
helped him to place it in position. The joiner, hissing
slightly in his concentration, ran his fingers along the
joint, then took some screwnails from his pocket.

There was some congestion in the passageway, but hands
were willing and the coffin was soon outside being roped
firmly in the cart. Jimmy took hold of a rein, and the joiner,
on the other side of the horse, grasped the cart shaft to help
him along. Presently one of the fishermen called to the
joiner to jump up. And this he did.

'He's not fit for it,' said the fisherman calmly to Dougald.

'No,' muttered Dougald, who was dressed in a blue serge
suit, rumpled and unbrushed, with an antique bowler hat
above his hairy face. A red gleam shone dully from his
cheek-bones.

The second fisherman, Norman Macleod, who was
walking behind them, with Charlie, referred to the recent
storm. He had always noticed that a storm from that
particular airt had stirred up the sea-bottom and set the
lobsters on the move.

'Were you out last night?'

'Yes,' answered Charlie. 'I set a few pots round the skerries. But I hadn't much bait.'

'Ay, there's that,' Norman agreed. Charlie wouldn't have had much time to go out and fish for bait. 'Did you get many?'

'There was a lobster in each pot,' said Charlie.

'We were very well fished ourselves. And some need for it. The hot, close summer didn't do us any good.'

'No, we didn't make much of it,' Charlie agreed. 'We're a bit far from the market when it comes to hot weather.'

Norman glanced at him. Charlie's blue serge fitted him, and the black felt hat he wore, instead of the customary bowler, gave his clean-shaven face an air of distinction. Norman remembered that Charlie had been meant for the Church.

'That's true,' he answered. 'And it brings up Kenneth Grant again and the talk of the lobster pond and better transport.' He smiled. 'You always back him up in that.'

'I do,' said Charlie, smiling also. 'And I thought you were of the same opinion.'

'It's right enough. If we're doing a thing we might as well do it properly. But it's difficult to change the old ways.'

'That's so,' Charlie agreed. 'But we'll have to do it some day or fade out altogether. And there's been a lot of fading out.'

Their talk was heard by those walking in front except when the cart wheels jolted in loud cracks. But the miles were long and presently a silence fell, relieved now and then by the difficulties of the track. The joiner and Jimmy, apart and free from any need for talk, were each wrapped in his own thought or lack of thought. William, who was walking beside Dougald, gradually gathered about him the sea's calm silence. Charlie and Norman having spoken at some length could walk within themselves. At the bottom of this silence, so deep that no more than a wayward gleam penetrated it, lay the face of the seaman who – as they all knew, as every one in the district knew – had been strangled.

A dark knot of men were seen in the distance. The cart drew near. It stopped. The black bier lay on the grass by the roadside. 'Well, Dougald,' or 'Well, Charlie,' said a man in unobtrusive friendly greeting, as they moved about and got the coffin on the bier.

The procession started walking along the public road for the burial ground. A young lad, holding the horse, waited until he felt he could with respect jump up on the cart and slowly follow. To walk back to Cruime would be too much for the limping joiner.

Turning off the main road, the procession came to a halt on the level sward before the cemetery wall. There the minister met them and prepared to hold the service that was normally held in the home of the dead.

The mourners for this foreign seaman had the extra feeling of hospitality to the stranger to quicken their natural respect for the dead. He was here among them, far from his home and his kindred.

From their own villages, wide-scattered, in all times folk had adventured forth or been driven forth into strange lands in the ends of the earth. As they would be done by, so would they do now. For it was the one earth, the one earth, and the one charity, the one respect from mind to mind, the one end.

This quiet, intuitive understanding anticipated the minister's words. But there was a realm in their mind, too, where they wondered more curiously what the minister might say touching certain things, and as they stood there listening, their hats lifted and held a little above the head in the traditional manner, a pair of eyes would now and then, out of a far-away stare, as the body shifted its balance, suddenly focus on the face of Charlie or of Dougald for a moment, before going on into distance again.

That the minister had command of the occasion, they also felt deep in their understanding. They were aware of the power of the man who knows and who will fashion his subject out of words with the inevitable assurance and proportion which the joiner, in his humbler craft, displays with a piece of wood.

But the minister did not refer to Dougald or Charlie directly. What he did do, with vivid metaphor, was draw the picture of human life on its storm-tossed sea. We were all in that ship. Glimpses of the ship were caught, not on any sea, but on the sea they knew, and the ship was the ship that had foundered. The minister drew his picture with sure strokes, giving the void shape and the suggestion of more dreadful shape, so that though it was their sea it was at the same time *that other sea*. They saw the ship in the black night and in the roar of the storm. They heard the seamen cry, and the seamen were themselves. Valiantly the seamen fought the terrible dangers by which they were encompassed. As brothers they fought. For there is no other way to fight, no other way, when hell has let loose its hosts and destruction roars out of its brazen throat. Then is the last, the ultimate, moment, in which faith, faith *in man* and faith *in God*, is the only light left in the darkness. To that faith they cling, to that lighthouse. Here is a trust that cannot be betrayed. For that trust to be betrayed would make of life a vile treachery, and of death a hideous mockery. The minister's eyes were shut, for this was the prayer to God in the presence of the dead, but as he spoke of the betrayal of trust he lifted his blind face to the sky and his words travelled into the regions of the air and far across the histories of mankind even unto the beginning of the world. And even in the beginning of the world there was a man who betrayed his brother, mocking the work of God, and God set a sign on his brow. And we remember that, and come as men who are brothers unto this seaman, and take him among us as one of ourselves, as one who strove greatly to bring his ship and his companions to land, as we, too, would hope to have striven, and we would commend him and all his brother seamen to God's infinite mercy, as we ourselves hope to be commended, when, in a short time, our ship founders in the darkness, even as theirs.

A great stillness had come upon the men.

After the minister in his final words had asked for divine comfort upon the hearts of the women and children who would presently sorrow in distant lands, he opened his eyes and looked upon the world, and the men were delivered from their visions. As they observed the minister's eyes steady, they turned their own and saw, near them, Mr. Sandeman and his guest standing with their hats by their sides.

There was a little pause, then the coffin was lifted and borne into the cemetery.

CHAPTER NINE

'Well, I'm only telling you what my wife said,' replied Norman. 'The nurse was up calling on the policeman's wife and it's from the nurse my wife got it. There will be no trial, no case.'

Smeorach's eyes broke their distant look. 'Her news is good indeed. It's me that's glad to hear it. It's a weight lifted off this place.'

They were silent for a little.

'It was an extraordinary business altogether,' said William, the jovial one, solemnly. 'And I didn't like it.'

'Who did?' asked Smeorach, his bright eyes on the fire.

'For myself,' said Norman, 'I never had any belief in it at all. And it's the great pity it was ever spoken of.'

'Have you seen Charlie lately?' asked Murdo.

'No,' replied Norman. 'Not since I walked beside him the day we took the remains from Sgeir.'

'Has anyone seen any of the brothers?' asked Smeorach.

No one had seen them for a fortnight. But the boy Hamish stirred. 'I saw Dougald one day,' he said.

They all looked at him.

'When?' asked William.

'Last Saturday,' said Hamish.

'Where?'

'Near Loch Geal.'

'What were you doing out there?' asked Norman, his uncle.

Hamish looked self-conscious.

'Never you mind what he was doing,' said William. 'Did you get any?'

'One or two,' admitted Hamish.

'Och och,' said Smeorach, who was fond of a trout, 'and

you never as much as asked an old man whether he had a mouth on him.'

This was a relief to the dark tangle of their thoughts.

'It's you I was thinking of,' admitted Hamish.

William laughed. 'I always had an excuse myself,' he said.

'What were you fishing with?' asked Norman.

Hamish remained silent.

'Did it work?' asked William.

'Yes,' said Hamish.

'If you are trying to tell me that you were working an otter—'

'Who's trying to tell you?' William interrupted Norman. 'Go on, Hamish.'

'That's all very well,' said Norman. 'But Mr. Sandeman has the fishing rights. It's his land. We don't want any trouble from him.'

'Who's talking of trouble?' asked William largely. 'Have you forgotten what it is to be a boy yourself?'

'That's all very well,' said Norman.

'When you've finished talking, maybe Hamish will tell me why he didn't bring me a trout,' said Smeorach.

'They weren't very good,' said Hamish, in a low confused voice. He was clearly vexed he had spoken.

'How that?' asked Smeorach, in his bright friendly tones.

'Because—'

'Yes?'

'When I got hold of the first one, he was black and slimy and the milt squirted out of him.'

'Did it now? It would, indeed. Of course. Of course.' He nodded. 'It was a bit late. What a pity!'

They smiled at Smeorach's genuine tone of regret.

As the questioning began again Hamish flushed slightly. He was nearly twelve, with dark hair and intelligent eyes. The eyes glanced hither and thither and looked down. Clearly he had had a story to tell. Norrie sat closer to him, also looking down. They were inseparable companions.

'If they ran into Dougald,' said Smeorach, 'it wasn't because they didn't keep a look-out. I'll be bound for that. Am I not right, Hamish?'

'Yes,' said Hamish. 'We were watching. But he was there before us.'

'And you never saw him?'

'No.' Hamish's eyes lifted. 'I nearly walked on him.'

They all waited in complete silence.

'You couldn't tell him,' muttered Hamish, excusing himself, 'from the hillside.'

Smeorach's face exhibited fabulous appreciation. 'His whiskers like the dead bracken, and his homespun like the rock.' It sounded like a line of poetry in his mouth.

William began to laugh. A bit of the dead moor rose astonishingly into life. The latch clicked and a man entered Smeorach's cottage.

'What's the joke?' he asked Smeorach, rubbing his hands.

'Young Hamish here was telling us a little story. What's your news? Sit down, Ian. Sit down.'

'Not that much news,' said Ian, the smile twisting the left side of his mouth.

They all looked at the twist and waited.

'It was Kenneth Grant,' said Ian. 'A few of us were having a talk about the October sheep sales. Kenneth said that Charlie went south to-day.'

'You mean he's left the place?' asked William.

'Well, as to that, who can say? for Kenneth did not see him himself. But he was in his best clothes and he was carrying a bag.'

'I thought it would come to that,' said Norman in a sudden downright voice. 'I thought it would drive him out.'

'Did you?' challenged William. 'That's not what you said before.'

'Maybe not,' said Norman calmly. 'I was hoping that his pride would hold him. But I feared it.'

'A man must do what he feels he has to do,' said Murdo.

'Maybe,' said Norman. 'But he often does what he is driven to do – and not always by himself.'

'Who drove him?' asked William.

'All of us,' said Norman in his steady sea voice. 'The doctor, then the Fiscal, then the minister putting the mark of Cain on his brow. Then the silence of ourselves.'

'Would you dispute what the doctor found?' asked Murdo.

'Whatever the doctor found,' said Norman, 'and I'm saying nothing against him, for he's a good doctor and a reasonable man, whatever he found it was not enough for the Fiscal to lay a case against Charlie. That's all I know.'

'You cannot blame yourself like that, Norman,' said Smeorach thoughtfully. 'No, no.'

'No?' said Norman, a sardonic note creeping into his voice.

'No,' said Smeorach. The old man shook his head. 'You liked Charlie.'

'Well?'

'It is the highest reason.' Smeorach's old thin voice was gentle.

'We should have done something,' persisted Norman, but with a remoteness in his manner.

'What?' asked Murdo.

Norman did not answer. William shifted his eyes from him. There was silence.

'I did not like it,' said Norman, speaking out of his mood and the remoteness. 'When the funeral was over, no one spoke to the two brothers, and they walked away, and they did not walk together.'

Smeorach raised his head, looked at Norman, and asked, 'What could you have said?'

'I could at least have spoken to Charlie.'

'But you did not speak because you were shy of entering upon him. And the moment passed. That moment,' added Smeorach, 'always passes.'

Fate stood quiet as an alien fisherman among them. Then Norman stirred.

'He was a seaman,' he said. 'And in all the traditions of the sea, no seaman behaved – in that way. On the land, a man will behave after his nature. But in the danger of the sea – it is different.'

Silence added the words that were left unspoken, drawing the images that swelled into focus even as they passed away. Like images in the night, in the night of a storm. Or like those more intense images of the daylight, a daylight translated by the eyes of the mind. *And they did not walk together*.

In that leave-taking, in that laborious parting from the grave, when the breath has grown stale in the breast and the Sunday clothes are stiff about the body, one or two drift slowly off together, and another one or two, and a quiet word is spoken, and all drift away up to the public road. But Dougald has turned to the moor, to the trackless way, and Charlie, after standing for a little alone, undecided and swaying in his bitter thought, a glitter in the switch of his eyes, turns and follows him.

From the highway, as they return on foot to Cruime, with the joiner's cart among them, and while they talk about everyday things, weather and labour and the prospects for the harvest, eyes now and then look over a shoulder at the moor and behold the two figures, ever growing smaller, but ever apart, Charlie following Dougald as in some strange but ominous compulsion. This picture haunts Norman.

Even little Hamish, though he was not there, sees something of it, for every word that Norman had used came from him with its burden on its back. But his own haunting picture is more vivid, and he had perhaps tried to get rid of it by telling it to grown men who might laugh, for it had twice held him in the cramp of a nightmare. It was that moment when he had nearly stepped on Dougald, and Dougald, like a piece of the earth, had moved. Had he not been looking over his shoulder, looking into the distance – for how could danger be at his very feet? – he might have seen Dougald earlier. The homespun like the outcrop of rock; the beard like the dead bracken. That appalling moment when the thing moved, when the heart leapt and weakness went down the legs like a flush of warm water. That was the moment which nightmare chose.

And under all their images, pervasive as an ancestral memory, the crime that had been committed.

Crime.

Norman could not come out of his mood.

When they had all gone, Smeorach sat by his fire, warming his thin hands. The fire that had once shown the pink of blood between the fingers showed now but the grey skin.

The fingers moved and shut themselves and opened and shut, in a dry hiss, trying to gather warmth.

It was as well Charlie had gone.

The two brothers, shut within four narrow walls, the two of them, and no word spoken upon the living air.

There is a limit to what may be borne by mortal man. There is the other limit to what he may do – the final and fatal act.

Smeorach lifted his eyes to the blind window, and it seemed to him that life was all shadows, and the movement of shadows, and blindness, and had no meaning, and when you hearkened for its sound, it had no sound.

CHAPTER TEN

As Flora came down the stairs, the cairn terrier started his dance in the hall. Usually she quietened his mad excitement, but to-day she said, 'Going for a walk?' At this, in one of his wild turns, he collided with the hat-stand. Walking-sticks and umbrellas rattled so fiercely that he lost his head altogether and barked with a rapid splitting sharpness.

The study door opened behind her. 'Be quiet, Fraoch!' she commanded, turning the knob of the half-glass door, through which he shot as from a catapult. She closed the door carefully without looking round, and walked out.

She was dressed in brown tweed, brown brogues, and a plain brown felt hat with its brim tilted slightly over her right temple. The colour in her smooth face shone flower-fresh in the westering sun. The flush, indeed, seemed to have invaded her eyes, filling them for the moment with too deep a light.

She walked along the pathway that went through the trees directly to the west, and her body had the straightness and grace of a young tree. Her feet were long, like her hands, and she moved with a flowing healthy stride.

A smile of innocent cunning touched her features, for Fraoch had disappeared in the other direction. She was in full sight now, as she knew, of the study window. Fraoch might rush on half a mile before discovering his mistake. This path that led on to the Ros had been avoided so long that his mistake was understandable. But she did not turn round. She would not turn round until she reached the stile and the manse was hidden.

She knew her father would be standing in his dark clothes looking out of the window. Perhaps standing back a little from the window. Perhaps not. Just as this path to the west had never been expressly forbidden, yet had been forbidden.

She heard the rushing Fraoch behind her, saw him shoot past, whirl, come dashing up and whirl once more. She spoke to him and he barked. She kept speaking to him and he barked out of his delirious happiness. He tried the fence recklessly but could not manage it. Afraid he would hurt himself, she ran up. He could hardly wait to be caught. As she lifted him in her arms, he wildly licked her face though he was in a desperate hurry. His tongue was very wet.

'Foo!' she said, twisting her face away. The two steps on each side of the stile were narrow slats on simple uprights. To save herself she had to let his wriggling body go before she had quite got her leg over. She grabbed wildly at the hand-post, caught it, was swung round off her balance, and fell with a choked cry on the other side.

Fraoch, who had landed on his feet, flattened his front legs, lowering his head over them, watchful for the next move in the game.

Flora sat up and looked about her and back at the trees which screened the house. Pain twisted her face. Slowly she rubbed her haunch bone. A fleck of blood was on her right wrist where it had grazed the fence. She knew there was nothing broken. As the stunning pain ebbed, she sat where she was, suddenly tired, not caring about getting up. Her eyes filled. She began to cry.

Fraoch's head, still on his paws, cocked sideways a little, then slowly lifted. His legs straightened. His tail wagged uncertainly and well down. Once more his head slewed, ears very erect, as he considered her out of his deep brown eyes. Then, nodding, lips curling back, needle-sharp teeth showing in a laugh, he advanced, his whole body twisting unnaturally, towards her knees.

Her left hand lay dead. He licked it. The hand rose and went round him.

'It doesn't matter any more,' she said, 'whether we go this way or not.'

She wept now heavily like a beaten and defeated child. 'It doesn't matter,' she said.

Her words released the flood of tears and her sobs choked her. Fraoch tried for her face and she pushed him away. He began to whine in thin bat-like cries.

'Nothing matters,' she said, and her long full body writhed slowly, the convulsion moving upward in a wave. 'Oh,' she moaned, her mouth lifted at last. Her blinded face fell away from the sky. She stuck a knuckle in her mouth, began breathing heavily, choking the next uprush of feeling. Desperately resisting the impulse to throw herself face down on the grass, she staggered to her feet.

For a moment she stared wildly, as at something invisible approaching her, then, gulping and sniffing still, she began methodically putting herself right. There was no one about. There was no need to hurry.

Fraoch gave a small yelp, hardly a bark. She looked at him and a smile struggled into her face. She wiped her eyes and smoothed her cheeks; she wiped her nose and tucked her handkerchief away.

For a little while, as they continued their walk, Fraoch restricted his circling movements, returning every now and then to make sure that all was well, but at last he got a real scent and life found its true purpose in a race with the invisible.

Down on her left, towards the inner end of the wide bay, Flora saw the roofs of Ros Lodge among its plantation of pines. Far beyond and in the same direction lay Ardnarie with its croft houses and small coloured fields. Across the calm air came the rapid barking of a motor-cycle and the slow barking of two collie dogs.

The white launch lay to its red buoy in the unruffled blue-green water, which broke in lazy impacts on the shore. Someone was sitting on the slipway below the boathouse with its dark-green roof. The sun was sliding down the sky and already the sea far to the west was gathering the silver that presently would become a molten glitter.

Flora continued along the breast of the gentle slope. It was going to be a wonderful sunset. The long bands of marmoreal cloud above the western horizon were waiting in their dream for the glory that would descend upon them.

It was a land of sunsets, of a beauty that, dying, could be too much for what is born in loneliness. Yet she loved it, too. It brought in its aftermath the relief – which she now experienced after her storm of tears, a strange detached relief in which the body lightened and in some way passed out, with its own light-headed gaiety, upon the air. But delicate, too delicate, and vulnerable, yet defiant, too. At any moment, under an uncontrollable waywardness of impulse, it could cry out or cover its head.

Those impulses, those wayward moods, that in the moment of their being were all life, all and everything!

She knew their surge too well, the formless beginning of the wave, its oncoming, that awful suspense of the faculties, the flight of reason, of control, the waiting, the terrible intolerable waiting.

Fraoch shot past with little urgent yelps, his back no higher than the heather. The purple had faded but not completely. She picked a sprig on which the florets were wide open, no longer reserved and bud-pointed but flat open in a starry eagerness, a radiant maturity, a giving-up.

She called Fraoch but he ignored her. No sooner had he rushed one scent to earth than he flushed another. Though normally an obedient dog, in his hunting he seemed actually not to hear the human voice, the cry of command. A thrashing made no difference. Once the scent and himself were joined, nothing could part them short of brute force. But he had no interest in wild game or sheep. Only in rabbits, which he continued to hunt in his sleep.

She so understood this law of his being, that it had become a bond between them. Sometimes she teased him about it, tickling his pads as he dreamt on the hearth-rug and whispering, 'Rabbits!' When he wakened up and found there were no rabbits, she accused herself: 'What a shame!' and laughed and pushed away his more urgent demonstrations of affection.

The Lodge sank out of sight as the slope curved round upon the wide broken expanse of the Ros. Away on her right lay the inland mysterious region of Loch Geal, full of tales, and some said there was still a ghost. She herself had known its silence in a summer noon.

Mostly these tales had to do with lovers, though there was one, bitter with the harsh violence of murder and the evocation of the murderer's pale face in the night.

Her father, in one of his interesting playful moods of long ago, had tried to explain it all by saying that it was the place between the two coasts of the Ros where folk would go when they had secret things to tell or to do. Thus it had always seemed to her that before a girl would dare the terrors of the night in order to meet her lover here, she must have had upon her the hand of Fate. She would have moved under that curious compulsion which could still be felt in the ballad about her or the song. Even the voice has changed, and her simple acts and her words can be reduced no further and so have upon them the fatality of the end.

Flora did not reason thus about it. Or rather, even while her father had been speaking or the song was being sung, her reason produced its own profound logic in the form of images, visualizations. She saw reason happen, and it had bearing and dignity. This kind of reason permits no shadow of misunderstanding as it moves to its inevitable conclusion.

At the end of the Ros lay Charlie's cottage . . .

She visioned the inside of the cottage, still and disrupted. Charlie's room gaped in the silence. Things that he had left behind lay twisted.

Dougald might root about like an animal in a den, but the den was not listening to him. Charlie was gone.

She did not ask herself questions about Charlie's going. The why? crying in her mind dissolved about the figure of Charlie who was leaving the Ros, who was walking away into that far world, where neither eye nor cry could follow.

Passionately she had told herself that Charlie had never done the foul deed, the awful unthinkable act. But these were just words crying in her mind. Behind them were the human bodies, the bodies of men, and the minds of men, stalking through the possibility of all deeds and of all crimes. In that dim hinterland they moved and struck out of the compulsion of the fatal mood.

When she herself had disobeyed all the rules, she had not thought about crime. She knew she was doing wrong, she knew she would bring disgrace on herself and on her parents, but these were thoughts that merely tied the feet

and the arms; and all the resources of her mind, with an
unthinkable calm and cunning, had set about trying to
break clear. She had hoped, of course, that she would not
be found out. She had made herself believe she wouldn't.
Actually, in a way she didn't understand, she didn't care
what happened – once she had broken through and reached
Charlie.

How astonished the other girls had been! And some of
them so clever, too, that in comparison she was stupid.
They had looked upon her as simple, as one with so small
an endowment of brains that she could hardly explain in
words an obvious affair of history or geography. She had
had to learn her school tasks by a process of continuous
repetition. True, once the lesson had come alive in her
mind, and her voice, which some of the girls so frankly
admired, expressed it with assurance, then she was for
that moment redeemed even in her teacher's opinion. In
this fashion, she had struggled on. In the polite arts, like
drawing, she had held her own, though again without
facility and therefore in a characteristic manner. In the
use of watercolours, for example, the art-mistress always
said that her drawing was over-simplified and her use of
colour altogether too primitive. She herself had known
they were childish. Secretly she was very ashamed of
them. But when she tried for shadings and clever per-
spectives, she merely smudged. So she stuck to her
simple lines and her clean colours. And, at least, her
colours always had been good. When class work was
being inspected by an outside examiner, it was always a
certainty that Flora's work, for whatever reason, would
command most attention.

But her sole personal triumph among her fellow students
in that Edinburgh girls' college, lay in the way she carried
her two tweed suits on special occasions. When they asked
who her tailor was, she laughed. When they asked where
she got the fascinating tweed, she mentioned a remote
country weaver. One was a soft green, with yellowish flecks
in it when closely examined. The other, a dun brown. But
her particular friend, Elizabeth Cameron, a dark stumpy
girl, knew why Flora's clothes fitted her so perfectly,

because she knew that had she herself been the tailor she would have been inspired by Flora's figure and style. It was bliss for Elizabeth to walk with Flora along Princes Street at a certain hour on Saturday afternoon.

And on Princes Street she had first met Charlie. She had known him, of course, as a schoolboy at Cruime, but as he had been four years older, naturally there had been no communion between them. None. Charlie had been one of the 'big boys', and little girls merely talked about their fights or other desperate doings. Charlie had been her particular hero. That was all.

And then there he was on Princes Street, and with him the places which she loved, the Ros, and Cruime, the paths, the little burns, the sea. And Charlie sees that she is all grown up.

Charlie is shy and very polite, so he talks and laughs quite a lot to show how much he is at his ease. They have their college manners, their Edinburgh *savoir-faire*. They are not yet near each other at all. They are laughing across whole wastes of the Ros. The old names are talismans in their speech. She completely forgets about Elizabeth, who is coming behind with Charlie's friend. They are walking along together. And she knows that Charlie, too, has this subtle thing called style. It is all about him, in his movement, in his manners. An easy grace of the body, a flowing on. They breasted Princes Street and felt its passing eyes upon them. Oh, it was exciting!

Fraoch appeared, panting, brown earth on his whiskers and forehead.

'Where have you been, you rascal?' she asked.

But he made only a half-hearted attempt at laughing. There was clearly no need to propitiate her. 'What a face!' she cried. She laughed. 'Come here till I clean you.'

She looked about for a place to sit down. Her own world was now left behind, and the cool intimacy that inhabits lonely places was suddenly with her. Seated on a heather cushion, she called him, but instead of coming, he began ploughing a grassy verge with his head. Then flat on his stomach, tongue hanging out, he looked at her. She admitted he had improved his appearance. At her gentle

words, he made all the motions of approach without,
however, advancing more than a foot.

She looked at him for a long moment, smiling thoughtfully, then her eyes unconsciously slid away.

Some of the long bars of cloud above the western horizon
were already catching a faint warmth. They were so arranged, one floating behind another, that the sky flattened
and receded to an immense distance. Spaces and shapes
and here and there an extra vividness gave variety, so that it
became a sunset land of many provinces and far-travelled
countries. One ocean of emerald, glimpsed through an arch
of cloud as through a grotto, led beyond all temporal
boundaries. Sails setting into those far seas would never
return. The silver and the golden apples, and the last sound
gone beyond the earth and beyond the sun.

The ultimates. Where no reason is any more.

One loses reason altogether. One doesn't care for anyone's opinion. She had been taken before the Principal of
the college. She had been spoken to at length, more in
sorrow than in anger, but very firmly none the less, for if the
girls of this college were not to 'set an example', then who
would?

Flora had appreciated it all. She had indeed been so
overwhelmed with shame that in the very moment of the
interview it had hardly seemed to be happening to her at all,
but rather to some numbed person in a dream.

She had not meant to be late, she said. She had not
noticed the time.

'But it was after midnight!'

'I came back before, but when I found the door shut, I
was afraid to— I didn't know what to do.'

'Was the young man with you?'

'Yes, Ma'm.'

'Who is this young man?'

Flora remained silent.

'I cannot force you to tell me. But I have my duty to your
parents who entrust you to my charge. I have a similar duty
to all parents. I have the honour of the college to uphold.
When a student forgets how to behave herself then it is my
duty to inform her parents – and to ask them to withdraw

her, if such a dishonouring course should be necessary.'
The voice had hardened, the dark eyes caught a pattern of
severe and threatening dignity.

In the end, Flora had told everything. That Charlie was a
divinity student, who had known her as a schoolgirl, was
taken into account, and she was let off, but only after her
solemn promise was given that she would never again
transgress against the rules of the college. As for the young
man, should there be further evidence of clandestine
intercourse of any kind with him, then Flora's parents
would at once be informed.

In the end, the Principal had spoken, firmly still, but
kindly. It was this final thrust of explanatory kindliness that
had preyed on Flora.

For a few days she remained in a quietened state, which
even her inquisitive companions, forever secretly pestering
her for details, could not dissipate. When at last she felt she
must let Charlie know, she found she had never had his
address.

Then Charlie's note came.

It started all over again, only, oh, a hundred times worse.

For Charlie was getting into a strange erratic mood.
Something was happening to him. But he would not tell
her anything. He laughed aside her reproaches. Occasionally there seemed something bitter, even cruel, in him. She
caught it in the sound of his voice, especially when he
laughed.

Also at other times – at other times – in an embrace.
Then his protestation of sorrow, of regret. That was when
he was most formidable. He had not meant to hurt her. She
must understand that. He would not hurt her, hurt her
feelings, would not hurt a hair of her head to save his life.
The words did not matter. It was the way he said them.
There was a warmth in him that got round the heart. A
movement, a pliancy, a variety, a gay detachment, intimate
and wholly unexpected little courtesies in a culminating
moment that took the breath.

A madness. A walking beyond. She lived in this terrifying
and enchanting dream even while she was doing her
lessons. As a background, it accompanied her always.

She mentioned it to no one, but her companions knew of it. They would have guessed, even had Elizabeth kept her mouth shut. And Elizabeth could not quite do that. Oaths of secrecy and whispered tidings. On such fare the girls kept alive and even bloomed. Flora was not the only one, by any means. But the girls knew, with the intuition that begins where logic ends, that Flora was the only one upon whom the absolute had come. In a profound way they respected this and watched. The brilliant Sally Henderson changed her attitude and unobtrusively began to be friendly, to help.

For one final month, what an extraordinary life that had been!

The absolute stood back into the region where no sun shone. Dark tracks led to it as to some awful Loch Geal at midnight.

Whenever Charlie declared his religious scepticism, the source of his money would dry up. That thought brought shame on him, too, for even his brother Dougald was assisting him.

Flora's father had helped to get him one of his bursaries. There were others, who had written letters, signed papers. An uncle on his mother's side, an elder of the Free Church, had given fifty pounds. They had all been anxious to help a lad who showed promise, and whose parents had died, the father from drowning while lobster-fishing off the Stormy Isles and the mother following a simple accident by which she damaged her spine. His mother's illness had been prolonged, and during it she had shown so patient and cheerful a disposition that Charlie had grown more affectionate to her than ever before. It was during this period that he had said he might have gone in for the Church, had that been possible.

Then the important ones had made it possible. And their number – as if he had been a gift to the Church from a whole community – was what now haunted Charlie in those sensitive places which torture selects for its more delicate manifestations.

He got past the unwillingness to tell her, past the obscurities and dark if lightly-delivered hints, the slight air even of swaggering carelessness, past everything –

because at last she realized that he had come to care for her. This was an extreme revelation, because it also made clear that up to this point he had simply been enjoying himself as any lad will with a girl he likes. It had also made clear something in herself, made it terribly and finally clear.

In a way, she had become a different girl. In the back of her mind, she was really changed. The meaning of everything had altered. The college rules were still there. But she no longer stressed their difficulty to Charlie. She had to deal with them herself. They were obstacles that had to be overcome, while that queer and culminating debate went on.

The awful thing was that she was no good at argument. Sometimes this annoyed Charlie. He craved words from her, understanding, discussion. She was little help to him. Sitting there in the darkened world by a whin bush on the Blackford Hill, she must have seemed often little more than a deaf mute. He could have had no idea in the world of the intensity with which she lived those moments.

The burden of them occasionally did really grow so great that she became insensible and her hand lay so heavy that she could not have moved it. When he caught her then in some wild clearing mood of his own, she could not respond.

For to her, the situation, however tragic for Charlie, or for herself, was simple. If Charlie could not be a minister, he could not. That was all.

One knew, without words, when that dreadful truth was reached. In fact, she knew it before Charlie himself quite knew it. Before he had taken his decision, she was already wandering in the bleak regions beyond.

No one who has words ready, whose words come rushing forth or whose words are swift and logical, can understand what it is to perceive a situation so completely and fatally that nothing can be said, nothing can be added, nothing taken away.

Words then are noises and sounds that obscure, that cover up, that evade. For this reason they are warm and human and desired. But the point is reached when they won't come, and the breast chokes and feels like a dumb animal's breast. Room then in space only for simple words, for simple statement of the fact.

'It will make no difference to me,' she said.

From her own mind, the words went into all space and time. Hand in hand they sent her with him.

But they did not quieten Charlie's restlessness. And there were a couple of long desperate nights when she saw Charlie was trying to break with her. But he could not bring himself to do it. And in a way which she profoundly understood, but for which there could be no words ever, she saw Charlie torturing himself and torturing her deliberately, yet now hardly knowing himself why he did it. A little more, a little more of this mood now, and the break can be made, the inexorable departure can be taken, the obliterating laughter be indulged. She touches him with her hand. 'Charlie!'

Until that last night when she was caught climbing back to Elizabeth at the window. Every girl in the place seemed awake. They all knew. They had been thrilled by the use of the window and the double rope with the knots which made a short ladder.

It was the sort of escapade so completely alien to Flora's nature, to the very movement of her body, that now, nearly seven years afterwards, it seemed quite unreal. It was like expecting some well-behaved young lady, innately conscious of the need for the social observances, suddenly to become a tight-rope walker in public. Not only grotesque, but physically impossible.

She could still remember, however, very vividly the swing round when she had got her right foot pushed in between the ropes over the first knot. Her body had thumped against the wall and her right leg had shot out. It was the first time she had tried to climb back. It had taken her an age to conquer eight feet; she had destroyed her shoes and her gloves completely, and had lain in Elizabeth's arms sweating and exhausted.

Never again! she had vowed. She could even remember how she had said her prayers that night! For days she had been painfully muscle-bound.

Next time Elizabeth dropped down the torn shoes and the patched gloves to her before she started the climb.

It was the third time that she got caught.

The humiliation was so absolute that she remained cool. For the girls, this was drama's master climax. She had the air of wearing her clothes on a special social occasion when one must be very correct. She had overheard an amusing conversation between two girls. One said in a somewhat awed voice: 'Whoever would have believed it was in her?' And the other replied: 'I always told you these Highland girls may look simple, but they're deep.'

During the days that followed, her brain would not work. She was kept under observation and denied class work while 'her case was being considered'. There was nothing for her brain to work on. She simply had to wait. So she waited.

Then she was called to the Principal's room – and left with her father. That night they travelled north by train. That nightmare journey, all through the night.

She never heard from Charlie. She got it from her mother in time that he had gone to South Africa.

Over a year ago he had come back. Her mother had died. Her father had spoken to her in a way that left no doubt as to what he expected from her. There had been a hidden and terrible menace in his attitude to Charlie. Charlie's denial of religion had something to do with it – but not all. It began in that region of denial. But there wasn't any kind of words for it. It was like blasphemy and horror, and the figures of the night to which they give birth.

She could understand it in a way, too. Charlie had betrayed everything on earth and in heaven her father stood for. And he had betrayed it in a vile and ungenerous way. So much had been made clear to her in the Principal's room, for her father had seemingly made inquiries about Charlie before coming for her. And then Charlie had stepped beyond his own soul's betrayal to betray his benefactor's flesh and blood. There had been something dark in her father, full of flesh and blood, when he had said that. This was what went beyond religion and all things of the mind.

Charlie, so far as she knew, had made no effort to see her since he came back. And she, of course, had made no effort to see him. There was a sense in which their love was like something that had happened long ago, and happened so terribly, that it had been completed, and could no more be stirred from its long brown grave.

Fraoch began yelping down in the hollow. He was tearing at a burrow. Her eyes rested on him incuriously, then lifted to the infinite regions of the west where colour heaped its living waves over the sinking sun.

The silence touched her heart.

Then, oh then, the silence became a footfall on her heart.

The breath heaved in her breast. She was stifled. She could not move. But her head, as in a story, turned slowly over her left shoulder, and there, coming down the path towards her, was Charlie.

CHAPTER ELEVEN

Charlie had not far to come before he reached her. He wore a new grey mackintosh, a new tweed cap, and carried in his right hand a strapped gladstone bag.

Flora could not turn away. She could have turned away to call the dog, but it did not occur to her. Thought and movement were arrested outside her head and she stood in a kind of trance that was like an unbreathed breath falling infinitely slowly towards the ground.

On Charlie's face the smile was at once awkward and strangely bitter. He did not lift his cap: he touched it in what seemed a slow ironic salute. He stopped some three paces from her and said in a simple voice: 'Well, Flora?'

She turned her head away but still could not call to Fraoch.

'After the rabbits, is he?'

'Yes,' she answered. Then suddenly released, she called, 'Fraoch! Fraoch!' But the gutturals went harsh in her throat, and the name sounded ugly and meaningless.

'Why grudge him his bit of sport?'

But she could not turn her face round. The only thing to do was go down for the dog. She could not call again.

'Leave him,' suggested Charlie.

'Excuse me, I'll go for him,' she said over her shoulder and started off.

'Flora!'

His calling of her name stopped her. She looked round. Against an immense compulsion to walk slowly back to him, she held to her course moving sideways a step and stumbling. Internally she was now in a complete wild tumult.

Fraoch, dodging to the other end of the rabbit burrow, saw her coming. But he went to the end and stuck his head

in. Realizing that there could be no immediate issue to this
quest, he backed out and began to circle away, exhibiting
all the usual signs of laughing guilt. She spoke random
words of blame. His body performed the propitiatory rites
while keeping at a safe distance. Then she turned and
began walking back. Charlie was waiting. She went
straight, if slowly, towards him.

The exercise and tumult had heightened her colour. She
saw the acknowledgment in Charlie's eyes. His smile was
paler, and caught in its faint lines was a troubling of
bitterness that was like guilt. She was afraid of its hard-
ness. He laid down the gladstone bag.

'Well, and how are you, Flora?'

'Fine, thank you.'

'A long time since we've met, isn't it?'

'Yes.' She kept her head up, though she did not now look
at him.

'We always were so very polite,' he said. 'It's nice to see
you again.'

She did not answer.

'You have nothing to say to that?'

She had nothing to say.

'You don't seem to have changed much – except that you
have grown more beautiful. Have you changed?'

She could not face up to the mockery, with the awful
denied warmth in it. The tribute to her beauty stole about
her in an unbearable way.

'What's the matter?' he asked.

Swiftly she looked straight at him, searching for the
accusation.

'Nothing,' she answered.

'Quite sure?'

'Yes,' she answered, looking away.

It moved him instantly, in the old way. She had nothing
to say to words, but whenever the heart of meaning was
touched she responded at once. It was as if in these last few
words they had carried out a long explicit conversation
about the dead seaman and Charlie's alleged guilt. It was
extraordinarily delicate and enlivening. His breathing came
a little faster.

'You never got a long letter I wrote you from South Africa?' Her face came full upon him. 'No.'

'I sometimes wondered.'

'No, I never got it,' she said. And she looked at his features as if they might tell her why she never got it.

He turned his eyes to the west. 'It must have got sunk – somewhere, I suppose.'

'Where?'

He looked at her. 'How do I know?' Then he added: 'Perhaps it was as well.'

'Do you mean – it got sunk at sea?'

'Do you think that's what I mean?'

'I don't know,' she murmured, and her eyes looked into a nearer thought, a nearer cause for the letter not having been delivered to her.

'It was perhaps just as well,' he repeated.

But she was not interested in this remark. She was interested in the letter, the concrete letter. For she knew that the letter would have told her something she would never now find out. Besides, it was her letter.

He laughed softly. 'Flora. The same Flora.'

'Why?' she asked, referring now to his repeated remark about its being just as well, as if she had just reached it. She did not want to ask the question, but the way he repeated her name was still more difficult to bear.

'Why? . . . Well – it gave so much away . . . that could come to nothing. When we were in Edinburgh, I could always see you. During the whole time, I could always see you. You were there.'

They stood for a little in complete silence.

'I don't know that I ever told you the real truth either,' he said.

She looked at him. He smiled in the same dry way. 'Truth about my religious doubts and all that,' he said. 'Not about anything else. There's an odd thing about us – I've had plenty of time to think this out – odd thing about us, who really belong to the Highlands. We're only moved really by personal things, personal relationships.'

The words helped her to get used to his presence. Both

their bodies could gather a certain ease behind the screen. The personal . . . personal . . . how well she knew!

'It was that lecturer, Tommy Agnew,' he said. 'I could never explain to you how much he meant, how he worried me. I must have spoken of him often, but you did not understand.'

'I did.' As she uttered them the words were somehow strangely out of character.

'No, you didn't,' he answered.

She was silent.

'I think he spotted that I saw he had his own doubts. For that reason he pursued me. A queer state of mind it bred in me. It worked like a poison. It obsessed me far more than anything else – far more than you. I could not sleep because of the arguments that twisted in my mind. It was not – I saw this clearly afterwards – it was not finally the doubts about religion. Most young fellows have doubts. But there are books that answer doubts. Make arguments about them anyway. It was when the doubts took on a human shape – like Tommy Agnew. Then they grew terribly real. It was Tommy Agnew who pursued you – and whom you pursued. He was the sheep-worrier.'

They were amazing words to be speaking there at that moment. They were like words in an old rite. And Tommy Agnew had not been in life quite as he drew him now. There had been another element, an element of sympathy, in which there had been an understanding, but an understanding which could never be admitted, so that the sympathy was like a strange and fatal bait.

And besides, Tommy Agnew may have been making himself a test, taking on the guise of the concealed doubter to find out whether the capacity for religious experience was innately in the student. Or he may have been doing this to justify himself to himself in that far region of the imagination which nihilism haunts. It was in that region the conflict took place.

But the mind had simplified all that in the long processes of time, and Tommy Agnew was now the human symbol of the sheep-worrying dog.

'It took me a long time to see that,' he said. 'It was as if I had to go away in order to look back and see everything moving in its own place.'

They could not sit down. If they sat down, words would stop and their bodies be more awkward than the bodies of strangers. She was looking away very far toward the south. Every second her face became more known to him.

'It was when I looked back like that that I saw you. Tommy Agnew now had no size. He was like a little thin black dog slipping away into the dark. He was of no interest to me at all and I wondered at the great trouble he had raised, that black fever.'

'I always hated him,' she said.

He nearly laughed outright. 'A voice like yours could never hate anything,' he said with dry detachment. 'Never. It was things like that I saw.'

'I always hated when you were going to talk about him,' she corrected herself, for she had never seen the lecturer.

He looked at her side face. 'Did you?' he asked, with understanding.

She did not answer.

'I suppose if you felt it enough, it would choke you against saying anything?'

She glanced at him swiftly and saw the speculative smile on his face. She stirred on her feet, because of the awful something with its pallor behind the smile.

'I was just so taken up with myself and the grand drama I was going through,' he said with easy mockery. 'But when I looked back, I saw you. You were the only real figure in that drama. But I thought perhaps you'll fade a bit too, given time. You didn't. You only grew more real. So in the end I wrote you.'

She stirred again.

'Would you like to sit down?' he asked reasonably.

This ease in his voice was terrible to her.

'That's really all I wanted to say to you,' he added, as if to end the burden 'I wanted you to know that you were more real to me than anything else. I felt you were due that. I may have been thoughtless, but – you had all of me.'

She suddenly looked at him with her full face. There was pain in her face, a silent cry for forbearance. He saw the hurt intimate light in her eyes. But he knew, too, that this was Flora's face, and in it that which had cried across space and haunted the long valley of time.

As he took the two steps towards her, he already saw her giving way. As his arms went round her, her weight fell forward, her face turned from him. He held her there firmly and still, without stirring, without movement of the mind, as though time, after its long journey, had gone to sleep.

The tide ebbs and turns. The first stirrings come with a tenderness. Her head moved, bringing the forehead against his shoulder. Her whole body firmed, and he knew she was going to lean back from him, and lift her face with all the courage she had and say what she had to say to him.

Her face came clear, all colour and light – and in an instant the colour drained and the light went out.

He turned his own head to follow her appalled gaze. Coming down towards them, tall in his dark clothes, was her father.

A wild gust of fighting life tore through Charlie. 'Flora,' he said, 'you'll meet me here – tomorrow night.' He was like a man getting ready to fight.

She broke away and began walking homewards. She went towards her father and passed him.

The minister stood looking down towards Charlie. Their faces stared, one at the other, then the minister turned and followed his daughter. A thin darkening wind came from the sunken sun.

'God damn you!' muttered Charlie, deep in his throat. As he took a stride after the minister, he staggered.

Fraoch went shooting past him. When they had disappeared, Charlie gazed about him, at the gladstone bag, at his own hands, and sat down.

CHAPTER TWELVE

That same sunset also attracted Mr. Gwynn as he walked upon the high road.

Near the manse he saluted the doctor, who was on his way to Cruime. The doctor stopped his motor-cycle and acknowledged remarks about the evening colour. Mr. Gwynn was on his way back to Ros Lodge, after an expedition into the forest that had taken him a little farther than he had meant to go.

'Don't you know the short cut down here?' asked the doctor.

Mr. Gwynn didn't, and in no time the doctor had his machine on its stand and was conducting the politely protesting Mr. Gwynn through the lower trees of the manse plantation and onto a path that ran directly down towards a small gorge, from which it issued upon the pines that sheltered the Lodge.

'As a matter of fact, I am glad to have this chance of a few words with you,' Mr. Gwynn admitted as they walked along.

An odd thought struck the doctor's mind. It was that Mr. Gwynn stood the daylight better than he had expected. The dark-green felt hat was well down on the head; the light overcoat and muffler were comfortable without being hot. There was fresh air about him and even a suggestion of adventure. Though he had perhaps over-walked himself, his eyes were bright and alive.

'It's about Michael,' continued Mr. Gwynn. 'I won't excuse myself for mentioning it, because I was so relieved at finding the friendly relations between you. I think the photographic business was a stroke of genius.'

'I hope you're not implying I'm due any credit for that.'

'No. Not altogether. Let us call it a stroke of chance or

fortune.' He gave the doctor a glance. 'I suppose a good doctor may not always be aware of – of—' he hesitated and made a slight gesture, 'even of how his own mind may work at certain critical moments.'

The doctor smiled.

'You were not to know,' continued Mr. Gwynn, 'that Michael was really interested in the stage, in theatrical production – in, of course, a very highbrow super-realist way!'

'Did he ever *do* anything at it?' asked the doctor.

Mr. Gwynn appreciated the question. 'You would not expect him to?'

'On the contrary,' said the doctor. 'I would.'

'Good!' said Mr. Gwynn and he laughed pleasantly. 'That is very good. The only trouble is, of course, the lack of theatres and audiences for that sort of stuff. Naturally. Not to mention money.'

'Quite,' said the doctor thoughtfully.

'So it develops into – well, I mean when that kind of thing is frustrated in a group – you follow?'

'Not quite,' said the doctor.

'But you have studied psychology?'

'In the sense of psychiatry, no.'

'Please don't think I have either,' said Mr. Gwynn, in his frank way. 'But you can appreciate generally what might take place, how minds of a certain kind, denied an outlet, might express themselves by turning what is called normal healthy living into a somewhat shocking process, deliberately shocking?'

'Yes – generally. But without the practical detail, it is not always easy to get the picture.'

'He never told you anything?'

'An odd detail, perhaps, that slipped out.'

'You never encouraged him to—?'

'No,' said the doctor at once.

Mr. Gwynn looked at him. 'Why?'

They walked on for a few paces in silence.

'I don't think that sort of thing should be done in a hurry,' said the doctor at last.

'I hesitate to ask your reason – but at least let me assure

you it's not mere curiosity,' replied Mr. Gwynn soberly.
'Do you mean you would rather resent the intrusion – on
yourself?'

'Perhaps,' said the doctor. 'It's – in the circumstances –
hardly a professional matter.'

'I entirely agree.' Mr. Gwynn nodded. 'And thank you
for being so frank.'

They had to go single file for a little way, and then
they came to the brink of the descent down the little
gorge.

'Lovely, isn't it?' said Mr. Gwynn. He stood, breathing in
the pale gold of the small birches that seemed to grow out of
the boulders and rocks. 'Extraordinary country. You think
there's nothing but bleak brown mountain and moor, then
all of a sudden – this.' He made his slight characteristic
gesture, the palm of the right hand finishing upward.
Something foreign and charming and detached about it,
the doctor thought.

'The path is quite clear.' The doctor was pointing.
'You'll just have to watch your step.'

'Thank you very much, Doctor – and not only for
introducing me to this.' His eyes were merry.

The doctor looked at him, and shook his head with a
smile. 'I've done nothing. You see, actually I feel this
mental business is very difficult. We all can help with
analysis now and then. But it's a difficult, and perhaps
treacherous business – for the inexpert.'

'You mean when it really goes down into consideration
of – the split mind – and so on?'

'Yes.'

'I agree. Apparently they can do fairly wonderful things
to the mind nowadays – the experts.'

'Apparently.'

'You are very cautious?' suggested Mr. Gwynn.

'It's not that really. One can often have some idea of the
trouble. Just as *you* feel you know what's pretty well wrong
with Michael. Then there are psychopathic conditions
which have to be analysed very very carefully – often with
surprising results. But not all conditions are psychopathic
in that way. There's not always the hidden trigger, so to

speak, that you can ultimately find, and pull, and so clear
the gun barrels.'

'What precisely are you getting at?'

'This set that Michael moved among – what would you
say was wrong with them?'

'Lord, that would take a time to tell! These were the
regions I inhabited.'

'In that case – we'll postpone it!'

'Shall we?'

At once all air of urgency was dispelled, as if Mr. Gwynn
had suddenly realized the hopelessness of talk – with this
country doctor. A freshness died out of his expression,
though he was charming and friendly as ever.

The doctor's response was curious. He said: 'I rather
fancy that if Michael unloaded himself on me, he might
then feel somewhat empty – and resentful. He might
suddenly, indeed, dislike me very much. That may not
be the usual result, I know. However, if the main trouble in
all this is a loss of faith, a sort of nihilism, then what is
needed is an integrating process, something that will bring
the split bits together. The technique for doing that might
have to be pretty subtle, and very individual.' The doctor's
face wore its easy professional mask.

Mr. Gwynn looked searchingly at him. Then his face
broke into a smile. But before he could speak, the doctor
said, 'I must be off or I'll have the dark on me.' As he
turned his head away, he paused. Well up the slope, and
proceeding in the direction of the manse, went Flora,
followed at about ten paces by her father. Even as he
stared, he saw a movement behind Flora's heels. It was
Fraoch, with his head down.

The sun had set and there was a darkening over the
withered heath.

'Is that the parson?'

'Yes,' answered the doctor without turning round.

'Rather intense sort of man, isn't he?'

'Actually,' said the doctor, 'he's a kind man. Helps his
flock in unobtrusive ways quite a lot. Most of the old folk
swear by him.' He had turned and was talking casually.

'We heard him at the burial service,' said Mr. Gwynn.

'Oh. In religious matters, well – he believes.' The doctor took out his cigarette case.

'So we are back at belief?' said Mr. Gwynn with humour, as he refused a cigarette.

'I suppose so,' said the doctor, and he smiled through the cigarette smoke.

'Do come down and see us soon. I wish you would.'

'Thank you very much. I will.'

After a few more courtesies, the doctor started back, casting his eyes along the slope and seeing the ominous procession pass into the trees.

CHAPTER THIRTEEN

His dream wakened the doctor, it was so vivid. In an endless minute, he lived it all over again, and so complete was the illusion that he had not to hunt for a forgotten part, did not feel, as normally happened, that it was already fading. On the contrary, it so troubled him that he had deliberately to repel it, to make himself realize it was still dark, to wonder what time it was.

Listening, he heard a movement in the kitchen. He came fully to himself and thought: There she is! There was no need for his mother to get up. Iosbail, the maid, could have got all he wanted. Striking a match, he looked at the time, lit the candle, and swung out of bed.

To his mother he said, 'I told you I didn't want bacon. You needn't have bothered getting up.'

'You do need bacon,' his mother answered positively. 'You know very well you don't know how long you'll be: perhaps all day.'

He did not answer, feeling irritated. Turning away, he got his medical gear into the brown bag.

He made no comment when the plate of bacon with two fried eggs was placed before him. He just sat waiting until his mother had poured him a cup of tea. Slowly and somewhat noisily, for it was very hot, he began drinking the tea. Finally he ate one of the eggs and a rasher of bacon.

Outside it was still dark but with a suggestion of the grey of the morning. He did not think of lighting his acetylene lamp, and waddled off into the gloom. There was a slight decline for twenty yards and when he dropped the exhaust valve the engine fired. This pleased him.

The dawn grey was quite distinct by the time he was above the manse. It was a perfectly still and chill morning, and the manse roof and the trees were very quiet. This dark-grey of a motionless world had the quality of pure dream, the arrested stillness, the absolute quality.

An irrational impulse came over him to stop his machine, look at the manse, and listen.

He did not obey this impulse but he looked at the manse until his machine swerved.

The extraordinary thing about his dream was its air of earthly actuality. Usually there is a strangeness in a dream, odd symbols to disentangle and recognize. However vividly real it may appear, it has its own dimensions of time and space. This dream of his so belonged to normal earthly dimensions that it was still completely clear as if it were in simple fact the record of an actual happening.

Normally he could satisfy himself as to the starting point or cause of a dream. This time he was baffled, and there was something about the dream so horrible that it necessarily cast an odd light into the dark recesses of his own mind.

He had seen the minister's face as he walked restlessly and softly, like a caged animal, had seen it with that kind of clarity which Michael sometimes got in his photographs. Up and down his study; pausing, going on; listening, going on; swallowing his spittle, hesitating by the door, coming back.

Completely horrible, because he had known to its last quiver of feeling what was in the minister's mind. The dead of the night and this same stillness on the world, with a deeper waiting stillness in the manse, the stairs, about the doors.

The minister should have been in bed hours ago, but this had been working on him, gradually working up to a fever, this now frenzied desire to go into his daughter's bedroom and chastise her.

For the doctor knew, what the minister did not know, that beneath this desire to chastise her flesh there was not merely a father's outraged authority, not only those promptings to sadism which at bitter moments affect most of mankind, but also a very deep incestuous motive.

And what was horrible was that the doctor should find this motive even while he was certain that the minister would neither find it nor act upon it. As the minister's hand closed stealthily over the door knob of his study, the doctor awoke.

Soon Cruime was there before him in its deep twilight. Here and there a gable-end showed white as a sheep's face. The sea had the sky's dim reflection and the skerries were black. A dog began to bark. Old women would turn in their beds and as they listened to the sounds of the motor-cycle fading away into the forest they would wish the game-keeper's wife an easy delivery, poor thing.

At an early hour like this, one lived with humanity in a curious detachment. And despite his dream, perhaps even because of it, the doctor was aware of humanity in its age-old, childlike simplicity of sleep. The symbols and the terrors of sleep, the distant calm death-sleep, the sweating terrors out of primitive religions, ancient myths. Children all. So that the minister himself is like a child wandering and weeping in the night.

This disembodied, translating quality of the grey dawn twilight! How often he had known it, how intimate and faintly unearthly it was! To get it in its fullness, one needed to be worn-out and empty, with its grey chill on the skin.

The road into the forest of Garuvben was narrow but smooth except for two thin green lines where the grass was beginning to grow. The bare glen wound round to the left, with flowing mountain lines against the sky. Down where the burn ran there were low bushes, but elsewhere all was heather, broken by occasional boulders and outcrops of rock. The head stalker's house, hidden by the near mountain, was some three miles away. The rise in the road was gradual and continuous and the doctor opened throttle. He was just a little anxious about his patient, for she had been developing lately (her husband had hinted it with a touch of embarrassment) odd fancies about the mountains. However, the nurse would be there. He had needed a few hours' sleep. Work came occasionally in a spate.

He was now travelling at speed with his eyes on the road directly in front, for he had to watch the slight green ridges which lay between the track of the horses' hoofs and the wheel-tracks. He certainly anticipated no traffic at that hour and was among the sheep before he quite noticed them. There was a harsh yell which he heard even above the sound of the engine. But he was so used to the unexpected on these roads that his thumb closed the throttle and his foot jammed on the brake automatically and he found himself sitting still while the sheep took the hillside. He had hit none of them, though one collided with his front wheel now in passing.

The sheepdog had set up a half-nervous barking but was already on the slope after the sheep, while the shepherd stood and glowered. It was Dougald MacIan.

'On the road early, Dougald,' called the doctor.

In that half-light Dougald certainly did look like a wild apparition of himself. Had he appeared out of some hole where he had been drunk for days, he could hardly have bettered that hairy glowering. The doctor felt its animosity touch him. Then Dougald broke out of his stance and took to the hillside after his dozen ewes. As he stepped on the heather, he staggered.

The cool smile was still on the doctor's face, but now it developed a hard humoured twist as he started on the tiresome business of getting his machine going against the gradient. Half a mile farther on and just short of the house, he was stopped by the head stalker.

'Oh I'm glad to see you, Doctor.' The warm voice was full of urgency and distress.

'How are things going?'

'I don't know. Oh, I'm glad you've come.'

'Don't worry. We'll soon have her all right. The nurse is with her?'

'Yes, Doctor.' And in his eagerness he was helping the doctor to pull back the cycle onto its stand.

Andrew Mackinnon was a man of the hills, straight, strongly built in a spare way, with weathered face, brown moustache, and steady blue eyes. The eagerness of an over-anxious boy was now struggling against the reserve of the man. As they approached the door, there were some scarcely human cries. The doctor glanced at Andrew whose cap had got tilted in his effort to help with the cycle, and saw that the hair over his forehead was licked smooth with sweat.

As the doctor unslung his bag, he said, 'What were you doing to Dougald MacIan so early in the morning?'

Andrew looked bewildered. 'I don't know.'

'Is he drunk?'

'Maybe he is a bit.' He tried to smile, in agony that the doctor could stand there making a joke.

'Don't worry,' said the doctor.

'Oh hurry!' said Andrew, and he turned away, pursued by the cries.

Some two hours later, Andrew stood with the doctor who was pulling on his gauntlet gloves beside the motor-cycle.

'I don't know how to thank you, Doctor.'

'A healthy boy. And she'll be all right.'

'Oh, yes, yes,' said Andrew, the sibilants hissing in his mouth. The doctor saw that reaction had produced a jerkiness in the man's muscles.

'But she'll need to take things carefully. I'll say a word to the nurse.'

'If only you would, Doctor. Yes, yes.'

'And, by the way, you were right in what you said about the mountains.'

'Do you think that yourself, Doctor?'

'Yes. They're getting her a bit down.' He remained thoughtful for a moment while Andrew, who was several years older, stared at his face as a boy at a master's. 'When did this – fear of hers start?'

'It's some time now. Maybe when the boy first started coming. I had some difficult times – particularly when the light would be going – in the evening.'

His words, almost painfully dug out of him, were extra-ordinarily pregnant with image for the doctor.

'Hasn't she been happy here, then, the last year or two?'

'I don't think so. Before, there would be comings and goings with the girls up by at the big house, for they were girls from the district. But the year before last they started taking the whole staff from the South . . . it's different.'

'There was some trouble?'

'I don't know that it was anything much. But there came

upon her – a loneliness. And then the hills. . . . She was brought up on the east coast.'

'How would you like a place on the east coast?' Andrew looked at him. 'Yesterday I promised her that, before my Maker. Though indeed she didn't ask.'

'I'll tell you what I'd like you to do some time, Andrew. Come down on your bicycle one evening to Ardnarie and have a talk with me. We'll get to the bottom of this and put the whole thing straight. It's important.'

'I will, Doctor. Thank you indeed. You're very kind.' Then he gave a deep smile. 'Some of us will be cursing the new engines like that one at times,' and he cast a glance at the motor-cycle, 'but never did I hear sweeter music out of a chanter than the sound of her coming this morning on the road.'

The doctor gave a quiet laugh. 'I wouldn't say that Dougald MacIan thought it sweet.'

'Oh Lord,' said Andrew in a rush, 'didn't I just stop him coming in at the door. It still makes me cold.'

'Why, where was he?'

Before the doctor's steady look, Andrew, rapidly becoming his normal self, now said, 'To tell the truth, I wasn't taking him all in. He was wanting to give me a dram and to go in and give the mistress a dram. I had a great job with him.'

'Where did he come from with the sheep?'

'He came,' said Andrew, clearly only now realizing the enormous fact, 'he came over the old drove road across the mountains.'

'The old drove road,' repeated the doctor. 'But that would take him days. No one ever goes that way now?'

'No. And if the old Brigadier at the big house had seen him he would have given him what for. He'll be giving the same this morning to myself for being so late!' Humour was now seeping into Andrew. 'He must have started off drunk. Though that's not like him at all. I never thought about it till this minute. It is queer.' His voice sounded as if it wanted to laugh – but it didn't.

'I happen to know he didn't come back with Kenneth Grant from the sheep sales. Kenneth lost him.'

'I wondered myself,' said Andrew. 'And to tell the truth I remember now saying to him, "Who's buying sheep at this time?" For, of course, I was thinking of the Club, and I knew the Club wouldn't be buying sheep.'

'What did he say?'

'He got a bit angry. "Why wouldn't I be buying sheep for myself?" he asked. "Isn't it more than high time?"'

'For himself?' repeated the doctor, with a quiet searching emphasis.

'Yes,' replied Andrew. 'That's what he said. But I didn't want to argue with him. I didn't care who he was buying the sheep for. And I never saw Dougald before prepared as you would say to argue. I thought it was the drink entirely.'

Andrew was still not fully conscious of what he was saying. Relief from the awful night through which he had wandered, hardly able to sit in one place ten minutes at a time, was now fully upon him.

'He had a grievance?' said the doctor.

'He had indeed,' replied Andrew, almost merrily. 'Here he was, he said, with the right to have twenty – or was it twenty-five? – on the ground, and not a sheep of his own there. Wasn't it high time for him to have some? I told him it was indeed and that he was lucky to have the money to buy such a nice lot of ewes. But there was no pleasing him. Why was he lucky? he asked in a threatening voice. At that, damn me, Doctor, if you'll excuse me, I lost my temper with him. I told him I did not give a curse for his damn sheep. I told him my wife was at death's door.' Andrew suddenly paused, with a half-shamefaced expression. 'I'll always think well of him for what followed. I was a little beyond myself. If he had gone against me, I – I wouldn't have been responsible. It would have been a terrible thing.' Thought of it suddenly silenced him.

'What did he do?'

'He just looked at me. And there's no fear in yon man. He just looked at me. Then he sort of grunted and pulled out his bottle and handed it to me. I took it from him and had a good pull at it. That sobered me.'

'Then?'

'Then he had a pull at the bottle himself, put it back in his inside pocket, and walked away with his sheep.'

'*His* sheep,' said the doctor. He looked at Andrew with the detached expression which his profession had made second nature. Andrew began to look back with the expression in which a thought is being born. *Where had Dougald got the money to buy his sheep?* The doctor heaved his cycle off its stand, straddled it, 'I'll look in before the day is over,' and pushed off.

CHAPTER FOURTEEN

The executive committee of the Sheep Club had received Kenneth Grant's report of the October sheep sales and were well content. The price for the cast ewes was the best for many years and the wether lambs had not only done well but had done a shade better than lambs in their own class from long-established sheep farms in the district.

So pleased were Kenneth's five listeners that he went on to describe the auction mart, the press of buyers and onlookers, how some of the old grim dealers began to nod against one another, how Dougald kept the lambs moving in the ring, until the mart came into the attic that looked like an underground den.

Then to the statement of figures, all neatly detailed on a sheet of double foolscap, liabilities on one side and assets on the other, with straight lines drawn at an angle to fill in blanks. Everything for the whole year was there. Heads nodded. Yes, everything was there, straightforward and above board, supported by receipts for expenditure and the auctioneer's statements. In Kenneth's neat writing, it looked a beautiful bit of work.

They agreed with Kenneth that snatching a profit didn't help in the long run. Some of them may not always have agreed with this, but they somehow didn't feel now that they hadn't agreed. Items were expounded and discussed. There was no hurry. Time was a concern only of tides and seasons. This tide in their affairs rose as Kenneth gave his additions and subtractions, and it hung brimming at the full as Kenneth went over his effort in long division and said that in his opinion for every holder there could with safety be a payment of seven pounds.

It was a large sum of money. It was two rents. There were farms on the east side where many a ploughman worked half a year to get as much. And all for doing nothing! And they were paying Dougald nine pounds in the half year, all of seven shillings a week. If wages were going up, then, as Kenneth said, prices would have to go up also. So that however you looked at it, things were pretty good and shaping better.

Kenneth Grant produced a bottle of Ord whisky. They shifted on their wooden seats. Things were shaping well, indeed!

'I didn't notice,' said Peter MacInnes, the chairman, 'that you had this item in the statement of the account.'

They all laughed, but softly, out of a deep warmth.

'The glasses are not in it either,' replied Kenneth, producing six of them where one would have done. A lavish display. And not the glass of ordinary usage, which was a sherry glass, but the neatest half-size tumblers they ever saw.

The cork came away with a loud plonk.

'Hisht, boy, they'll be hearing you!' said Robbie Ross, a small man with a barrel chest and quiet black eyes.

They laughed again.

Kenneth half-filled each tumbler. Eyes were turned on the chairman, for out of an age-old conception of courtesy no man there could taste the liquor until something had been said about the occasion, and about life, and about the wave of goodness that now flowed around their affairs.

'There's only one man we have to thank for this,' began Peter MacInnes, 'and that man is Kenneth Grant.' So literal a statement of the truth delighted them. It was the right note for a beginning. 'He must have been thinking about it long beforehand, and that's what he's always been doing, as we know this night.'

'Indeed that's true,' declared Robbie.

'Foresight was needed,' continued Peter, 'and patience, but that would have availed us little without the knowledge of business, and that knowledge was given to the Club in a way we all know. We have had a good year and it will bring a blessing to us all, if we have the heart to deserve it. I hope our affairs will continue to prosper, and things be made easier for all those dependent on us. And maybe they will do that, if we continue to deserve them. But I am not making any speech now.' He paused, took off his cap, and caught the glass. They all took off their caps. 'Here's good health and long life to our Secretary, and to all those in his household.'

They stood up and with individual expressions of compliment drank off the neat liquor, for to have paused halfway would have been to make a face at generosity.

Faces they did make, but of pleasant wonderment, for they were a people who took the drop only when it came their way, and it was, by individual asseveration, an unusually good drop.

They waited for Kenneth.

He thanked them and said if he had done anything it was in his own interest as well as theirs, 'but particularly,' said Kenneth, and his eyes came level, 'in the interests of the place. For I would like to see this place thriving. And we could make it thrive, if we just planned a little bit ahead. Dead we have been too long with all the best lads leaving us, and the young girls, too. But you have heard me on that before! However, I'm not going to despair. I have a few plans in my locker. Thank you again, and fill your glass, Robbie, and pass the bottle round. We can talk then.'

And talk they did. There was a glow of good fellowship, of rich optimism. When the last of the bottle had been evenly measured into the glasses, Kenneth said, 'There's one man maybe we've been forgetting. It's Dougald MacIan. He's worked well for the Club, if ever a man did, cutting the bracken and making bog hay, when there was no need for him to do either, and many another thing as well.'

'That's true indeed,' said Peter MacInnes.

Yes, indeed, it was true, they all agreed with solemn expressions and movements. But no one somehow made a toast of it.

'I was going to have suggested that maybe we might have made him a small present. What do you think?'

There was silence for a little, then Peter MacInnes looked directly at Kenneth. 'What do you think yourself? He has certainly worked well.'

And Kenneth, despite himself, was at a loss. 'It's whatever

you say,' he replied, but there was no conviction in his voice. There was enough over after the division to give Dougald a pound, or even two. It was the kind of present that would pay them, for it would give Dougald good heart.

'I hear he's been buying ewes,' said Donald Grant, a burly medium-sized man with a greying beard. 'Has he said anything to you about it?'

'No,' answered Kenneth. 'But he will. I missed him after the sale was over. I don't know what happened. But I will say this: I'm glad to hear it.'

'Yes,' came from here and there as a glass was turned thoughtfully in a hand.

'Perhaps, then,' said Kenneth slowly, 'we might as well leave it meantime. There's still a little while before the general meeting.'

'Perhaps it might be as well,' said Peter, '—if that's agreed?'

It seemed to be agreed.

But the meeting had fallen flat. And this irked them, for they had been in the mood to enjoy making a gesture, enjoy giving. It was the mood they liked being in. Kenneth had always had to guard against it, for in business affairs it meant: let us divide the spoil now, let us do the handsome while the going is good and take no care of the morrow.

Kenneth knew what was in their minds, and saw the shadows stalking in the hinterlands. But the main question remained unuttered: where did Dougald get the money to buy the sheep? They knew Charlie had returned with a new coat on him, a new cap, and a bulging gladstone bag. What had he gone south for? To change foreign money? . . . *There had been no key for the seaman's chest* . . . And next day Dougald had left for the October sales, and returned across the mountains, driving twelve of his own sheep and full of drink.

The lamp with its double wick and bright reflector was on Kenneth's left and shot its light across the statement of accounts and the brown-painted table. Peter MacInnes was on his right and the remaining four in front. He looked at their faces, hardly consciously, for he was also preoccupied with what was in his own mind and in theirs. And their faces held shadows above the stronger beam of light and were individual and solid and haunted by the dark potencies of life. Robbie Ross's face was round as a turnip, the skin tight on the bone and the small eyes all the blacker for their pin-points of light. Donald Grant's face was solemn and heavy. William Nicholson, the jovial man, looked like one in whom a wild jest had been frozen and the head made small restless movements to keep the throat free of the ice. The fourth was Ian Maclennan, a tall powerful man, dark, who spoke slightly through his nose, and had in the ordinary friendly way a casual snicker on his face which tilted the left corner of his upper lip, and he loved great bouts of laughter. Usually he was forthright. Kenneth now saw him move on his hard seat.

'I suppose,' asked Ian, 'he will always have kept up his payments with you?'

'He's in no debt to me,' answered Kenneth.

They waited. But Kenneth did not amplify his statement.

'In that case,' said Ian, 'it is no affair of the Club's.'

Peter MacInnes spoke slowly and temperately. 'I think as a Committee we have gone as far as we need go with that. At the general meeting, I'll say some good things about the work Dougald has done and how much the Club is indebted to him. I'll say that, if it's in your minds that I should.'

Certainly! Certainly! They leaned back, relieved. Yes, he was certainly entitled to that! Optimism began to rise again and good fellowship.

'Here's to the very best!' said William.

Here's to it! They drank the glass off. A good drop indeed. And they had money to declare. It was not every day there was a pig to kill.

They laughed, and moved slowly away, and stood, and went on, and faded into the dark.

Kenneth returned to gather his papers and put out the light. He gazed at the account sheet and folded it over. He stared before him as if the faces were still there.

He had gone soft for a little to-night, soft and indecisive. He had meant to take a strong line about Dougald. What the devil did it matter what Dougald did privately? He was a first-class shepherd. He was a man who did his job with a will, among so many who were well-meaning enough but feckless.

No one knew, as Kenneth did, how much diplomacy and careful agitation, how much thought and sheer labour, it had taken to get hold of the Ros and start the Sheep Club. How often he had been near throwing the whole thing up! The jealousies, the trifling doubts!

But he had done it. And, dammit, he would do more. He would get the mails contract. He would organize the collecting and transport of lobsters in his own vans. And people were saying that some day there would be motor vans, even in the Highlands. He would make money out of this place, and if they did not come with him, the harder he would screw them.

But he must watch that softness in himself, the welling up of the mood, the friendliness that laughed in the moment and for the moment's sake, that weakness.

The faces and the solid bodies, the persistent presences, faded out as he turned away abruptly cursing he hardly knew what, with a spurt of irrational anger against Dougald, whom he would support through thick and thin.

'Going home, William?' asked Ian Maclennan, as they parted from the others.

'I am, but I thought first I might look in at Smeorach's.'

'I wonder what old Smeorach will have to say about it?'

'He'll have something, you may be sure. Dougald never goes home with his messages without calling on him.'

'That's true,' said Ian, and he gave a small snicker of a laugh. 'Begod, it's extraordinary right enough!'

Their voices became charged with humour. The night was dark, but already they were clear of the central cluster of houses and beginning to distinguish the grey surface of the road. As they came to the path which turned off to Smeorach's cottage, they paused, suddenly aware of the sound of the sea. It had been blowing a bit in the early part of the day, and the waves beat with a long heavy roll on the strand.

It was a sombre sound, coming out of a distant dimension of its own, toneless, mindless, blue-green, smothering.

'God, boy,' said Ian, with a touch of awe, 'it's a terrible
joke!'

They listened to the night, then went down to 'draw
Smeorach out'.

CHAPTER FIFTEEN

Flora got out of bed quietly and stood listening for a sound within the night. So used was her ear to the wind in the trees, that its seething, like sea-water down a pebbly beach, enclosed the house and made it easier for her to concentrate on the spaces within its walls, its stair-landing, its rooms, its kitchen region below – that well of the house where the housekeeper slept and Fraoch had his basket-bed.

On her bare feet she went towards the door, right hand outstretched, until the finger-tips crawled round the box of the lock and found the knob. The hand closed on the cold brass, gripped hard, and turned slowly. The door came towards her with a tiny protest. She laid her ear against the inner silence of the house.

But the sound she wanted to hear was not there, and with the held breath bursting softly from her, she pushed the door back, but did not close it.

Breathing now like one who had been running, she half-turned and staggered so that there was the distinct pad of her feet on the floor. She held her breath again, then made for the bed. The bed came to meet her so that she hit it near the foot. There was a weighty creak. She groped for the pillows, got under the clothes, and lay listening beyond the threshing of her heart.

If only it had been possible to go out by the window! To go out by the window would be to fly into the night like a bird. . . . All the time she was listening. Nothing came upon the inner silence. Everything lay waiting as before.

Her father had come up over an hour ago. He made a curious sound when he slept. It was not a real snore. The roots of his nostrils closed against the outrush of breath and there was a soft explosive 'Ha-a-a', easily audible on the landing to an attentive ear.

Around this landing there were five doors. Her father's door was almost directly opposite the top of the stairs and her own was the second from it to the right. A very short passage led on her side to the bathroom. There was no water-closet in the bathroom. The water-closet had three steps going up to it from the last turn of the stairs.

It must be now well after midnight. Even if she managed to slip out, it would be one o'clock before she got near the spot where they had met. Charlie would not be able to understand why she was so late. He would say in his man's mind that she had decided not to come. He would not understand the difficulties. She saw the expression on his face, the satiric expression, the scoffing defeated expression: *so she wouldn't come!* She saw and felt his body turning away.

She did not blame him. It was her problem, the thing she had to arrange and do on her own, never even telling him. But he would have to wait. He must give her time. He mustn't be too impatient.

Her father was everywhere, for he inhabited the back regions of her mind, an imminent deadly menace. But he was her father. Farther back than her first memory, he was there. The relationship was as real as life itself. It was part of life and had its compulsions and its duties. She did not think about these. They were there.

Thus conscience was not something to argue about. If she could have argued about it with conviction, all her behaviour would have been different. Her conscience worked deep in her unconscious life, and whatever it was made of, it had the nature of an instinct. Thus she simply knew that the relationship itself, that which existed behind all moods, all acts, was right.

She had to contend against this, she had to evade it in order to reach Charlie. She had to evade her father. That would leave the relationship intact.

There was tremendous danger in this evasion, because, if discovered, it would bring upon her the menace of her father. And the menace was as real as the deepest stir in her blood.

That menace she would one day have to meet. But she

must meet it then, not evasively, but terribly and face to face, and oppose it and tear it away. She could never afford to be caught by it before she was ready, for if it caught her and beat her down before she was ready, then she might never have the need to oppose it again. She would be finished for the rest of time, and beyond time.

She had been beaten down once already. She knew what it meant.

The wind must have been veering round, for all at once the slat of wood at the foot of the blind rattled against the window which was open a foot. Her head lifted. Her door banged, not loudly, for it had only two inches of a swing. But to Flora the clash cried through the house. She could not move. It clashed again, less loudly. She got out of bed, pulled the door open, and listened. The wind poured through her nightdress. There was a rattle downstairs, a window rattle. Then something fell softly outside. She heard, quite distinctly, the smothered growl in Fraoch's throat.

She shut the door noiselessly and got back to bed. She was trembling and felt slightly sick. There had been no sound from her father's room.

She knew he was awake. That appalling silent wakefulness, not a word spoken; the words of grace before food, the two or three quiet sentences to the housekeeper, but, to her, no word. Nothing but mounting suffocating silence.

If only he had not found her in Charlie's arms! That was the awful thing. That was the thing he could not get over. It was a privacy that no mortal eyes should have seen. Oh, he should not have seen it! The cry came from a profound source, hot and dissolving in its own blind shame. For she knew how it would work on him, how it fed on his silence. She knew it with a profound intuition, so that her flesh of its own accord writhed and contracted in order to crush it out. And all the time she had to deal with Fraoch's growl.

For Fraoch she had seen as the real difficulty. With her father asleep, she could have tiptoed downstairs. Old Johan would be asleep. And even if she wasn't there was the whole depth of the house and three doors between her bed and the night outside. But Fraoch could catch her lightest step on the stairs. When he heard the outer door being opened, he would whine. He might bark. He very likely would, the anxious thin bark, which he used when he wished to call attention to himself.

She had thought of taking him up to her bedroom, had worked out a plan for doing it after the housekeeper had retired, but had decided against it, afraid of how he might act, both in the house and immediately he got outside. Rabbits occasionally troubled the garden at night. Besides, she wanted to be free, even of Fraoch.

But all he might do would be to come to the kitchen door – she had made sure it was shut – sniff under it, and whine. Should this waken Johan, she would threaten him in a husky angry voice from her bed. Fraoch would then lie on the kitchen floor, his nose to the wind coming under the door, until she returned. Then he would get to his feet again and whine, but when he knew she was in her own room, he would go back to his bed.

She could picture all this with complete clarity. There was a risk. But all was risk.

Time was going on. Charlie would not wait past two o'clock. That was absolutely certain.

All at once, she imagined him at the stile, where she had fallen. Then, as it were, she lifted her eyes and saw him there. She saw his face. She was so distracted that she said, 'Charlie.'

The distraction turned her on her back. A flush went down her body. Out of the momentary exhaustion came the words: *except that you are more beautiful.*

Of all he had said, these were the only words that needed no remembering.

They had been the shell against her father's silence, permitting her mind its secret freedom, leaving life secretly to live.

They had inhabited not her face but her body, giving it ease and grace of movement, smooth upon the muscles, the long muscles, the round breasts, the curved shoulders, upon the whole body composed in a chair, giving to it all, as if it hardly belonged to her, an enchanting comeliness.

Then she suddenly and clearly realized that Charlie would be at the stile, staring into the trees, waiting for her. He would come to meet her, would not let her walk all that way alone in the dark to where they had had their brief meeting.

To go out and see, and come back, need only be a matter of minutes. Half an hour away from the house would give her time to convince Charlie how impossible it was for her to be sure that she could meet him at night. They would have to arrange something else.

The need to tell him this was of extreme urgency. Nothing else mattered. The whole reason for their meeting became precisely this. She thought of it solely in terms of talking to him about it. Even the need for making another arrangement was only an after-thought, while anything else that might happen (for she knew how Charlie would envelop her) would be a terrible distraction, and utterly dangerous, because if they forgot themselves, even standing together, even for a minute, then the house and the menace would come alive behind her, would come alive in that minute.

All this was perfectly clear in her mind. It simplified her problem, made it practical, straightforward, and placed its execution in so short a duration of time that she could not be overtaken and caught in Charlie's company.

Her eye went back to the stile. He was leaning on the fence, dark body, face invisible, staring into the trees.

Very quietly she got on to her feet and began to dress. She had laid her clothes all ready, but the room itself had taken a slightly different aspect, its orientation had most subtly changed, so that it drew her hand a little beyond where it should have to go before an article of dress was delivered up.

She knew exactly where the dressing table was, with its simple detached mirror. The candlestick with its box of matches was on the rush-bottomed chair by the head of her bed. But the sound which a struck match would make she now dared not risk. She dared not risk a light either for that would be a distraction, a blinding of the senses against the known dark.

She could not find the dressing table. She groped about in the air above a floor which grew in size. She felt completely lost, and helpless. Unless she was very careful something would hit her legs.

She stood quite still, for she knew that it would be dangerous to become more bewildered. She must now be very near the dressing table. Although she had her long brown hair already wound round her head in two twisted plaits, she wanted to feel the teeth of the comb over her brows. She wanted to comb back the roots from her forehead and above her ears. The hard cool teeth would bring her to her more normal self and she would be dressed.

She was not afraid of the room, and as she stood quite still she made a clear mental effort to settle it in its proper position and proportions. As if in answer to her effort, the bottom slat of the blind tapped against the window-frame, tapped in small hard notes, slowly, as if meditatively struck by the toneless mind of the world outside.

At once she realized that the dressing table was not in front of her as she had thought, but to her right hand. She stretched out an arm and let her hand descend. It landed on the comb.

From the dressing table she walked with quiet certainty to the door and at once the long folds of her cloth dressing gown met her fingers. She put it on over her tweeds. In each pocket there was a shoe. Her Sunday shoes, for her week-day ones were in their proper place in the kitchen.

She stood quite still for a moment, then very carefully she began to open the door.

On the threshold, listening, she heard nothing except the noises of the wind about the house. No sound came from her father's room.

She closed the door behind her and walked along the strip of carpet. Opposite her father's door she paused. In an instant its silence gripped her heart as if it were listening and alive, appallingly alive in its inner darkness.

Automatically she began to go down the stairs, and it is probable, indeed certain, that had she not already worked out a plan she would have gone on and away into the night.

But she had thought of the lavatory as an emergency refuge in the event of things going against her, such as her father's silence, clumsy sounds by herself, Fraoch's barking. She hardly hesitated a moment, went up the three steps, and stood almost swooning in the small place.

The decision to pull the chain drained the last ounce of energy out of her. She was weakened now by the dark menace to a degree that made her gulp oxygen in to her lungs. The rush of the waters was shattering. She got back to her room as quickly as she could, closed the door and fought for a dizzy moment against throwing herself on the bed. She could not wait to take off her dressing gown. Drawing the bedclothes over her, she stopped the cry, the bitter cry against this terrible indignity, this crime against the movement of her life.

A little time after that, she heard, as if she had all the time been listening for it, her father's door being opened. She heard, not the rattle of a knob, but the door itself, which fitted closely, coming unstuck.

Now she knew that she had had no fear that night until this moment. This was fear itself. It was black, and charged with unthinkable power.

Clutching the bedclothes about her neck, she held on to them. Whatever happened, whatever was said, it must not be seen that she was dressed, for that would expose her design, would tell everything. Nothing more final could happen than that.

He was standing now outside her door. Her fingers knotted in the bedclothes. It did not occur to her to ask herself what her father would do. She knew only the awful menace of her father and of his anger. It was of the spirit, not of the flesh. The anger of the unknowable god that destroys.

As the blood was swelling inside her to deafening point, she suddenly heard his footsteps going into the bathroom. There was the distinct clink of a tumbler, the gush from a tap. He was drinking cold water.

Now he was coming back. There was a swishing sound in the night outside, and all at once Fraoch set up a full-throated barking. Something was moving outside.

Her father was going downstairs. She got up on an elbow. A strong urge to go to the door and listen almost got the better of her, but she resisted it. She mustn't expose herself, not for a moment. Fraoch kept on barking – until her father entered the kitchen. She knew the moment he entered by the change in Fraoch's throat. At once she was out of bed, her door open, listening. She must know if anything happened, if anyone . . . And her thought stopped on Charlie. The kitchen door lock gave its rusty squeal. Fraoch must have darted out, for her father was yelling. Fraoch, barking madly a little beyond her window, suddenly stopped. There was complete silence. Her father's voice started calling him again.

Now she could hear Johan's voice and her father shouting that someone was about the house.

Fraoch knew he couldn't be seen and could therefore afford to ignore an order.

Her father was outside, calling the dog in an intense voice, thick with anger.

Presently the kitchen door banged and the lock shot home. 'He can stay out!'

Swiftly Flora got into bed. She felt she was safe now. Her father's steps came heavily up the stairs. His door slammed shut. Flora breathed, and presently, slipping to her feet, began undressing.

Trembling a little, she lay in her bed, thinking of the night, wondering if it was Charlie who had walked round the house.

But somehow all stress was now eased, as if even her failure to meet Charlie was no longer of tremendous importance.

She accepted her defeat. It could not be helped. Almost, in a way, life was easier now, curled here in her bed, with its wave of exhaustion and sadness washing her softly. The wave came over her in a languor, in a soft, sad, drowning sleep. She gave way to it, letting it come, but just when it was about to wash her away altogether, it began to recede.

In the region that lies behind closed eyes, pictures formed and faded without any volition on her part. Then one formed and stayed. It was Charlie's face.

She tried to turn away from it, because it had that same pallor of guilt. It's not that the face was pale. It was a whiteness of guilt coming through, straining the features a little, making small thin creases. This expression naturally searched for its own satire, its bitter dryness.

She turned over on her face. Oh, she did not care about crime or guilt or anything. It wasn't that. It was Charlie. Her heart was wrung.

The only meaning of life on earth for her was to help him. Compared with doing that, nothing else had any meaning at all. She should be there, out there.

When this emotion ebbed, she began to think again, and her real thinking, as always, was concerned with doing. The torturing hours started weaving their fantastic schemes.

Towards the morning she fell asleep, and was awakened by the housekeeper knocking on her door.

So astonished was she at this unusual summons – for she was always down in good time to tidy the study while breakfast was being got ready – that she leapt out of bed. She knew at once she had overslept. As she pulled up the blind, she saw her father, fully dressed, standing by a rose-bed, examining the imprint of a man's boot in the black earth.

CHAPTER SIXTEEN

The doctor looked at Michael Sandeman in that objective way he had. But now there was the suggestion of an incredulous humour about his eyes.

'You doubt it?' challenged Michael, holding the look.

'There is the possibility that you may have been deceived.'

'Just how?'

The doctor took up his glass. 'In the way we all deceive ourselves at times.' He drank, set the glass on the low table and shoved it away a little with the tips of his fingers.

Michael laughed abruptly. 'I can hear the same thought creaking in your head as in Gwynn's. Do you imagine,' and he gave the doctor a piercing glance, 'that I am incapable of estimating the possibility of a hallucinatory experience?'

'Surely not,' said the doctor simply. 'As an educated man, you naturally are aware of the possibility.'

Mr. Gwynn smiled.

'Damn you both,' said Michael, his voice rising. 'I tell you I heard the playing. I *know* I heard it. I listened to it for God knows how long. That's a *fact*.'

'I am not doubting that.'

'Then what the hell are you doubting?' Michael's voice was getting its intolerant lash.

The doctor saw the affair was really serious. 'The only place – and you must excuse me for putting it like this – the only place we hear a thing is inside our own heads. Normally we can establish its cause outside our own heads.'

'Blast you, why not say I was deluded and be done with it?'

'As you like,' answered the doctor calmly.

'You simply don't believe,' suggested Mr. Gwynn, 'in – well, in—'

'In the supernatural?' said the doctor. 'No.' He shook his head.

Mr. Gwynn looked at him thoughtfully.

'Who said I thought it was supernatural?' demanded Michael of the doctor.

'Well, what do you think it was?' asked the doctor directly.

'How the hell should I know? I'm only telling you what I heard.'

'So I gather,' agreed the doctor.

Michael jumped up. 'Blast you two bloody people,' he said. 'Don't you think it's bad enough for me to have to doubt myself?'

The doctor got to his feet with a responsive courtesy. 'And how am I to know that you are not pulling my leg? You make statements and hurl questions at me. If you sit down and tell me frankly all that happened, then I'll tell you equally frankly what I think of it.'

Michael threw himself into his chair. 'I know.' He was silent for a few moments, then all at once went on: 'It was such an odd bloody experience. Gwynn and I were up in the Loch Geal region. A fair number of woodcock there and a marvellous assortment of duck. That was yesterday forenoon. I have ideas about them and want to put up one or two hides. There's something about the shape of a woodcock, about its head, and there's a duck – but never mind that. Though, by God, it's marvellous, if I can just get it. I am satisfied that in wild nature there are certain shapes – I *mean* shapes – certain physical forms – that touch the unconscious – no, no, that's not it. I mean this: these shapes touch something in our ancestral unconscious, what Freud calls the archaic heritage, and this touch is literally magical in the way that it creates a sort of responsive image, something that we have the feeling we knew before, and that, by God, we did know before, as the psychologists, the scientific ones, may yet prove. Hell, there I'm off!' He lay back, as if this kind of effort exhausted vital energy, and laughed.

'I think,' said the doctor, in his normal voice, 'that that's very interesting.'

Michael's mouth twisted. 'Thanks very much.' Then he looked at the doctor challengingly. 'Why do you think it's interesting?'

'That's difficult,' replied the doctor. 'But your words somehow suddenly caught – how can I put it? – not caught but evoked a sort of totemistic response. The bird – the totem – the tribe – the clan. Very vague, I'm afraid!'

Michael's look held and sharpened.

'Interesting, yes,' said Mr. Gwynn, who had continued drinking port against their whisky. 'Tell me this, Doctor. We realize we are outsiders here – at least, I am. The people here are no doubt as normal and ordinary to themselves, as we all are to ourselves, in London or elsewhere. But to us they seem to have a lot in them of this primitive nature – using the word in its anthropological sense – in the way that Michael is searching it out – or even you yourself just now . . . You don't mind my question?'

'Not at all,' said the doctor. 'Please do not think I'd be touchy about anything real like that, even if I am one of them. I'm afraid, then, my answer would be that, on the whole, you come with the outsider's eye.'

'I flatly deny that,' said Michael.

'One minute,' said Mr. Gwynn. 'And we may not really be wandering from the point of Michael's experience. Take your parson, by way of instance. And it's an important instance because it deals with religious belief, with what is, in other words, the development of that old totem system which you have just mentioned. Christian philosophers admit as much themselves – if not perhaps in such simple terms! Now am I wrong in having an impression that this man is – it's something more than intolerant, harsh – it's something in a certain sense dark and weird. It's as if there was somehow an incomplete relationship between him and the people. Something hasn't been bridged over somewhere. Does that make any sense to you?'

'I don't know about sense,' answered the doctor. 'I think, if I may say so, I feel what you're getting at. But would a single instance be worth discussing – in a general way?'

'Of course it would,' said Mr. Gwynn. 'He may be the

one instance left! However, I understand that he is in this respect rather typical of his brethren in these remote Highland places. I gather – and it's wonderful how you gather information when you're hunting it – I gather that they have, in their no doubt efficient Presbyterian way, for a long time now exercised a gloomy power, frowning on concerts and dances and similar expressions of communal gaiety. And not merely frowning, but denouncing and prohibiting. Is that fairly true on the whole?'

'There are exceptions, but on the whole perhaps yes.'

'You mean definitely yes,' said Michael.

'Well?' said the doctor.

'Why?' asked Mr. Gwynn.

'Because, no doubt like men in every walk of life, like, say, landlords and doctors, or kings and tyrants, they want to hang on to power.'

'You think so?' asked Mr. Gwynn. 'Purely the gratification of the will to power?'

'On the whole, I'd say yes.'

'Seems a bit obvious or easy?'

'But why should truth necessarily be difficult or obscure?'

'Outside arithmetic, it generally is. That's the trouble. It's a very old question: What is truth?'

The doctor smiled also.

'You say,' continued Mr. Gwynn, 'that a doctor wants to hang on to power. Does he?'

'Of course he does,' answered the doctor. 'He is completely intolerant of the interference of old wives. He does his best to prohibit all sorts of practices which he considers inimical to general health. He does so because he believes his health system is the best. In the same way the minister believes that he knows the only path to heaven.'

'Afraid I've merely introduced a red herring.' Mr. Gwynn shrugged apologetically. 'I agree with you, of course, in a superficial way. But it must go deeper than that. Much deeper.'

The doctor remained silent. Michael eyed him. 'You are,' said Michael, 'Highland and damned perverse.' Then he laughed, as if, all the same, he enjoyed the perversity.

'I don't see it,' said the doctor, his expression apparently quite frank.

'Perhaps we are a bit obscure,' admitted Mr. Gwynn thoughtfully. 'Michael and I have been on this topic, and once you've been on a topic it's not always easy to go back clearly to the beginning. To show you how sincerely interested we are, let me put it like this.' Mr. Gwynn paused and looked directly at the doctor. 'Are you really interested?'

'I am,' replied the doctor. 'You must understand that I have not much opportunity of discussion with – with—'

'With your intellectual equals,' concluded Michael, getting up to fill the glasses. He glanced at the clock on the mantel-piece.

'It's an enormous subject,' said Mr. Gwynn, 'and you might naturally be sceptical of our interest in it. Perhaps you won't be altogether if I tell you that I'm interested in a certain manifestation of modern painting sometimes called "primitive". I am at present digging into this. Trying to get at the root of it. I was even unfortunate enough to have stayed in last night in order to jot down some notes, and so missed Michael's remarkable experience – or hallucination! For Michael's interest is creative, as you will have gathered, against my mere metaphysical or analytical interest. Now you mentioned the word totemistic. At once I was enormously expectant – and correspondingly disappointed when you switched to the simple commonplace of will-to-power. For in that early tribal or primitive state of society, with its totems and magic, life was completely integrated. It was completely integrated because it was lived within a dispensation that was magical, that is, imaginative. The signs and symbols, the totems, had power in that weird absolute way which we very occasionally experience in the work of our highest artists or poets today. The magic casements opening . . . on the light that never was on land or sea, if I may mix my poets. That *kind* of thing, in the sense that its nature was – and is – absolute. Am I making sense at all?'

'Please go on,' said the doctor.

Mr. Gwynn hesitated. 'I hardly know where to go first. If

I were to follow these painter fellows, for example, I might find them hunting back to the primitive, not simply to start a new craze, or do something "different", but to discover again that integration, that magical wholeness, which the modern world has so completely split, if not destroyed. There is thus about it at once an air of frustration and of re-creation. It is rather a profound entanglement and on its elucidation, in my view, depends nothing less than humanity's future health of body and mind. That, I suppose you will agree, is a rather tall subject!'

The doctor smiled back. 'I do.'

'Yes?' prompted Mr. Gwynn as the doctor hesitated.

'This equating of art or poetry with the primitive – surely that's going a bit far? I do not quite get your Shakespeare as a primitive.'

'Naturally. He wasn't. No modern person can be – though I'm beginning to think that there are persons in remote places – and perhaps in slums, not to mention certain high-art circles – who may be nearer it than others! What Shakespeare did do, possibly, apart from his *magic* which made him the supreme poet he was, was pose the whole question of the split mind in *Hamlet* and leave a host of followers, among whom a fellow like Dostoevsky stands out, to carry on the business. But that's away near the end of my argument. Are you really troubled at the moment by my seeming to leave out the intellect, logic, scientific knowledge?'

'Afraid I was,' admitted the doctor.

'Naturally, because in your profession you must come across any number of half-mad minds!'

'Plus the one he has added to his collection from this house,' said Michael. 'And that was before *you* came, Gwynn. *Words, words, words.* By God, Shakespeare had it all!'

'But not before he had used a few words himself,' replied Mr. Gwynn. 'To proceed. What I am trying to do is to show you a groping attempt at using the scientific method in this very elusive business. Let me illustrate with a homely example. Erchie, who attends to the outside affairs of this house, was waiting for me the day before yesterday to take

me out to the *Stormy Petrel*. I took the oars and was turning
the dinghy round when Erchie, who is a quiet man, all but
yelled. I thought he had put his foot through her bottom.
All that had happened was that I was turning her round
against the sun, turning her widdershins, instead of turning
her *with* the sun, what he called *jeeshil* – or so it sounded.'

The doctor nodded. 'That superstition is still alive.'

'Now listen, doctor,' said Mr. Gwynn. 'I don't mind
what you call it, superstition or anything else. What interests me is not the label but Erchie's state of mind. The
conclusion I came to was this. And it is here you can
definitely tell me whether I'm right or wrong. Had I
continued turning her widdershins and gone on, then for
the whole of our subsequent trip Erchie's mind would have
been ragged and he would have been, let us say, half-
expecting something calamitous to happen. Whereas when
I obeyed him, by turning *jeeshil*, his mind was set at rest,
that is, he was whole within himself, properly integrated.
Right or wrong?'

'Perfectly right,' said the doctor.

'And what would have happened,' asked Michael, 'if we
had run upon calamity *after* turning *jeeshil*. How do you
spell that blessed word?'

'D-e-i-s-e-i-l,' spelled the doctor, 'but your pronuncia-
tion is good.'

Michael laughed as though he had expected a spelling
oddity, and swept his eyes across the clock. 'What would
have happened, Gwynn?'

'It would not, so to speak, have mattered then. For, of
course, in any primitive society they have their logic of
practical happenings. This coexists with the integral imaginative. Nothing would have overtly happened to raise a
condition of conflict in the mind.'

'Is it your contention,' asked the doctor, 'that the
minister is pulling the boat widdershins?'

Mr. Gwynn looked at him steadily for a few seconds. 'If I
thought you were getting the full implications of that, I
should not spoil so marvellous a picture by adding a single
stroke.'

The doctor automatically put his hand in his pocket, but

Michael abruptly shoved the cigarette box across the small table. 'Thanks,' said the doctor, and then began tapping his cigarette with an air of reserve. 'I shouldn't go so far as that. And in any case, you seem to be putting a premium on superstition.'

'Are you being obsessed by the label again? The psychological result – and that's what we are being concerned about in the first instance – in Erchie's case was that he became a whole-hearted seaman and therefore literally a more capable and efficient seaman, a more harmonious man. To become capable, efficient, and harmonious both within oneself and in relation to one's environment, is surely the highest concept of a way of life. Can you suggest any other?'

'No. But doesn't this instance presuppose that one believes in what one knows to be a superstition, that is, something contrary to scientific knowledge? An obvious contradiction, which surely therefore makes harmony impossible.'

'For you and me, yes. This instance does not apply to us. So far as it goes, we are unbelievers. What our true instances may be – or whether we have become chronic unbelievers, with an absolute split in our personalities – is an ultimate to which our argument would have to rise. It is possible that when it did rise to it we might find a tremendous amount of light shed upon our present condition *and* the present condition of the world with its war scares and possible – in my view, highly probable – outbreak of universal war.'

'Oh hell, you're bogged now,' cried Michael. He arose. The clock struck eleven.

'Wait a bit,' said the doctor. 'I should like to know where you think the minister stands.' He looked at Mr. Gwynn.

'Haven't you said it? He is pulling the boat widdershins. Erchie knows he is doing it. The minister himself knows he is doing it. He is doing it deliberately. He is going to smash the superstition. That's his job. But the superstition stands for a whole way of life. He is therefore smashing that. And what is he offering in its place? Not a new way of life, here and now, on earth, in relation to sea and land, with the natural happiness and mirth which come out of a wholeness of living, magic, imagination, all the emotions and desires in the one integrated pattern – not that, but a quite other thing, namely, the salvation of the soul in a *future life*. Now I am not offering any moral reflection upon all this. I am only trying to see what is happening, what is happening in Erchie's mind, and, in particular, what must be happening in the minister's mind. Fear is the weapon. *Thou shalt not* is the commandment. Now in our no longer primitive world you cannot act like that without enormous consequences, which will be found at work not merely internally in the mind but externally in social relations.' Mr. Gwynn, suddenly finding himself leaning forward, straightened up with his characteristic gesture. He laughed with soft humour. He cast a glance at the doctor as he nodded sideways towards Michael. 'We have certainly given his adventure an airing!'

'Are you coming?' Michael asked.

They both looked at him.

Towards the end Michael had listened with mounting impatience.

'Where now?' asked Mr. Gwynn.

'I am going out,' said Michael in a flat factual voice, 'to see if I can hear that pipe again.'

'Oh, are you?' Mr. Gwynn arose as if Michael's notion was a perfectly normal one. 'Feel like coming, Doctor?'

'Oh, I don't know,' said the doctor, now also on his feet. Michael turned to the door. Mr. Gwynn looked meaningly at the doctor. 'Unless you have anything urgent?'

'Not as it happens,' said the doctor.

'Good! Come along, then.'

They went out and put on their coats.

CHAPTER SEVENTEEN

They were simply both giving in to Michael's sudden ill-humour, thought the doctor, as he followed Mr. Gwynn, who followed Michael, in silence along the shore path from the house.

The moon must be rising somewhere behind the mountains, for the night was growing brighter. The white hull of the *Stormy Petrel* lay very clear just inside the curving spit of land, her bow to the shore for the wind was in the north-east. The doctor kept looking at her for a little time. A boat at anchor had an air of peace, especially at night. Like a cow in a meadow. But more still than the cow, more lost in its wooden dream.

An odd company, this that he had dropped into. And shrewd, very clever. There was something in them both that he liked. It was a frankness, an open way of discussing anything. The reserve was entirely on his part. And Michael, with that flashing look of his, sometimes spotted it. Something a little mad in him. It would not need much to push it over the rational border. It was almost possible to feel the fellow's mood as he went stalking on there in front.

The doctor became aware that he was arguing himself out of a hardening that had come over his own mood, a certain vague antagonism.

What was it he resented? Assuming Mr. Gwynn had taken the usual visitor's tack of smiling at the poor native's superstition, then he, the doctor, would at once have taken the opposite point of view and supported it by specific instance of second sight and what not and based the whole on a real lack of scientific investigation.

Instead of that, Mr. Gwynn had taken the scientific approach to the ganglion centre itself of the whole matter.

And he had been acute. There was no doubt about that.

The man was rationalizing in a pretty sound way. The doctor himself had felt the largeness of the issues involved; no one could feel them better, simply because of his contacts with the native mind when it faced the final issue of life or death . . . An incomplete relationship between the minister and his people, something 'dark and weird'!

Did he resent this subtle intrusion and almost automatically take the minister's side, so that even at this very moment he felt more friendly to the minister than he had yet done, felt he understood him better?

The doctor looked about him and smiled. The land was still and the inshore sea pale with the sky's light. The way the two figures kept striding on in front was physically comical. Such silent determination on so utterly mad a quest! Somebody should speak. It was uncivilized. It was idiotic. A silence it would be wrong to break!

But this was characteristic of them, too – to go on this totem hunt. They were not afraid of failing, of being laughed at. If nothing happened, Michael might be unbearable. But meantime he was going. And Mr. Gwynn was backing him up, and not merely loyally. For all his years, he was prepared for experience!

Michael had heard a weird archaic music, he had said, played out of a wood-wind instrument that no orchestra had ever known. When he had crossed over the hollow to investigate – there had been nothing!

Had he heard Erchie tell the legend of the music that sometimes haunted the midnight hour by the shore of Loch Geal? . . . Whereupon the doctor's mind, lifting as it were to the far space of this legend, suddenly encountered what must obviously be the complete solution. Charlie had been playing his bagpipes at Sgeir, and the wind had brought the 'weird archaic' music in faint eddies! Certainly nothing of the orchestra about that! It was laughable, almost exciting. He would keep the solution up his sleeve until Michael, having failed, would need some backing!

After about twenty minutes, Michael stopped. The other two closed in. 'This is where we go up.' Michael's voice was lowpitched. 'I think we should move as quietly as we can.'

'Very well,' agreed Mr. Gwynn. 'And you can remember

a man's heart at fifty-seven is not what it was at twenty-seven.'

Michael smiled. 'Have I been forgetting again?' His face turned to the doctor. 'Enjoying your scepticism?'

'Look here,' said the doctor softly, 'it's a lovely night. There can only be the slimmest chance of a second performance. We've got to be careful. Where did it happen exactly?' His voice carried conviction.

'There's a path here, little more than a sheep-path, that goes right to Loch Geal,' answered Michael.

'I know it,' said the doctor.

'It's about half-way – less than half-way.'

'Not at Loch Geal?'

'No. Quite a new place I discovered all on my own.' His voice was mocking but friendly, as if the night had sucked his bad humour away.

'How did you discover it?'

'I was at Loch Geal, in connection with these hides. Certain things I wanted to find out about what happens at night – not only to the birds. I was on the way back – a little later – not much – than this. It was an extraordinarily beautiful night. I had sat down. Then I heard it – as I told you. It seemed to be at some little distance – as if being played out of the earth – or by the earth.' He paused, clearly to give the doctor the benefit of the moment. 'As I got up, of course the earth saw me. The music stopped abruptly. I tried to find it. I was tripped by the earth and went headlong. I said a few things upon the night.'

'Was that the end?'

'No. Then I was followed.'

He must have felt the doctor's sudden piercing glance, for he added, 'I thought that might surprise you!'

The doctor waited.

'I never got a clear glimpse. The thing was above me. Once I heard it, and once it started a boulder thudding down.'

'How far did it follow you?'

'At least half-way back the way we've just come.'

'You didn't make any effort to—'

'To intercept it? No. I was afraid. That's why I'm here

now. And would have been whether you'd both come or not.'

They stood in silence. 'Why don't you ask me why I was afraid?' inquired Michael.

'Well, why were you?' asked the doctor directly.

'That's better,' said Michael. 'I had the feeling that the thing was a man – a man who had committed murder – perhaps long ago at Loch Geal. I felt the murder in him.'

The doctor was silent.

'No comment at all?' probed Michael.

The doctor was looking out to sea. Near at hand the water was bright, but far off it darkened under the wind. Then upon a darkened patch came a glitter. The moon must be looking over the mountains. He turned his head round.

'When you strike a stone with your foot,' said the doctor, 'the sound carries a long distance to listening ears. We'd better go pretty quietly.'

Michael stood a moment gazing at the doctor, then turned to the slope.

In the same order, they now went carefully and much more slowly. Twice Michael stopped, clearly to let Mr. Gwynn have his wind. 'You might have told me,' whispered Mr. Gwynn at the second stop, 'and I would have drunk nothing.'

His two companions smiled. The doctor, who had dropped in on them some time after dinner, had had his own meal about six o'clock. The three whiskies – and Michael's was a careless hand – were now inducing a certain empty bodiless feeling, with the forehead slightly cold and the mind abnormally clear.

At the third stop, Mr. Gwynn's breath was audibly wheezing. The doctor gestured downward with his open hand, then sat down. Mr. Gwynn at once flopped beside him. Michael stooped and whispered. 'Not far now. Another hundred yards or so.'

'Sit down,' whispered the doctor.

Michael sat down. The doctor bent to his ear. 'If we keep to leeward . . .'

Michael nodded. The wind was blowing down past them

and now, away from the shelter of the shore, it was a fair breeze.

Mr. Gwynn began to button his coat round his throat. The weather was mild for late October, but the wind was searching. The doctor cast about him and saw a sheltering bluff up a little and to the right. Their heads came together and he pointed. 'For shelter. Otherwise our hot skins will have us sneezing like donkeys.' Having to keep his voice low induced a near feeling of friendliness. Laughter issued softly from their nostrils. They followed him, stooping slightly, and came under the shallow bluff where it was quite windless when they sat down.

'Ah-h,' breathed Mr. Gwynn.

'Sit on your gloves,' breathed the doctor.

When they had made themselves comfortable, the doctor whispered: 'This is the moment when I believe in your "primitive"!' Something of boyhood had come back upon him in this freedom of the night, this nocturnal adventuring with all day-light responsibility gone.

Mr. Gwynn jerked up his head in silent laughter. 'It doesn't matter what happens now?'

'Not a bit,' whispered the doctor.

'Shut up, you blithering toughs!' whispered Michael.

'He's actually expecting something,' the doctor informed Mr. Gwynn.

Mr. Gwynn tilted his head again. With the doctor, he entered into fathomless conspiracy. 'He does not understand yet!'

'Not he,' agreed the doctor.

'I suppose you call this primitive mirth,' murmured Michael sardonically.

'B' the holy powers an' he's got it!' declared Mr. Gwynn, and from the control of his voice, the sudden Irish brogue, and the slight but perfectly finished gesture, the doctor knew that this man had once been an actor.

Suddenly the whole outing was a delight. Mr. Gwynn, with a careless confidence, swayed on top of his form. He quoted lines from Shakespeare of at once an exquisite beauty and idiotic aptness. And all was suppressed, suppressed by Michael, until it cried out silently upon the night, and the doctor, like one in truth half drunk, swayed with shut mouth and husky throat, while Mr. Gwynn half shrugged a shoulder or lifted a spread palm and breathed out his immortal magic on the air.

There was an extraordinary charm about the little man at that moment, a natural gaiety, an exquisite yet controlled inconsequence.

This went on for quite a long time, but it had its natural end, conquered by the night, by the moon, by the smooth heather breasts, by the black shadows, by the chill that searched for the heart even within their windless horseshoe of shelter.

Mr. Gwynn shuddered softly and stared over his knees. Then in a voice that for the first time firmed beyond soft syllables to the monotone of the wind moaning round this bleak tumbled land, this barren haunted place, he said very very slowly as if he had forgotten his companions, forgotten everything:

> A savage place! as holy and enchanted
> As e'er beneath a waning moon was haunted
> By woman wailing for her demon lover!

These lines from Coleridge left a hollow of silence around them and deep within their marvelling minds, and upon this hollow, without any warning, came a flurry of piped notes.

The suddenness, the complete clarity, of the piping, its weird archaic character, so gripped Mr. Gwynn that his face hardly rose from his clasped knees, it only tilted upward a little to let the mouth fall open.

A harsh sound in Michael's throat held an immensity of triumph and relief.

The player could not be more than a hundred yards away, above them but to the left; though it was difficult to be precise. There was a bubbly floating sound in the notes and yet at the same time an inner thin buzzing of a reed. Not of any reed, not a dry reed, but a reed wet as the tender green corn stalk which the schoolboy cracks between his lips before blowing its low shrillness. 'Archaic' was the very word; and 'weird'. It ran all about the ground, rushed away on the wind. It had abrupt pauses, as if for breath. It had a curious compressed quality of frolic. Then suddenly it went slow and intensely sad. The theme notes were held, but between each two intolerably drawn-out notes there was still a rush of short swift notes.

Mr. Gwynn had an involuntary vision, quite extraordinarily vivid. The mouth that blew the pipe was as wide as the face, with the deep upper lip curving over. The eyelashes curved over the eyes in the same way, like drawn hoods. The skin had the pallor of clay. Perhaps the face of a frog-like leprechaun out of some long-forgotten story book of childhood.

Michael was the first to come to himself. He leaned towards their heads. 'Let us rush it,' he whispered.

And at once the doctor replied: 'For God's sake, no!' The intensity in his whisper made them stare at him.

Michael had not been interested in receiving any impression from the music. The fact of its being there intoxicated him; justified him in so wild and magnificent a way that he could have rushed it and grappled with it, though it were murder itself that played.

But upon the doctor the effect was very different. Whether or not there was anything in Mr. Gwynn's talk of the 'ancestral unconscious', certainly his ancestors had a hold on the doctor now. It did not matter that he knew the theme of the slow piece being played. That only intensified his emotion, gave it shape and somehow an appalling knowledge. When an old pipe tune was so profound in its revelation of human experience, of inexpressible sorrow, that its creation was clearly beyond human power, the folk knew then that the master could have got it only from some other power, and they talked of magic chanters and the fairies, the small wise people of the green hills. There is a defeat that is bitter in the mouth beyond all bitterness of the bitterest herb; a sadness that has agony and the breaking of the heart in one's own hands. This is the music the doctor heard, and his mind was charged with a dreadful unknowable foreknowledge.

He knew the two were staring at him, but he paid no

attention to them behind the chill mask of his face. Their words and theories were less than noises in a spent wind; a prattling of clever children long ago; but their presence here was a mortal danger and he had got to get them away somehow.

Slowly he raised his head and peered towards the place whence the music came, taking care to keep the rough old heather on top as a shield, though he knew the moon, behind him, would not shine on his face. When he heard Michael rising, he at once gripped his shoulder, keeping him down, and felt the shoulder wriggle in pain. He forced Michael down and sat beside him. 'Hush!' he breathed, shaking his head in warning but looking at neither of them.

The music stopped.

The doctor sat for a little time without moving, his whole being listening to the night, then, motioning them to remain as they were, he slowly rose again. He remained standing so long and so still that Michael began to stir.

As he sat down, the doctor laid a strong detaining hand on Michael, who whispered intensely, 'Is he gone?'

'No.'

'Did you see him?'

'No.'

'You know who it is?'

The doctor's expressionless face looked at Michael's face, looked beyond it, and made no answer. 'Hsh!' he warned.

The music started again, and clearly the player had come under the fatal spell of the one theme. The same notes, the long-held and intolerable cries with the swift notes between bubbling like blood in the heart.

'I'm going to have a look,' whispered Michael.

The doctor held him for a moment. 'All right. But listen. Keep your face hidden behind the heather.' Then his voice dropped two full tones. 'Don't let your head be seen. And whatever happens, don't move. Do you understand that?'

'Yes,' whispered Mr. Gwynn.

The doctor started at Michael.

'Yes,' whispered Michael quietly.

There was nothing to be seen but the night as they had already seen it, the dark heather, the frozen movement of the earth, and the lines that ran against a sky pale blue in the east and passing by imperceptible gradation to a deep blue in the west.

Mr. Gwynn knew that, as never before, he was held in thrall to the living night, and as the marvel of this was something that could not be exceeded, he turned his head away from the invisible source of the magical notes, to look, as he had so often looked, at the moon. It was a carelessness, beyond fear, of the secret spirit in a new dimension, and in this weird dimension he wanted to see how the lady moon walked.

She was walking now above the hill-tops of Garuvben deer forest, and a trail of passing cloud going in her direction set up the familiar illusion of her walking the opposite way. Her light came on the breast of the near slope passing upward on his right hand and as his eye ran along the slope – his breath caught, and in the same moment the doctor's fingers closed over his arm.

By an odd chance, the head of the approaching figure passed across the moon. The whole figure was completely silhouetted and in the same moment the three watchers knew it was a woman.

She looked very tall upon the hillside and came slowly and without sound. The doctor had no need to press down his companions. Anxiety not to be seen was purely instinctive, and balanced by the instinct which dared not release the eyes.

They saw her stop when she heard the music. She stood quite still, as if she might stand like that for ever. But in a little while she was coming on again, only more slowly, as if each footstep now were an adventure not on the breast of the hill.

She was almost opposite them, barely thirty yards away, when the music stopped abruptly as if the pipe had been struck from the player's mouth.

She stood again, and now they knew she was waiting and would never go on.

They heard him coming, heard the reckless thrust of his

feet, and there he was, the moon shining on him, swiftly approaching, coming close to her, with the cry 'Flora!' in his mouth. Without another word – no cry had come from her – they stood locked in an embrace, his face fallen over her shoulder, without the slightest movement, clearly without thought, lost at the end of an experience that needed blindness and rest.

His voice began whispering, softly and hidden. They heard her sighing breath and voice smother against him in a small cry. He put his arm round her and, leaving the right of way, by which she had come, they began walking into the heart of the Ros, towards Loch Geal. Within fifty yards, they had passed from sight.

Upon the silence came Michael's low voice:

'So that was the murderer!'

The doctor did not move.

Mr. Gwynn looked up at the doctor and was held by the tense immobility of his body and face.

'Charlie!' Astonishment and wild humour raked out of Michael's throat. 'Hell, could you beat it!'

'Hsh!' said Mr. Gwynn, feeling Michael was about to laugh wildly upon the night.

'Let us go,' said the doctor in a drained voice. He stood for a moment or two perfectly still, then turned away. Mr. Gwynn followed him, with Michael behind.

They went on in silence, and not until they had reached the shore path was a word spoken. There Mr. Gwynn expelled a loud breath. 'I'm tired,' he said and sat down.

'It was Charlie, wasn't it?' Michael asked the doctor, both of them standing.

The doctor turned his head and looked at him. 'Do you think so?'

'Of course it was!'

The doctor moved his head and looked about the ground.

'Don't you?' persisted Michael.

'Here,' said the doctor to Mr. Gwynn, 'the low ground at this time of year is always damp and treacherous. I shouldn't advise you to sit long.'

Mr. Gwynn got up. 'I think you're right.'

'We'd better keep going,' said the doctor like one automatically offering medical advice.

Michael gave a small laugh as he followed. Presently he said, 'It's up there that he dislodged the stone.' His voice, being raised to a natural pitch for the first time since they had started out, sounded astonishingly loud. 'What the hell was Charlie's game, following me?'

Neither of the two in front replied.

'Have you no idea, Doctor?'

'None,' answered the doctor.

Michael laughed. 'You sound so bloody mysterious.' The amazing justification of his previous experience, which had been so doubtfully received, the fabulous happenings of the night with their new and incredible implications, had induced in him a vast and unconquerable gaiety. Perhaps the doctor had gone all quiet and non-committal because of the rather obvious way, now that things about money and what not were leaking out, in which the magnificent Procurator-Fiscal and himself, not to mention the policeman, had mishandled the affair of Charlie and the throttled seaman! Though it was hardly fair to bait the doctor – that's the way Gwynn would put it – because he was professionally involved! Hell beneath, it was laughable!

And that a girl should be in it! That tilted the whole applecart! No city civilization could 'produce' a show like this. It hadn't the background, the backcloth *sub specie aeternitatis*! His mind roared upon the night. They – haunters of hotel lounges and night dives – said nothing ever happened in the country beyond the birth of a cow. 'They' flashed through Michael's mind, their known faces, their eternal hectic laughter, their swift movement and gabble and glitter of faces in artificial light. Their languorous moods. He knew them all. He cheered to them derisively.

Christ, these women! he thought, his teeth on edge but only in the moment's spasm.

A girl walking somnambulistic upon a tilted heath. It couldn't be 'produced'. By God, a man daren't produce it. The rotten world wouldn't believe it. Imagination was dead, choked, damned.

A girl's head passing across the gibbous moon! It had become artificial, poetically made-up! Michael shook with silent laughter that ran in a shiver over his skin. A girl . . . what girl?

Gehenna, it must be a girl in the place! . . . *Flora*! The cry came back upon Michael. Flora! The minister's daughter! The thought, like a fist against his chest, stopped Michael in his tracks.

He saw the other two go on, go steadily on. Gwynn was taking short quick steps, trying to keep up with the striding doctor. The small figure seemed to waddle in its urgency, purposeful as ever, but waddling a little.

An intense imaginative bout in Michael often reached a sudden satiety, when his mind refused to function. Stress fell away and exhaustion flowed softly over the brain. The eyes of the imagination closed and sank; sometimes his physical eyes closed for a few seconds also.

Now he simply could not move, and he stood, letting the other two walk on. They rounded a rocky bluff, and he stood alone.

They were waiting for him at the gate.

'The needs of the night,' explained Michael. 'Come in, Doctor, and have a drink.' His voice was friendly.

'No, thanks,' said the doctor quite firmly. 'I must get home.'

'I was asking him,' said Mr. Gwynn, 'what was the instrument. It's called a chanter, the pipe which a piper practises on.'

'Was it?' said Michael incuriously. 'Sorry to disappoint you over the supernatural.'

'But don't you see,' said Mr. Gwynn, 'that it's far more marvellous than any supernatural.' His imagination was not yet exhausted, perhaps because it dealt now so much in theories. 'That there should be a pipe like that! That's where the imagination—'

'Staggers and reels,' suggested Michael as Mr. Gwynn paused.

Mr. Gwynn made his gesture and rolled his head a little.

'I must go,' said the doctor. Then he added, 'It might be as well if we kept this to ourselves.'

'Good God,' declared Michael, 'what do you think?'

'Right!' said the doctor, backing away a pace or two. 'Good night.' Then he went along the path between the plantation wall and the sea.

CHAPTER EIGHTEEN

Robbie Ross came out of the door of his mother's cottage to take the air of the morning. Yes, dawn's twilight was creeping over the land. He looked at the sky and decided it was going to be a fresh but broken day. The wind was still asleep and the small fields lay quiet. As he slowly scratched his whiskered chin the familiar scene was translated into a far past through which his boy's feet went running and his boy's mouth cried sounds that no mortal ear now would ever catch. The final moment of parting had come, the severing with all that had been.

His hand fell away from his beard but only a few inches as if it, too, were affected by the moment's vision, while his eyes stared at the little barn. Then they were staring past the barn, and only when they focused of their own accord on a figure coming into view beyond it, was the past pulled away like a grey translucent veil. His brows gathered over the small black eyes; he backed a couple of steps into the doorway; then turned and entered the room which he had just left.

'The minister is coming up the field,' he said quietly.

The faces of two women and a man were turned to him in the yellow lamplight. They stared for a little while as if they had not heard aright. Then one of the women, with a small cry, got to her feet and began tidying the room, removing dishes and fragments of food, whisking this away and arranging that. The other woman, smoothing back her hair, went to the box-bed and leaned over. 'Mother,' she said, putting a glad earnest note into her voice, as if she were talking to a child, 'the minister is coming to see you.'

The old woman, who was eighty-one years of age, lifted her eyes to her daughter's face but did not speak.

'The minister,' repeated her daughter, a little louder. 'He's just coming.'

The veined wrinkled hands stirred, their long nails faintly scratching the hard texture of the counterpane.

'Aren't you glad?'

'The minister,' breathed the spent voice of the woman, whose death they had been awaiting all night.

'Yes, the minister himself. Aren't you the proud woman to be having him calling on you on the Sabbath morning? Whoever had the like before?'

The daughter straightened the pillows and smoothed back the white hair from the worn forehead and tucked it under the goffered linen cap. 'You look like a picture,' she said, on a rush of feeling. As she turned away, there were tears in her eyes.

'Go to the door, one of you,' said the other sister in a harsh voice.

Robbie went out again. The minister came up to him, breathing a trifle heavily, for the croft lay on the high slope above Cruime village.

'How is your mother?'

'She is still with us,' replied Robbie.

They spoke quietly as they shook hands.

Robbie made way for him.

The minister went into the room and shook hands first with Robbie's brother, Callum, because he was nearest to him, and then with the two sisters, Ellen who had tidied the room, and Martha who had spoken to her mother.

'I awoke thinking of your mother while it was yet dark,' he said and turned to the figure in the bed.

Martha hurried to place a convenient chair for him, but he stood looking down on the dying woman, a smile on his face. He caught her right hand gently. 'And how are you to-day, Mrs. Ross?' She did not answer, but her eyes were on his face. 'Not feeling very strong to-day?' He pressed the cold hand firmly. 'I thought you might like to see me. We are very old friends.' He felt the fingers of her left hand creeping over the back of his own. Then she held his hand in both of hers. She could not speak, for the emotion that was just capable of showing itself in her expression took all

her strength. 'It came to me to come and see you and I am
very glad,' he concluded.

The head moved in a small slow nod which was all that
courtesy and weakness could manage. She had always
retained the old-fashioned grace, the traditional manners, of her Gaelic folk. This grace was most deeply
expressed when the heart was touched, for then it caught
a warmth and a welcoming. Its light was in her eyes.

Martha, understanding all, put her hand to her mouth
and turned away. It was as if, in some strange way, the
minister had brought death with him, and the long-sealed
fountains of emotion felt the final pressure. Ellen threw her
a sharp glance and turned to the peat fire, where she swept
the pale yellow ash noiselessly back along the hearth stone.
As she had done this recently, there was little to sweep. She
then felt the weight of the iron kettle and retired with it,
walking softly. The brothers heard the two tin jugs of water
being poured quietly into the kettle from the covered
buckets which stood just inside the front door. Then she
returned with the kettle and hung it over the fire. She would
have liked to have gone out with the brown earthenware
teapot, as she had done several times during the long night,
but now the minister had sat down on the chair by the bed.
Martha had handed him the family Bible and was setting
the wick to its highest point. Ellen, watching her – for
Martha was the younger – saw that the funnel had become
discoloured. Martha had turned the wick a little too high in
the middle night when Robbie had read a chapter.

But nothing more could be done now and Ellen, sitting
on a small hard chair, dropped her hands in her lap and
stared into the fire.

Martha thought that perhaps the minister was reading
passages her mother specially liked, for her mother had
been living here alone for many years, ever since her
father had died. The four members of the family now
present were all married, two brothers were beyond the
seas, and one sister dead. Callum worked the croft along
with his own. That two brothers of the one family should
have remained in their birth district was very unusual.
Martha had arrived two days ago from the east country.

She was the youngest of the four, being only forty-three.

But already the minister's words were stealing their senses away. From long habit, his voice took on its pulpit intonation, and once more Robbie felt himself being translated, not now into the intimate scenes of his own boyhood, but distantly to places that were places of pilgrimage, far lands, and towns that, seen from a plain, were Nazareth or Nineveh or the City of David. No voice could be familiar with those names. The voice had to be translated a little, too.

Yet the minister's voice was more familiar than it was in the pulpit, it was nearer to them and softer in its cadence, so that all was seen in a more intimate light. The resounding force, which held authority and therefore fear, fell away from it. Here in this house now they were at one, and the oneness came upon them, and came upon the minister, too. The intonation caught a strangely poetic or imaginative quality, and Martha heard the voice of her grandmother, dead these thirty years, telling her a story at the end of the day, in the listening twilight, when the eyes grow large, and the sudden clucking of the hens outside, or the arrogant *kok-kok-kok* of the cock, or the lowing of a cow across the fields, or the distant barking of a dog, takes on a significance that is inexpressibly known and will for ever haunt the mind.

Robbie and Martha had the dark eyes of the dying woman, but Ellen was thin and had the assessing grey eyes of her tall brother Callum, yet all four of them now became as children again, under the minister's voice and the potency of the mother who had been firm in her kindness, reprimanding and guiding them, gentle and laughing often, but with that calmness in hard circumstance, that providing of their endless needs, which now, as parents themselves, they acknowledged to be the wisdom they could never hope to attain.

'Let us pray,' said the minister. He stood up, clasped his hands in front of him, and bowed his head. They all stood up and bowed their heads.

The oneness now grew upon them more strongly. For Martha, somehow, this was not 'religion'. She had always had an instinctive repugnance – in earlier life not unmixed a little, perhaps, with fear – for the dolefulness of religious observance. But now when the minister in his eloquent, strongly felt prayer came to the part where he referred to the dying woman in terms of her goodness as an exemplary mother and lifted up his face with its closed eyes to bring his pleading more directly 'on high', Martha opened her own eyes, for her love was all for her mother, and looked at her mother in a great quickening of love, and cried inwardly: 'Oh, it would be lovely if she died now!' This was a shattering cry within her, but it gave her face a great sweetness.

When the prayer was ended, the minister sat down, and turned the leaves to one of the Psalms of David, not yet looking at the woman in the bed.

They all joined in the singing, knowing the familiar words, all except the woman in the bed, who had so often led it. Martha had her mother's voice, and as it poured through her like an eternal stream, she looked at her mother directly as if she would draw her, too, into it.

Her mother's head turned slowly on the pillow and the dark eyes looked at the singers and came to rest on Martha's eyes. Martha smiled to her, crying silently: *Mother! Mother!* even as she sang. Then a smile went over her mother's face, a faint tired smile, and the head, as though what held it had suddenly let go, fell flat against the pillow and the chin sagged. This time Martha cried aloud.

It was full daylight outside when the minister, having shaken hands with the four soft-voiced sorrowers, turned the corner of the barn and looked far upon the morning sea and then more closely upon the houses of Cruime spread away below him. Not a smoke yet ascended from any chimney, and would not for another hour. This was the Sabbath day when no work was done and even early rising would have shown an indecent haste in worldly affairs. The day of rest for man and beast. The boats were drawn far up on the beach and the houses were quiet and seemly.

The effect of communion in the death service was exceptionally strong upon the minister, cleansing and cooling his mind, and giving it a renewed assurance. He was glad now that he had obeyed the urge to go and see Mrs. Ross with whom he had had many a quiet and pleasant hour, and allowed himself only half consciously to think of it as divinely inspired. He could still feel its wondrous healing power and was content to leave it thus within the miracle of God's grace to His servant.

He stood looking down upon the familiar scene, broad-shouldered and powerful. Then suddenly something made him turn his head, and in a surge of incredulous amazement he saw a man driving sheep along the slope above the arable fields, as if it were an ordinary weekday and he were driving them from a market. There was something in the very gait of the man that was like a curse. It was Dougald MacIan.

A faint darkness from a flush of blood came over the minister's vision. Rage at what he saw, black hatred of its abominable desecration, had him in an instant. That a man, accursed already, should so dare!

As Dougald altered course to cut in below the dead woman's croft and so open out on a direct drive for the Ros, the minister bore down upon him.

'What's this you're doing, Dougald MacIan?' cried the minister.

Dougald looked round, and staggered, and stood.

'What's this you're doing on the Lord's Day?'

Dougald glowered at the minister as if his wits were struggling back to him like black sheep.

The wrath in the minister's face gave it a wild and piercing power. The hairy eyebrows stood out stormily. He was half a head taller than Dougald and overbore him from the slope.

Dougald's expression narrowed dangerously; the mouth parted and the under jaw shot out a little showing the tips of the small strong teeth.

'Do you hear me?' cried the minister, and in the quiet morning his voice was heard by those stirring in near cottages. From the gable-end of their childhood's home, Robbie and Callum looked down upon the naked scene.

'Huh!' grunted Dougald, and from the wind of his

onward bodily thrust came the smell of whisky to the minister's nostrils.

Swiftly the minister overtook him and barred his way. 'You will answer for this!' he cried.

Again Dougald stopped.

'You will answer for this before God, you desecrator of His holy day. You will not carry on like this, making foul His very air with your vile breath. I will not have it. Do you hear me?'

The minister was now shouting, and here and there a halfclad figure appeared by a door-jamb or a gable corner. As his denunciation rose, his very words could be made out.

'. . . You, treading our holy earth to mire with your sheep's feet and your own drunken feet! I tell you, Dougald MacIan, that a day will come upon you when the wrath of God will burn you up. Burn you up, you—'

Dougald suddenly lurched forward to pass the minister, but as he did so his left arm shot out. It was the shepherd's gesture to his collie when he wanted the dog to round up sheep on the left flank, and it was accompanied by the shepherd's cry, now a harsh half-choked brutal cry, but in the same instant the two brothers in the croft above heard the clear skelp of the back of Dougald's hand against the minister's face.

The minister staggered and stood as Dougald lurched on.

It was often afterwards conjectured in Cruime what might have happened next, for the minister was a very powerful man and he started after Dougald, but Robbie Ross, running down the slope, called in his sea voice: 'Minister! Minister!' and the minister stopped and looked up. He was trembling when Robbie spoke to him.

There was a full congregation in the church that day, including for the first time Michael Sandeman and his guest Mr. Gwynn, who had come innocently enough, or at least with a strong desire on the part of Michael to look at the girl Flora and with a general interest in his peculiar theories on the part of Mr. Gwynn.

And Mr. Gwynn had a lot to think about that seemed

mysterious enough. That they should sit for the singing and stand during the minister's prayer had its interest, but something portentously quiet about the minister's bearing and voice and an air of expectancy in the congregation which he could feel somehow surprised him. Here was an inward as well as an outward unity which he had not quite anticipated, and clearly the unity was not one of easy acceptance, of purely religious peace, not anyhow as Mr. Gwynn had hitherto understood acceptance and peace. Underneath it all, something was curiously, avidly, alive.

Mr. Gwynn shifted his stance, for it now looked as if that first great prayer were never going to end – it lasted twenty minutes – and discreetly let his eyes rove a little to each side.

The men's faces appeared completely stolid, utterly without feeling or subtlety. Earth and clay and stone. But curiously strong, enduring, and openly there. They were a marvellous array of masks. The individuality of each, the difference of one from another, was extremely striking. He tried to think of a city congregation but could vaguely call up only smooth pale faces of an indistinguished uniformity. The women had not the weathered openness of the men. They retired, seeming indeed to have their shoulders rounded by the pull of their black clothes towards the hidden breast over which their faces inclined in a still composure.

When the minister began to talk of 'our sister' who had been called away that morning, Mr. Gwynn at once experienced a gleam of light upon this enigmatic under-current of being. Death, dark and round-shouldered, with hidden face – oldest of all the enigmas. He almost got a glimpse of it, like a presence in a crypt below them. He heard the intoning of the minister's voice and the worship-ping silence.

Death.

He looked up at the minister (for he was only five seats back from the precentor, who sat under the pulpit) and studied the face with its closed eyes, the darkness of short hairs on the cheek bones, the clean-shaven jaw and sensi-tive upper lip, the clipped hair that grew down in front of the ears, and the strong grey-dark growth of hair on the head. The closed eyes were smudges of shadow under the heavy eyebrows. The absence of a beard was somehow noticeable.

How apt his words were, how dignified, yet kindly and beseeching. This was no professional panegyric. The man, Mr. Gwynn decided, was moved, deeply moved, and only as his voice rose a little did Mr. Gwynn perceive that, with just propriety, he was making of her 'an ensample' before his flock. There was a moment of suspense when it seemed he was going to introduce contrast, direct and forceful, but the short dramatic pause ended and the minister, with reverent reticence, went on. Mr. Gwynn detected the faintest stir in the congregation and was surprised that so elusive a moment should produce so delicate a response.

Moving his head slowly, he glanced at Michael and found him staring directly at the girl who was standing beside the housekeeper in the manse pew. It was a front pew and as his line of vision bore slightly to the left, Mr. Gwynn could see the right side of her face foreshortened.

Well made, rather, with a smooth grace of body; a navy-blue costume cut to lie on real shoulders; a personable young woman. Clothes would fit her with an easy natural-ness. She no doubt saw they did! Strands of hair, with a brown glisten, curled over the pale nape of her neck. Her grey straw hat was large, and had a slight tilt which, when she moved her head, as if her eyes had wearied staring into the pitch-pine of the pulpit, gave her full profile so soft a surety in its line that Mr. Gwynn could have made a compliment to a summer day.

Smiling faintly – for it was an odd sort of feeling to have suddenly had – Mr. Gwynn, as she moved her head again, turned his own away towards a pointed window in the white-plastered wall. The panes of glass were small but transparent. There was not a square inch of coloured glass, or coloured anything, anywhere in the church.

Colour! A red, say; or a blue robe?

Utterly transparent glass, for the white light. Beyond it, the upcurled fingers of an elm, the extreme tips, bare and elephant-grey, swaying in an invisible wind.

Hardly a summer's day! . . . That cold moonlit midnight, and the figure walking down upon them. His eyes were drawn back to Flora. Very slightly now her head was bowed, with the pallor of the nape showing more distinctly, like a waiting, unconscious sacrifice.

Mr. Gwynn had his extravagant fancies. There was plenty of time for them, immeasurable time.

Very distinct, this feeling of unobstructed time, this movement of the free mind unhindered by colour, by scents, by emotion. When the voice in the pulpit, coming at long last towards an end, called for a blessing upon the King and the Queen and all the members of the Royal Family, Mr. Gwynn withdrew his eyes from the window with an expression of such innocence that he knew his face, too, was a mask.

Coughings and stirrings and scraping of feet. The body had its short interlude before settling down again.

The sermon lasted over an hour. The long narrow seat with its straight back was of pitch pine, varnished, and innocent of any covering. Normally, to have sat there for an hour would have been for Mr. Gwynn a fine exercise in physical torture. As it was, he had occasional aches and cramps and, after the great dramatic denunciation, experienced the 'needles and pins' forgotten since boyhood.

The large open Bible on the pulpit cushion, the quiet but very effective reading of the verse:

And the Lord said unto Cain, Where is Abel thy brother? And he said, I know not. Am I my brother's keeper?

With his left hand the minister slowly closed the great book in a final and authoritative small slap.

It was beautifully done, thought Mr. Gwynn. The beauty lay, of course, in the fact that the minister was not consciously acting the profound restraint behind that authoritative closing of the 'Holy Word'.

Moreover, the words of the text had in themselves roused Mr. Gwynn, for at once he perceived their extraordinary aptness to the ferment of socialistic theories which stirred certain intellectual groups in London. The Fabians had produced nothing at once so compact and so dramatic! Here was not merely the theory, but also the actors. The

brotherhood of humanity and humanity itself. And also –
also – God. It was terrific. And all inside a dozen words!
Where is Abel thy brother? . . . Am I my brother's keeper?

The fundamental questions, the questions which had to
be answered first, if any subsequent theory of action were to
fit! Fabianism, communism, socialism, anarchism . . . here
was the starting point, poised on surely the shortest of all
antiphonies between man and God, action and Justice, the
human mind and That which it seeks. In that remote
beginning, the curtain was lifted, the drama was set. The
theme, the plot, was then as it was now, and as it would be
'world without end'.

Oh, and here were the human actors reduced to their
simplest economic terms! For machines may come and
machines may go, but upon the man who tills his fields like
Cain and herds his flocks like Abel, all human life finally
depends.

The minister was in no hurry. He drew that picture of a
primitive agriculture with homely illustration. They tilled
their fields in Cruime and Ardnarie. For the fields were
there before man was. And man came and worked the
fields, and destroyed the weeds. Yes, he dug the weeds out
of the soil, and gathered them into little heaps, and set fire
to them, and destroyed them utterly. That was what had to
be done with weeds – wherever they grew. Then he sowed
the good seed, and he tended the crops, and if he did all this
as a good husband-man, then he reaped of his seeds, some
an hundred-fold, some sixty-fold, some thirty-fold.

He drew the parallel between the good tiller of the soil
and the good man, between the field and the mind, those
two fundamental elements given by God. He did it in
simple language, going over the parallels, illustrating
them, leaving nothing obscure, until all was unavoidably
there before them. Then he began to rise to the implicit
meanings, the higher questions. How were these elements
given and why? What harvest was the human mind ultimately to reap and where?

And there, all the time, beneath his face, his words,
silently beneath his extended hand, lay the great Bible,
holding the answer.

He turned from Cain to Abel, and it was only now, when he uttered the Biblical words: *And Abel was a keeper of sheep*, that Mr. Gwynn began to feel a coolness run over his skin. At the same time he heard the great silence in the church.

A memory of the burial service of the dead seaman came back. Very very clearly the minister had time to work out the subtlest implications of his theme!

Abel was a shepherd. As the land had to be tilled, so the flocks had to be reared. The Bible had many references to shepherds and to sheep. Christ was known as the Shepherd and as the Lamb. Great sentences from Isaiah rolled over the congregation. God Himself, in His inscrutable insight, had preferred the offering of Abel the shepherd to that of Cain the tiller of the soil.

Mr. Gwynn had sometimes wondered as a little boy why God should have shown this preference for Abel's offering. Now he saw the minister use this very preference to enhance any sin that might be found in the shepherd. For it was not Abel the shepherd who had killed Cain. Abel had been the favoured of God.

The implications began to grow painful. Even Mr. Gwynn felt that the preacher should come to the point and be done with it. But the preacher was far from the point yet.

For when God asked Cain, *Where is Abel thy brother?* he answered, *I know not: Am I my brother's keeper?*

My brother's keeper. Are we all our brothers' keepers? To answer No would be for each man to have his hand secretly lifted against his brother in readiness to slay him. The world had borne this out in many a terrible crime and on many a bloody battlefield. To answer No is for man to destroy himself.

The brotherhood of man.

But this conception of the brotherhood of man and its inevitable necessity, the minister lifted into the brotherhood of man in the fellowship of Christ. Herein lay the ordering and the meaning and the sanction; herein lay the harvest and the completion; the final purpose; the ultimate, the eternal, end.

The sin is then not only against the brotherhood of man

but also against the fellowship in Christ, not only in life but also in death, not only in time but also in eternity.

And the Lord set a mark upon Cain, lest any finding him should kill him. And Cain went out from the presence of the Lord.

The minister turned away and turned back, his voice quietened, and he spoke for a little time on the meaning of brotherhood and fellowship in terms of understanding and kindliness as they went about their daily tasks, each in his appointed place, of the manners that sprang from such understanding, of the sweet solace of courtesy.

Then he paused for some seconds and they knew it was coming.

He began quietly, telling how he had been prompted in the darkness of this very morning to visit the sick bed, and of how God, in His infinite grace, had seen fit that His servant should arrive in time to give consolation and assurance to one whose life had been so finely and wisely lived under the hand of God that he had ever considered it a high privilege to enter at her door, and from whose door he had never departed without feeling strengthened and refreshed. Then when all was over he had stood there looking down upon the houses of Cruime quiet in their Sabbath calm.

As he painted the picture of their native place so familiar to them and yet now so strangely beautiful, his hands opened the Bible and he read:

And on the seventh day God ended his work which he had made; and he rested on the seventh day from all his work which he had made.

And God blessed the seventh day, and sanctified it; because that in it he had rested from all his work which God created and made.

And then the minister described how, shambling through this seventh day, which God had blessed, came one Dougald MacIan driving his sheep and making mock of the holy day, turning its ordained rest into the drunken riot of a common market.

The money-changers had gone before the thong of the Lord, but Dougald MacIan had turned against the Lord's ordained servant and struck him in the face.

Wrath in its streams and rivulets poured into the minister and Mr. Gwynn had the impression that he began visibly to swell as he took upon himself the powers of judgment and condemnation, under the avenging hand of God.

Something out of that ancient world came into the church, the world of the patriarch and the prophet, evoked almost bodily by words; and the words, crying in their powerful rhythm, threshed down upon the congregation as a wind upon a wood.

Dark and archaic words out of the mouths of prophets, with the power in them of the sign and the symbol. Not the power of daylight and order but the avenging power that hunts the fleeing heels of sin into death's uttermost abyss.

The last psalm was sung with a quietness as of exhaustion and the benediction had within it the calm that is the weary end of all thought.

Mr. Gwynn did not care to look openly at the faces as he came out with them and so saw many of them in a way which his memory would the more vividly recall. But once he was out among the tombstones, he turned to Michael — to find he was not there.

The folk flowed past him, and now here, walking by the housekeeper, came Flora, with a faint mantling of colour in her grave face, and light in her eyes, lovely eyes, and a glisten of pain, wakening and walking out of a dream of . . . Mr. Gwynn had no word, no image, for it, so that he became completely unconscious of his stare, and only when the housekeeper glanced sideways at him, and Flora's eyes passed across his face, did he come to himself fully and raise his hat.

Michael was now at his side. Mr. Gwynn looked at his face and saw the whitening of the skin and the dark glow in his eyes.

CHAPTER NINETEEN

'But I thought the thing was finished and done with,' said Kenneth Grant.

'Oh no,' said the policeman.

'But surely once a case has been decided, it can't be opened again?'

'This case was never decided.'

Kenneth Grant looked at him, saw the conscientiousness of duty in the smooth face and the troubled but persistent eyes. He always thought of the policeman as an overgrown school-boy, simple and agreeable but capable of being very stubborn. Then Kenneth glanced at the doctor, but on that face found no particular expression.

'Well, I'm dead against it,' Kenneth said flatly. 'And – though it's none of my business – I'd warn you to think twice about raking all this business up again.'

'It's hardly being left to me,' said the policeman. 'Since Sunday the people are all talking. And what steps do I know the minister will be taking? Besides, it's my duty.'

'Well, you know your duty best,' said Kenneth. 'But before I started in, I'd be sure I had more evidence up my sleeve than folks' talk.'

'That's what I've got to get,' said the policeman, looking at Kenneth.

Kenneth looked back at him directly. 'Well, I've none to give you.'

The three of them were standing on a patch of green over from Kenneth's shop. The motor-cycle was on the edge of the gravel a few yards lower down. The doctor saw the lively dark-eyed Sarah standing back from the post office window staring out at them.

'You can be asked to give it – if it's needed,' said the policeman.

'Oh,' said Kenneth. 'Who'll ask me?'

'The law,' said the policeman. 'The Crown can call anyone as a witness.'

'What for?'

'About how he got the money. He buys his messages at your shop. You're the secretary of the Club and he's the shepherd. He draws his wages through you.'

'I see,' said Kenneth.

The policeman shifted his weight, feeling Kenneth's hostility.

'What's your idea?' asked the doctor in simple tones, looking at the policeman.

His question surprised them.

'Well, where did he get the money from?' asked the policeman. 'Here's a man who could never buy any sheep for himself. Then suddenly – after what you know took place – he buys them.'

'Your idea is that the way Dougald got his money has something to do with the strangling of the foreign seaman?'

'I'm not saying it has. But the circumstances are suspicious. If Dougald can prove that he came by the money honestly, then that finishes it.'

'And if he can't?'

'Then surely it is my duty to investigate it. Anyway, they will come on me to do it. If anyone writes about it, the Inspector will be here on my top. I'm not wanting to force anyone to tell me anything. But – it may not be left to me. I'll have to show that I tried to do what I could.'

'Naturally,' the doctor agreed. 'Supposing Dougald just says that he had the money – had saved it up, let us say – what more could you do?'

'There might be a lot more,' said the policeman. 'There's some things might be followed up.'

'You mean the money he paid out could be traced?'

'Yes.'

'Not the money itself,' said Kenneth. 'And you already know that. It was ordinary money and you know them he paid it to. If that's all—' Kenneth smiled drily.

'That's not all,' replied the policeman, nettled. They had

always been good friends, and this exasperated the difference now between them.

'No?' said Kenneth sceptically.

'No,' said the policeman with some heat. 'There's also Charlie's trip south. I understand it was to Edinburgh, but that can be found out. If he changed any foreign money there – his visit to the place where he changed it may be remembered by them in it.'

'I see,' said the doctor, taking out his cigarette case. 'You mean that, without any evidence, you would be prepared to collar Charlie – charge him with – it would have to be a crime of some kind – and parade him before the – the money-changers of Edinburgh?' The doctor looked pleasantly serious.

'We might get some evidence first.' The policeman was more nettled.

'How?' asked the doctor simply.

'Well,' said the policeman, plainly now feeling compelled to divulge what was his own secret idea, 'we could make preliminary investigations in Edinburgh. We could find out if any Swedish money was changed within a certain two or three days and we could have a photograph of Charlie to show.'

'You mean you could compel Charlie to have his photograph taken?' asked the doctor, throwing the burnt match away.

'I saw a very good photograph of him when I was at Ros Lodge concerning the dead seaman's photograph,' replied the policeman, shifting his weight again.

As the doctor lifted his cigarette to his mouth, his eyelashes drooped and his eyes crawled over the policeman's face.

'Very interesting.' The doctor nodded thoughtfully. 'The only difficulty I see is this. On medical evidence, Dougald could have had nothing whatever to do with the death of the seaman. As you know, he wasn't there. There can therefore be no crime against Dougald – nothing, in fact, but that he spent some money.'

'I know,' said the policeman. 'But if the foreign money was changed—' He was troubled, for hours of meditation had shown him the difficulties.

'Even if that could be proved – what about it? It would then be a simple matter of not having reported what was washed up on the shore. I understand that that is not regarded as a criminal offence – hardly even as a civil offence – on any shore!' The doctor smiled in a friendly way. 'You'll have to be pretty careful.'

'For myself,' said Kenneth, suddenly full of words, 'you know I don't want not to help. But I always have a feeling against telling how I may help anyone. It's private. If I loaned a man some money and went blabbing about it – he would be hurt. You know you would be yourself. All I will say is this. There's no difficulty about where Dougald got the two lots of sheep and the kind of money he paid for them and the total amount of it. He was entitled to have that exact number of sheep for himself privately as the shepherd. That's the usual thing on every club farm. For the rest, I'll just say this – and you can take it down if you like – that before this happened Dougald owed me nothing in his dealings at my shop and everything was fair and square with the Club.'

'Well, thank you for that,' said the policeman.

'I must be getting back,' said the doctor. 'If I can help – look in. So long!'

As he went along, he smiled to himself at Kenneth's mollifying speech – after the hostile reticence. What had taken place inside Kenneth's cunning mind while the talk went on was very simple. He would now tell Dougald, if questioned, to say that the money was all his own savings. Kenneth could be depended upon to work out the arithmetic of that all right! He would also tell Dougald to deny having found foreign money, either by Charlie or himself. If, however, foreign money was traced to them, then – and only then – Dougald might confess to its having been washed up on the shore. There need be no connection with the strangled seaman!

What was troubling the honest policeman was that Charlie and Dougald *had* suddenly got money. That was dead plain. Dougald could not have saved three or four years' total wages, *plus* what he had paid Kenneth for purchases, all at once! If he had saved it gradually he

would naturally have bought the sheep gradually – say two
or three last year or the year before. Not in this way, all at
once, and getting drunk, and driving them home by the old
drove road, on a Sabbath, too, and – of all things –
smacking the minister in the face! Before the simplest
man would do all that, such obvious stuff crying out for
detection, plainly a guilty conscience had played havoc with
his mind. And whatever Mr. Gwynn might say about the
primitive, its basic elements in a man like Dougald MacIan
to-day were precisely cunning and suspicion, often in an
extreme form. Such cunning could be overborne only by
some shocking derangement throwing up an idiotic defiance. The minister was probably lucky to have got off with
the one smack!

The doctor's mind steadied for a moment – and drew
back to the old question. Could it be possible that Charlie
had strangled the seaman on discovering the money in the
chest – the seaman, lying on the bed, may have opened his
eyes and seen Charlie rummaging in the chest – rolled off
the bed – a fight? Charlie killed him – and then his nerve
failed?

Charlie had looked as if he had come through some such
experience. The psychological shock had been almost
painfully evident in his face on that morning after the
death. The body lying in the somewhat darkened bed,
would be avoided, they would not think of looking for
marks on it. The news of the strangulation had been a
complete shock to Dougald. Charlie would have hidden
that from him. He may have told it to him since – with
devastating results.

The doctor's mind steadied – and this time contemplated the effect of the attack on the minister. The news
would spread far beyond the district. Behind the policeman's attitude to his duty, there was also his self-interest. If
he did nothing at all, how would his superiors take it when
the rumours began to flow in? That was troubling him –
very naturally. He would have to do something.

The doctor's mind slid from the minister's face to Flora,
and his breathing quickened. It was an appalling vision – the
girl being led into that dark and hellish mess. And being led

she was! The scene on the moonlit hillside came back upon him with a sudden effect of vast and tragic catastrophe, and blotted out his thought. The cycle bounded on some loose gravel. He was passing the manse. He would have to do something. There was no one about the manse. But what? As the cycle took the long gradient for Ardnarie, he saw a girl on the roadside, calling a dog out of the way. But Fraoch, wondering why he was guilty, paid no attention to the oncoming cycle. The doctor stopped his machine.

'I'm very sorry,' said Flora, with a hot glance of apology, then she drew the bewildered Fraoch to one side.

'I'm glad to stop this noisy contraption occasionally,' replied the doctor, resting on his machine. 'Giving Fraoch a walk? Well, Fraoch?' He put down an inviting hand, and Fraoch politely twisted his body, flattened his ears, and showed his laughing teeth, but stayed a yard away. 'He's taking no chances!'

She smiled. 'He's often a very naughty dog,' she said.

'How old is he now?'

'He's nearly seven.'

'Is he really?' The doctor looked up with an air of surprise. He had this trick of making conversation in a natural way about ordinary things. It dismissed all personal stress and left the mind free.

The colour which had come into her face was ebbing and gave the skin a delicate transparency. The light in her eyes, which had flashed hotly, was now a glistening pure light, alive, as things in nature are alive. Her body, with its full lines, swayed naturally. The daughter of the manse, the conventional lady – this innocent, naïve creature.

'He's getting a few grey hairs about the mouth.'

'Do you think so? What a shame!'

'He enjoys himself.' A smile came into his eyes as he glanced up again, this time a trifle more directly. 'One scent of a rabbit and the whole problem of life is solved.'

Women often blessed him for his cool friendly ease.

'I know,' she said, looking at Fraoch, who was aware that he was being trapped by this interest.

The doctor, knowing what was in Fraoch's mind, said in a low hissing voice, 'What is it? . . . Rabbits!'

At once Fraoch cocked his ears, glanced this way and that, and shot off the road.

They laughed.

'My mother,' he said, 'is not a very good visitor. She finds a long walk a little tiring.'

'I'm sure she does.'

'So if ever you felt,' – and he looked at her now with a more intimate expression – 'like resting half-way, she would be pleased to see you.'

'Thank you very much. I – I am always afraid of troubling anyone.'

'You mean the manse has to be received?'

He knew she was not quick-witted intellectually, but his casual emphasis on the word *received* she caught at once, and was delighted as if a whole amusing social relationship had been made clear. She looked at him directly, at his half smile, and laughed, swaying back.

The direct look of her eyes in wonder, in communication, had been in some way a flash of illumination. The doctor experienced a distinct warmth.

All at once Fraoch set up his yelping. They glanced down the slope and saw Michael Sandeman coming up towards them. Fraoch's stern waggled from a burrow.

'I must go,' she said.

'Please don't.'

His tone drew her into the moment's conspiracy against Michael's appearance, and she instinctively obeyed it. She would be a faithful ally.

'So if you care to drop in, you will be received,' he began again in his light voice, and now his eyes were bright with humour.

'Thank you very much. I—' as she hesitated she looked directly at him, shyly smiling, her eyes burning, aware of herself between the two men, 'I like your mother.'

Michael was now only a few paces away. This heightened the feeling between them.

'Well, please do come,' he said, answering her look directly. Then the moment's expression was withdrawn inward, out of sight, and he turned to acknowledge Michael's greeting.

Michael could be a very fascinating fellow when he liked. Now there was a lash of colour in his face. His teeth flashed. His smile was brilliant in a way that seemed to cover a fundamental shyness. Where he might have been, out of all his exhaustive experience of women and the world, rather casual and blasé or deliberately charming, he actually appeared excited, gay, like one to whom the world was still new and fresh. A camera in a brown case was slung over his back. He started talking at once, without personal greetings.

'I often do wonder if your dog ever does catch anything?' He flashed his look at Flora. Her colour was rising. He turned to the doctor and speculated, in exaggerated language, what might be done about registering on a photographic plate the obviously extreme amount of emotion exhibited by Fraoch's tail when the head was well and truly into a burrow crawling with primeval scent.

They all laughed.

'You must let me have a shot at it some day. Will you?'

'Yes – of course—' Flora stuttered. She was embarrassed before his direct, engaging look.

'Don't see quite how you are going to manage that,' said the doctor with dry thoughtfulness, 'the emotion being expressed by the movement rather than by the tail.'

But Michael was not to be led away from Flora, to whom he at once turned. 'You see,' he said, 'that's what he always tries to do to me – in spite of the fact that he knows perfectly well my whole aim is to suggest dynamic movement in the static pose. You see what I mean?'

Flora laughed, and the sound of it, because she was embarrassed, was rounded and deep in her throat. Michael's eye swept over her features, then he turned swiftly to the doctor, waiting, with the laugh leashed in his face.

This kind of talk went on for a little while until it became clear to the doctor that the moment had arrived when something must be done, and he was not going to leave Michael in charge.

All at once Flora said, 'You will excuse me, but I must get home.' She turned to look for Fraoch, who at that moment shot across the road farther up. She smiled to the doctor, 'Good-bye,' and was passing on her slight bow to Michael, when he said, 'I'm going that way. Do you mind—?'

The doctor waddled his machine off.

As he drew it back on its stand by the side of his home he looked and saw two figures standing on the crest of the slope. Even at that distance there was no doubt it was Michael and Flora.

Presently his mother came to the back door. 'What's keeping you, David?'

He bent down and began to tinker with the carburettor. 'I'll be in a minute,' he replied without looking at her.

'Hurry, then. Your food is more than ready. You can see about that again.'

He did not answer and she withdrew.

Her voice had suddenly irritated him. He felt the blood flooding his temples as he stooped.

CHAPTER TWENTY

'I would have been down with the fish earlier,' explained Betsy to Smeorach, 'but I looked in to see Sarah in the post office and she kept me until she could lock the door.'

'That's right, blame me,' said Sarah.

When Angus and George dropped in, Smeorach's eyes lit up. His house was used for many things, and the present occasion was not among the least of them.

As the gaiety grew, the girls, all alive, baited the young men up to the danger point. When that point was reached and physical violence threatened, their art of balance was extremely complicated, being only just enough. Then Betsy, in passing, flicked cold water from her fingers down Angus's neck.

She had gone over the score now. Angus got up, and she dodged him, and yelled that she would throw the lamp at him, but he was on the old male warpath. She saw it in his eye. She danced nimbly round Smeorach, calling for his protection.

'Fair is fair,' said Smeorach, 'and you brought it on yourself.'

She fled and Angus caught her in the dark passage. There was much commotion and door-rattling and a voice lifted from outside: 'What's wrong?'

Betsy came swiftly back into the room, face flushed and hair not so tidy as it had been. 'That big fool!' she said, but softly.

'One minute!' cried Angus in the passage-way. Then the door was opened.

'Lord, boy, what's gone wrong?' It was William's voice.

'It's the door,' said Angus, a big-boned, normally slow-witted young man. 'The bar must have fallen down. I was trying to open it for you.'

'He's coming on!' murmured Smeorach and laughed softly.

Betsy tried not to look pleased at this compliment to Angus and was deftly putting her hair right, when William entered and looked at her.

'Ho! ho!' said William. 'So that's the way the wind blows?'

'The wind,' answered Betsy promptly, 'bloweth where it listeth, and we hear the sound thereof but cannot tell whither it cometh or whither it goeth.'

George tilted himself so far back in his pleasure that he had to grab Sarah's shoulder, but Betsy was quick, and collapse and its spectacle were avoided.

'I would have expected you to keep better order in your house at your time of life, Smeorach.'

'There has always been order in my house, William, and there has always been life. There has also been time. You are right, as usual.'

'Boy, you don't grow any older,' said William, drowning Smeorach's thrust in a sudden admiration for the old man.

They were all laughing, pleased with the way William let the better thing uppermost. Besides, the four younger folk had used the occasion to seat themselves in a certain order and they were prepared to laugh at little.

Presently there was a rattle at the door. A couple of men came in. They were no sooner settled than Norman entered, followed by the two boys, Hamish and Norrie.

In the uplift of voices, Hamish whispered to George.

'Am I hearing you were caught at Loch Geal again, Hamish?' cried Smeorach.

'I wasn't going to Loch Geal,' mumbled Hamish.

'What's all this?' inquired Norman.

'Can none of you leave a boy alone?' demanded Sarah.

'Surely it was nothing against him. I only heard myself that he was playing with the Red Indians,' said Smeorach.

'Where were you?' inquired Norman, who was always the last to hear of Hamish's doings.

In the end, Hamish, who had to establish his innocence, told his story.

It appeared that he and Norrie had hurried off immediately school was over 'in order just to see' the two hares that big John-the-roadman had said he had seen quite close to the main road in the grey of the morning. He said that they had a strange yellowish colour on them and made off into the Ros in a way that caused him to wonder what they were indeed.

But though the two boys went on and went on, never a sign of the hares did they see, until at last they were near at Loch Geal itself – 'though we weren't going there'.

They were moving very carefully now, for the sun had set, and all at once they came on a wee house built of divots. They knew it hadn't been there before and this made them think, and they couldn't think who could have built it, and there was no sign of the hares, though they looked around carefully, so they thought it was time to go home.

'It was indeed,' agreed Smeorach.

'But I thought I would just have one look round the corner.'

'Was this at Loch Geal itself?' asked William, as if talking to a man of his own years.

'It was,' said Hamish at once. 'Just at the outlet yonder. So I went on as quietly as I could go. And Norrie came behind me. And then – I saw a tuft of heather and it moved. So I thought it might be one of the hares. So I didn't know what to do. So I threw the stone at it. And it rose up. And it was a man.'

Smeorach leaned back in astonishment.

'And then a great lot of ducks got up and they quacked and quacked and flew away. And there was the man and he had heather tied all round his bonnet and standing up, like – like a Redskin.'

All eyes were on Hamish.

'It was,' said Hamish, 'Mr. Sandeman from the Lodge. And he roared at us – and began coming – so we – we ran off. That was all it was,' concluded Hamish, hardly glancing at Norman.

'Did he catch you?' asked George.

'No,' answered Hamish, 'he just came only a little way.'

'Did your stone hit him?' asked Angus.

'It only just scliffed him.'

Angus laughed.

'What did he roar at you?' asked William.

Hamish, after a side glance at his Uncle Norman, hung his head.

'Perhaps it wasn't very nice,' said Betsy, 'and the boy has more sense than most of you.'

'Never mind the women, Hamish. Out with it!'

'I'll leave it to himself,' said Norman.

'He roared: "What the—" and he used a bad word "are you doing here?"' concluded Hamish.

The boy's reticence was a relish. And the picture of a grown man with heather in his bonnet hunting ducks for no more than a photograph was an odd marvel to men who were hunters in the blood. The whole affair had the delight of a half-mad fairy story. They grew droll about it from all angles.

'Whenever Hamish goes on the Ros it seems to rise up at him!'

'If he's not careful it will be another case for the police one of these days,' said Norman.

'Nonsense! Nonsense!'

'That's not what he was saying to me just now,' said George.

'Not saying what about what?' asked William.

At once they were all waiting, looking at George.

'What he told me when he came in,' said George. The silence deepened. 'He told me,' continued George, 'that Dougald MacIan is at this moment in Kenneth Grant's shop.'

'Is he?' said Smeorach, his voice a whistle as he looked at Hamish.

'He is,' said Hamish.

Heads were lifted in the instinctive motion of listening.

'I hope he doesn't buy the entire shop and leave us nothing,' said William on a note of concern.

Laughter broke out again in small searching chuckles. The strangled seaman and the minister hit in the face on a Sabbath morning were beginning to inhabit that nocturnal land into which ran yellow hares, guarded by a wealthy landlord from the South with heather in his bonnet, a skein of quacking duck, and a wan loch face in the failing light.

And in front of it all – money; money as the thing with which to play, the magic fact, the worker of miracles at sheep sales, the real witch's broom, the solid cash.

Even the girls could not keep out of the verbal fun, the fantastic idiotic humour. 'I hear the doctor,' said Sarah with an innocent air, 'told old Catriona to look after her chest – and she wondered.'

But Smeorach did not care much for this talk, though it was, too, a great temptation to him, for with the dreadful perversity in things it is only at such a moment that the clever saying comes naturally from nowhere.

'Be quiet, my heroes.'

The humour began to wither, the delicious fun was wilting in the cold wind that blows off dead flesh and crime. The moor was going black and hag-holed.

Dougald MacIan stumped through Betsy's mind, his bag on his back, and his bag held more than groceries. She gave a small shudder and got up and put peat on the fire.

They all noticed her shudder and to some faces it brought a wry smile.

'Feeling it a bit cold, Betsy?' asked William.

'Ach, be quiet,' said Betsy, no longer in a mood to play. There was a resentful note in her voice, as if she suddenly hated Dougald and all he stood for.

Everyone understood. As she swept back the ash with more spirit than care, one or two laughed.

Then they heard the footsteps coming and at once there was dead quiet. Heavy footsteps, pounding the ground, passing the window, and now at the door.

No one spoke. No one moved. The door rattled harshly and the slither of the bag against the jambs was heard. Smeorach got up and went forward.

'Well,' he cried, in his high welcoming voice, 'if it isn't Dougald MacIan himself! Come away in, man! Come away! I'm glad to see you.'

'It's a full house, Dougald,' said William in a loud pleasant voice. They were making way for him. The face, the beard, the small quick eyes that shot back the light, the humped shoulders under the swollen bag.

'Huh!' He came forward to the chair he was always given by the right-hand side of the fire. Those behind him glanced at one another swiftly. The bag hit the floor in a soft squashing shudder and the black collie with the white star looked up at Betsy, sensitive, hardly daring to expect anything.

'Down!' At that growl from his master the collie slid in behind the bag and lay down. Betsy saw the green glisten of the eyes in the shadow, and her heart contracted in a silent cry. She turned her back on the fire and found a seat with others on the form by the wall.

'Ay, man,' cried Smeorach, full of welcoming action, 'and how are things with yourself, Dougald?'

'All right,' answered Dougald.

Smeorach sat down, his eyes bright, his whiskers restless. 'Good for you! I haven't seen Charlie for some time. But I hear there are a few lobsters on the travel just now. And isn't that good, too? Betsy here just came in with a fine blockie for me. Indeed what I'm saying is true, and if it's true it's no lie – I would rather have a bit of fresh fish than all your meat any day.'

'Huh!' said Dougald, and his eyes now shot swiftly about the company.

'And that was the way in our fathers' time, too,' continued Smeorach, his voice catching the story-teller's mood. 'Fish every day of the week and maybe meat on the Sabbath – and maybe not – and we never missed it. Wasn't that the way, Murdo?'

'It was,' said Murdo.

'Yes, and I have seen it, all along the coast, from everywhere the small boats would be going out and bringing in the cod and the ling. And what a splitting there was then, and a drying! I have seen it you couldn't step on all the Claddach but you would be stepping on the spelded fish.'

'I can almost remember that myself,' said William, 'and I haven't got your whiskers yet.'

There was a movement, a daring murmur.

'There's nothing wrong with my whiskers,' answered Smeorach. 'And when you have earned your own as honourably there will be time for you to talk. But no, you must go scraping away at that razor of yours, William, thinking you will make more of yourself than you are. But I'm telling you when razors were as scarce as cheap shop boots, we had the boats, and the young men, and the fish, and there was life in the place, and great warmth in that life, William, great warmth and friendliness, and not like what it is now, when the one or two of you that's left will be dropping in to see an old man for the poor fun of trying to pull his whiskers. What do you say yourself, Dougald?'

'Huh!' said Dougald.

Smeorach nodded in courteous acknowledgment.

'The trouble is nowadays,' said William, 'that the young women will hardly look at a fellow with a whisker on him.'

'Ho! ho! ho!' laughed Smeorach with jutting beard. 'So that's your trouble! Well! well! Who would have thought it!' His head drooped and waggled and the beard brushed his chest.

Soft laughter and smiling wary faces.

'Oh, it's easy to laugh,' retorted William. 'But if you take a handsome fellow like George, there, or Angus, and supposing, just for the sake of argument, that two girls, like, say—'

'Never mind your likes and supposings,' interrupted Smeorach. 'All I'll say is that when the whiskers were in it, the girls did not find them overmuch in the way. You can take that from me, William.'

'God bless me! Has a man of your years no shame in him at all?'

'No, William. None. And if you can say the same when you have the same number of years, you'll be lucky. But why would we be listening to him?' said Smeorach, turning to his guest. Then he turned to Betsy. 'Will you put the kettle on, Betsy, like a good girl, for it's a long walk Dougald has before him.'

'No tea for me,' said Dougald. 'I'm just going.'

'Hits, man!' replied Smeorach. 'You'll need something to warm you up. It's a good night. What's your hurry?'

'I'm going,' mumbled Dougald, looking about the floor for his bag.

'You'll not go out of this house without something!'

'Another time,' mumbled Dougald. 'I have things to do.'

Betsy hung the kettle on the crook. Dougald got up.

'Surely you're not really going?' cried Smeorach. 'Man, I'm vexed at that, for I haven't got half your news out of you yet. It's been a good year for the crofters. No wonder they're speaking well of your good work. Things weren't so easy in my young days!'

Smeorach smiled as he rose.

Dougald slung the bag on his back with a swirl that drew smoke from the chimney. Then he stood for a moment, filling the whole room. As he turned away, voices called good night after him.

Smeorach saw him round the corner of the house.

When he came back, they looked at him.

'I don't know,' said Smeorach quietly and stood for a moment on the middle of his own floor.

Their minds lifted to the man striding darkly across the moor, the sack on his back, and, for a few seconds, only the tongues of flame stirred.

CHAPTER TWENTY-ONE

'Ha, the very man! Just in time to save Gwynn's mind!' Michael gave the doctor a hearty welcome, turning away from him, hunting out another glass.

'Good evening, Doctor. Glad to see someone. Have a cigar.' Mr. Gwynn was smiling. 'Michael, as you will perceive, is cock-a-hoop.'

'Another masterpiece?'

'I shouldn't call it that, but it has a certain enigmatic quality,' admitted Mr. Gwynn.

'And he can't find a word for it!' Michael spilled some of the liquor. 'The subtle analyst of mental conditions is stumped. Floored. He's reduced to epithets, to German! Do you know what's the nearest he can get to it? *Primordial innocence.*'

'You are naturally a bit mystified,' said Mr. Gwynn. 'But as a matter of interest, do the words *primordial innocence* convey anything to you?'

'Well,' began the doctor doubtfully.

His expression of doubt was too much for Michael, as he lay back in his low chair and thrust his legs out.

'I was about to say,' continued the doctor, 'that it does sum up a possible condition, but I should have thought that, in a state of nature, the word *innocence* hardly applied.'

'Oh, the nail on the head!' cried Michael.

'Pay no attention to him, please,' Mr. Gwynn begged. 'Merely the usual creative frenzy.'

The doctor smiled and asked Mr. Gwynn lightly, 'What sort of bird is it?'

Michael rolled in his chair, groaning, 'O God!'

Mr. Gwynn glanced directly at the doctor. 'I beg your pardon, Doctor. How stupid of me! It's a woman's photograph. The photograph of Flora, the minister's daughter.'

There was a second before the doctor said 'Oh,' and lifted his glass.

Michael's glittering eyes were on him. 'That fairly got you!'

'Well, naturally,' said the doctor.

'You are so used to his birds, Doctor – and, by the way, he has done a beauty. Stalking a duck, he got a kittiwake. Heeling over, wings outspread. The parallel lines of the feathered quills and the *shadow* of the flesh from which they spring – like an X-ray photograph of pure motion. Marvellous!'

'Yet he can't find one simple little word,' prodded Michael.

Mr. Gwynn's gesture acknowledged the remark.

'And you can't help him out, Doctor,' Michael concluded in ironic appraisement of so unusual a situation.

'How could he – when he hasn't seen the photograph?' suggested Mr. Gwynn.

'But he has seen the girl,' replied Michael, settling deeper in his chair. His eyes flashed on Mr. Gwynn, and then shot round. 'Haven't you, Doctor?'

'All this is hardly fair, Doctor, I admit,' said Mr. Gwynn in his easy frank manner. 'You see, Michael, who can stalk anything now, studies what he calls the habits of his prey, so there was no accident in that encounter the other day.'

'The doctor was the accident,' said Michael.

'After you had gone, he set about wasting a shot or two on the dog.'

'Try it on the dog,' said Michael.

'And then,' proceeded Mr. Gwynn, 'it appears the lady got interested and sat for her photograph.'

'She did really,' Michael cried, unable to contain himself. 'With the most charming and shy innocence. *Not* primordial. Very conscious indeed. It was delicious.'

'And then,' said Mr. Gwynn, 'he got himself and myself invited to tea. Can you beat it – for sheer nerve? We were there to-day.'

'And to-morrow night they dine with us.' Michael's side-long glance steadied on the doctor. Then he suddenly sat up. 'Would you like to come?' he asked impulsively. 'Do.'

'Afraid – not to-morrow night,' considered the doctor. 'Thank you, all the same.'

'Pity,' said Michael, lying back. 'You have no idea how Gwynn here gets on with the father. You would positively think they were birds of the same feather. Perhaps they are! So I'll be left to entertain Flora. Couldn't you possibly arrange your sick list so as to help me out?'

'Afraid not.'

'Too bad.' Michael laughed.

'He is really an extraordinary man, the minister,' said Mr. Gwynn thoughtfully. 'It's as if his mind – which in its fashion is as sensitive – and hidden – as one of Michael's plates, had written on its darkness all that his people have come through from primitive times, all crushed down, hunted by landlords and other beasts, their way of life gripped by claws, economic claws, Calvinistic claws, and torn – like that.' (Mr. Gwynn made slow-tearing claws of his fingers, his face having come alive, vividly expressive. He was being carried away. He didn't mind.) 'You can see them, running to hide. Into dark corners. The dark corners of the mind. Their social pattern – getting torn. So they appear dark and gloomy, as individualists. Why? Because they are so intensely social. They prove, as no other people I know prove, that man can fulfil himself only in social life. And they have carried over this feeling for social life, almost pure, because they carry it over from the integrated imaginative life of the primitive world. When they gather together they tell stories, they laugh, they sing.' He paused and threw a hand up. 'Oh, you wonder how I know? When Erchie tells me of "the times that were in it long ago" I know what he is getting at. I have been to one or two what they called "ceilidhs" in London. Very correct. Rather forced gaiety. Tartan and so on. Boring. But, in time, a drink or two and a few break away, who are now hungry for the real thing. They find a room, away, hidden somewhere. They sing. I was embarrassed – it seemed so without true singing or real music, maudlin, nostalgic. They swam in it. They laughed. They drowned in it. Terrible! But I know now what they were hunting. They were hunting the lost social life. The rhythm of it was in them. Class distinction

forgotten. The hunt for the classless expression of pure
being through the social medium. The hunt' – Mr. Gwynn
made his gesture – 'that the whole world will one day
pursue.' He paused and then suddenly smiled. 'Michael
is getting bored. He thinks I ride my hobby horse! But you
will forgive me, Doctor. For how else can I understand
what moves in the mind of the highly sensitized, highly
civilized, modern "primitive" painter?'

Michael shot to his feet. 'Would you like to see the
photograph?' He looked searchingly at the doctor.

'Thanks,' said the doctor, getting up.

'You always do sound enthusiastic!' Michael led the way.

The doctor found his feet heavy. He had to drag them
against a dead weight of reluctance. Why had he come at
all? He might have expected something like this. But he had
been pursued by that growing foreboding that something
terrible was about to happen. The black ring was closing in.
The policeman. Closing in about Charlie – and Flora. Flora
would be found out. By her father. It did not bear thinking
about. A nightmare of night – and God alone knew what
fatal and bloody act. Going to see her photograph . . . it
made him feel slightly sick.

And there she was.

She was there, sitting with her hands in her lap, her head
up, looking out of a background that gave an impression of
immensity, facing past the camera to an immense distance,
but with an air of . . . it was impossible to describe it. So
simple, so natural, that it touched the heart with something
perilously like pathos.

Yet the word pathos was idiotic. There was no pathos in
that figure. Unless indeed something of pathos is the
ultimate condition of humanity, and some exquisite poign-
ant kinship of the spirit realizes it in a final moment.

Michael, alive in his showmanship, was waiting.

Out of a sudden perversity, believing the reaction was
utterly personal to himself, the doctor, feeling he could thus
secretly laugh at them, for he was bitter, said in quite
normal tones, 'A bit pathetic, don't you think?'

Michael's face hardened.

But Mr. Gwynn emitted a long soft breath through

pursed lips. Then he turned his face to the doctor. 'That's an extraordinary word to use . . . Do you feel that it affects you – strangely – with a sense of tears?'

And the doctor knew, profoundly, that that was what it did.

He smiled, refusing Mr. Gwynn's quiet and genuine wonder. 'I would hardly go as far as that! I certainly never saw any pathos in her. She is, I think, a rather solid, hefty lump of a girl, don't you?'

'Why did you use the word pathetic?'

'Merely a comment on the photographer's work, I suppose?' said Michael in so flat a tone that it held more searching irony than any laugh.

'Possibly,' acknowledged the doctor.

Michael turned away swiftly. 'Possibly you'll appreciate this better.'

'Ah, that's good,' responded the doctor. 'That's a speaking likeness.'

'God!' Michael groaned.

'That's really remarkable,' said the doctor. Actually he had never before seen a photograph like it. She was smiling directly into the camera. She was alive absolutely as in life, as in that moment when she had looked at him on the road before Michael had come up, only here she was amused, she was gay, with a hint of the wild shyness.

In the next one she had her hat on.

Michael, watching the doctor's face, said, 'Yes, in time I got her to take her hat off.'

'Uhm,' said the doctor. 'Striking. Really attractive.'

There were two more.

'That smiling one. Please let me see it again,' the doctor asked.

He looked at it and smiled back. It cheered him. He actually felt the gloom, the tiredness of spirit, falling from him. In some companionable way, it gave him courage. 'I must say I like that.' He turned to Mr. Gwynn. 'What do you think of it?'

'Vivid, wonderful,' said Mr. Gwynn. 'As you say – a speaking likeness.'

'I'm glad you agree.'

Michael gave his harsh chuckle.

'But also,' said Mr. Gwynn, 'I find a trace of it – the pathos – there as well. Do you not?'

'I'm not a critic,' replied the doctor. 'I always say what comes into my head – as Mr. Sandeman told me to do. He said that might help him. It gives him his laugh.'

'All right. All right,' said Michael. 'You needn't think you can drag anything out of him, Gwynn, if he doesn't want to let it go.'

'Have I ever refused you?' asked the doctor.

'No,' answered Michael. 'And you're not going to refuse me now.'

Something in Michael's tone made the doctor glance quickly at him.

'I want to take your photograph.'

The doctor's face went bleak. 'No,' he answered with cool humour. 'Not mine.'

'And I'm going to take it,' said Michael, 'in artificial light.'

The doctor turned away as if amused, but actually to cover the tremor that had come to his muscles. The flash of internal anger had been electrically fierce.

'I am going to take Gwynn,' continued Michael, 'sitting on a green meadow, like Buddha, but instead of contemplating his navel he will just have completed that gesture of finality – for which there is no word.'

Mr. Gwynn laughed softly and mockingly.

'But I cannot think where,' said Michael, 'I am going to place the minister. In the ravine up at the back there, with the black rocks and the water tumbling into its whirlpool. But that seems too obvious.' He added, after a moment, with sudden intensity, 'Too damned literary!'

'That, you will appreciate,' said Mr. Gwynn to the doctor, 'is one for me.'

'Yes,' said Michael, the pallor in his face, caring for no one's reactions. 'The classical. The classical, hell! Gwynn, the classicist, hunting the primitive! The neoplatonic Christian philosopher searching for his roots – in totemism!' He didn't even laugh.

But Mr. Gwynn laughed, mostly in a movement of the

shoulders and the hands. But he was watching Michael. 'Why the doctor in artificial light?'

They stared at each other, the doctor completely forgotten. Then Michael turned and looked at the doctor. His eyes went slowly over the doctor's face, over each feature, in a cool searching objectivity. They began to travel down, studied the hands, and, from the stance of the feet, lifted to Mr. Gwynn's face.

'All the same, I am right,' he said, with complete conviction.

'He disdains even to explain to us. The abounding vanity of the creator!' Mr. Gwynn's irony had its edge for the doctor's sake.

An extraordinary expression came to Michael's face, a sort of wild unearthly surprise. 'The Creator never did explain! Christ! I *know* why He didn't!' He cried the words, his face flaming white, and took a stride or two about the easel.

Mr. Gwynn continued to stare at him, but his eyes had gone dark and his lips had parted. The room was held in Michael's private revelation, his moment of light. Gargantuan shadows of blasphemy were shot through with this light. Egoism had gone beyond itself.

The doctor was quite cold. He could have slashed this distorted arrogance, this sheer mental unbalance, but there was something now, something somewhere, beyond them all. He experienced an angered piercing bitterness, at the same time as he felt somewhere this wildness of light. Michael's eyes had stiffened him. He broke now out of his stance, and, as his head moved on his shoulders, the gallery's deliberate lighting drew his glance to the easel.

Flora's face, laughing in its gay shyness, vivid in the flesh, flesh and life, human and lovely, immediate, now secretly holding itself away from Michael, laughing in the green brown world.

Suddenly the doctor laughed back.

The others, startled, followed his look.

They, too, began to laugh. Michael rolled round the easel, laughing from the belly.

When the jest was exhausted, Michael had become normal, or sub-normal, almost physically weary.

'Pathos!' he said. 'At least she has disproved that now. As I told you, Gwynn, there is only one way of taking her, and that is stripped. Venus. The Highland Aphrodite!'

'Back to the classical,' suggested Mr. Gwynn

Michael smiled wearily. 'How you feed on words! I am thinking of the woman who generates. Have you lost your feeling for – for texture?'

'No,' answered Mr. Gwynn, and all at once his voice had a simple earnestness. Unknowingly, his right thumb kept feeling along the finger-tips. 'I agree with you. She would be superb.'

Michael removed the smiling photograph and set up the first one.

'You see?' said Mr. Gwynn at once.

Michael stood looking at it.

'It's more than flesh,' continued Mr. Gwynn. 'There is a strange passivity. A pure state of being. Non-intellectual, in the sense that there is no curiosity. That's what I mean by innocence. And primordial – because you get the feeling of something timeless.'

'Walter Pater,' murmured Michael, in good-natured mockery.

Mr. Gwynn shook his head. 'No. The very opposite. There is no smile there, no knowingness. She does not sit amid us, with a woman's knowledge of our sins, sins she has helped to create and secretly knows as her own children. Here is woman a little remote from us. She does not sit, but goes wandering.'

'I suppose all that that means,' said Michael, in a quiet voice, still looking at the photograph, 'is that she hasn't had the Lady Lisa's experience.'

'No,' answered Mr. Gwynn. 'However complete her experience, however devastating, even tragic – finally, alone, she would sit like that, and a man thinking of her, and therefore inevitably thinking of her *like that*, would break his heart.'

'And actually she is a very conventional creature,' said Michael.

'Very,' said Mr. Gwynn.

Michael turned his face to him and smiled. 'We know how conventional she was – wandering on that bare hill-side.'

'Wandering,' said Mr. Gwynn, and held Michael's look.

Michael turned his head. 'What do you think, Doctor?' There was now nothing provocative in his voice. It was friendly.

'I'm afraid it is all a bit beyond me,' answered the doctor.

'You don't like giving anything away, do you?'

'Afraid I have nothing to give.'

'Not even your photograph?' Michael turned to Mr. Gwynn. 'Do you know what I think? I think the doctor refuses his photograph because he feels, in the purely primitive way, that it might take some virtue out of him. It might steal away his likeness.'

'Well, it might,' answered Mr. Gwynn. 'Is a person who has been painted – or even photographed – ever the same? Is not some magic taken from him? If you turn me into a caricature of a Buddha, how can I ever be whole again?'

Michael almost broke into a laugh.

'You may smile,' said Mr. Gwynn, 'but there it is. At some moment when I try to achieve a harmony within me, the tail of my inner eye will see that Buddha, and harmony will be split. When this occurs more than once, I shall become "disillusioned", my hidden mind, to protect itself, will adopt a certain cynicism, very cultured no doubt' – Mr. Gwynn's shoulders and hands acknowledged the point for him – 'but there I'll be, back in our modern disease – the split mind. The doctor and I will form a trade union against you. Do you agree, Doctor?'

The doctor, who was taking a cigarette from his case, paused to hand one to Mr. Gwynn and to Michael. They lit up.

'I think it mightn't be a bad idea,' agreed the doctor. 'It isn't good for anyone to get too much of his own way.'

'A bunch of toughs,' said Michael. 'You prattle about your science and your metaphysical or analytical processes or whatever they are, but whenever you come up against the artist, the one man who sees a thing whole, you instinctively fight him. You're afraid of him, and that's the truth.'

'Saving your presence,' said Mr. Gwynn, 'sure an' why should we be afraid of him?'

But Michael refused Mr. Gwynn's lead to let the conversation slide away. Mr. Gwynn had realized that their guest may have had to bear a lot.

'Dammit all,' said Michael with just a touch of spirit, 'here I am in a place like this. And here you come to meditate on your profound – so profound – theories. We used to talk in grandiloquent terms of Balzac's Human Comedy. But always it was away in the world, in France. Somewhere or something big and vast. But when I try to bring it down to a god-haunted forgotten country place like this – why, then, it is provincial. Ah, to hell with you!' concluded Michael, suddenly tired of talking. 'By the way, Doctor,' he added, 'I don't think you have seen one other member of our human comedy.' He removed Flora, and, going over to a stack of enlargements, selected one and set it on the easel.

It was a photograph, almost in profile, of the policeman with his notebook in his left hand and a stub of pencil in his right. The figure was slightly out of focus, but just beyond it, seen between the bent head and the recording hand, was the picture of Charlie, standing up from his boat, against the black skerries, and upon him the lens had clearly been deliberately focused. The slight indistinctness swelled the figure of the policeman in a menacing way.

Michael looked at his work for a moment, but he no longer seemed vitally interested. 'That's the lot – so far,' he said. 'Come along, let us have a drink.' He turned to the electric switches.

CHAPTER TWENTY-TWO

The two boys laughed in husky glee as they peered back over a heathery knoll in the direction of Cruime and the highway. They had come by different routes without being seen, especially by other children who might have followed them – or told at home.

It was delightful to be free, it was full of the greatest fun, of hidden glee – which could now come out and frolic around. The wind suddenly blew Hamish's jacket up off his back and onto his head. They both laughed.

'I think it's going to be a dirty night,' said Hamish with a change of tone.

At once they got up and started forward, and their voices grew friendly in a low and marvelling way.

'It's funny John-the-roadman said they were yellow when the one we saw was white,' said Norrie.

'I asked old Peter if he ever saw a yellow hare. And he said to me Who told you that? So I said it was John-the-roadman. Then he said that when a hare was changing it sometimes got a sort of yellowish look. He had seen that sometimes himself, he said, specially about the hind quarters. Then he told me that there are two kinds of hares and they are both quite different.'

'Our one is the white hare.'

'Yes,' said Hamish, 'but it's also called the blue hare and it's also called the mountain hare. And it's just the same hare.'

'I didn't know all that,' Norrie admitted.

'And the other one is called the brown hare and it never changes its hair at all and that's the difference.'

'And where does it stay?' asked Norrie.

'It stays on big farms on the east side of the country and it's nearly as big as a young calf.'

'How do they catch him? They would need a big snare for that fellow!'

'Have you got your snare on you?' asked Hamish suddenly.

'I have. Have you?'

After each had grabbed the bulge in his pocket, Hamish proceeded with his description of how the mountain hare – which was the one that concerned them – changed his coat from heather colour in the summer to snow white in the winter. Norrie wanted to know if the hare knew how to change its coat or what happened, and in this way their conversation took a very interesting turn.

The sky was an angry grey and they could hear the sea in the cliffs. It was blowing hard.

'The wind is well into the north,' said Hamish in a seaman's voice. Every now and then they looked over their shoulders, but as they came near 'the place' they forgot to look. 'The place' was where they had seen the white hare.

By the time they came to it they decided the light was just right, for it was already going fast. No hare would go into a snare in daylight, for though a hare might be many a mysterious thing it was no fool.

They now began looking about for 'traces'. But they found none, and as the idea of finding them had been Norrie's, Hamish suggested that a running hare would not drop his 'traces' and him running.

'No,' said Norrie, 'but we saw him sitting once.'

'But he wouldn't do it every time he sat,' said Hamish.

'No, but he must do it some time,' said Norrie with inexorable logic.

So, doubled over, they made another search, and when Norrie cried in excitement, Hamish was with him in a moment. But Hamish shook his head. 'They're too black. That's sheeps',' he said.

'Yes,' said Norrie. But he was disappointed. 'Have you ever seen a hare's?' he asked.

In the end, they agreed that the hare had been running on the narrow sheep track. He wasn't such a fool as to go leaping through long heather if there was a track handy. Trust him!

So they searched for a patch of old unburnt heather, where the track narrowed to little more than a hand's length, and agreed with a profound feeling of certainty that this was the very spot.

First a stone and the driving home of the stake. Next the setting up of the thin hazel stick notched on top to hold the golden wire. Finally the smoothing out of the noose, the difficult tricky job, and the argument over its height above the ground. On hands and knees they worked like two beavers, and then drew back and flattened themselves to the ground, seeing themselves as a hare charging along, and decided that their handiwork was good. And then they heard the whistle.

One wild look at each other and they were up and racing on.

From behind a bluff they peered and waited. First the sheep, then a dog, and finally the unmistakable head and shoulders of Dougald MacIan rising against the sea.

Without a word, as birds have no word, they were up and off.

If a sheep went into the snare by a leg! If Dougald himself tripped headlong in it!

They fled inland towards Loch Geal.

Presently, through the deepening dusk, they saw the dread figure and his wide flock and his rushing collie not going towards Sgeir but coming straight for them.

Deeper into the tumbled land about Loch Geal they went.

Like something terrible and inexorable, the shepherd and his flock and his dog still advanced upon them.

Deeper and farther they went, into places which they had never seen before and which looked queerly at them but made neither move nor sign.

'Did you hear yon?' breathed Norrie.

Listening, they heard the pounding of their hearts.

'Come on,' said Hamish.

A wild quacking and whirring of ducks withered their hearts.

They stood, stricken, seeing the corner of dim water and the dark reeds.

'Come on,' whispered Hamish in the terrible instinctive fear that the quacking would betray them.

They ran down, and now with trembling muscles they stumbled headlong in boggy ground, and swarmed about, pulling their feet out, uttering choked swift cries.

Through the place they got, tearing themselves out on hands and knees, grabbing at the heather, up and off, pursued by their own cries and the memory of the quacking duck.

Exhausted, they fell at last, and lay, panting so fiercely that it induced a darkness in the head and the fear that can no more run from that which comes behind, leaving nothing but a last cry for the thing when it jumps.

Nothing jumped, however, and soon their breathing could be held to let their ears listen.

Whispering is the darkness in the heart of the wind. It hears itself under the night. The wind passes. The whisper listens.

In a paralysis of the throat, the whisper becomes a grip of the hand.

Hamish, with Norrie's fingers in his flesh, followed Norrie's upward look.

Neither of them stirred or whispered.

'Where?' whispered Hamish.

'Up there.'

Nothing happened.

'What?' whispered Hamish.

'That tuft of heather – it moved.'

It was now almost quite dark, but Hamish could see the tuft against the grey-dark sky. Their mouths, open for silence, grew dry again.

'It's only the wind,' whispered Hamish.

They watched it.

Hamish brought his mouth to Norrie's ear. 'Come on,' he breathed, and slowly he got into a stooping position and slid away. When Norrie made up on him they started running. A cockgrouse split the night: *Err, kek, kek, kek, go-back, go-back!* Norrie pitched by the shoulder and rolled over, choking, after the first scream or two had ripped out.

Hamish crouched by him. 'Hsh! Shut up!'

Norrie was crying, whimpering, his head down, gripping his leg, slowly rolling.

'Let's go on a bit,' whispered Hamish and he began to lift Norrie to his feet.

But Norrie's right leg would not take his weight.

'Get on my back,' said Hamish.

When he could carry Norrie no farther, he stopped. They sat and listened. Then they began to examine the knee, where the pain was.

'If you're able to work it at all, it can't be broken,' said Hamish encouragingly.

'I don't know,' mumbled Norrie. 'I can't feel it.'

'It just got stunned. The best plan is to rub it. Will I rub it for you?'

Hamish's warm friendliness was a comfort to Norrie. The night covered them over.

When at last they got up, they continued in the same direction. Hamish had the idea that if they kept circling to the right they must eventually get round Loch Geal and so in time reach the sheep track which they had abandoned when they first saw Dougald.

Norrie was hirpling. He said his leg felt very queer.

Soon, however, it was so dark that they had to go very slowly, swerving away to right or left before high obstacles.

The idea that they knew the way was very strong in them, especially in Hamish, who led.

An hour after that they were still going, but Loch Geal had vanished.

In another hour, Hamish said he thought it must be the sea in front of them, because the blackness looked less black and it seemed 'away down'. But it couldn't be the sea, because if it was the sea they would hear it. Besides, it was in the wrong place!

This feeling that it couldn't be the sea conflicted, how-ever, with a sensation of empty space. It was very dark now. They had to stick close together. This sensation of empty space below them was frightening. It brought a special emptiness into their empty stomachs.

'Here, lean on me,' said Hamish, 'and we'll go together to a sheltered spot and rest for a while.' His voice was low and earnest in Norrie's ear, for the wind was buffeting them, blowing into their ears, making them tired and stupid, stealing their senses, and Hamish knew that tears, the awful slow soft-sobbing tears of despair, were near Norrie now.

He took Norrie's left arm round his neck and put his own right round Norrie's back. His foot, landing on a rounded stone, nearly upset him. And then a very strange thing happened. It was not altogether anger against the stone that made him heave it forward with his boot, nor yet the moment's relief which springs from such a diversion, but also, down in him where the pure sensation of empty space had been born, an unconscious desire to test that sensation. No sooner, however, had the stone rolled away, than he gripped Norrie and said with a renewed confidence: 'Come on!' The ground, which was always going up or down, was now going down. They had taken two short steps forward when up from what seemed the cavernous bottom of the world came the startled shrieking of sea-birds, as the stone exploded on skerries two hundred feet below them. They stopped on the edge of the cliff.

They stopped, and they shrank in on themselves and back, and they turned, and the cliffs of the world rose against their faces.

As they crawled away, chasms yawned on every side and blinded them. But they gripped the earth, and their hands were feelers. They lay and panted in dizzy weakness, but only for a moment, only for a second or two, because they felt the earth itself was treacherous, was heaving up to throw them back, throw them over, empty them away.

After that – the endlessness of time having come upon them – the two boys were curled up in a sheltering hag, their skin a pale rime, their teeth chittering.

Presently Norrie said in a queer calm voice: 'They'll be searching for us. They'll think we're dead.' Even his teeth had stopped chittering while he said that. It was like the voice of a child.

They had been dogged by the fear of the awful retribution awaiting them at home. Now Hamish saw the matter solemnly and distant a little from him. Death made a great difference.

They wanted to discuss the effect that their death would create on certain persons, but they could not speak of it, so they thought about it in silence. Death would have its revenge on many a hand and tongue which had in times past been lifted against them.

Hamish lifted his head and looked about him.

'Do you know,' he said, 'I think it's getting lighter!' He stood up. 'It is! There must be a moon rising somewhere.' He scanned the dark starless sky and saw in the east a distinct lightening of grey-dark cloud.

He stooped and gripped Norrie. 'Come and look!'

Norrie got up but in a moment gave a horrid choking gasp.

A figure, like a condensation of the dark night, was coming towards them, without outline, enormous. It strode on two feet. When about to bear down upon them, it strode past. In no time it had gone out of sight down into a hollow.

Without a thought, without a word, the boys started off the opposite way and Norrie forgot the pain in his knee. But after a few yards they drew up, casting wild glances about them, and backing a little as if about to be hit.

'Wait!' gasped Hamish. He had realized they were on a path. 'This way!' And he struck inland off the path, and they threw themselves down in the lee of a small knoll, listening in so horrible a fear that the ears had to strain beyond the blood stream.

After a time, Hamish said in a low voice, 'It was a man.'

They listened again. Nothing was coming at them. But the wind, the dark wind, was searching. Round the knoll it came and licked them. Over there, it whined. High above streamed the riders of the night, invisible eager heads shot forward like the heads of wild duck.

'I think,' breathed Hamish in low valiance, 'it was Charlie.'

Norrie could not speak. But something like a tiny eye, far in Hamish, remained watchful and wary. And at last it lifted itself on its thin stalk and looked about its primeval shore.

But Norrie was curled in the back end of his burrow, where the weasel of life could gnaw at him.

Hamish, with his voice, began drawing the weasel away, pulling it off from behind, and the pain of renewed hope was worse than the pain of the weasel's teeth. The figures of the night and the ghosts of all the stories, the murdered men and the drowned women, were coming back to life, outside in the night, beyond the covered head.

Suddenly, as if waiting for this extreme moment, the night began to speak. Far off they heard its voice, so far that when it was gone it was like a cry damned in its own forlorn death.

The boys got up in terror and stumbled away from it. They fell and crawled once more into the hag from which the dark figure had driven them. In this hag, the wind shot clean over them. They pressed against its inner bank.

They heard another torn cry.

And then – out there – coming up towards them – coming along the path – a figure . . . two figures, two dark bodies, and a woman's voice gave a small cry, and a man's voice was low and quick, and they were together, darkly striding, and the sound of their footsteps was on the earth, and they passed on, passed away into that region from which the solitary figure had come.

A louder cry went through the night, a pursuing cry.

And inland, a cry here . . . a cry there . . . faint and torn, like the cry of spirits wandering and for ever lost.

And all cries were hunting them, and everything was coming upon them.

Nearer now, a striding figure, a vast staggering-onward figure, the figure of the pursuing cry, and it followed those that had gone before, and was lost.

Hamish dragged his body from the bank and inland he saw a yellow eye, and it stared at him and went out.

He crouched down beside Norrie and did not speak.

All at once, the near night was shattered by a great hallooing cry, and following that cry at a breath's distance: 'Ha-a-amish!'

Hamish's flesh ran soft upon the bone. It was his Uncle Norman.

Norrie came back to life. He started crying out, weakly and urgently. Hamish followed his staggering body.

Norman heard, and saw, and came striding to them. 'Thank God!' And his voice was thick and fervent. On his knees, he took the boys in his arms. 'Are you all right?' His breath was warm and the strength of all the world was in his arms and body. He had no bitter word for them, but only kindness and strong fondness. For the first time that night, tears burst from Hamish's eyes.

'You were lost, were you?'

'Ye-es,' said Hamish.

'And you were hiding there? That was the wise thing to do. I knew you had sense in you. I told them that. For to keep going in the black dark – that's fatal. Are you terribly cold? Come, Norrie, I'll rub you a bit—'

Hamish gave a cry. Another figure was upon them.

Norman turned his head. 'Is that you, Doctor?'

'Yes.'

'I've got them!'

'Good!' said the doctor. 'Are they all right?' He was stooping beside them.

'Fine.'

'Did you see anyone passing?' asked the doctor.

'Passing?' repeated Norman, held by the doctor's voice. 'No.'

'Didn't you?' The doctor was at once wrapped in his own thought.

'Why?' asked Norman.

'Did you see anyone?' the doctor suddenly asked the boys.

'Yes,' said Hamish. 'A man and a woman went that way. Then another man.'

'My God!' said the doctor.

'What is it, Doctor?' asked Norman.

'Charlie and Flora. A smash-up. The minister is after them.'

'Here, Doctor!' cried Norman. 'Wait!'

The doctor called back: 'There's no time.' Then he was gone.

Norman took a second or two. 'Come with me, boys.'

They started off after the doctor. Presently he stopped, turned towards the moor and let out three cries. An answering 'Ay! Ay!' came from far away. A yellow eye showed. Another eye came on a skyline. The moor passed on the cries. Norman got to his knees and took Norrie on his back.

Hamish, whose hand drew strength from Norman's firm grasp, ventured, 'Where are you going?'

'To Dougald's cottage,' answered Norman.

Presently they emerged on the flat western tip of the Ros, and there the wind blew powerfully, and Hamish changed to Norman's lee side.

They came to the cottage, and Norman went round it to the front door, Norrie still on his back and Hamish at his hand.

At the door, Norman stopped and quietly lowered Norrie to the ground, and then he listened. The door was open. Norman shoved his head round the post. 'Anyone in?' There was no answer. The lamp was burning.

A cry came from the rocks.

Norman turned swiftly. The boys followed him.

'Stop there!' ordered Norman, who had forgotten them.

They stopped, as if his voice had hit them, and then he disappeared over the cliff.

The dark-grey of the sky had thinned, its heaviness now being ominously driven under the risen moon. Norman went down the steep zig-zag clean-footed as a seaman on a tilting deck, and the shingle crunched as he jumped. He strode past the minister and Dougald to where the doctor on the water's edge was yelling.

'What is it?' he demanded.

The doctor swung round. His voice lashed high and sharp.

'They're gone – in the boat!'

Norman's skin ran cold. In a great voice he yelled imperiously, 'Charlie!' He saw the movement of the boat, coming black from a skerry. 'Charlie!' The throat was lacerated by that cry. The boat passed away and the channel was empty.

Norman turned round. The looming figure of the

minister was there. A vast wrath engulfed Norman. There was something in Charlie which he had always loved. And if Charlie hadn't been madly driven he wouldn't have so gone to his doom, taking the woman with him. The full storm, to which the night had been working up, sent its smashing volley, whizzing through the teeth of the skerries and lashing their faces with its spindrift.

'God forgive you,' roared Norman above the roar of the sea, 'for driving them to their deaths!' Blinded by his wrath, he turned to the cliff, his heart crying on within him, crying to those in the grip of that sea, and crying helplessly.

CHAPTER TWENTY-THREE

The sensational news ran along that coast through the grey of the morning and the thunder of the sea. Kenneth Grant haunted his post office, rapping out telegraphic messages to white-faced Sarah and drawing the words from her one by one as they came in.

There had been one wild hope – in which none of the seamen could believe – that Charlie's boat might have made the sheltered harbour of Glaspool in the deep inlet of Loch Savach twenty miles to the south'ard. It was the first hope to be definitely dispelled. For most men it was also the last.

For Charlie was no fool. Charlie did not just go wildly into the sea. If he could have made Glaspool, he would have had plenty of time on his hands to dispose of his boat and, with Flora, catch the early morning bus for the south train. That had been undoubtedly his wild plan, and he had made the seaman's instant decision, cut adrift and taken the fight in freedom upon himself.

He would never have crept in upon some lonely beach, even had that been possible. Not Charlie. It was his own boat and he would have sold her openly and gone. His defiance, his action, was final, with all a seaman's last impatience for the landsman's temporizings and fears. Fate had come upon him and he had instantly, instinctively, taken to his own boat and headed for the open.

In the group of men standing in the lee of Kenneth Grant's shop waiting for news, such thoughts slipped, sometimes halfspoken, from one or other mind to many.

'He took his chance,' said William. 'He thought he could do it.'

'No,' said Norman slowly. 'He did not think.'

'It's easy for us to think that now.'

'Charlie is a good seaman,' said Norman. 'None better. He knew there was no earthly chance of the weather taking off.'

'He might have done it – had it got no worse.'

'I doubt it. I was there, at Sgeir. It was hitting the skerries in solid lumps then. We know a November storm. We all knew here it was coming upon us fast. Charlie knew.'

'Do you mean he was? . . .' William did not like to use a disparaging word even in argument.

'No,' answered Norman. 'He was driven. And in the wild moment he went his way. And he took his woman with him.'

'So would you or me,' said William, his voice rising.

Norman stared far, saying nothing.

The wind had its thin persistent howl, packed with fury. A sheet of loosened zinc rattled somewhere behind the shop like a piece of artillery. An elderly woman, going from one gable-end to another, was blown from her course, her black clothes flattening against her body like a loose sail against a mast, before she turned, leaning over, and slowly staggered to shelter. She nearly fell as the wind suddenly left her, and in that islanded moment a remote smile touched watching faces, for Kittag was quick with her tongue when men in their lordly way looked upon feminine struggle.

Angus, whose wit was heavy and slow, turned his rawboned reddish face – and the smile died.

They all turned their heads and beheld the minister, one hand holding on his black felt hat, coming along the road. He was leaning forward, and sometimes he staggered and sometimes he stood. Upon each face came a narrowing look and younger eyes glanced to right and left for a way of escape. But no one moved, for the moment had its own inescapable dignity.

As the minister drew near, all eyes left him and stared seaward, a blindness in their expression. Far as eye could reach, the sea was a smother of white-caps, of breaking grey-green water, a tumultuous onrushing stream, blown and tossed, in which no boat of that coast could live for ten minutes.

As the minister hove into the shelter beside them, the older men turned their faces to him, calm and level.

He was panting and the struggle had drained all colour out of his skin as if the heart, over-taxed, had drawn the blood inward.

'Any word?'

'No, Minister,' answered Norman with solemn calm. 'There is no word.'

The minister swayed, as though the wind had left him dizzy.

Just then Kenneth came out of the post office door. As he saw the minister, his whole expression steadied and sank inward.

'Any news?' asked the minister quietly, in a fatal friendliness.

Kenneth glanced away. 'No, there's no news so far.'

The minister kept looking at him, his eyes hot and hungry.

'If I get any, I'll tell you at once,' added Kenneth. 'They're searching now – all down the coast.'

Silence held them.

'How long do you think the storm will last?' asked the minister.

Automatically the seamen's faces looked at the sky. No one spoke. Then William said, 'It may take another day or so to blow itself out.'

There was silence again and they felt the dread question coming. Then it came: 'Do you think there's any hope, men?'

At last Norman turned his face and looked levelly at the minister. 'It's too early to say yet. Charlie was a good seaman. It's a long coast.'

The minister searched Norman's face, but he might as well have searched the face of the sea.

'So be it,' he said, and he bowed perceptibly, and turned and walked away from them. Whenever the wind got him, it threw him forward. He came about to fight it, rolled, and pitched on his side like a drunk man.

They ran to him and helped him up. The palms of his hands had got the gravel in breaking his fall and were bleeding.

'Come up to the house,' invited Kenneth, handing him his hat.

'I'm all right,' said the minister. 'Thank you.' His calm was like the calm of one in a fatal sleep.

'Come away!' urged William. 'Come up to Kenneth's.'

The minister looked at William, then his eyes went into distance. Their voices had been lifted against the wind. Now a tearing gust got them. 'I'm going home,' said the minister, but they only saw his lips move.

No one dared lay hands on him. Lying back against the wind, he went on.

'Follow him,' said Norman to Angus.

Angus and George followed the minister at a distance. Opposite Smeorach's the minister gripped the low stone wall, leaning over it like one about to be sick. The wind blew his hat away. George raced after it. Angus went up to the minister.

'Come on in to Smeorach's,' said Angus awkwardly but strongly.

The minister turned his head slowly and looked at Angus. The skin was livid. The eyes burning. The hair blew on his head. Angus could not think what to do, so he did not think, but took the minister by the arm, as he would an ordinary man, and said in a rough inviting way, 'Come on!'

The minister went with him, weakened by that human grip. Smeorach saw them pass the window.

'Minister!' cried Smeorach. 'Come in! Come in!'

Angus pulled the door shut and went back to the road, in time to catch a glimpse of George disappearing over the crest after the flying hat.

Angus, opening his mouth, let the wind choke his laughter. This relieved him.

George's head reappeared and Angus waited for him. George did not think much of Angus's heavy humour. 'Here – put it on you!' he cried.

But Angus would not take the hat. Neither of them wanted to go to Smeorach's. At last George, aware that eyes were watching them from sheltered house-walls, went with the hat. He knocked on the door – a thing he never did – lifted the latch, and went in.

The minister was flat on his back on the floor, face white as death and eyes shut.

'Run,' called Smeorach in his piping voice, 'to Kenneth's for a drop of spirits.'

George shouted his news to Angus and together they swept into the gale.

When George returned with a half-bottle of whisky, he caught a glimpse of the minister sitting in the chair to the right of the fire. 'I think he'll be all right now,' whispered Smeorach at the door.

'He could not be in better hands,' said Norman, when George bore back the news.

As the forenoon wore on, the men drifted away.

As the day sank into night, every house on that coastline for fifty miles had its own construction of the story. Nothing else was discussed. It lived with them. It was present, not like their own bodies, but in a movement of figures charged with destiny, and before it their apprehension was humbled and judgment was a presumption to which their brows dare not lift. Ears of young children hearkened to the wind and to the roar of the sea. Here and there men returned with the darkening, weary and wordless after their empty search along cliff and shore. Doors were shut fast, the old thick walls contained them, and outside the night streamed and rocked.

Through Sarah's bright, dark-eyed face the spirit shone like a bird arrested in flight. Betsy was still as a pool in which the reflections are clear and deep.

'Who would ever have thought it?' asked Sarah of Betsy and the night.

'Perhaps they were going together for a long time,' said Betsy to Sarah and to the silence that wondered and wandered under the night.

'They must have been.'

'Meeting on the moor at night.'

The night swept over them, its vast edge like a screaming scythe-blade.

'She couldn't have been afraid,' said Sarah.

'She might.'

'Yes, she might,' agreed Sarah.

Their argument brought them closer.

'The years in Edinburgh. All that time. And when he was away. They never forgot.'

'What are you girls doing through there in the cold? Come away in!'

'We're coming, Mother,' cried Betsy.

'Which window was it she got out of?' asked Betsy, as if her mother had never called from the kitchen.

'One near the front door. She must have come down the stairs and then went out the window, so that no one would hear. The minister must have heard something. He went to her bed and it was empty. Then he found her dressing gown by the window. But I couldn't catch all they were saying. Kenneth is against the minister. And the minister followed her and came on them. Wasn't it awful?'

Their minds tried to picture love betrayed in the night.

'Did they . . . what happened?' asked Betsy.

'High words. High wild words. Charlie challenged him. They are two big strong men. Flora came between them and turned to her father, and cried "Father! Father!" And she was there between them. It was dark and wild, and no one now will maybe ever know all that was said. But it had come at last and there was no going back. It had to be one way or the other now.'

'And she went with Charlie.'

'Yes,' said Sarah.

'Flora!' cried Betsy softly and listened to the far night of the world into which Flora had gone with her lover Charlie, and as she listened a great wave raced in thunder along the strand. Warm tears began to trickle down her cold face.

Sarah became similarly affected.

Up in Sarah's little post office, the shop closed and all lights extinguished save for the candle on the counter beside them, Kenneth Grant and the policeman were talking.

'But I wasn't against you,' said the policeman. 'I had to do my duty. I had to find out if Dougald could have had the money on his own. I am satisfied from the little I could drag out of him and from yourself, that he could. That ends it.'

'Hell, it's ended all right,' said Kenneth.

'I didn't want—'

'Oh, I know,' muttered Kenneth, turning his shoulder impatiently and lifting the bottle. 'Here!'

The policeman let Kenneth pour more whisky into his glass, but his expression was reserved and hurt.

Kenneth said, the glass tilted in his hand, 'Look here, Ranald, I know how you feel. You know how I feel. In your place I'd have done the same. We're all human. We've all got to live. But damn it all, man, it's the loss, the terrible loss. What's the use of us living in this dead hole if we're not going ahead? Charlie – Charlie had intelligence. The fellow liked the sea. He had ideas. He had seen the world. I have ideas, too. Norman is steady as a rock. William has salt in him. The young fellows would take a lead – if there's money in it. Money! Damn, didn't they take their sheep money? Wouldn't they take their lobster money and their fish money? Wouldn't they take the money I could save them on carriage? They don't know how to go about it. But I know. And I wouldn't be doing it only for their good like some bloody charity. I'd be doing it for my own good. And your good. And everyone's bloody good. And now Charlie is snuffed out like that – hell, like that!' He drank.

The policeman drank.

'I liked Charlie,' said Kenneth in a quiet voice, staring at the floor.

There was a scrambling at the door.

'Who's there?' called Kenneth.

'It's me, Peter MacInnes.'

As Kenneth unlocked the door and pulled it open, Peter came in carrying a dead lantern. 'I saw your light,' he said.

Kenneth at once made Peter sit down. 'Where have you been? Here, take a dram.'

'Wait,' gasped Peter, 'till I get my breath.' He breathed heavily for a little while, then said, 'I was at the manse.'

'The manse! On a night like this!' Kenneth looked shrewdly at him.

'One or two of us had to go.'

Kenneth had forgotten that Peter was an elder of the church. He often forgot, because Peter had some fun in him, and was wise, and possessed little of the heavy solemnity which Kenneth hated and so often derided in suitable company.

'Is the minister all right?' asked Kenneth.

'Yes.'

'In that case, you can take your dram.'

Peter contemplated the glass for a moment, then glanced at Kenneth. 'Slainte!' He emptied the glass and shuddered a little over the neat spirit. 'Ha-a-a! that will do me good,' he said slowly. He looked at the policeman. 'I hope this will be no more trouble for you, Ranald?'

'No. Why would it? There's nothing wrong,' answered the policeman earnestly.

'No,' said Peter nodding. 'I suppose there's nothing wrong.'

'You know what I mean,' added the policeman quickly, for Kenneth had turned away with a hunch to his shoulders.

'Yes, we know,' said Peter quietly. He nodded slowly. 'We thought the minister would not want to preach tomorrow, and we thought we could make simple arrangements among us.'

As he paused, Kenneth asked sharply, 'He's not going to preach?'

'Yes, he's going to take the service as usual,' answered Peter, and his face steadied in a thoughtful way.

Kenneth kept looking at Peter. 'I see,' he said ironically.

'What?' Peter lifted up his bearded face.

'Oh, it's all right,' said Kenneth. 'He wouldn't give in.'

'You sound a bit bitter, Kenneth.'

'No,' answered Kenneth bitterly. 'Merely the fact. He doesn't give in. That sort of power never does. It goes on. It's as strong as death.'

'Would you have it give in?'

'No,' answered Kenneth with sharper irony. 'Why should I?'

'You judge harshly. And from one point.'

'It's a good point,' answered Kenneth.

'You're a young man, Kenneth,' said Peter. 'There's more than one thing in the world.'

'Maybe,' replied Kenneth, who was thirty-five, 'but there's death in it – all the time.'

'Yes,' said Peter, looking at him. 'There's death.'

'Will you have another dram?' asked Kenneth politely.

'No, I'll have no more. Thank you for it. I'll be going now, for they may be anxious at home.'

'It's time I was home myself,' said the policeman.

Peter got up. Kenneth put the two glasses in an outside pocket and the bottle in an inside pocket. Then he opened the door.

The roar of the night came at them.

The policeman went one way and Peter MacInnes the other. The gloom enveloped them with the good night on their lips.

Kenneth locked the door and stood for a moment in its shelter, looking far in the direction of the roaring sea. The hounds of power on the hunt of death. Power – and death.

He shuddered from the cold and his own bitterness, and the high cry that was in him came out in a bitter curse.

From that cold, the boy Hamish snuggled in his bed beside his elder brother. They had spoken together in low voices for a long time, but now Neil, who was fifteen, had suddenly fallen asleep, for he had fought the wind that day for many hours along the southern shores of Loch Ros.

Hamish's mind always came back to the white hare. They said a witch could change into a hare. Maybe that had been in John-the-roadman's eye! But that was silly, too, because if so, why then would the gamekeepers, like Andrew Mackinnon – and Kenneth Grant getting a day, and others besides – why would they go on a great shoot of the white hares if they were witches? And everyone liked thick dark hare soup, with the meat broken up in it, and eating it with bursting hot potatoes on a cold day. Saliva made a small trickle on its own into Hamish's mouth. But the whiteness was beyond his mouth. And the figures in the dark of the Ros.

The way the minister had walked off blindly into the Ros, saying no word to Uncle Norman who had spoken calmly to him on the cliff-top . . .

And Dougald's cottage, where they had rested a little while, though the doctor had not stayed long, for Norman had said there was no need for the doctor to come back with

them. It would be out of his way and they could manage
fine. And while they were talking like that, there was
Dougald, silent, pouring the water in the teapot and
spreading the cups like a woman. And all the time there
were thoughts and things behind the surface. And Hamish
knew fine that the doctor left to follow the minister lest
something queer happened on that road.

And another thing – the way Dougald stuck the kitchen
knife in the big jam-pot, and pulled the knife out laden, and
tilted the jam on the thick slices of bread, and they had to
eat fast and keep licking the jam back from the edge. What
would Hamish's mother have said to that way of doing? It
was good, though! Strawberry jam. There was no jam in all
the world like strawberry jam.

The colour red went back into white. For now they were
on the moor. (And it was a strange thing, wasn't it? that on
that moor grown men were not against them seeing them as
bad boys, but were tall full men, and even Dougald himself
had been a silent man, spreading no fear, but spreading
strawberry jam thick as though he wanted to empty the
pot.)

And there they were going on and on, Uncle Norman
taking the storm on his left side and sheltering them, little
thinking! And then they passed Loch Geal, and then they
must be coming near 'the place'. Near and nearer. And
then they saw the white thing.

'God bless me,' said Uncle Norman to himself. 'What's
that?'

And Hamish had taken the two quick steps forward. And
it was the white hare, stretched full out, dead in the snare.

The wonder that had come on him then! Without
thinking, he cried in triumph that it was their hare! They
had set the snare and it was their own hare!

'Boys,' said Uncle Norman, and his voice was quiet and
friendly, 'do you think it's right doing this?'

It was terrible, terrible, and Hamish wanted to cry. For
there was the hare, the white hare, and they had caught it.
They were all on their knees above the hare. And a great
feeling came over Hamish and he wanted to go away.

But Uncle Norman put his heavy hand on his shoulder.

'I know,' he said. 'I was once a boy myself. But you see what can happen, and your mothers nearly out of their minds?'

Hamish could not speak for he saw everything through the kind tone of Uncle Norman's words.

And then a great blatter of wind came and nearly flattened them and Uncle Norman groaned, and looked over his shoulder far away where the sea was, and the earth quivered under them.

It was a terrible instant, for Uncle Norman gave a low cry out of his throat as though he was seeing someone being struck.

After that he said no more about the hare. He took the noose off the head, and pulled out the stake, and handed the snare to Hamish.

'It's food. We cannot leave that,' said Uncle Norman and he carried the hare in one hand.

But Hamish knew now why Uncle Norman had cried out. He had cried out because maybe yon was the very blow that sank the boat and drowned Charlie and Flora.

Drowned them.

Perhaps because the only human bodies Hamish had ever seen in the sea were bodies swimming and diving, he now thought of the drowned bodies as a whiteness in the sea, each a whiteness sinking far down.

He did not feel grief for the bodies, but drew away from them, drew away swiftly so that they would not touch him, and the whiteness became the whiter whiteness of the hare, and then it began to float away, ever more distantly and dimly like a banner.

CHAPTER TWENTY-FOUR

The morning broke with the storm raging fiercely as ever. Though late for breakfast, Michael and Mr. Gwynn found the light dim and the room raw and cold despite the bright fire. The roar of the wind in the pines was incessant, like a sea for ever threatening to flatten wall and roof.

They scarcely spoke. Even Mr. Gwynn, who was used to Michael's moods, made no particular effort at social behaviour. They had sat up a little too late, had drunk a little too much, and had been further intoxicated by an outpouring of talk.

They had turned the 'story' into magnificent 'theatre'. They had discovered the vivifying 'life influence'. Their enthusiasm, as the pines bent and the wind-devils shrieked, had found expression in an exalted vision. Everything was seen against eternity now, man and woman, cliff and bird, sea and air. The alcohol, sipped at the excited moment, heightened the intensity. Man must for ever renew himself in the primeval elements. Man must for ever move, like a liberator, through his own unconscious. Otherwise power dies, dignity perishes, and 'theatre' becomes 'a show'.

'This bloody light!' said Michael, as he wiped his mouth, dropped his napkin unfolded on the table, and got up.

Mr. Gwynn helped himself to a spoonful of marmalade.

'Not a damned thing can a man do in this light.' Michael turned his back to the fire and blew a first long mouthful of cigarette smoke.

'It's Sunday,' suggested Mr. Gwynn. 'What did you think of doing?'

'What do you think I want light for?'

'Want to take the sea, do you?'

Michael shot him a glance. 'Yes, I want to take the sea.'

Mr. Gwynn ignored the challenge in Michael's voice.

'Not thinking of going to church?' Mr. Gwynn folded his napkin and stuck it in a silver ring.

'Why, are you?'

'Yes.'

'Good God! I suppose the whole place will turn out to gloat.'

'The community meets.'

Michael gave a sarcastic grunt.

'All the same,' said Mr. Gwynn, 'that's what it does. A living community always meets.'

'I thought you thought it was a dead community, searching back for what it once did spontaneously.'

'Even so.'

'Religion?'

'And ceremonial.'

'And the parson using the occasion to exploit his power? Standing upon his dead daughter? Exhibiting himself?'

Mr. Gwynn got up. 'No,' he said. 'Not quite.'

'You positively find my tone offensive?'

Mr. Gwynn ignored his look. 'Not quite.'

Michael laughed shortly. 'By God, if you don't watch out you'll be getting old.'

'I am getting old.'

'If you feel like that, why not?' said Michael moving away, and, being on the move, he left the room.

Mr. Gwynn went up through the pines and sat for a little in the shelter of the ravine, watching the waterfall boil in the whirlpool, which was contained in a round rock pot five yards across. He felt a strange need upon him to discuss things with men of his own age, men who had experienced and winnowed. He felt it would only be decent to say a few words to the minister. The man was lonely.

Pride and arrogance could come out of a loneliness of power. They were the fuel that kept the power going. Backed by divine power, the affair was complicated, the issue uncertain. But fuel, wildly blown upon, ate itself up. Nothing then left but the structure of loneliness – and ashes.

The man could not speak to his elders. Not as a man. The structure had to be maintained.

There was an ashen look in the minister's face as he towered over them. The elevated box of the pulpit shut him in. His voice was drained clear.

The manse pew was empty.

Mr. Gwynn listened. The congregation was much smaller than usual. Many of the old folk, the regular attendants, could not come because of the storm. But there was someone from nearly every house, out of respect.

The sense of harmony in the worship grew. Such curiosity as may have moved many to come and see how the minister would bear up, to hear what he would say and what judgment deliver, was quite certainly consumed.

The sympathy, born out of community, reached the minister. Mr. Gwynn saw him, not becoming aware of it, but being unconsciously touched by it. His voice, which had been hard and automatic, though quiet and clear out of – and here Mr. Gwynn reckoned he knew – a public man's response, which is an actor's response, to the dramatic need of a situation, that most subtle need charged with a unifying if invisible force, now caught a softer note as the personal, the dangerous personal, touched the universal.

But this again could be contained, and acted upon, thus producing an ever deeper unity, the state where the concept is all but lost in the thing itself.

Mr. Gwynn waited, with astonishingly little sense of discomfort, for the inevitable moment when the logos would lose itself and the Book close.

It came in a context which Mr. Gwynn had only half followed for his mind was moving in places beyond the spoken word. An ancient – was it Abraham? – how could Abraham have wandered into the Sermon on the Mount? – an ancient calling: 'My son!' Mr. Gwynn, caught by something in the voice, looked swiftly at the minister. The minister lifted his head. He tried again. 'My son!' But there were no words beyond these. Suddenly there were no words. In the silence an old woman sobbed. The Book was closed. The sermon had lasted barely twenty minutes.

Mr. Gwynn sat on in his seat until the church emptied. Then he went round towards the vestry. Peter MacInnes looked for a long moment: 'You would like to see the minister?' Then he stood aside, and closed the vestry door.

It was a Sunday of shifts, of odds and ends, of grey wind-driven gloom, of cold brown tangle writhing on seething shores. Young men found escape into it, escape from the Sabbath, from the gloom, hunting along cliffs, their hearts in their mouths as they adventured dangerous descents to booming caves, shouting exultantly above the sea.

Michael cursed the day, for the waves fascinated him. The exquisitely lovely curves – with the incredible power. He wanted sunlight, flashing sunlight, and his camera. He had crossed the Ros to get into the storm's face. To reach the cliff-edge he had to crawl flat. There were sucking back-eddies that were quite extraordinarily dangerous. Once he felt himself being lifted. His heart stopped and his nails dug in. Backing away, feet first, he began to laugh.

The power of the wild day came upon him. He grew a little mad, wiping out Gwynn and his endless theorizings. 'All that bloody gabble!' cried Michael at Gwynn and himself.

Like a seaman, he wore no overcoat. Thick woollen pants under tough blue serge trousers; a thick blue fisherman's jersey under a tweed jacket; a cap pulled well down, the light from dark-brown eyes shooting under its snout. If he fell, he would bounce!

Then he saw the gull. Perhaps, driven here, it had been resting in a nook, perhaps he had startled it, but suddenly there it was, heeling over, and in an instant the wind had it.

Little Hamish had been watching Michael through a spyglass. His brother Neil, who had borrowed it from old Daniel-the-sailor, had miraculously gone off without it. Hamish had shoved the glass up under his jersey and drifted out of the house when his mother wasn't looking. Keeping the end of his home between him and all harm, he came ultimately to a sheltered nook, with the sea before him and the whole north coast of the Ros. When he had pulled out the cylinders and got the telescope focused, he searched everywhere for his brother, who was bound to miss the glass and come running back. Then there would be ructions! And the boys of his age were not allowed to wander even along the shore on the Sabbath day . . . There was Mr. Sandeman from the Lodge, plain as though he was before your very nose! Hamish steadied the telescope on a boulder. The wind blew Mr. Sandeman about. It was funny! And fancy him looking for them there! As if Charlie would have sailed *into* the storm! It's little they knew, the people from the South!

All at once the end of the telescope shot up. Hamish stared as if he might see better with his unaided eyes. His face had gone white and now he was running for his home, the extended telescope gripped against his body. 'Is Father in?'

'What's that?' answered his mother sharply. 'He's not in, and if he was—'

Hamish ran on. Uncle Norman was coming up from the beach.

'What is it, boy?'

'It's – Mr. Sandeman. He fell over.'

'Fell over what?'

'The cliff – yonder!'

Norman saw the boy's wild distress and the telescope.

Within a minute, he had the glass on the spot, searching the cliff-foot, the cliff-face.

Hamish could see his uncle was finding nothing. 'I saw him!' he cried. 'He was trying the edge – and then he went.'

The glass was now steady. It wasn't moving.

Hamish watched it without breathing.

Uncle Norman turned over on his side. 'He's there,' he said in a curiously quiet voice. 'On the blackstone ledge.' His eyes crinkled thoughtfully, then he was up and off, Hamish trotting after him. 'I'll get a length of rope,' Norman called, for William and old Sandy had been watching the curious proceedings. Hamish gasped forth his news to them. Women's voices rose shrilly even though it was the Sabbath day. Men buttoned their jackets and pulled their caps down. Norman, with a light mooring rope over his shoulder, led the way. Sandy had taken the telescope from Hamish. In the lee of William's cottage, he got ready to follow what might happen. Other old men and women and children gathered round him.

'He's still alive,' said Norman to those going with him. 'If only he lies quiet!'

They knew the blackstone ledge. It was, in fact, a sea-mark, a bite in the cliff, very noticeable from the water. It was no more than fifteen feet from the top. Beneath it there was a sheer drop of at least eighty feet.

They had to make a considerable detour to get round the beach, but soon they were on the Ros, and, of the streaming tail, Hamish was not last.

When at last they reached the spot, Norman called to everyone to stand back. Crawling to the edge, he looked over.

Michael Sandeman was on his feet studying the cliff directly in front of him. His shoulder was to the back of the bite, which was straight rock, and his eyes were trying to find a possible way up the edge of the bite which was broken and began to fall back from above his head. Even on a calm day, the climb would be very difficult. Now, when to stand, as he was doing, gripping a rock-crack at his hip and with both feet braced against a slight boss, was taking a grave risk with the wind's inexhaustible resource in ferocity, he knew it was utterly and absolutely impossible. Yet his eyes, implacable as the forces that had trapped him, studied the rock, and rose with it, hold by possible hold – until they steadied on Norman's face.

Norman yelled to him not to move, then he backed away.

The arranging of the rope took only a minute. Squatting men, with heels dug in, paid the rope out between their knees.

Norman's arm was helping his voice in directing Michael how to fix the noose of rope round him. Then the arm directed those behind.

Lying back against the rope, Michael walked up the rock. When he stood among them, they could see, however, that he was not without pain. The right leg of his trousers was ripped, the back of his jacket split, there was blood trickling down both hands and down his right temple. His face was very white and his smile had a curiously writhen sharpness.

Taking his left arm, Norman led him back into a sheltered hollow.

To Norman and some of the others, who had often gone into real danger in rescuing a sheep, the incident was of the slightest. Had it happened to one of themselves, such a one would have been mercilessly chaffed.

Meantime Michael became aware that eyes were concentrating in a fascinated way on his chest. He looked down and saw the movement of his jacket. Pushing a hand carefully under it, he brought forth a gull.

No magic could have held them as did that gull. They gaped at it, at the strange white deadness which is sometimes caught in a living gull's head. The head moved this way and that.

'Its wing is broken,' said Michael.

Norman's brows drew down. 'Do you mean you risked your life to save that?'

Michael saw the cold disapproval in the face. He kept looking at it in a detached way. 'Not exactly,' he answered. 'I wondered if I could get down. It was decided for me.'

The wry humour was about to be appreciated when suddenly the gull shot its beak into Michael's wrist.

In an instant the bird was flapping and tumbling among them. Hamish was third in the dive but he caught it. He brought it back to Michael.

'Thanks,' said Michael. Then he looked at Hamish a second time. 'I think I have seen you before.'

Hamish retired beside William, who nudged him secretly. Michael smiled with his eyes as Hamish's head disappeared.

'It was him who saw you first to-day anyway,' said William.

'Was it?' Michael looked at William.

'Yes,' answered William. 'Otherwise no one would have seen you.'

There was silence.

'I am his uncle,' said Norman. 'If the boy has sometimes gone to the Ros, after a trout or whatever it may be, it's not with our consent.'

The words came with a simple gravity. Astonished

laughter, his natural reaction, was furthest of any emotion from Michael. He looked upon their waiting faces, with their reticent understanding of the moment. He was feeling little pain, hardly anything at all except a very odd sensation of disembodiment.

'What's his name?' he asked Norman.

'Hamish,' answered Norman. 'Hamish Macleod.'

'Then I wish publicly to declare,' said Michael, 'that so long as I am landlord of the Ros, Hamish Macleod will have free access to the Ros and to all its sporting rights.'

A dozen brown faces broke into light laughter. Bodies swayed, trying to catch a glimpse of the hiding Hamish.

'It's very good of you to take it like that, Mr. Sandeman,' said Norman, relieved.

Michael looked at Norman again, and then looked down at the gull in his hands.

But in a few moments his eyes were back on Norman's face, as if it might be capable of further incredible oracles.

'Do you think there's any hope of finding them now?' he asked.

The question was unexpected and gathered heavily in Norman's face. The others waited.

'Since this morning, that has troubled me. There has been enough time now, wherever boat or oars were washed up, for word to have reached us. I will say frankly that I was waiting for that word. His boat could never have lived in that sea through the night.'

'That's certain?'

'As certain as I know of anything in this world. She had neither the size nor the crew. We all agree on that.'

'What about the Stormy Isles?'

Norman looked at him. 'Do you know them?'

'Yes.'

'Well.'

'Cliff walls,' interjected William.

Hamish whispered something to William. William bent over, then straightened himself with a small smile.

'What does Hamish say?' asked Michael, fighting off a fainting weakness.

'He said: The Roaring Cave!'

There was a smile.

'I think I'll get home.' As Michael stood up, the bird fluttered out of his hands.

'You should kill it,' said William.

Michael slowly nodded.

One of the men swiftly drew its neck and threw it aside.

As Norman was watching Michael, who stood swaying, Kenneth Grant came riding up bare back.

'Just in time, Kenneth,' said Norman. 'We'll give you a leg up, Mr. Sandeman.'

'I'll walk across with you,' said Kenneth, after he had had a look at Michael, 'and then I can ride her home. We can wash that blood off in Loch Geal.'

They all stood watching Michael ride slowly away.

CHAPTER TWENTY-FIVE

'Behold, I come!' said Michael.

Mr. Gwynn, breathing heavily, looked at him.

Michael was grey and swayed slightly but with dignity. From the pony's back, he looked down tolerantly upon his friend.

'The procession proceeds,' said Michael to Kenneth, who thereupon led on the pony.

He staggered as he got off and would have fallen but for Mr. Gwynn.

'Come in and have a drink,' said Michael to Kenneth.

'No, thank you, I'll be going.'

'Come along!' Michael looked at Kenneth's face, then he turned for the door.

From his low long chair, Michael took the glass. It shook a little in his hand and audibly clinked against his teeth.

'You will perceive,' he said to Mr. Gwynn, as he set the glass on the floor, 'that I am acting the laird of the manor.'

'What on earth happened?'

'Merely fell over a cliff.' He turned to Kenneth. 'Your timing was unusually good.'

'We were watching,' said Kenneth, 'through a glass.'

'Ah!' Michael nodded.

'Their faces,' he said to Mr. Gwynn. 'Really remarkable.'

'Whose faces?'

'You must pardon this divine incorporeal feeling. I'm going to pass out presently. No one should drink whisky – except at such a moment as this. The faces of the men of Cruime – not forgetting one boy. They all rescued me with a rope.'

'Only just, apparently.'

Michael nodded. 'And only by the skin of the boy's eyes. Hamish . . . What's his uncle's name?'

'Hamish's uncle? Norman Macleod,' answered Kenneth.

'A profound fellow.'

'Yes, he's one of our best men.'

Michael regarded Kenneth thoughtfully. 'You are keen on – on doing things here?'

'Well, I try to do what I can.'

'Sheep Club and all that?'

'I admit I fought for the Ros,' said Kenneth.

A glimmer of humour shone in Michael's eyes. 'If ever you have any other scheme, Mr. Grant, and I can help . . .' The glass fell out of his hand. 'Pray don't mind it,' he murmured to Kenneth.

'You're going to bed,' said Mr. Gwynn decisively, 'and you're going now. Then I'll get the doctor along to look you over.'

'The doctor!' Michael laughed softly, lolling his head.

'Come! Get up!'

The doctor turned up after supper.

Michael was in a deep sleep, so they left him alone. From the answers to a few questions, the doctor was satisfied that no bones were broken.

'Exhaustion. When he's at it, he burns himself up pretty quickly.'

Mr. Gwynn agreed. 'That was always his trouble – living at an intense pitch when the mood is on.'

'He has,' ventured the doctor, 'got rather a – distinct ego.'

'Yes. Very. But it's more than that, Doctor. If you don't mind my saying so, I know he gets you a little on the raw occasionally. I – have admired your restraint.' Mr. Gwynn smiled in understanding. 'When the ego gets going like that, one feels in it – something destructive – a sort of teasing out that cares nothing for another's feelings – a tearing down to the root, a tearing out. Do I make sense?'

'Yet in his case, saved from being vicious, you think, because of the creative impulse in him?'

'Precisely! Yet – for we should follow his frankness – not always saved. I've seen so much of it. Oh, so much! Brilliant young fellows. I don't merely mean they lose what we call

the moral sense. Promiscuous sexuality and all that – well!'
Mr. Gwynn's gesture signified that that mightn't matter so
much. 'It's that their minds, their laughter even, becomes
avid, sadistic. They squeeze the juice into a sort of poison.
They pervert, destroy – themselves.' Mr. Gwynn added: 'I
should know.'

The doctor was silent for a moment, then reticently
passing over Mr. Gwynn's last sentence, said quietly, 'I
suppose they start off hunting for something – some sort of
belief.'

'And there's no belief. That's the essence of it. Between
the period of belief that was and the new belief that may
some day come again, there is this desert, this dark wood.
It's the land we inhabit.'

The doctor lit a fresh cigarette. 'I wonder if you are
exaggerating? You see, the number of people who are
destructive, or nihilistic, those brilliant fellows you talk
of, they are really only a few. They have been probably
in every age.'

'Yes. But they don't much matter in an age that has
belief. In an age that has lost belief, they do matter. They
may be few in number, but they ultimately destroy their
society. Always. They are your symptoms.'

'This word, belief?'

'I know. It's difficult. We don't want to use the word
religion, because it particularizes too narrowly. Denomi-
national. But, for example, away back in your primitive
world here you had absolute belief, a complete fusing of
intelligence, of imagination, of all the faculties. They did
not *believe* in belief. It was the breath they breathed, the life
they lived.'

'As an example, I see what you mean. But, after all, if
it was as easy as that . . . I mean if the thing wasn't
conscious in them, was just like the breath they
breathed, then did it amount to much? Was it really
belief as we try to know it?'

'Ah, now you introduce the word *conscious*, as we know
it. When intelligence stopped being fused with their belief,
it came apart by itself, it began to ask questions, to inquire –
and so began scientific inquiry. So the split in the whole.

The spontaneous belief that gave wholeness was gone. Now if we could grow a new whole out of scientific inquiry and material phenomena alone, then we could see our way ahead. But apparently we can't. When a man is happily in love, or listening to a piece of music, or creating something, then he has the complete sensation of wholeness. Immediately he pauses consciously to inquire into it, he ceases having the sensation itself. By sensation, I mean the act of experiencing, the breathing of the breath.'

'The conscious and the unconscious. They have got badly divided? I suppose this is science – applying psychic measurement to your philosophies!'

'And the conscious and unconscious are very much divided in us moreover, so what?'

They smiled and drank.

'An odd thing happened to-day,' said Mr. Gwynn. 'You would have been amused. That a platform of rock should have been there and that it was level – the least incline to the sea and he would have bounced off it – was the sort of miracle Michael enjoyed. Then he was hauled up, and he sat among the people, as you know. Then he came home, conscious that he had been, not just among the people, but among his people. He was acting it all, of course, throwing out the hint that he was coming riding on an ass's colt – but without the bitterness of blasphemy. It was all light-headed, but it also had for him a light and delicious feeling of reality.'

'The laird of his people?'

'No, no. That was the humour, the play-acting, based certainly on the fact that he is the laird. It was beneath that, the sense of having been one with them, of knowing them simply, in a moment that, after all, must have been for him a heightened, even revealing moment.'

'Sorry, Mr. Gwynn.' The doctor shook his head. 'I can't take it in. Half an hour with them, trying to get them to talk – for they can't talk as you or he does – and he would be irritated, bored stiff.'

'Yes, yes, yes,' said Mr. Gwynn. 'No doubt. But he gets bored with me, with you, with himself. That's the trouble. You miss my point. The storm, the cliff, the sea, the bird, the men, the men's faces, death missed by a hair's breadth, life. He got life. Not an intensification of the split, but unconscious wholeness in simply breathing and not feeling alien among these men.' Mr. Gwynn shrugged. 'I make too much of it. A trifle, that you'd really have had to see to appreciate.'

'Perhaps I can see. Anyway, as you tell it, it's a nice distinction.' The doctor smiled through a slow exhalation of cigarette smoke, amused, as if the picture were there before him.

Mr. Gwynn smiled also, almost quizzically, at the doctor. 'Odd that one should smile or laugh when vision suddenly does its work.'

The doctor laughed. 'Yes.'

'Makes you feel good.'

The doctor glanced at him.

Mr. Gwynn nodded with the same humour. 'How pregnant the colloquialism! Makes you feel *good*. Interesting?'

'It is, when you think of it that way.'

'The old primordial goodness of the human heart,' said Mr. Gwynn.

'You believe that's there?'

'Always. Basic. And you can measure its strength by its evil opposite, its perversion – and the one hell's broth it brews. The need to feel good must in nature have an outlet. When it doesn't get it – when it gets dammed back for any one reason or another, economic, theoretic, intolerant, religious, witch-doctorish – then it bursts through, with mad scaldings and bloody wars.'

'It's a hopeful philosophy!'

'Or a scientific assessment. But our only hope, definitely.'

The talk went on for a long time, then, finding Michael still asleep, the doctor left.

Immediately he was alone in the storm, under the threshing trees, all words left him. Not much primordial goodness, here, in the black destroying heart of the night! Nothing but sheer nihilism!

He leaned against the outside gate, staring into the

storm, sheltered from it, staring up in the direction of the manse.

Curiosity and something calling out of the heart of the storm drew him towards the manse – as it had drawn him the night the boys got lost.

That night he had been in Cruime and had formed one of the scattered search party. Once alone, he had argued that the boys, afraid of the thundering cliffs, would probably have struggled back inland and so might easily land about the manse.

One excuse was no doubt as good as another if it took him down the manse way! He had already rationalized the half-incestuous dream – or rather its explanation had suddenly leaped upon him when actually engaged in delivering the head stalker's wife. It had been motivated by his unconscious anxiety, his anxiety while he slept, for a difficult case. He had transferred the woman's flesh to Flora, for in his dream he had seen Flora's flesh, the small of the back, the buttocks, the part that was going to be voluptuously thrashed.

His unconscious had done this for him, simply because it had apprehended, in its own odd fashion, that the black wrath of the father – desire that was dammed – would be visited upon the daughter.

The unconscious acted in this completely irrational way. That's all that need be thought about it. If there was any cause for shame or alarm anywhere, it was in his own dreaming mind!

Yet – something was going to happen. Charlie and Flora could not go on meeting as they were doing and nothing come of it. Life did not work in that way.

He had come down that night by the cemetery wall, through the trees, feeling his way. Emerging from the blackness of the trees, he had seen the vague bulk of the house. His eyes had lifted for its outline against the sky, then shot down to something like a human figure moving across the lawn. He thought he was deceived, but waited, holding his breath, then crept nearer.

Movement within the house. A momentary glimpse of a light. He waited.

The key turned with a sharp scream in the front door. The doctor flattened himself against the wall. The minister came out, shut the door, and started across the lawn. Fraoch barked inside. The barking passed into a high whining. The doctor slid away from the wall, across the lawn. Flora must have come out by the window!

The doctor's eyes were extremely wary. The darkness, the swaying and noisy trees – it was very difficult to be sure of a movement, a sound. Once he thought he heard a cry and quickened his steps – and fell into the fence.

There were cries about, cries from the moor of the search party for the boys. For those he was following, the night must have been suddenly haunted!

After the trees, the moor path was almost distinct for a yard or two ahead. Every now and then he stopped and listened. Charlie was bound to have come and met Flora. Where were they? He kept going on.

Then he heard voices, not the crying voices of the moor, but two men's wild voices, and then Flora's cry: 'Father! Father!'

When he reached the spot there was no one there. He cast about, crying in a low voice, searching for a body, for someone left behind in the heather.

Then on again – to Norman and the lost boys.

Dismissing that memory, the doctor now lay down in the shelter of a rocky outcrop, looking across at where the manse must be.

Flora and Charlie were already storied figures flying through the night, for ever now flying through the night. Grown tall. Symbol figures. He thought of Flora, the living girl, in a sharp catch of the heart.

A flicker of light in a window of the manse. A flicker – and it was gone, like a blown match.

The minister, restless in the night, would find her room empty! A grinning bitterness came upon the doctor's mood, a harsh irony that streamed away on the tearing wind.

There was no irony in the minister's heart that night, only darkness and the sounds of the tempest. These sounds had, however, a vivid life-semblance. Listened to, as he lay in his bed, they developed their force to an extreme pitch. For ever defeated, they rushed upon their defeat, piling up their force, bursting through and away, with the whine of defeat in their rushing throats. Harrying, harrying, and empty, empty, getting hold of nothing, themselves nothing but the anger and the whine, the defeated emptiness rushing upon the far emptiness of the air, upon the vast vacant interspaces, where death, curling over, head to knees, thins to a wind eddy, to a last bodiless howl passing away into ultimate nothing. . . . Then at hand, quite close at hand, about the gable-corner, in the corridor beyond the bedroom door, beyond the shut doors, the sob of the force that knows it will never find, the dark figure standing, head down, the quiver of the sob in the throat, and the terrible terrible silence.

Ah, away, away, into the seas! The seas – the backs of the waves – the herds of the ocean – the tumultuous, onrushing, wind-driven seas – spindrift-lashed and blinded – piling up – and up – and over . . . O God!

The minister got out of bed and stood in his white nightshirt staring at all he saw and could not see beyond the darkness and in the darkness, far and for ever lost, and here, at hand, close to him.

Groping, he found the door, and opened it, and listened. The corridor was cold to his bare feet, it was still, both hearkening and dead, with invisible eyes for his back.

He turned the knob of her door and went in. His intrusion came upon him so strongly, so desperately, that softly he called 'Flora!' For one extreme moment he heard, not a sound but an intensity of listening from the bed. This so wrought upon him that he floundered about and hit into a chair and heard the rustle of a candlestick and matchbox.

Before human sound could be made, before anything could be uttered, he grabbed wildly at the candlestick, upset it, groped about the floor, muttering quickly, harshly, found the matchbox, pushed it open, pushed it out of his hand, found it again, broke the first match, cried silently for everything, for one thing, to wait, wait – and with hands now so trembling that they could hardly strike the match, struck it.

The bed was empty. The pillows were white and smooth. The sheet was folded over the counterpane, smooth and white. Everything was straight, straight lines, untouched, spotless and quiet. The red cinder of the match dropped from his stung fingers, hesitated a moment, and, in a red wink, went out.

A man of sixty does not change radically, not readily. His structure has taken so long to build, has stood so many stresses, from without and from within, from powers that undermine, from acids working corrosively in the dark, from hidden sins and desperate self-knowledge, from all that which would destroy it, that at last its uprights have become rigid, and when the storms of emotion, suddenly liberated, assail it, it stands of itself, gathering about it an impervious heedlessness, a withdrawn weariness, an automatic endurance.

The minister knew that even he himself could not get through this structure now. In the pulpit, to-day, he had not got through it, for all that he had been deeply moved, by communion with the people, by the cry of Abraham for his son Isaac (that cry which had rung in his ears to-day for the first time), and afterwards by the approval of Mr. Gwynn, the civilized man with the quiet eyes and the perfect manners, speaking his few words with deep understanding, beyond the understanding of the personal tragedy to that tragedy which sits far and lonely in the heart of each one, working with his few words, of sympathy and learning, dear to the minister's own learning and its memories.

And the structure came out of it as out of a mist, smoother a little in its pride, in its endurance.

Here was the structure set up for the people. In power it had been set up for him to sustain. The personal backed by the eternal; pride lifted to the realm of the non-human by divine sanction, to judgment beyond all earthly judgments. The structure upon a hill, remorseless as a gibbet, setting the wind to divine harmonies about the swinging bodies of the unbelievers.

He had wearied of his tired wife. When a person dies sorrow may enter the heart – but behind the sorrow there is freedom. The body in freedom moves away from the grave, throws off the old entanglement. From all graves, people thus turn away and the sun is shining or the rain soft in the face, and there is one less, but not the one that is each one turning away. And the sins there may have been are buried with the dead.

The sins are buried, and, expiated or not, they crumble in the grave and in the heart that turns away. Turns away to freedom.

But the structure remains . . .

Flora stood suddenly beyond the room. Her body upright, full-size as in life, but with the bloom faint and evanescent, moved down slanting shafts of space, passed through him and passed away, came again and passed away, came and was gone.

She was his lost youth. The youth that had been lost in his earnestness and studies, in his divine idealisms, in his repression of secret sins, in all the horrible shifts and makeshifts, the feverish strife of youth, collecting in the gloom, already the gloom of pride, little talismans of learned metal that will one day be welded into the ideal, the heavenly structure.

And Flora grows up as his lost youth and he loves her. Not now with youth's wretched carnal love, but freely in the mind, as that which he has created and sees moving about and delights in, while the structure stands behind him, strengthened in grace.

The structure is assailed by the same human force as steals his daughter and sucks away her love. Wrath stirs, jealousy moves darkly, the jungle comes to life. Paths here he had never known, swamps that horrify and fascinate, wrath that lures, anger that hates, and a driving force that is beyond reason.

The structure remains, and on that structure he will crucify love and hate.

But at least once each one turns away from a grave, and the sunlight is on the face or the soft rain, and lo! that which is buried is not buried but is the sunlight and the rain, for love knows no burial but remains everywhere.

The framework of his body, the skeleton of bones,

collapsed towards the bed, the knees hit the floor, the arms lifted but not to God, they lifted upward and over the structure in a blind cry, and they crashed it down on the bed and his head fell between his arms and he sobbed heavily.

CHAPTER TWENTY-SIX

'Good morning, Doctor. It's a better morning.'

The doctor returned the greeting cheerfully, asking after the patient.

Mr. Gwynn, who was taking the air at the front door, looked over his shoulder with a conspiratorial air. 'On the warpath, I *think*.'

'That's good!'

'Is it?'

Just then Michael came round the up end of the house. 'He's gone. Damn him!' His brows were drawn.

'What's wrong now?' the doctor asked pleasantly.

'Oh, it doesn't matter. We can do without him,' replied Michael. 'Damn funny thing that you can never find a man when you really want him.'

Further talk disclosed that Erchie had set out that morning for either Cruime or Badloan, which lay south of Ardnarie. The doctor suggested that the old boy, knowing there would be no call on the boat—

'But there is a call,' interrupted Michael. 'That's just what I want him for.'

'You don't mean you're thinking – of putting to sea?'

'That's just what I do mean. Now. At once,' answered Michael, with a challenging impatient flash of his dark eyes.

'But, look here – though the wind has dropped a bit, outside there's a terrific sea running.'

'I know. Well?'

'Well – why?' challenged the doctor.

'Because I want to have a look at the Stormy Isles,' answered Michael, holding the doctor's eyes.

To further talk, Michael replied with a swift – 'Damn it, I have the only boat with power on this coast. Am I going to sit here while others, like your precious friend in the manse, sits in – whatever he does sit in?'

They saw that nothing was going to stop him.

'If you fellows don't care about coming,' said Michael, 'right! I'll manage her.' He turned his back on them and entered the house.

Mr. Gwynn looked at the doctor.

'I can't,' said the doctor. 'Besides, it's quite mad.'

'I know,' agreed Mr. Gwynn. 'He has got some sort of feeling about it. At breakfast he mentioned a "roaring cave".'

'Good God! If he tries to land there, he'll simply be heaved up and smashed to atoms.' The doctor grew alarmed.

'You couldn't possibly? . . .'

'How can I?' It angered the doctor that a fellow like Michael, just because of his mood, should so tyrannize over others.

Michael came out, buttoning a black oilskin.

'Wait a minute,' said Mr. Gwynn to him.

'I'll get the dinghy ready,' called Michael, and he strode away.

The doctor, in his weatherproof coat and leggings, walked down with Mr. Gwynn, now like an elderly gnome in a sou'wester and a black oilskin that nearly reached his ankles. Michael was baling the last drop out of the dinghy. The three of them handed her down stern first to the water by the low stone jetty.

'In you get,' ordered Michael.

The doctor hesitated, then stepped in.

Michael pushed off from the jetty and, taking the oars, began to turn her round.

'Here!' cried the doctor sharply.

Michael paused and flashed a look at him. As he realized he had been turning the dinghy against the sun, he dug his oars in to hold her, and let out a laugh. Mr. Gwynn laughed also, throwing his head up. Michael swung the dinghy *deiseil*, his expression full of life. 'Good old Doc!' he shouted. In an instant the temper of his mood was completely changed.

'I feel nothing can harm us now!' called Mr. Gwynn.

'Hush, be quiet!' said the doctor, smiling but inwardly thinking them fools.

'Why?' asked Mr. Gwynn.

'They might hear you,' replied the doctor, with a narrow ironic look.

'*They*,' murmured Mr. Gwynn, and he gazed upon the vacant air.

The *Stormy Petrel* had a four-cylinder fourteen horse-power Kelvin petrol engine. The effects of Michael's cliff fall became apparent when he tried to swing the fly-wheel. Pain stung sharply from bruised flesh and his face went ghastly. The doctor insisted on probing him thoroughly. Satisfied, he turned to the engine which was cold, but after one or two false starts, it kept the roar going. Michael transferred the mooring to the dinghy, came back along the top of the high deck and stiffly down into the open cockpit aft. The doctor, who had used up too much energy too quickly in swinging the engine, was pleased to breathe without moving and let Michael carry on. Michael shoved the engine into gear. There was a rumble in the water beneath them and the *Stormy Petrel* was at last under way, with the dinghy falling astern. For a long moment the doctor looked at that dinghy, which they were leaving behind, with deep misgiving.

Michael was now in the highest spirits. Standing upright, with the tiller by his right leg, he could see over the high cabin, could see the waves far ahead, with a white cap showing here and there. The *Stormy Petrel* was a thirty-foot craft, gracefully narrow, indeed under eight feet in beam, with a neat forefoot capable of over eight knots, and painted white.

'Pretty good, isn't she?' called Michael.

The doctor who was leaning against the house, staring ahead, turned his face. 'We'll soon see,' he answered.

Michael laughed and chaffed the doctor for wanting to visit his mouldy old patients when he could come on a trip like this.

She began to feel the sea as they moved from the lee of the Ros. The storm was certainly broken; the wind was going down, but with all the uncertainty of November in its going. The clouds had lightened and one patch of blue was for Mr. Gwynn as bright as summer.

Then she began to roll. Until they cleared the Head at the south entrance to Loch Ros, they were going to have the seas nearly beam on. Had the doctor been at the tiller he would have headed more directly into the weather until the time came to put her about and run south. But he did not like to say anything to Michael.

As they drew near the Head, however, the motion of the boat became alarming. The waves were nearly as heavy as they had been under the storm, only not now dangerous, if the boat were handled properly. They were opening the sea beyond the headland of the Ros and the doctor knew that that vast body of ocean ran back right to the Arctic. He didn't like the look of things at all. . . . Now they were taking it! He saw the big one coming. It threw Michael off his feet. The boat yawed away. In an instant, the doctor had the tiller. Mr. Gwynn was drenched, but with an eye for Michael's reaction. There was a tense moment after Michael had righted himself. The doctor was seated, the tiller gripped in a hand that showed white knuckles. His face, drawn and cold, was to the coming waves.

'Where away now?' cried Michael, for they were making into the seas, taking them at a comfortable angle.

The doctor did not answer.

'Here, where are you going?' called Michael. 'We want to see the shore.'

The doctor did not look at him, but said calmly, 'If you think I'm going to sit in this boat while you run her along a lee shore, you're mistaken.'

'Why? Not frightened are you?'

The doctor's expression hardened. It was Michael's boat. He should give up the tiller, which Michael was waiting for. The trial of strength tautened.

'All right,' said the doctor, without any heat. 'It's your boat. But if you want to run her along that shore, then you must first put about and land me. I'm not going.'

'Who asked you to come?'

'You said you were going to the Stormy Isles. I'll go with you. But not along that shore.'

'No?'

'No.' Then in a moment the doctor called, 'Look out!' He took her over the shoulder of the high sea.

'Oh, all right!' called Michael. 'Didn't know you had your certificate.' He laughed and the tension was broken.

'Close the throttle a bit,' called the doctor, as the spray came over in a curtain.

'How's that?'

'Better.' The doctor's spirits immediately began to rise now that he had charge of her, and under reduced speed she rode the waves like a bird. 'She's a nice craft,' he said with a gleam.

'You keep her steady till I check the oil drip, you twister,' cried Michael.

Mr. Gwynn laughed, and turned up the front of his sou'wester.

The doctor became even more comfortable when he saw Michael feel parts of the engine for heat. She had a fine steady beat.

Presently, choosing his moment, he put her about and now they were running before it. Far to the south they could see the Stormy Isles, with flecks of white that were rock-spouting seas. He laid a course on them.

Michael, through his powerful field glasses, began sweeping the shore.

In a little while, he decided that a certain scrambling figure searching the cliffs was Dougald MacIan. Mr. Gwynn had a look. Then Michael handed the glasses to the doctor and took the tiller.

The doctor picked up the figure. It was undoubtedly Dougald MacIan. Small and lonely he looked, curiously pathetic, hunting that wild shore like a persistent, bereft animal. The doctor watched him for a long time. Then he lowered the glasses and nodded to Michael. 'It is,' he said.

Michael immediately took the glasses and abandoned the tiller to the doctor.

The Stormy Isles began to define themselves more clearly. Even on a calm summer day, landing was, more often than not, quite impossible because of the swell. Mostly they were sheer cliff wall, with great colonies of sea-birds inhabiting narrow ledges, and with skerries on which cormorants spread their wings or seals sunned themselves. Now and then a lobster fisherman was lost or a naturalist marooned.

Looking on that stormy scene, Michael dropped his glasses and turned to the doctor with a smile.

'I have a confession to make,' he said. 'Do you know a little boy named Hamish Macleod? His uncle is Norman.'

'Yes.'

'Well, he – Hamish – on whom I have conferred the freedom of the Ros – mentioned "The Roaring Cave". I awoke some time during the night with the name in my ears. That's why you're here.'

The doctor switched his eyes to Mr. Gwynn. They both silently shook their heads and Mr. Gwynn added a negligible shrug. There was nothing one could do about this sort of thing. Nothing.

Michael, whose pallor was whipped with colour, laughed at them. 'All the same, to-day it is to the leeward side of Puffin Island. I have been there.'

'And landed?'

'Well, no. The wind wasn't right.'

'Supposing you were in a sailing boat, in the darkness of night, in a storm—'

'With my lady love,' interposed Michael. 'Go on.'

'Would you – or would you not,' inquired the doctor, 'give that scene in front of you a wide berth?'

'Like to turn back?' asked Michael, a teasing humour in the challenge of his head.

'Why not?' replied the doctor. 'You could then root us out of bed in the middle of the night to do the trip in more realistic conditions.'

'Jolly good idea!' cried Michael. 'What do you say, Gwynn?'

But the engine replied for Mr. Gwynn with a distinctly sarcastic cough. The effect was very dramatic. Their faces froze and waited. The engine coughed again, spluttered, picked up, spluttered, and stopped.

Michael dived upon it through the door, for it lay bedded on the threshold of the cabin. He tickled the carburettor, caught the starting handle and swung it round and round. The engine went off with a roar. The doctor got the boat straightened up and was hesitating which side of the islands to head away for, lest it happened again, when it happened. This time Michael's wild swinging had no effect.

'It's either the plugs or a choke in the petrol feed,' said the doctor, joining Michael at the engine.

Michael was white and wildly erratic. 'She's never done this before!' he cried across the engine. 'Damnation!'

The doctor was trying to flood the carburettor when the *Stormy Petrel*, having lost way and broached to, was lifted on a wave and thrown bodily. Michael pitched right across the engine and yelled as his bare hands came against hot metal. The doctor, thrown on his back, could not help him. Mr. Gwynn was rolling on the floor of the cockpit, having bashed his head against the side of the door through which he had been staring. As she righted herself, the boat threw Michael off the engine.

'Take a hold!' yelled the doctor, back at the carburettor. It would not flood. 'The feed is choked. Where's your tools?'

As she was flung wildly again, Michael this time held on, though his feet were thrown against the engine. He got round to a locker on the doctor's side. Suddenly they were facing each other.

'Your petrol tank?' asked the doctor in a level searching voice.

The petrol tank, painted white, was pinned flat against the wooden wall, on the port side of the door. Michael turned to it and rapped it. It rang like an empty drum. It *was* empty.

'Have you a spare tin?'

Forward through the cabin staggered Michael, followed by the doctor, past the tiny galley and lavatory, into the bow of the *Stormy Petrel*.

'Christ!' cried Michael. 'He's taken it out of her!'

There were odds and ends of gear but no petrol tin.

'The blasted fool! The damned idiot!' His invective grew. His rage consumed him.

'Have you a bit of sail?' asked the doctor sharply.

The boat threw them. They collided. 'Have you no sail?'

There had been a triangular sail that could be laced to the mast. But it had been getting mouldy. For several weeks it had been drying in one of the outhouses. It had never, in the life of the boat, been needed.

There was no sail.

Nothing, thought the doctor, as he stared at Michael, could now save them from being smashed on the cliff walls. Nothing.

Michael left him, in a wild mad energy, to search lockers, to do something. The doctor stood where he was, his eyes going over the useless junk in that narrow heaving space. A steep sea, catching her at an awkward angle, might fill the open cockpit at any moment. She was top heavy for this game.

He turned and a noisy snore in the lavatory drew his eyes. This white porcelain lavatory, with its pump handle and seawater flush, had had an extraordinary attraction for the local youth. They had never seen anything like it. The very thought of it made them laugh. Many of them had visited it in the dead of night when Erchie was fast asleep. The lavatory boat!

The doctor found Michael stretched on the floor. He had cracked his head, but he was squirming, he was getting up. The doctor helped him. The crack, however, had only increased his wrath. He was in a vile temper. The doctor saw that the desire to destroy, to smash what had brought this upon them was now psychopathological. It usurped the fear of death. It drew for a moment a blind anger across the doctor's own eyes, but he steadied himself, and turned away.

As he got to the cockpit a wash of green water came over the square stern. Mr. Gwynn was working back and fore the handle of the round pump. The sight eased the doctor's mood, but when he turned to the Stormy Isles, they seemed to have come much nearer, their cliffs rising out of the sea, curtains of foam, ever renewed, hanging in the air, the skerries boiling. Half an hour away at the outside.

'Can't you get her right?' called Mr. Gwynn.

The doctor, hanging on as they got thrown into the trough, looked down into Mr. Gwynn's eyes. 'No petrol.'

The eyes looked back. There was no humour in them now. But they were steady.

The doctor nodded, then turned away to look on the seas behind, as Michael lurched out.

It happens sometimes that one may catch sight of such a boat coming through seas in a dream. The up-jut of bow, lost, then rising again, lost, but coming on, the peak of sail dark as the fin of a basking shark.

The sight of it, less than half a mile away, had a powerful effect on the doctor, somehow powerful and piercing sweet, like music.

They followed his look and saw the lobster boat, creaming on the wave top, falling away, but coming again, coming.

Mr. Gwynn got to his feet. No one spoke.

'What'll she do?' cried Michael.

'I don't know,' answered the doctor.

'They can never take us off.'

'No, they can't take us off.'

'Well, what the hell! What can we do?'

The doctor turned from that wild voice to stare at the Stormy Isles. There was sea-room yet.

Norman. Norman at the helm. William and Angus. They made no sign as they drew near. Their faces were quiet and impassive, their eyes on the *Stormy Petrel*, on her white pitching bulk.

The calm faces, the steady eyes, the silence among the three men. The music went over the doctor again and stung his eyes. It was a lovely thing to watch. His own people, the men of the sea, with seamanship in them. He could have yelled to them in heart's greeting. He could go down with them.

The wave that lifted the three men, left them, rushed on the *Stormy Petrel* and threw her. There could be no nearness, no precision. All a mad wallowing and tossing. Danger in nearness, fatal danger.

They were coming straight for them, straight at the cockpit where they sat, gripping the gunnel.

Then Norman must have spoken, for Angus, the slow-witted youth with the big bones and the ginger hair, whom Betsy loved, took up an end of rope and passed it under his armpits.

They were coming for them, right down on them. Norman turned his head slowly over his shoulder, looking back at the seas. Angus twisted round and faced the *Stormy Petrel*, crouching. William lay back, a rope fender between his knees.

Norman had the sheet, which passed through a wooden purchase hole, in one hand, the tiller in the other.

They rose to be thrown at them, and fell away. Then they were coming. They were coming now. Listing over, see-thing, the sheet eased, the tiller pressing slowly against Norman's side, racing, racing in on the *Stormy Petrel's* stern, but already easing away, Angus crouching on his feet, no word spoken, nothing cried, and then Angus is up, he leaps, the *Venture* dips from his foot, but his open hands just reach the cockpit edge and grip, the doctor dives at him, so does Michael, Mr. Gwynn gets a hold, and Angus wet to the neck is in over, smiling to them in his awkward way, even while he is already laying on the rope with strong hands.

William, from the *Venture*, raises a hand in salute and smiles. A neat bit of work, desperately tried in a desperate moment.

Hand over fist, in comes the rope, the *Venture's* mizzen sail tied to the end of it. Angus throws a glance at the *Stormy Petrel's* twelve-foot mast. Near its top there is an opening, like an eye in a needle. He nods to the doctor and says, 'I'll take the mast down and maybe you could shove this end through?'

'Yes, yes,' said the doctor. The fellow looked as if he were asking a difficult favour on a quiet afternoon. But the doctor had hardly gripped the rope-end, when Angus was on top of the deck, flat against the skylight as she heaved over, then on to the mast.

It was stuck, he couldn't loosen it, couldn't get it free. It came suddenly and at the wrong moment. It fell with a crash and, as the boat heeled over, Angus was swept away.

But he had seen the small iron posts, set far apart, with the thin wire rope threaded through them and running right round the edge of the high deck. Even as he fetched up against an iron post he dived for the mast and held on. As the boat righted herself, mast and man were swung the opposite way. Angus grabbed the skylight. The doctor got hold of the mast-top and threaded the rope through the eye over the single wheel. Before he had finished, Angus was spreadeagled, ready.

At the balanced moment he rose to his feet, light as a dancer, and stepped the mast in a trice, then was down again, busy with his ropes. All at once the wet sail flapped out, enveloping him. The *Stormy Petrel* began to nose round. The doctor leapt to the tiller. She was coming alive, rising out of her sickness, staggering a little, but rising, shaking herself, shaking the waves from her. Angus crawled aft, taking the sheet with him, slid off his stomach into the cockpit and trimmed his sail. Then he turned to the doctor. 'You can feel her?'

'Yes,' answered the doctor. 'Here, come and take it.'

'Och, it's all right,' said Angus, but he took the tiller.

'Think you have plenty of room?'

Angus did not reply for half a minute. 'Yes,' he said. 'She's doing better than I thought.' Then he added, 'Though I wouldn't like to have to try and sail her into a wind!'

The doctor laughed, easing the pressure in his breast. Angus looked modestly pleased.

'What brought you out?'

'Someone saw you,' replied Angus. 'And someone said that Erchie said last night he was going this morning for petrol to the merchant's at Badloan. So we wondered.'

'I see,' said the doctor.

'It's taking off,' said Angus. 'It will be a good evening yet.'

'Where are we going now?'

'She can't do much but run before it. So we could just fetch Glaspool by keeping on. I suppose it's the petrol you're out of?'

'It is,' said the doctor.

'We'd get it there,' said Angus.

He took the outside passage, following the *Venture*, and as Mr. Gwynn stared at the cliff wall of the first island, spouting its white plumes on the air, he realized the merciless nature of what would have been their end. Michael was on the other side of the cabin door, also looking, with a slight congestion in his face, a stormy moodiness in his eye.

Mr. Gwynn called to him: 'I think your *deiseil* worked after all!'

Michael's mouth twisted. 'I shouldn't have given it the chance,' he muttered.

'This business of getting them to save you is becoming chronic.' Mr. Gwynn laughed. He was full of mocking exhilaration. He could see Michael was having his difficult moment. So he prodded him again, taunted him.

Michael began to react. 'It would have been a cleaner end, a damned sight cleaner, than some of you deserve.' His teeth flashed, but the colour deepened in his face.

'Is the Roaring Cave far yet?' inquired Mr. Gwynn, with mirthful satire.

Meantime the doctor and Angus, both of whom Michael ignored, were seated by the tiller.

'It's not like Erchie,' Angus was saying. 'He's very canny and he knows the sea. Did you look everywhere?'

'All over her. He used to carry a spare tin for'ard in the bows. It's not there.'

'He would have taken it up to the house likely. Though why?'

'Why? as you say.'

'You're quite sure?'

'You mean you'd like to look yourself? Go ahead.'

'Oh no. I don't mean that.'

'Go on.' The doctor took the tiller.

Angus somewhat shame-faced but with his light-blue eyes clear as sea-water, got up. A comfortably broad seat ran right round the cockpit. A wooden skirting dropped from its outer edge to the floorboards. Angus tried the skirting with a sharp kick from his toe that drew the attention of Michael and Mr. Gwynn. The skirting was nailed into position. All three watched him as his eye ran along it and came to rest on a simple swivel catch, painted the same colour as the wood. He stooped and with difficulty turned it. A section of wood fell out. Slipping to his knees, he removed from its carefully wedged position a two-gallon tin of petrol.

'I felt sure he would have it somewhere,' said Angus smiling.

No one moved for some time.

Michael caught the tin, weighed it in his hands. It was full. 'God!'

The doctor kept staring at the tin. Then he lifted his eyes to Angus's face. 'Did you know it was there?'

'No,' answered Angus.

'A bad business, Angus. We'd have gone to glory – with that tin there.'

'But why did he shift it?' asked Mr. Gwynn. 'He always kept the tin forward in the bow. Didn't he, Michael?'

'Always,' answered Michael. 'Forget him, for God's sake.'

'Excuse me,' said Angus.

Michael paused and looked at him. 'Yes?'

'It will not be the same tin. The one that he kept in the peak for'ard will be up at the house right enough. This will be the one that he will have hidden on himself.'

It was as if he gave all Erchie's character there, and the humour of it got hold of them and released them. It weakened them, too. They sat down and swayed in a mirth of nonsense and friendliness.

Then Michael dived into the cabin and came out with the petrol filler. The doctor screwed off the cap of the tank and together they emptied the tin into it.

'How far will that take us?' asked Angus.

Michael turned at the cabin door. 'That's a thought, isn't it?'

The doctor looked at Angus. 'Like Erchie, you want to have something up your sleeve – in case?'

'Maybe it would be as well,' suggested Angus.

They laughed and held a meeting.

'I am wondering,' said Angus, 'what they are going to do.

So long as they keep going ahead, we can follow at our leisure for a bit.'

The others had forgotten the *Venture* in their excitement. When Angus was questioned as to Norman's intentions, he answered, 'He may run for Glaspool, too, and then maybe you could tow us home?'

'Splendid!' cried Michael, coming to full life.

'It's the tide,' said Angus. 'It's with us just now. If it wasn't it would have been a different story.'

'How?' Michael looked at him.

'If the tide had been going against that sea . . .' He smiled.

'You seem to have run us into a few risks, Doctor,' said Michael.

The doctor smiled and looked at Angus.

Thus encouraged, Angus said, 'He was also wanting to have a look at the Roaring Cave.'

'Was he?' Michael's voice was unexpectedly quiet and piercing.

'Yes,' answered Angus. 'He's making in now.'

Their heads shot round. They were past the first island and coming abreast of the second. The *Venture* was now running on a course that would give her a fair view of the tail-end of the third island and the Roaring Cave. As Angus drew clear of the second island, he made no effort to follow. Angus was waiting for the moment when the *Venture* would fall away on her southerly course. She did not fall away. She was coming round in a sweep.

'She may be seeing something,' he muttered out of a drawn expression.

Michael went white, unable to speak.

'Start her up,' said Angus.

When the engine was going, Angus handed the tiller to the doctor, leapt from the seat to the top deck, ran along it nimbly, and in no time had the sail secured. Back in the cockpit he at once took the tiller from the doctor. He never spoke. He had forgotten them. Round in a slow sweep came the *Stormy Petrel*. The *Venture* had passed from view beyond a vast lump of cliff and seething skerry.

'Stand by her,' said Angus.

'Right!' called Michael, by gear lever and throttle.

As they came round, they saw the *Venture*, sail down, with William and Norman on the oars, pulling for the narrow beach of the Roaring Cave. To one side of it, on a shelf of black rock, they saw a boat.

'That's Charlie's boat,' said Angus.

CHAPTER TWENTY-SEVEN

Angus ran the *Stormy Petrel* up towards the *Venture*, slowing the engine with a flattening gesture from his hand. At his final gesture, Michael slid the lever into neutral. It was sheltered here, but there was a heavy heave in the water.

'What now?' shouted Angus.

'Hold her there,' answered Norman.

They stared at the abandoned boat. There was no sign of life.

'Come with us, Doctor,' cried Norman.

William fended off as the doctor changed boats.

'We're wasting petrol,' said Angus to Michael. 'I'll try for bottom.'

As Angus got a hold with the anchor, the *Venture* drew near the beach. Landing was a nasty business and for a little while the two men hung on the oars. Then William took both oars, and, when the bow touched for a moment, Norman and the doctor leapt. As the water came surging about Norman's thighs, he heaved against the *Venture*, then waded ashore. As they lifted their eyes, Charlie appeared in the Cave's mouth, clad in a torn shirt and trousers.

They all saw him and Charlie saw them. He put a hand against the rock and stared out of his clay-grey face.

None of them spoke. No one called. Norman and the doctor went up the slithering stones.

'Charlie,' said Norman, in a slow voice, warm with affection, 'I'm glad to see you, boy.'

Charlie did not answer. He turned and went into the cave, staggering on the stones.

They followed him until he stopped. Lying under a ledge was the body of Flora, covered to the chin with the sail of Charlie's boat. The doctor got down on his knees. She was not dead.

The doctor got up and looked directly at Charlie. 'She's sleeping.'

Charlie looked back at the doctor, but in a moment his eyes seemed to lose their focus. 'I think so,' he said.

'Don't worry. It will be all right.'

The eyes came back and focused on the doctor's face in a curious arid expression. 'All right,' he said. As he staggered, Norman caught him. 'It's all right,' Charlie repeated, drawing himself to his own stance.

'Has she been like this long?' asked the doctor.

'I think so, yes, for a time.'

'We'll wake her up, and take her along.' Under the brown sail, Charlie's jacket and jersey covered her.

As her eyes opened and turned upon them they held for several seconds a curious wet glitter of blind light. Consciousness came through the glitter and dispelled it.

From the doctor's face to Norman's the eyes travelled. 'Charlie!' she muttered out of a hoarse throat.

'Here's Charlie,' said the doctor.

Her eyes found Charlie. 'It's all right,' he said, without moving. 'They've come for you.'

She pushed herself into a sitting position, swaying against her supporting arm. She began breathing heavily. 'Charlie!' she cried like a wild frightened child.

He came to her then. He made to stoop but fell over on his hip. 'It's all right,' he said. 'They've come for you. You're all right now.'

It was an extraordinary moment, because though she had not yet got back full consciousness, something deep in her detected an alien element in Charlie's voice and suddenly she gripped him and clung to him.

He held her for a little, staring over her head at the black rock wall.

The doctor decided she had a touch of fever. When they got her up, she swayed weakly on her feet. Norman put his arm round her. 'Come you, Miss Flora,' he said with the warm courtesy that was native to him. 'You lean on me.' His voice was gentle, his body strong and sure.

The doctor turned to Charlie. 'Put these on.'

Charlie looked at the jersey and jacket, then put them on.

'Now! Come along.' The doctor's voice was normal, friendly. 'I smell smoke, do I? Did you manage a fire? Lean on me, if you want to.'

'It's all right,' said Charlie.

They came out of the cave. Norman was now near the water line and carrying Flora. The doctor hurried forward. As William nosed the boat in, Norman and the doctor waded into the steep surf with Flora in their arms. They got her on board and then turned for Charlie.

But Charlie had stopped just outside the cave mouth, and as all eyes were turned on him he went slowly over towards his boat.

Every soul there knew, in one terrible moment, that Charlie did not want to come.

The point had been reached when it was easy to take life apart, one's own life, cleanly, and dispose of it. Beyond bitterness and the last clotted mood, life comes clean and clear again, and final, like a brittle stalk, like clean sea-water. This point lies beyond the place where all defeats meet and make living no longer possible.

Having come so far and been defeated, been defeated in his pride, his manhood, his seamanship, it was no longer possible for him to go back. Charlie could not go back. He could not go.

Norman knew this in his blood, knew it in so dreadful and intimate a way that he dared not go to Charlie, dared not move. Norman knew that Charlie's legs would not answer him.

The seconds got drawn out beyond bearing while the *Venture* heaved dangerously and the water soused the two men standing in it to the arm-pits. Suddenly high above the pounding of the sea on the outer rock, rose the cry: 'Charlie!'

Charlie, who was looking into his boat, turned his head.

'Charlie!' Her voice broke. The tears were on her face and she scrambled to her feet to make out of the boat.

Charlie came walking down towards them and Michael knew, where the marrow crawls inside the bone, that there came a courage, carried lightly, without expression, of a kind he had never before encountered.

As Charlie drew near the water, William, lying strongly on the oars, lifted his voice cheerfully: 'It's all right, Charlie, we'll come back for your boat.'

Thus William passed it off for Charlie's sake. As Charlie was helped into the *Venture*, Michael turned to Mr. Gwynn and beheld in the eyes a glimmer of profound feeling. 'I'll light the stove,' said Mr. Gwynn and he went into the cabin.

From the *Venture* they all got on board the *Stormy Petrel* except William, who kept the heaving boats apart with a fender.

Charlie was quiet, did not look at any of them directly and spoke reasonably. With his three days' growth and bare head he had the appearance of an outcast, but there was a detached dignity about him.

Flora, after her outburst, was strangely composed. She had thanked them as they helped her into the *Stormy Petrel*, and had at once sat down, her body upright, but with a burning light in her eyes, quite different from Charlie's grey distant look. They were both obviously in a terribly weak condition.

Michael came out. 'Right, Doctor!'

The two berths, which folded against the walls of the cabin, had been let down, and now the doctor took Flora inside. When he had got her stretched out, he felt her pulse.

'The water, Doctor,' said Mr. Gwynn, poking his head round from the galley, 'is a week old. Will it be all right?'

'Fine,' answered the doctor, then continued his light comforting words to Flora. She smiled to him slowly and with such bright eyes that he thought, in her weakness, she was going to weep. The expression pierced him, and he turned away, hesitating for a moment before he stepped into the cockpit.

'You'd better have a lie down,' he said to Charlie.

'I'm fine,' said Charlie.

'In you go, Charlie,' said Norman. 'The lie down will do you good.'

Charlie murmured 'All right' and went in.

'Well?' questioned Norman.

'I have enough petrol for about two hours' running,'

answered Michael. 'On a calm day I have done it under an hour and a half.'

Norman looked at the weather. The blue was stretching over the sky. The wind would yet fall away completely. The sea was going down.

'If you could give us a tow for a bit,' he pondered.

'Naturally,' said Michael.

'Only you mustn't cut it fine. If you could take us clear of the islands, we'll manage then. What do you think, Doctor?'

'The sooner we get her into a warm bed the better. They're both far through.'

Norman nodded. 'The tide will soon be on the turn. It'll be slack for a while. You get something hot to drink. You're pretty cold looking yourself and wet to your middle.'

'It's a cold sea!' The doctor smiled, feeling the cold crawling over his skin.

Nearly three days of it, without food! . . . Involuntarily his eyes lifted to the great hole in the rock. Day and night, through the howling strom. Charlie would be a good companion to a woman then. He knew that by the way she had turned blindly and clung to him, turned to the warmth that body and spirit had already given her.

Mr. Gwynn narrowly missed a bad scalding when the Stormy Petrel all at once began to rock violently from side to side. Charlie was thrown out of his bunk and seemed for a little while to be unconscious. Flora, who had first been heaved against the boat's side, got an instinctive grip that held her.

More water had to be boiled, but in the end tea, with sugar and condensed milk, was served all round. The doctor attended to the two in the bunks. He did not ask them any questions, but treated them as normal patients who had come under his care. He had to support Flora with an arm round her shoulders while she drank. But neither of them seemed hungry. Charlie was completely uncaring. As Flora lay back, her eyes closed and the breath came from her as if her chest had been squeezed. Norman was anxious to be off. He had had a talk with William and Angus, who were now in the Venture. On a short tow rope, with William and Angus seated aft, the *Venture* did her best to keep her nose up, as Norman, at the tiller of the *Stormy Petrel*, swept out the way they had come in.

The spreading blue of the sky brought a freshness to the sea. Norman got the engine speed he wanted. After a time, with the islands well astern, he turned to the *Venture*. William nodded, raising his hand. Norman pulled the slip knot and heaved the rope clear. Already the *Venture's* sail was taking the wind. Her head fell away and she started on her first long tack.

Again the doctor knew a swift surge of feeling at sight of the gallant craft and the two men in her. His eyes took a secret look at Michael and Mr. Gwynn and found them unconsciously staring at the climbing and plunging lobster boat, already falling behind, falling away, in the seas. They could not break the fascination. The doctor went into the cabin.

Charlie was on an elbow, about to get out of his bunk. Flora was finding the pitching distressing and muttered something in a rambling way, but the doctor eased her head upward as well as he could. When he glanced over his shoulder, Charlie was on the flat of his back with his eyes shut. He stayed there beside Flora, looking sometimes on her face, at the eyelashes, the fine temples, the delicate skin texture, the curves of the mouth, the nostrils, and finding behind the outward shape and the closed eyes that something of the lonely woman – which they had sought one night to give a name to, but could not. In unconscious rest, without the need to draw back, the nameless in her was very near. It was asleep like something in his hands, like something in a still place far within him. And suddenly, in a solemn way, as sleep or death is solemn, it was for ever distant from him, this face, this spirit, that was so near. In many a death scene, he had realized the uniqueness, the ultimate loneliness, of the human being. Now there was added something neither of life nor of death, that brought the realization: *This is woman*, and the revelation affected him with an untranslatable strangeness.

As the pitching slackened, he went out into the cockpit. They were entering Loch Ros, making for the calm of its northern shore. Norman was taking no chances. If the engine stopped now, he could fetch Balcreggan on the southern shore under his mizzen sail.

The *Venture* was not following them. She could be seen well out to sea, fighting to give the Point a wide berth – and so home to Cruime. They would want to have her ready for the morning and the lobsters that the storm may have brought to their fishing grounds.

When the doctor saw folk making for the jetty below Ros Lodge, his face hardened. It was going to be difficult for Charlie. Then another problem struck him. Should he order Flora to be taken to Ros Lodge or should he have her driven direct to the manse?

He could order either course, whether the minister was there or not.

The problem so tormented him that his face became expressionless. He didn't know what to do. Ros Lodge was the last place in which he would wish to leave her. Yet to think of her in the manse, with her father . . .

Norman put the tiller over. Michael closed down the throttle and slid the gear into neutral. The *Stormy Petrel* glided into the stone jetty towards Erchie's waiting hands.

There were about a dozen onlookers and they had their dramatic moment. Then an elderly woman cried out and came waddling and sliding over the slimy stones. She was the housekeeper at the manse. The doctor looked into her face and turned to Michael. 'If you get the trap ready, we can send Flora and the housekeeper to the manse.'

Norman, the policeman, and the doctor carried Flora up the jetty. Michael told Erchie to get the old mare into the trap.

'Very well, sir,' replied Erchie, with a look at Charlie.

Charlie was on his own feet and began walking forward. Erchie caught his arm as he staggered.

'It's all right,' said Charlie, stopping.

'You'll come up to the house, Charlie, and rest there,' said Michael. 'Let me give you a hand.'

Charlie bore their attentions for a little while, then on the dry gravel above the uneven stones, he stopped again. Erchie hurried away to get the trap ready.

'Take it easy,' said Michael to Charlie.

Mr. Gwynn, finding the earth moving like the sea, swayed slightly and cast his eyes over the watching faces.

Charlie disengaged his arm. 'I'm all right,' he said. His lips were bloodless and his eyes like glass. Then he walked away from Michael, going slowly and with great care like a drunk man.

For a moment, Michael could not move. No one moved. Charlie turned away from Ros Lodge, taking the shore road towards Sgeir. A figure came through the watchers and began following Charlie at a little distance. It was Dougald, his brother. The path curved round the plantation wall and in a little while they had passed from sight.

CHAPTER TWENTY-EIGHT

The following afternoon, in bright sunshine, several men were lounging about the joiner's shop. The joiner was handling planks and hissing thoughtfully as he hirpled around.

'It's very good of him,' said Norman, for Erchie had brought the news that if the carpenter got ready what was necessary to mend Charlie's boat, the *Stormy Petrel* would run him down and tow the completed job home.

'Yes, Mr. Sandeman seems all right,' agreed Kenneth. 'I think we might get a lot out of him if we went about it the right way.'

There was a smile at that.

'All the same,' said Kenneth, 'that's the way to look at it. I hope I won't be grey before I see an engine in each of your boats.'

They laughed then.

'Did he give you tally-ho?' William asked Erchie.

'He said something right enough,' admitted Erchie, who was sixty-five, with hair showing grey under his cap, a rather long nose, and a tired friendly face. 'Yes, he said something.' He looked a trifle embarrassed and they waited for him with complete attention. 'I didn't know what to answer. Sure as death, boys, I didn't know what to say. He asked me what he should pay you for having come to their rescue.'

William was the first to break the silence. A chuckling note or two came from deep in his throat. 'There you are!' he said to Kenneth. 'Right first time!'

'Why not?' Kenneth answered him in a challenging voice. 'It's the law of the sea that you get paid in such a case. It's salvage.'

Norman was looking at Erchie. 'What did you say to him?' he asked quietly.

'To tell the truth, Norman, I did not know what to say, and the words came out of me without thinking, and I said you were not the kind of men to expect to be paid for saving anyone's life, not at sea.'

Norman nodded. 'Nor anywhere else, I hope.'

'Man, Erchie,' said William, enjoying the situation, 'couldn't you have thought of a bottle of whisky for the New Year itself? Or two bottles – for Angus is only a boy and he didn't do much whatever.'

Angus grinned. 'I'll be remembering that when I come round with my bottle at the New Year to your house, William.'

'So long as you come round with the bottle,' said William. 'What do you say, Smeorach?'

'Och well, a present like that is maybe different. A decent man would like to give some little thing, and it would be a poor heart that couldn't help him by taking it,' replied Smeorach.

'He's smelling the drop already!' declared William, looking sadly at the others.

'As long as you smell no worse, William,' retorted Smeorach, 'you can blow your nose anywhere.'

They laughed.

'All the same, Mr. Sandeman is right,' contended Kenneth. 'You saved his boat. He realizes that he should pay something for salvage.'

'No,' said Norman. 'We did what any men would do. For myself, I would feel shame to be offered anything. Besides, wasn't it out to look for Charlie, one of ourselves, he went?'

'I had forgotten that,' said Kenneth.

Everyone glanced at Kenneth and chuckled. Norman had fairly caught him that time!

'I hear the girl Flora is coming on fine,' Smeorach remarked.

'She's a well-built girl, with a good frame to her,' said Norman.

They fell silent.

'You wouldn't think of taking a walk out to see Charlie to-night, Norman?' asked Kenneth.

'I did think about it. But he mightn't thank me.'

'He looked a pretty sick man,' said William.

'When you're like that, you don't always want to be bothered, maybe,' suggested Smeorach.

'That is so,' Norman agreed.

They shifted restlessly on their feet.

Presently Erchie left. He had a talk with John-the-roadman and one or two others. There was only one topic of conversation along that coast. Sarah and Betsy and a hundred girls like them could think of nothing else. Boys were thrilled by the daring rescue of the *Stormy Petrel*, and fences had to be taken in a flying leap, even as the hero Angus had leapt from one boat to another in mid ocean. But about the finest bit of the story was when Angus found the hidden tin of petrol. That capped everything. Oh, that was good! Think of them going to their doom with that tin there! And then in leaps Angus . . . and his eye finds the hidden tin. Like magic!

It was growing dark as Erchie saw a boy coming along the road towards him, clearly pursued by many fears or devils. It was young Hamish and Erchie stopped him.

But Hamish could not speak. The blood had been drawn from his face to keep his legs going.

'What's that you've got?' asked Erchie and his eyes were searching.

'He gave it to me!' gulped Hamish. 'He did!'

'Who?'

'Mr. Sandeman.'

'I won't take it from you. Let me see it . . . Ay, it's his best trout rod.' Erchie shoved back the smooth cork handle into its canvas case. 'It's a beautiful rod. Did he give you the reel for it?'

'Yes,' said Hamish, reluctantly producing it and handing it over, his eyes jumping from Erchie's hands to his face. 'He gave it to me himself.' When Erchie tested the reel's action, its lovely crying sound was too much for Hamish and his hand came out fearfully for it.

Erchie smiled and Hamish instantly pocketed the reel.

'What a pity you didn't get a fly or two to complete you,' said Erchie.

Hamish looked up from under his eyelids.

Erchie put a friendly hand on his head. Then Hamish produced the fly book. He had not yet had time to look at it properly himself, and as the pages turned over Erchie began to name the flies.

Hamish's excitement was like a flame in a wind. Grouse and claret, teal and green, march brown, zulu – the names were legendary sounds. He did not hear them properly. He could not hear anything properly, because he could not yet believe what had happened to him. In a malign moment these marvels might vanish. The fly book, for example, fell out of his hands, but he pounced on it instantly and closed it up. It had an attached brown elastic band that tried to outwit his fumbling fingers. But it gave in with a tight *flip*! that was a sound in itself.

'There's no need for you to hurt yourself running,' said Erchie in a kindly voice. 'They're your own now.'

'Yes. He gave them to me himself. I never asked him, I never spoke a word.'

'You thanked him, I hope?'

Hamish stared at Erchie. He obviously didn't remember. He looked distressed.

'Why did he give them to you?' asked Erchie.

'I don't know,' said Hamish. 'He never said.' His distress grew. 'I'll be going now, it's getting late.'

'He gave them to you because you helped him. They're your own, and not the richest man in the world has better. Take great care of them.'

'I'll do that.'

'Good night, then.'

'Good night.'

Hamish walked off, but presently, when Erchie looked over his shoulder, he was running like a hare.

He can't contain himself, thought Erchie, and his old eyes smiled far back through time.

After dinner, he went to report. The soft-voiced maid, Ina, after drawing from him such new news as he had gathered, knocked and announced him.

Michael got up abruptly. 'Come in. Sit down.' He poured a large neat whisky and handed it to Erchie.

Erchie thanked him, and though he did not say *slàinte*! he looked at each of them and gave a perceptible nod of courteous acknowledgment.

Mr. Gwynn bowed.

'Well?' demanded Michael.

'It's just as I said, sir. They wouldn't think of taking money.'

Michael gave him a sidelong satiric look, then smiled, not without amusement. 'Too proud are they?'

'It's not that, sir. There's many nowadays that would take the money however it came. But Norman and William, they have the old feeling in them.'

'What old feeling?'

Erchie looked troubled. 'It's difficult to explain.'

'You think I wouldn't understand it?'

'It's just the old custom,' said Erchie, with a subtle lack of any expression.

'Did you see Norman?'

'Yes. He was there.'

'What did he say?'

'He said he would feel shame to be offered anything.'

'Was he offended?'

'Oh no. They know it was out of kindness you meant it. They were not offended because William began making a joke about it.'

'Indeed! What sort of joke?'

Erchie hesitated. 'I shouldn't have mentioned it.'

'I shan't give you away.'

'Och, it was just a joke, but William said, "Now if he had thought of sending us a bottle of whisky for the New Year!"'

Mr. Gwynn laughed.

'You think,' said Michael drily, 'that if I sent them a case of whisky for the New Year, they wouldn't take it amiss?'

Erchie lifted his glass and looked at it. 'If you sent a small letter with it in your own hand, they would be very happy.' He drained the glass.

'Have another drop,' said Michael.

Erchie protested but Michael ignored him.

'Slàinte,' said Mr. Gwynn.

'Slàinte mhath,' responded Erchie.

They both drank.

'About to-morrow?' asked Michael.

'The joiner will be ready, but they don't think the weather will be in it.'

'They weren't offended again?'

'No, sir,' said Erchie. 'They thought it very good of you.'

'Very nice of them.'

Erchie did not appear to catch the dry tone, but Mr. Gwynn saw something harden in him. Then Erchie said mildly, 'They just saw you, sir, like one of themselves, doing what you could to save Charlie.'

'Have a cigar,' said Mr. Gwynn.

'No, thank you, sir, I'll just be going now, if that's all.'

Mr. Gwynn made him take the cigar and Erchie got up. Mr. Gwynn was smiling to him, and Erchie, by way of pleasant parting words, said, 'I met the boy Hamish running. I thought he had a ghost after him.'

Mr. Gwynn's face lit up. 'What was it?'

'The presents he got. He was running as hard as his legs could carry him, or maybe a little harder.'

'Was he frightened someone might steal them from him?'

'I'm thinking he was just frightened they would vanish.'

Mr. Gwynn laughed merrily, his eyes on Erchie, on the lined face with its slow deep humour.

'Will they be offended?' inquired Michael, from his satiric mood.

'No, sir,' answered Erchie without looking at him. 'On the contrary, they will think very highly of you for it.' Then he went, without hurry, giving them a respectful good night.

'And here endeth the first lesson in manners, I suppose,' said Michael.

Mr. Gwynn threw him a look but said nothing.

Michael walked out of the room. Listening, Mr. Gwynn heard the click of the electric switches in the gallery.

What had been haunting him, haunting them both, these last few days, thought Mr. Gwynn, even while his ears listened, was this mystery of the individual personality.

It had taken a body of its own, on the cliff, on the sea, the three men bearing down on them in the *Venture*, Angus in his leap, Flora, and Charlie walking calmly on the arm of Death.

Figures, individual figures, on the land, on the face of the sea.

The individual human being, the one whole being.

Michael's feet were moving about the floor, empty sounds. Thudding about the floor.

Back into the primitive? . . . no, back into themselves. That was the search. For oneness. Searching, with paint, for the primitive where wholeness began, but finally here, on the sea, in the leap, with death as life's shadow, under the sun, against the gale, the body whole and singular, with warmth in it, for one other, for others, for all. Man's strangely tragic story, so full of wonder and light.

The footsteps stopped.

Michael was, in fact, now contemplating his gallery of the local human comedy, with the strangled foreign seaman hung in the middle, 'on the line', against the light-coloured wall.

To his right, Charlie. God, he had forgotten to ask Erchie about Charlie! Probably he had now thrown himself over a cliff to join his strangled brother! Calm, there; rising above his boat. Calm.

To the dead man's left, Flora. There she uprose, with the earth about her, the earth and the far sky, meeting in her quiet smile, the wandering and vagrancy of mankind, caught and stilled here. Beautiful, in an inalienable beauty of the spirit. Innocent of self-horror at the core. Without death.

The looming policeman. Michael stared long at him, at the notebook, the pencil.

Dougald, the mythical human monster. Gwynn's primitive! Almost transparent, so that you see things through him. Or is it that he interpenetrates all? A master question!

The minister – looking into the lens, the lens now of the human eye – with a polite social smile.

Gwynn's concentrated upward look from where he sat on the grass, all gesture shed and grace. Raw. Lifting beyond the wound. The skin of his face was naked.

The doctor, in profile – he did not know *that* one had been taken! – looking from the extreme left across his local comedy.

From nowhere Michael's mind was hit by a swift lash. A couple of strides, and he flung his gallery into darkness. He went out and along the shore, disturbing sea-birds that screeched shrilly, and from his throat harshly he answered them, crying 'Simulacra! Simulacra!' An intense feeling of exhilaration began to well up in him.

CHAPTER TWENTY-NINE

The night fell quickly, and before Dougald got back to his cottage it was dark, the thin rain whipping his face out of the rising wind. There was no light in the window. Charlie must have stayed in bed. When, however, he found the door standing open, a grunt came out of him. He shut it behind him and saw the kitchen filled with smoke. He went straight for the hand lamp, lit it, and turned into Charlie's room, slowing his steps to peer over the light with a controlled expression. The bed was empty and in disorder. There was no one in the room. His expression opened. The lamp shook in his hand. 'Charlie!' There was no answer.

He went back to the kitchen and looked in the kitchen bed. Charlie was not in the house. His expression grew congested with wrath and fear. Stock still he stood on the middle of the floor, the lamp in his hand lighting up his angry-red bushy face. Then he set down the lamp on the table, his collie looking up at him from the corner behind the peat basket.

Suddenly he lumbered out, pulling the door after him, and went along to the byre. 'Charlie!' He lit matches. The cow mooed at him, the chain rattling on her neck. Charlie was not anywhere about the outhouses. He came back to the kitchen and stood on the middle of the floor.

'God damn him, where has he gone now?' His voice was harsh and defiant and the force of emotion in him thrust his feet about the floor. Then he stood again, listening. The wind whined about the house, coming in from the west. Rain beat across the small window. He saw the reflection of the lamp, outside, ghost-like in the night.

All day he had hung about the house. Then Charlie had quietened and seemed ready for sleep, his eyes shut, breathing in little gusts out of exhaustion. The storm was plainly coming and there were a few ewes in poor condition that would have been the better of sending away for wintering with the hoggs. He had known that, but also knew he could pull them through or, at the worst, make the crofts take them for a while. The cost of wintering was the heaviest charge on the Club. He would have been back earlier had he not, after rounding up the ewes into a sheltered valley, started out for the doctor. As Charlie had refused absolutely to see the doctor, Dougald had had to struggle against Charlie's will every yard of the road. Within sight of Ros Lodge, Charlie's will had fought him to a raging standstill. Then Erchie, driving home a couple of strayed stirks, had come on him. 'If you see the doctor,' called Dougald, 'tell him Charlie is not well.' Turning abruptly, he had made back.

The wind came in a gust again. The storm was rising. Then through the whine of the wind, he heard another whine, a dog's whine, at the door. The sound of it ran cold down the small of his back. His eyes swept the floor. Nell uncurled and, twisting, whined uneasily, her eyes showing the whites as she glanced up at him from lowered muzzle. The other dog he had deliberately left with Charlie.

He pulled the door open and Tang came in, tawny as seatangle, slunk across the floor, and flattened behind Nell, but restlessly, as if beaten and fearful.

'Curse you!' roared Dougald. 'Get up!'

Tang avoided him and slunk under the table. Dougald was already at the door. 'Come on!' he roared. The wind blew into the kitchen and sent the smoke in whirls and the flame leaping in the funnel of the lamp. Maddened, he returned and swept his boot under the table. Whimpering, Tang ran out before him.

Dougald thought he saw the dog making for the cliff path beyond the unblinded window light.

He could have found his way down the cliff path in pitch dark. Even when he slipped, his body knew how to twist over, his hands where to grab and hold. Now he went down it without any clear sense in the order of his going. For horror of what he might find – or not find – was already coiled round the root fibres of his life.

The seas were spouting over the skerries, lashing and seething on the narrow beach, for they were coming straight in from the west. The stones rolled from his feet as Dougald strode heavily down till the withdrawn water came again and rushed over his feet, up to his knees.

There was nothing there. Nothing. On the cliff wall of the Point to his left, the sea smashed and burst. Into faults and caverns beyond, the water boomed and choked, glutted. But there, coming into him, curling round the skerries, were black lumps of water, like black heads. The beach came alive in storm and wreck.

Dougald lifted his head in mad defiance. Roaring out of his throat came challenging sounds, eager for battle. The sounds cursed the sea and the black heads and dared them and damned them. 'Damn you to hell!' he roared into the teeth of the rising storm, the stones crashing under his feet as the water swept over them and staggered him.

He turned and stumbled up the stones – and saw against the black hole of the low cave into which Charlie thrust his gear for shelter, a pallor like a vague moon, like a piece of newspaper, and Dougald's rage ebbed from him in a coldness colder than the sea, for he knew it was a face.

He drew towards it. It was making sounds, but hardly human sounds. He went right up to it and stooped. It was Charlie.

'What are you doing here?' asked Dougald, in a voice gone strangely simple.

Charlie slid back on his haunches.

'Come on up home,' said Dougald.

Charlie sat staring at him.

'Come on,' said Dougald and put a hand out.

Charlie scrambled to his feet and hit the lip of the cave with his head. This released him and in a moment they had come to grips.

They staggered as they fought, Dougald trying to pin his arms. Charlie began to yell, but his voice broke into a scream, into a wild vicious gibberish. When Dougald felt Charlie's fingers at his throat, a great strength came upon him, a bear's strength, that crushed Charlie's arms and body until they suddenly fell limp against him.

Dougald laid him out on the stones.

For a little Dougald stared down, his chest heaving noisily, then he looked over his shoulder at the sea, and a cry came from him, of defiance still, but broken. He picked Charlie up in his arms, shoved his body over his left shoulder as the cliff path grew steep, eased it at the cliff-top so that the blood would not choke the head, and so bore it into the house and laid it on the kitchen bed.

He unfastened the shirt at the neck and then stopped and stared. Charlie's head had fallen over loosely. It never moved.

'Charlie!' called Dougald. 'Charlie!' His hand came like a searching paw on the chest. 'Charlie!'

His voice broke. He turned away from the bed and put on the kettle, moving quickly but in a kind of blindness, like a wounded animal.

The doctor was heading across the moor, for Erchie had intercepted him on his way home at the junction of the roads, and he turned away at once from the meal that was waiting for him, riding his motor-cycle right past Ros Lodge and on over the rough sea track as far as he could.

He had been expecting this message, indeed had been hoping for it and growing uneasy when it wasn't coming. There had been that withdrawn dignity about Charlie, that air of keeping one at a distance, which neither Norman nor anyone else had dared to intrude upon.

This dignity of the human individual that so fascinated Mr. Gwynn! This primal wholeness on its two feet with its two eyes!

The doctor smiled, lowering his brow against the stinging rain in a certain humoured warmth, a satiric mirth, where the satire gave strength and was healthy.

So many of his trips were like this, to the individual between whom and his fellows death had shadowily slipped in.

He could suggest a different kind of portrait gallery for Michael, very different, and much more revealing of his 'human comedy'! Faces came before the doctor's inward eye, came out of the storm into which he thrust himself, and lay each in a momentary pool of quietness, faces on their death bed.

It was when the struggle was over and the money was made, when age had to take leave of the struggle and the money, the struggle and the meanness, the cunning little cruelties, the tricks of 'success' – what a desert was there then in the face on its death bed! He was looking upon the face of the trader who had died last week in Badloan.

Other faces. For there is no concealment now. This is the judgment hour, the lonely hour of self-judgment, and all one's fellows fall away, and all one's possessions fall away, and the hour and the place are naked as the body, stripped as the body will be at the hour's end.

This was no fantasy. He had seen it. Seen it often. The human picture gallery in this our age. The end of the strife and the conflict, when greed had lain as prime motive at the core of self. What doth it profit a man . . . Profit!

Profit that ravaged the face like a desert and made the eyes, the glassy eyes, stare in knowledge from its waste, in that last knowledge, with the lips already desert-dry and salted.

The beds they lay on tilted the faces and bodies into the dark howl of the wind and, invigorated by his satire, the doctor struggled on, in a hurry to get at Charlie.

For somehow it was not really remarkable that Charlie was still alive. All along, at the back of his mind, the doctor had had the odd feeling that Dougald would have been Charlie's watchdog. Dougald had an instinct for Charlie's sickness, not his body's sickness so much as his spirit's. Dougald would have had a surer cunning about it than any of them. Dougald would know it in the pining sheep that left its fellows for the lonely spot, the stag that set out on his last trek, alone, for the sanctuary. Charlie had only got to begin to drift in a certain direction for Dougald to follow.

But the doctor was hardly prepared for the scene he came upon. It held him just outside the unblinded window of the cottage and gathered an extraordinary power because he could not hear what was said.

Charlie's white face was mad-eyed on the pillow. His

hands were clutching at the bedclothes. There came a roar of rainwind which made the doctor thrust a supporting hand against the wall. Charlie's fingers went up to his own throat. Dougald's red fists gripped them. Charlie struggled and the bedclothes heaved and tossed. Now the doctor heard Charlie's piercing yells. Presently Charlie fell back and his mouth opened for the breath to snore through. Dougald smoothed the bedclothes, folded them down from the top, and with the slow gentleness of a woman placed Charlie's hands upon his body, and drew the clothes back to the chin. After standing a little while looking down upon his brother, Dougald turned away. Another blatter of high wind stopped him mid-floor. He stared straight at the window, and the doctor thought he was being seen. The wind howled round the walls and the doctor saw Dougald's mouth move. In an instant, the doctor knew he was not being seen, or was certainly not being recognized, for Dougald's shoulders hunched with a terrific suggestion of fighting power. He was challenging the forces of the night. He was prepared to meet all the forces from the sea and from hell beyond it. He was his brother's keeper.

A small shiver went over the doctor, and he leaned back against the wall for a moment, and stared into the rising fury that came from the sea, challenging it also with his smile, challenging it and defeating it, out of something magnificent in Dougald's stand.

Rattling the door, he entered and closed it behind him. Dougald was swift to meet him – then stopped dead.

'How is he?' asked the doctor, watching the body in front of him losing its stiffening.

'Come in.'

The doctor entered, took off his coat and leggings, and unslung the brown leather-and-canvas bag from his back. Then he went and warmed his hands at the fire. The kettle was lazily spouting its steam. He asked for a clean bowl.

'No, no!' said Charlie from the bed. 'No you don't!' His breathing began to rise. His hands came clear.

'Keep hold of him,' said the doctor.

Charlie did not recognize them, of course, but he was fighting. The doctor saw that. His face was hard and bitter.

Scared in a wild wide-eyed way, but not broken. 'By God, you don't!' roared Charlie, and his fist smashed into Dougald's face.

The doctor, with the body spent and quivering, thrust a needle into the flesh and pressed the shot home. 'That'll keep him quiet. How long has he been like this?'

'Since the darkening.'

The doctor nodded, satisfied. 'I'll look him over. Meantime, I'll tell you what you might do for me.'

Dougald waited.

'You might make me a cup of tea.'

Dougald's mouth fell open and he stared at the doctor. 'Yes,' he muttered and turned to the fire.

From the corner of his eye, the doctor saw Dougald's body getting busier and busier and moving now with remarkable lightness. He went out and came in, white bread, oatcake, butter, jam, cup and saucer. . . .

The doctor folded his stethoscope. 'I couldn't take four eggs,' he said.

Dougald looked at him solemnly, gaping a little.

'He'll pull through, I think.'

Dougald sat down and then leaned over to find a small pan. Gripping it, he looked again at the doctor. 'Is he – is his reason—?'

Then the doctor realized that Dougald thought Charlie had lost his reason, had gone mad.

'No, no,' said the doctor. 'He has been delirious. Delirium. He didn't know what he was doing.'

Dougald looked past the doctor and then back at his face again.

'His mind is all right,' the doctor made it clear. 'If he has the will to get better, I think he'll get better, and fairly quickly.'

'Oh.' It was no more than a curious wondering breath. All the features softened. He put the four eggs in the pan.

'When did you have food last yourself?' asked the doctor.

'I don't remember,' answered Dougald correctly.

'Well, we'll have tea together,' said the doctor firmly, 'then I must ask you to go with a message from me, stormy as the night is.'

Dougald looked at him expectantly.

'My mother won't know I'm here. I'll write a note, and you'll take it, and bring back one or two things.'

'Yes, Doctor.' The prospect of such action clearly relieved him. But he gave the doctor a curious beseeching glance. 'Will you wait till I come back? I won't take long.'

The doctor looked at him. 'I am going to stay here all night.'

Then something happened to Dougald's features. He got up and went into the passage as if searching for a lost pan. The doctor listened and heard one or two thick gulps. Plainly he was doing his best to choke them.

CHAPTER THIRTY

There came some days of good weather, when the land lay quietly under the sun and the sea glittered. This often happened in November, and the dreaming mood that fell upon the earth had at once a memory of summer in it and a thought of spring. Violence lay asleep in the coils of the sea, and the brows of the cliffs were smooth and far-sighted. Loch Geal had the shimmer of a shield, and the outlines of the mountains, rising from the Garuvben deer forest, flowed far upon horizons which limited the illimitable skies. The wind ran about the heather like a soft-mouthed spaniel seeking a scent.

With twilight, in this month not yet fallen asleep, an ear listens and a mind is free to speculate and even to gather odd apprehensions of lost magics. Very intimate these apprehensions are, very near the bone, and the face can afford to stare like a cliff-head.

'Dougald was always like that,' said Charlie, staring through the small window of his own room at the twilight.

The doctor, on the chair by the bed, was also staring out through the window.

'So you can imagine,' Charlie went on, 'What he felt like when I came back home.'

'Yes,' replied the doctor. 'I hadn't thought it meant to him so much as that.' His voice was quiet and contemplative. 'I see it now. When you failed to fulfil his hopes it must have been a pretty deadly blow. He was father and mother in one.'

'I don't know if that's it quite,' said Charlie. 'He was my brother. And this feeling of a brother to a brother – it is a queer blood feeling. It goes – deep. I haven't it as Dougald has it, but I know it.'

The doctor was silent for a little. 'I think that is profound.'

'All the money he could gather, every penny he had saved, it all went on me. Only a few months ago did he pay off the last of his debt to Kenneth Grant. I had helped there, of course. But still – it was all his doing. And it had meant that he never got out of the bit, never got his sheep – or much else.'

'I understand,' said the doctor. 'I can also see that it was, in the altered circumstances, a bit tough on you. Did he show it much?'

'Not a great deal. You know him. But even in one of his rages, when he might look at me as if he might kill me, it was still the rage of an elder brother. And then – then it got into his mind that it was him and me against the world. He doesn't say much.'

'Did you find it difficult?'

'Very – often enough. But, you see, I had come back.'

The doctor was silent, for the fatal quietude of Charlie's voice had evoked Flora. A faint bitterness from the voice ran through the twilight, but did not stain it.

This mood, this hour, had opened like an evening flower, after the fight against death in which the doctor had not spared himself, nor spared his patient Charlie. The fight was over, and they both knew the hour had been won. But one false word, rising from the wrong kind of curiosity, and the hour would fade before the eye, without disturbance, quietly but irrevocably.

'Well,' remarked the doctor, 'you had to do what you had to do.'

'I have wondered,' said Charlie. 'However, it happened.' Then in the same voice, he went on: 'When Dougald came back that morning and found the notes of foreign money in the seaman's chest, he took them. He was in that mood.'

The doctor had the feeling that Charlie's eyes had switched on him, but he did not look round. His breathing became a conscious operation, but he controlled it. 'I see,' he said slowly. 'Dougald was against the world, so he was taking his dues.' His smile of irony passed beyond the window. 'Naturally, you understand, I wondered if anything of the kind had happened,' continued the doctor with frankness, trying to answer the silence. 'Afterwards, I

mean, when Dougald bought the sheep. The way I rea-
soned it out was this. Here, we look upon taking what
Providence washes up on the shore as being more our own
than even a smuggled drop of whisky or a poached salmon.
The old laws of our land. Up in the Orkneys and Shetlands,
I understand, they have still a recognized legal claim, under
the old Udal system, to anything cast up on their shores.
But usually, as with the smuggled drop, we hide it.
Dougald did not hide it. He bought his sheep and to
blazes with them. He was simply in rebellion against the
forces that had defeated him. That's what I felt about it.'
For one moment, the doctor wondered if he had spoken
too much, if he had taken Charlie's confession too lightly.

'I suppose so,' said Charlie and was silent.

Dougald passed the window. They listened to his footsteps. They did not come in.

'I'm not blaming him,' said Charlie. 'It's just what
happened.'

The doctor, feeling he had said too much, remained
silent. But at last he had to speak, so he said, 'The key of the
chest was on the sailor?'

'Yes,' answered Charlie. 'Some time during the night –
long after he was dead – I opened the chest. I don't know
why. I think I was still trying to do something. I had been up
and down the cliff – and to other places. I wanted to save a
life this time – perhaps to make up for the one I had
strangled.'

The doctor did not move.

'I don't know what I expected to find in the chest that
would help. There was nothing anyway. Dougald came
home. The key was in it. He found the notes. He took them
out. He locked the chest. I asked him what he was going to
do with them. "Keep them," he said. I was beyond caring
what he did with them. But, somehow, whether he was
trying to get something back on me or not, God knows, but
it all came out, and we wrangled. In the ordinary way, just
because it belonged to a dead man, he would never have
touched the money. But everything – everything that had
happened – for years – came to a head then. It came to a
head – on money. I told him not to take it. I went a little

beyond myself. There was a moment when the brotherly feeling turned to poison in the blood. I don't know yet how he forbore to strike me. Had he struck me at all, he would have killed me. His face . . .' Charlie paused. 'I am aware it is no more than a figure of speech, talking of poison in the blood.'

And now for the first time, the twilight was stained.

The doctor began to feel for his cigarette case, but left it in his pocket. 'It must have been pretty bad,' he said.

'It was,' said Charlie. 'Another odd thing, too, was this. Dougald could not apparently smash me. I think he might have – had he not somehow been diverted by the key in his hand. I have thought about it. It suddenly became something more than the key of the chest. It became – everything – in his hand. That's not much sense, I'm afraid.'

'Uhm,' said the doctor. 'It's extraordinarily difficult to put words to it. Symbol of triumph, perhaps, with terrific meaning for that moment.'

'Something like that,' agreed Charlie. 'The past. Money. His triumph over me. Over laws and churches. Anyway, he shouted that he would settle it all. He walked out of the house and threw the key over the cliff.'

'That certainly settled it,' said the doctor.

'It did,' said Charlie. 'It committed us.'

The doctor, after a moment, turned and looked at Charlie. 'How are you feeling?'

'Fine,' answered Charlie. 'Floating a bit, but fine.'

The blue eyes regarded the doctor with a faint objective smile. The face was pale and thin, with a stubble over the jaw and upper lip. Something of the outcast was there, as it had been when they saved him from the Roaring Cave, but now Charlie was more securely himself. The talking was taking little out of him. They both knew they were committed to it. A quick surge of fellow-feeling, of warm friendliness, came to the doctor's eyes before he turned to the window. Charlie was like one remembering a sequence of events that had found, in this twilit detachment, their recording hour, before he passed on.

'If Dougald had not thrown the key away then, he would have given it to the policeman?'

'Yes. Not, perhaps, if we had only found the chest. But
– the owner was there – and there in the strongest of all
shapes.' Charlie was silent for a moment. 'You see,
Dougald's whole action was irrational. There wasn't
much money in the chest. I actually got less than eight
pounds for it. And it was foreign money. Perhaps that
made it more symbolic, as you say, than ever.'

The doctor also smiled in irony. 'It makes it clear
anyway,' he said.

'The rest of the money he did actually find on the shore. I
think in a kind of kit-bag. It was wrapped round and round
in fine oilskin and quite dry. An odd find, wasn't it? But I
expect someone tried to bring it in – and gave up. Perhaps it
belonged to one of the two bodies found near Glaspool.
But who can say?'

'No. Not with life gone.'

Life gone. The doctor's mind lapsed for a moment in
which life became a formless something of deep significance, penetrating the twilight to far fields.

'There were some English notes among them,' continued Charlie, 'but mostly Swedish. I found no difficulty in
cashing them. The young fellow behind the counter plainly
took me for a foreigner. He spoke slowly so that I should
understand him. When I was going he said good morning
in German.'

The doctor laughed quietly. 'That would ease any
strain?'

'It did.'

'Had you tried Gaelic on him?'

'No. Not actually. Though I did feel – and it affected my
speech – I did feel at that moment a foreigner. My voice eet
was ferry peculiar. It went that way all on its own.'

Charlie's detachment was almost absolute. 'It wasn't that
I was trying to act a part. There was no need for that
anyhow. Though perhaps you think there was?'

'Perhaps you may have been doing it unconsciously,
making a good job of it,' suggested the doctor, 'when
you were at it.'

'Perhaps.' The humour dying out of his face, Charlie looked
through the window at the outcrop of lichened rock. 'I certainly

did not want to placate anybody, and certainly not the fellow behind the counter. I don't know why I did it. But it had its effect on me. When I went out, I could not help smiling to myself. Often that night, I smiled away, hearing my acting voice, seeing the eager look on his face as he tried his German. And suddenly angered I thought: I'll go back home.'

'You hadn't meant to come back, then?'

'No. The money was Dougald's parting gift. I was going abroad. There was nearly forty pounds of it.'

'I see,' said the doctor.

'You'll perhaps see better if I remind you of the funeral of the dead seaman and of the minister's sermon . . . and of the way Dougald and I had to turn away from our people.'

Charlie's tone had not altered but the doctor's eyes winced as from the lash of a very fine thong.

'That threw Dougald and myself together, if in a queer bitter way. We hadn't much to say. Nothing. Then one night he put all the money on the table before me. "You better clear out," he said. So I went.'

The doctor did not speak.

'We're a queer people, I suppose. Or perhaps it's only myself. Eyes, many eyes, looking round corners. We've got like that. At college in Edinburgh chaps who wanted to feel stylish, a bit grand, said they didn't know Gaelic – "Oh, perhaps a word or two" – when all the time it was their native tongue.'

'I know,' said the doctor.

'When your heritage is denied like that – what's left?'

'Not much.'

'No . . . It's a sensitiveness, I suppose. Want to forget simple origins and be on top of the world with the best. It's easy to be sarcastic about it. But it doesn't help. Something went wrong. We lost something.'

'Mr. Gwynn at the Lodge says we have all lost something. Belief, he calls it. For our case, belief in the actual culture we had. And, though it was poor in worldly gear, it was rich in other things.'

'What things?'

'A belief in a common life among ourselves, working happily, in having our traditions, our language, our songs –

and so on. Did you think I was going to use the word spiritual?'

Charlie met the humoured challenge in the doctor's eyes. 'In that case, we can afford to use it,' he answered, making the avowal with some harshness, as if his mind had been switched to the local church and all it stood for to him.

'But it's the worldly gear that matters. Finally, I doubt if we have any other standard now,' said the doctor.

'I agree,' said Charlie. 'And the thought of it for some reason made me mad, and there and then I decided to return. To hell with them, I thought, to hell with them all. I suddenly realized, too, the goodness of my brother Dougald. He may not be a brilliant specimen, but—Anyway, it was his money. I had robbed him long enough.'

'What did Dougald say when you came back?'

'Nothing. But I spoke to him. Brothers can get terribly reticent. But I spoke out. I planted the English money in front of him. I told him to buy his sheep. I said that he had been very good to me, and that henceforth we'd hang together. It was not easy. He was moved.' A touch of arid humour came back into Charlie's face. 'He did not quite understand it. Perhaps I didn't myself. But he understood all right the bit about our being against them who were against us. He got drunk and took his own road – even over the mountains.'

'The old drove road of his people,' reflected the doctor. 'The instinct was still sound!'

'But I could see he was worried. There was still something. We never discussed the thing, because he had heard all I told you and the policeman about the seaman, the strangling. Still – he wondered.'

The doctor left the silence alone.

'I suppose you wonder, too – and all the rest of you. I'll never live that down. Never. I know that now. I knew it before I came back, but in the mood I was in I didn't mind. Now I *know* it . . . However, the thing itself has worried me also. Damnably. I did not give you the full details. You see, when I waded out to get a grip of him, I had to go too far, lost my feet, and when my hand fell on his head – I suppose he thought someone was attacking him. It was dark, remember, and the storm roaring like worlds falling on your top. A hand lifted, over-arm, gripped me and pushed me under. I had to fight. It was a hellish foaming struggle. We fetched up against the skerry. The back eddy took us there. I had just hit him in the face. The only thing to do with a man like that is to knock him out. I hadn't knocked him out. But I had got a grip of the skerry with one hand. The other had him by the back of the neck. Up to this point we had been sort of face to face, like dogs, but now, whether he had lost grip of his chest and taken both hands to grab it or whether the eddy had sucked him past me – anyway, the back of his head was to me, as if he had turned over to swim on his back – and I had the straight pull on his throat.'

Charlie paused for a little and stirred in his bed.

'I heard him choking,' he said.

The horror of what he had heard was in his voice, more terribly in his low clear voice than if he had cried aloud.

When Charlie recovered from that sentence, his voice was weary, his strength spent.

'I should have done something more. I am a seaman. Had I let him go, he would have drowned. I *hauled* him to me. Somehow I got ashore. I carried him. When I told you I felt his heart beat, I can only say that I thought I did. I may have been deluding myself. God knows. Hell, I'm weak.'

The doctor got up. Charlie's face was wet; he turned it away.

The doctor did not know what to say. It all came back upon him in a surge. The policeman. The Procurator-Fiscal. Himself. The questioning. The appalling suspicion. The photographs. Charlie's own knowledge of what had happened by the skerry. Charlie's face now, because of his bodily weakness, was quivering. All at once the doctor said. 'My God, man, don't you realize that you acted like a hero? What more could you have done?' He gripped Charlie's hand, pressed it, and left the room.

An hour later he left the cottage. It was all but dark. Dougald and himself had made tea, and he had taken it with Charlie, who had recovered his calm. The doctor had felt full of optimism, his mind swept clean of the horrible suspicions that had at odd moments spawned their murder pictures. He had felt perfectly confident he could deal with Charlie now, could 'put him right', not only with himself, but, what was a more difficult business, with his people, the seamen, the women and children, the folk of his own place.

'You can leave it to me,' he had said. 'I'll see that everything is all right.'

And Charlie, his head lying back on the pillow, had looked at him distantly, and smiled that grey ironic smile.

But the doctor could afford to ignore it. In his mind he knew how he could place Charlie's heroism in its true light. For he knew, in that moment, how strong was his own influence over the people. The thing was certain. And easy, so pleasantly easy, and even good for the doctor's own mind. A proper cleansing all round, from which Charlie would emerge as the grand fellow he was – and more than that, having borne so much.

And Charlie said nothing, showed nothing except that withering smile in his eyes.

It began to shake the doctor, but he did not show it, felt still that Charlie was being pig-headed, so he came at the matter on another tack. A man owed his community something. Kenneth Grant had said that one or two men, like Norman and Charlie, could be leaders who would put the place once more on its feet. It was something like that was needed. Belief that they could do things for themselves had got lost. Not only lost here, but lost in every small place of the world like it. But here there was something worth finding again. A too rigid religion and what not may have helped to blot it out, but it was worth finding again, a whole way of life that had bred fine men and women, kind-hearted, strong, decent. Hang it all, a fellow just couldn't clear out when he was needed, not a fellow like Charlie who could think about these things. Least of all, the thinking *and* working kind, now.

The doctor had positively surprised himself with his own eloquence, which had come so easily that he had chuckled now and then at its pleasant obviousness, confidently. Had even been aware, somewhere at the back of his mind, of a professional exercise of mental healing.

Charlie just listened, the deepening twilight in his eyes.

The doctor had a warning instinct against mentioning it, but if it really was the only thing that was keeping Charlie obdurate – 'Of course,' he had said, 'what you have told me is between us. Folk know now how you did your best to save the seaman. I'll make sure that they believe it. And that's merely making sure of the truth. Any extra detail that you may have given me here, that's between us.'

Charlie's eyes left the window and rested on his hands. The doctor saw the eyelashes flicker like the long legs of flies. Then the eyes lifted to his face.

'Why?' asked Charlie.

'Why?' repeated the doctor, as if suddenly hit over the heart, but smiling. 'Well, there's no need to – to go into every detail.'

And Charlie switched his eyes away, forbearing to trouble the doctor with another Why? Indeed, as if he had known intimately the doctor's momentary embarrassment, he said in his quiet voice, 'You see, Doctor, it's no good. Whatever you said, or anyone said, it's an end of me here. You've only got my story. Even if I had children, and grandchildren, they would still be known as coming from me, and beside me always, beside the picture of me, would be the strangled seaman and the money. That's fixed, for all time, in this community by the sea.'

The last words had dropped like an echo of something monstrous out of a horror poem by Edgar Allan Poe, and just because there was deliberately in the words themselves, in the echo, a subtle last something of easing humour, the dreadfulness was inexpressibly final.

Pursuing his way home, the doctor looked about him and saw the quiet lines of the Ros darkling under the descending night. And in that quietude, in the dead heather listening for the wind above its living roots, in the rocky outcrops, in the flying horizon lines and great flattened wings of the sea, he felt the tragedy which lay at the heart of beauty.

He rebelled against this at once. He had a mistrust of abstract words. There was nothing that man should not be able to put right. Nothing.

But suddenly it was as if Charlie smiled to him again from the air.

So the doctor came at it from another tack. And the final point was: What could be done? The problem was perfectly clear. Abstract words and feelings merely cluttered it up. People suffered from idiotic delusions. Irritating, very irritating, when you want something sensible and healthy done.

Charlie himself could do no more. That had to be accepted, like any other kind of illness. So the action had to be directed towards Charlie by others.

By men like Norman, his own sea companions, his fellow workers who respected him. The doctor would have a quiet talk with them. In an unobtrusive way Norman could first have an hour or two with Charlie alone. Kenneth Grant might in due course even be allowed to rub some common sense in. Would they do it? Of course they would. And only too gladly.

No need for him to enlarge on Charlie's vivid descriptions. No need even to mention to them the money in the chest.

Why?

Well, hang it, I *can* mention it! Any of them might have done the same. They'll understand. They will go to Charlie. They'll do all they can. The doctor knew this quite certainly.

But his mind was beginning to slip. He was already feeling baffled, congested. They would go, they would do what they could, but Charlie's picture – that picture – would be in their minds. For ever in their minds. He knew it. He knew it. As profoundly in their minds as in Charlie's own, and Charlie would hardly have even to smile at them, would as far as necessary spare them his smile. And they would feel defeated, even sunk in misery, but they would *know*.

The question came crying silently out of the doctor in anger, but also in wonder: *What is this thing? this wordless knowledge?*

And suddenly, from the excess of his baffled mood, there flashed something like a vision, and he saw figures, figures like Norman and the others, moving over a twilit landscape, a timeless landscape, and they were the people of the community, and they had their way of living, the right way and the wrong way, distilled out of numberless ages, so that the right way and the wrong way became native to the blood, like an instinct, an instinct protecting the community, and this instinct, known also to the very birds and animals that lived together, this conscience, this thing which needed no words, was – morality.

His vision – at least, this flashing penetration, in which figures like Norman did momentarily appear at a little distance – excited the doctor profoundly.

There might be other moralities, divine morality, but *this* was what affected Charlie and what Charlie knew affected the others.

And there was no getting beyond it or round it. There was no 'putting it right'. Were he in Charlie's position, he, too, would go away. The fine spirit – the community's highest product – had to act so. It was inevitable. And with great clarity the doctor saw that tragedy lay only in the inevitable, in the thing that could not be 'put right'.

It had a quietening effect on him, the wonder balancing the sadness. But soon he felt weary of it, angry at it, and cast it from him.

A certain rebelliousness surged up. It flung his reluctant thought against Flora and her father. Charlie had never mentioned Flora in all his talk. Such delicate reticence! But that way, too, had been tried – and had failed, most bitterly of all for Charlie's spirit. That had been the finish.

Well, he, the doctor, could approach them now. Speak to the minister and to Flora, tell them. . . . But the doctor's mind suddenly balked. No! Morality there might be, and tragedy, and all the rest of the strange gear the human animal had gathered in a million years, but at least there was a last dignity in man, and Charlie had won that. To go running around, like some social worker, trying to arrange things! . . . What an intolerable intrusion! What a betrayal of the dignity and the reticence!

Don't worry, Doctor, came Charlie's voice again. *This time I'll work my own passage abroad.*

All right, Charlie!

Something deeper, older, than that compelling vision of morality was needed now, and there was nothing deeper or older except death.

CHAPTER THIRTY-ONE

'There's only a slim chance,' said Michael, drawing back from his camera. 'And the shot I want, pure Victorian décor. They swing in round the shoulder off there and then come up against the light for the reeds exactly as I want them.'

'They go flighting in the evening to the stubble fields on that flat stretch by the burn—'

'Yes.'

'It's a quiet world here,' murmured the doctor.

'Isn't it?' agreed Michael. 'These few days have really been lovely. When you have cursed the bloody weather and feel like packing up, these days come. Extraordinary country.'

Michael had his hide near the tip of the south-western arm of Loch Geal, which, in his own words (with their slant on Gwynn) 'sprawled like a primordial starfish'. Occasionally a catspaw of wind darkened the surface away inward, but here the reeds were still and the water darkly transparent.

'You get some marvellous effects, too, if you look closely enough. See this tiny pool, cut off. What colour would you say it is?'

The doctor thought for a moment. 'It's dark, perhaps blueish – I don't know.'

'Because the more you look at it, the more immaterial it gets? The other day I satisfied myself suddenly by thinking of it as liquid air. Does that convey anything?'

'Liquid air . . . liquid sky . . . with a chill in it.'

'Oh, good!' said Michael. 'Damned good!' He laughed with restraint. 'When the sun goes further down, the shadows come, the long shadows of the reeds, and the shadows of the smallest hummocks, and there is a glisten of light on each reed. But you can do nothing with that. Absolutely nothing.'

'It is a world cut off here,' said the doctor.

'You feel that?'

'I do. And I confess I wasn't too keen on coming.'

'Oh, I know. You think you live amongst it all the time. So we do. And then – you enter it.' Michael looked at the doctor with a sidelong humour. 'You need more of this. You do such a hell of an amount of work.'

'No, not really. There are spells, of course.'

'Anyway, you make me feel a slacker. I'll have to pack up one of these days. Your example has been too devastating. The communal good and all that.' He chuckled, but a slight touch of colour had come to his cheeks.

'Thinking of going into your father's business?'

'Business, hell. There's other business to be done. Think of an age that does not see the theatre, that does not see these reeds, this light, as business of the highest kind, that condescends to it! To hell with them! I *know* now.' There was a short pause.

'What's Mr. Gwynn doing to-day?'

'Writing!' Michael's body swayed. 'Terrific pressure of inspiration. If you heard him last night! He thinks he's got it at last, all the pieces, the whole pattern.' He looked at the doctor with a sudden shrewd humour. 'What made you think of him just now?'

'Well,' said the doctor, 'I suppose we are social beings.'

Michael laughed at the answering glint of humour in the doctor's eye. The moment caught an elusive intimacy, like the quality of the light.

'Extraordinary how he comes into all this,' said Michael, as if agreeing to unspoken words. 'All his theory about – you know – the search back for imaginative wholeness in the primitive and all that—' But words were a bore. Here was the moment itself.

The doctor nodded. 'I know. The theory can be so heady.'

Michael was delighted. 'Lord, it's good,' he said. 'It's rich.'

'Does he fancy he has now brought the wholeness

forward into life to-day?' asked the doctor, giving the humour a dry speculative twist.

'Hell, no – that's the whole lovely problem. But he fancies he knows now *how* it should be done. He's got the key pattern!'

'I see,' said the doctor.

'I wonder,' suggested Michael. 'Because, you see, *now*, at this immortal moment, I have a premonition of – of the wholeness.' He kept his laughing eyes on the doctor.

The doctor looked into his eyes. 'Do you think it will last?'

'God, no. Does that matter?'

'Not much – in that case,' said the doctor, the humour of the moment slowly invading all his face.

'You're a subtle devil,' said Michael, moving with a restless laughing delight. 'And Gwynn – he's had another pow-wow with the parson. All in the same boat!'

'Has he?' said the doctor, his expression imperceptibly firming.

'Yes. Nothing much eventuated – it wouldn't, of course – beyond Gwynn's feeling that there has been a remarkable change in the soul's weather.'

The doctor remained silent.

Michael looked at him in a sidelong measuring way. 'Tell me, quite honestly, do you think we're just damned interlopers, moneyed rich, full of words and fury, signifying a witless condescension?'

'No,' answered the doctor; 'not altogether.'

Michael laughed. 'That's pretty good from you.'

The doctor had half turned away, and as his face lifted across the loch, his look steadied. On the far side two boyish figures, Hamish and Norrie, had just reached the water's edge.

'Damnation!' said Michael swiftly.

'Wait.'

'But, curse it, the incoming duck will see them!'

'Steady,' said the doctor. 'They don't mean anything. Hamish obviously wants to try the rod you gave him.'

'But we can't wait—'

'Leave it to me. It'll break his heart if he thought *you* saw him. He knows it's the close season. Don't show yourself.'

'Hurry up, then! The light – it's perfect light!'

Across the water came the cry of the fishing reel. The doctor got up and began walking away, his back to the boys. They saw him, and in a moment were flat in the heather.

Michael's impatience grew. What did the doctor think he was doing? Give them a shout or it would be too late! . . .

The doctor, without turning round, stood for an instant, then began to walk slowly out of sight. Immediately he had disappeared, the two boys got up, raced over the low ridge behind them and were gone. The doctor reappeared and strolled into the hide.

Michael was flushed, his eyes glistening. 'I'll keep that one for Gwynn.'

'He's a nice boy, Hamish,' said the doctor. 'But that rod has gone to his head. He would be wanting to see what it felt like, throwing a line from a real rod. He can't wait.'

'But he couldn't get trout now?'

'He knows that – knows they're no use anyway.'

Michael's cap was always well pulled down over his head with the snout tugged a little to one side. He gave it an extra tug and laughed. As he twisted round, his face above the fringe of sheltering heather, he stopped.

The ground behind the hide ran level for a little way, then tipped over into a descending valley. Topping the breast of the slope on its eastern side were two figures, a man and a woman. The distance was such that Michael asked, 'Who are they?'

'The minister and his daughter Flora,' answered the doctor.

'They're not coming here now?'

'No, I don't think so,' replied the doctor quietly.

Presently the two figures stopped. They stood together for several seconds, then they parted, the father going back and the girl going on.

'Seems to have given her his blessing,' said Michael.

'Looks like it.'

'Must have been pretty grim without it. Gwynn will be glad they've made it up. Wholeness once more!'

As Flora dipped out of sight, the doctor said lightly, 'I'll go and make sure she's not coming this way.' And he walked out of the hide but not over the flat ground, instead he took the slope to the right and disappeared over its crest.

Michael's brows gathered. What exactly was the doctor's idea? Where was she going?. . .

Flat in the heather, the doctor waited. Far at the point of the Ros, he could see Charlie's cottage in the sun.

In time Flora appeared over the western shoulder of the valley. When the valley was shut off, she paused and the doctor decided she could see the cottage. She stood quite still for a while, gazing in its direction, then slowly looked about her. All at once there were a few sharp eager yelps. They drew her attention. In a moment she was running, her skirt pulled up. He heard her rounded golden cries. She was stooping over Fraoch. She was on her back in the heather, Fraoch aloft and struggling in her hands. They frolicked wildly. Then she got up, straightened herself, raised an admonitory finger at Fraoch, and continued on her way with proper decorum.

He watched her as she went across the moor towards Charlie's cottage, space about her and a light that ran and lifted clear over the Ros and the sea beyond to the remote horizon line of the west.

There was a strange final certainty in her going. Behind the movement of her upright figure, he knew that words had been spoken between her father and herself, words and silences that swept the dark places, cleansing them, and so at last there she went, carrying her father's submission, his blessing, lightly, already forgetting it as one forgets the sunlight and the air, in the delicious turmoil of the adventure ahead.

But he also knew, in this moment of watching her, more than she knew or her father, for his mind brought Charlie into the wide design – and all Charlie's secret thoughts as he had learned and listened to them no later than last night. Now she would sit and listen to Charlie as the grey light came, and then, Charlie being unfit, Dougald would see her home.

The moor was translated to a distant land, to the African veldt, to a plain in Canada, and Charlie was by her side, and they were walking along, golden and laughing. . . . That was the certain end.

She was going away. They were both going away. He felt something draining out of his heart, draining out of the land itself, leaving an imponderable shadow.

Leaving the shadow on the land. The shadow from the passing of the bright ones. Always . . . going away . . . driven away. . . . Leaving her shadow on his heart.

There, where she walked, he had had, in the ghost light from yesterday's dead day, his vision of morality. Now he realized there was one thing deeper and older than his vision, and it was walking over the vision on two light feet.

Out of the bright air, first like a silent singing and then with a whirr of wings, came the wild duck in a wide circle, heads out-thrust on long necks, eager, out of the heart of life, in a lovely swift sweep, downward, flattening out, wings pressing back the air, webbed feet thrusting forward, breaking the mirror of the loch into running dancing ripples and shaking the reeds.

CANONGATE CLASSICS

Books listed in alphabetical order by author.

Listen to the Voice: Selected Stories Iain Crichton Smith
ISBN 0 86241 434 2   £5.99 $11.95
Diaries of a Dying Man William Soutar
ISBN 0 86241 347 8   £4.99 $11.95
Shorter Scottish Fiction Robert Louis Stevenson
ISBN 0 86241 555 1   £4.99 $13.95
Tales of Adventure (Black Arrow, Treasure Island, 'The
Sire de Malétroit's Door' and other Stories) Robert
Louis Stevenson
ISBN 0 86241 687 6   £7.99 $14.95
Tales of the South Seas (Island Landfalls, The Ebb-tide,
The Wrecker) Robert Louis Stevenson
ISBN 0 86241 643 4   £7.99 $14.95
The Scottish Novels: (Kidnapped, Catriona, The Master of
Ballantrae, Weir of Hermiston) Robert Louis Stevenson
ISBN 0 86241 533 0   £5.99 $13.95
The People of the Sea David Thomson
ISBN 0 86241 550 0   £4.99 $11.95
City of Dreadful Night James Thomson
ISBN 0 86241 449 0   £4.99 $11.95
Three Scottish Poets: MacCaig, Morgan, Lochhead
ISBN 0 86241 400 8   £4.99 $11.95
Black Lamb and Grey Falcon Rebecca West
ISBN 0 86241 428 8   £10.99 $19.95

ORDERING INFORMATION

Most Canongate Classics are available at good bookshops.
You can also order direct from Canongate Books Ltd – by
post: 14 High Street, Edinburgh EH1 1TE, or by telephone:
0131 557 5111. There is no charge for postage and packing to
customers in the United Kingdom.

Canongate Classics are distributed exclusively in the USA
amd Canada by:

Interlink Publishing Group, Inc.
46 Crosby Street
Northampton, MA 01060–1804
Tel: (413) 582–7054
Fax: (413) 582–7057
e-mail: interpg@aol.com
website: www.interlinkbooks.com